£2.49

Derek Wilson is a biography and ficti credit, including *Rothschild: A Story of Wealth and Power* and *The Astors: Landscape with Millionaires*. After graduating from Cambridge he spent several years travelling the world, working by turns as teacher, antique dealer, magazine editor and radio presenter, and he still writes documentaries and radio plays as well as serving as an Anglican lay reader. Since their three children grew up, Derek Wilson and his wife have divided their time between homes on Exmoor and in Normandy.

Also available from Headline are *The Triarchs* and *The Dresden Text*, further chronicles of Tim Lacy's investigations in the artworld.

The Hellfire Papers

Derek Wilson

HEADLINE

First published in 1995
by HEADLINE BOOK PUBLISHING

First published in paperback in 1995
by HEADLINE BOOK PUBLISHING

10 9 8 7 6 5 4 3 2 1

ISBN 0 7472 4428 6

Typeset by
Letterpart Limited, Reigate, Surrey

Printed and bound in Great Britain by
Cox & Wyman Ltd, Reading, Berks

HEADLINE BOOK PUBLISHING
A division of Hodder Headline PLC
338 Euston Road
London NW1 3BH

The Hellfire
Papers

PROLOGUE: Nunc Dimittis

'Damn!' The chapel bell stopped ringing as Emma took the last flight of stairs two at a time. She yanked open the outer door and paused briefly to hug her gown around her. Grand Court was empty, stark, cold and dismal. Its Tudor façade was obscured by the driving rain, except where lamplight showed pools of yellow stone and glistened unevenly on the cobbles. Emma lowered her head and made the twenty-yard sprint through the deluge to the college chapel.

As she leaned her weight against the heavy oak, it opened suddenly inwards and she almost fell into the arms of Kenton, the junior porter. He stepped back, as alarmed as she was.

'Easy, miss! You'll just about make it.'

'Is the Dean here?'

'Everyone's here who's going to be here – all four of you. I rang the bell as long as I could but Dr Vare's a stickler for punctuality.'

Emma shrugged. 'Oh well, thanks anyway.'

1

She crossed the small vestibule, pulled open the baize-covered door and slipped into the dimly-lit chapel as the portal hushed shut behind her. The two rows of stalls on each side of the building were virtually empty. After the buffeting of the rain the warm silence made an almost physical impact. Emma moved on her toes to the reading desk in the far corner. She was aware of but did not glance at the kneeling figure of the Dean in his seat to the right of the door. Apart from the spots illuminating the plain altar, the only pools of light came from the lamps on the reading desk and the Dean's stall and the bulbs over the places occupied by the other members of the congregation, two of the college's small contingent of theology students.

Unlike larger Cambridge colleges such as King's and St John's, St Mary's House did not boast a large, impressive chapel. It certainly had no famous choir to fulfil the liturgical obligations laid down by its founder. But day after day divine office was said, attended usually by no more than a handful of fellows and undergraduates. Among them was the person designated to read the lessons, a task laid in rotation upon all third-year students who could not give convincing evidence of virulent atheism or adherence to another faith.

Emma reached her seat, checked that the Bible in front of her was open at the right place and curled herself into the corner of the wide stall, hoping against hope that her late arrival had gone unnoticed by Dr Vare.

She looked across at the dark head of the surpliced figure leaning forward over folded arms in an attitude of prayer. He certainly seemed oblivious to all around him. As well as she knew him, Emma had never thought of the Dean of St

Mary's as a devout person. He possessed a brilliant mind, an agile wit and a positively sulphuric tongue. His students went in awe of him and it was said that he even overpowered meetings of the college's governing body. Dr Vare's conduct of worship was usually brisk and imperious and gave the distinct impression to many that he was doing Almighty God an immense favour by being there at all. So it was quite a revelation to see this austere cleric apparently so absorbed in silent supplication as to be oblivious of time.

Emma looked at her watch. If the old boy did not get a move on they would be late for hall. As it was she was going to be hard put to it to grab dinner, get changed and be ready by the time Gavin collected her to go to the Arts Theatre.

One of the theologians coughed pointedly and looked across at her with raised eyebrows.

Emma mouthed, 'Go and prod him!' and pointed towards the Dean.

The young man shook his head and grinned.

When another two silent minutes had passed it was obvious that something was wrong. It was also obvious that neither male member of the congregation was going to do anything.

Emma slipped from her seat and walked softly across the patterned marble. She stood in front of the Dean's stall.

'Dr Vare.' She steeled herself for a sharp rebuff.

There was no response.

Emma peered closely but could not see the Dean's face. 'Dr Vare, are you all right?'

Emma turned to the others. 'I think he's blacked out. Come and help.'

She was aware that her pulse was racing. She reached out a hand to the Dean's shoulder. There was no resistance. Dr Vare fell slowly sideways and landed heavily on the floor between the seat and the desk.

'Oh my God!' Emma gasped. 'He's had a heart attack.'

Then she saw the crimson stain all the way down the front of the crisply laundered surplice.

I

DUSK

Thy hand, great Anarch, lets the curtain fall;
And universal Darkness buries ALL.

– Alexander Pope, *The Dunciad*

CHAPTER 1

Catherine Lacy felt uneasy and she could not quite say why. She was in an unfamiliar environment. But it was a very agreeable environment and all she had to do was sit back and enjoy it. She was among strangers – high-powered strangers in elegant evening dress. But she enjoyed meeting people and could hold her own in any company. She had no idea why she was here. But she had no reason to regret this example of serendipity. Yet there was something irrationally unnerving about this evening. She sensed a hidden agenda. She and Tim had been invited here for a purpose – a purpose as yet unrevealed. She shook her head. Perhaps she was being fanciful.

From her seat at high table the attractive thirty-two-year-old blonde looked along the vastness of the hall. The places where undergraduates had sat earlier for their dinner were empty, but huge logs blazed in the large fireplace halfway along one wall and the light flickered over portraits of long-dead masters of the college. Above, the hammer beams were illumined by concealed lighting. The polished oak before her was heavy with silver plate and candlesticks. The food and wine were excellent. Around her, intelligent conversation ebbed and flowed. It was all a fascinating insight into the arcane world of academia, especially as she and Tim had no close connections with that world. There was that pinprick of mystery again. Why on earth had they been invited to Cambridge to attend a dinner in honour of a visiting American lecturer?

'Are you being quietly impressed by all this English ancientry?' Stuart Longton, seated on her left, looked like what he was, a bespectacled thirty-five-year-old academic, well set on a distinguished (some said, brilliant) career. 'We confidently claim it as the oldest college hall in Cambridge. It was built for the Austin friars when they set up here in the thirteenth century – a full three hundred years before Henry VIII kicked them out and generously 'gave' St Mary's House their property. It hasn't changed much over the years. We've been made several offers for it by some of your fellow countrymen.'

Catherine laughed. 'If you're trying to bait me you're forgetting that I'm a fully Anglicized American now. I live in deepest Wiltshire. You can't get much more English than that.'

'That's as maybe. For me you'll always be Catherine Younger, the most devastating head-turner at Harvard, the girl I almost married.'

'Oh, yeah? If you'd ever plucked up the courage to propose, I just might have scared the pants off you by accepting. What would you have done then?'

'Hurried home triumphantly with all my research notes in one pocket and a beautiful young bride in the other.'

'If you were so smitten, how come you never kept in touch? Your invitation to this shindig came quite out of the blue.' She sat back to allow the steward to remove her plate. As she did so her bobbed fair hair glowed halo-like in the soft light. 'You haven't told me yet why you *did* invite us. If you're planning to fan the old passion into flame I ought to warn you that Tim spent a few years in the SAS. On our first date I saw him disarm a gunman and almost break his neck.'

Stuart gazed along the table to where Tim Lacy sat talking with (or, Stuart thought, much more likely listening to) Dr Ingrid Brunhill from Oxford, a thin-lipped woman with lank black hair. He saw a man with features that were strong rather than fine, framed with dark hair that had a tendency to curl. He seemed to be coping attentively and sympathetically with his garrulous, self-obsessed neighbour. For that alone he deserved a medal.

'Tim's good at his job, isn't he?'

Catherine thought she detected a hint of anxiety behind the question. 'What an odd thing to ask a loyal wife. Of course he is. He started Lacy Security ten years ago, when he resigned his commission. Now it's one of the leading international companies specializing in the protection of public and private art collections. Why the interest?'

The next course arrived and for several moments they were occupied in helping themselves to vegetables from the silver dishes proffered by college servants.

Dr Longton lifted his wineglass. 'To you, Catherine. I'm very glad you came. These occasions can be terribly boring without good company to enliven them.'

'I find that hard to believe. You have quite a few interesting and important people here, don't you? I presume that the idea of such events is maintaining the college's contacts in high places. Tell me about these VIPs you've assembled tonight.'

'Well, you met the Master, Sir Evelyn Masquerier.'

'Yeah, quite a smoothie. Not like my idea of a top academic.'

'Oh, he's not. He got a passable degree in economics. Did some research. Published a couple of things. Then he was head-hunted by Mercantile Pacific. He spent most of the last thirty years as a merchant banker.'

'So, why . . .?'

'Well may you ask. It certainly wasn't a unanimous election. But the college desperately needed money and Masquerier knows all the right people.'

'And did he deliver the goods?'

'That depends on your point of view. In the two years he's been here he's tightened up our accounts and wangled a couple of major corporate donations, but only at the cost of turning us into "St Mary's House plc". We have to capitalize on every asset. You wouldn't believe the number of conferences we cram in here during the vacations. St Mary's is becoming more like a hotel than a college. The current stage of his game plan is to become known as the man who produced the economic miracle at St Mary's. That should lead to a life peerage and prestigious chairmanships of as many City boards as he cares to take. That's why he's sucking up to Lord Everton, the great do-gooder and commercial baron.'

'Which one's he?'

'You mean you don't know Lord Teddy, the professional philanthropist? Dear me, his PR machine must be slipping.

10

He's the barrel of lard sitting between La Brunhill and the delectable Lady Masquerier.' Stuart indicated an elderly, balding man who was laughing vigorously at a story he had just told the attractive, auburn-haired woman on his left.

'*That's* Masquerier's wife?'

'Yes, that's the fair Deborah – every bit as beautiful and ruthless as her Old Testament namesake.'

'She must be all of twenty years younger than her husband.'

'Deborah is thirty-eight. Sir Evelyn is sixty-two.'

'Does it work?'

'Deb isn't around very much. She spends most of her time in London and Cheltenham as a TV executive. She's on the board of Chiltern Cotswold. Very tough and high-powered. All in all, I'd say she and the Master deserve each other.'

'My, we are in cynical vein this evening! Isn't there anyone here who meets with your approval?'

Stuart peered disdainfully up and down the table as though looking for a pound coin in a handful of small change. 'Finsley-Kerr's very much upwardly mobile but not a bad sort for all that.' He indicated a middle-aged man with aquiline features.

'I've seen him somewhere before.'

'Probably on the telly. He's a junior minister at the Heritage Department. He sometimes gets pushed out by the cabinet to do interviews when there are awkward questions to be answered and his superiors don't want to risk having their images dented.'

Before Catherine could respond, her other neighbour, who introduced himself as the Master of Caius, offered an opening conversational gambit. They identified a mutual interest in Scottish neo-expressionism and this subject carried them through the pudding and well into the savoury. Only then was Catherine able to return her attention to her host.

'Stuart, you still haven't told me why you invited us here.'

He frowned. 'Aren't you enjoying yourself?'

'Yes I am. More than I expected, to be honest. But . . .'

'Did you get introduced to your compatriot over sherry?'

'The guest of honour? Very briefly. Who is he?'

'Professor Zangster – Joseph N. Zangster. I have it on impeccable authority that the N stands for Nicodemus. He heads the modern history faculty at Princeton. He's over here to deliver this term's Devereux Lectures and to pick up an honorary degree into the bargain. I don't suppose that's all he'll pick up.'

'Meaning?'

Stuart shrugged. 'Sorry, just being bitchy. I suppose I'm fed up at the thought of having to go along every week and hear him spout. There's always a three-line whip out in the faculty on these occasions.'

'Isn't he an interesting speaker?'

Stuart shrugged dismissively. 'Zangster's a leading expert on mid-eighteenth-century politics but we could have had someone more prestigious. It was largely pressure from Masquerier that got him invited. I wish I knew what the old boy was up to.' He spoke the last words almost to himself.

Catherine pounced on the silence which followed. 'Now, perhaps you'll tell me—'

Stuart put a finger to his lips. Someone banged heavily three times on the table. The Master of St Mary's House rose to propose a toast to the guest of honour.

★ ★ ★

After dinner the party retired to the senior combination room for dessert and port. These were taken at three smaller tables and guests were encouraged to move freely between them. At one turn of the musical chairs Catherine was introduced to Lord Everton.

The rotund, slightly perspiring figure took her hand gently in his own podgy fingers and stooped to kiss it. 'Mrs Lacy, I've so looked forward to meeting you.' He drew up a chair which creaked as he lowered himself onto it.

'Oh yeah! My Lord, I know flattery when I hear it.'

'No, I assure you – and please call me 'Teddy'. Now, let me prove to you that I'm not what the youngsters call "handing out a line of chat". I really do know quite a lot about you. You live in a charming house in Wiltshire from which your husband runs his highly successful security business and you operate an art gallery and educational arts centre. You have very rapidly established a reputation as a discoverer of new talent. Now, when Catherine Lacy puts on an exhibition the art world sits up and takes notice. There, how's that?' He beamed at her and Catherine felt herself falling under the spell of his charm.

She said, 'You've obviously done your homework. Unfortunately, I can't claim to be as well briefed about you. Tell me about yourself.'

He shrugged. 'Oh, what's to tell? My time is largely taken up with charity work. I hope you've heard of the Downham Homes?'

Catherine had. Most people were aware that the Downham centres for disturbed children and juvenile offenders were remarkably successful private enterprise contributions towards the solving of a growing social problem. She said, 'Yes, indeed. They're doing a great job.'

'Thank you, Catherine, thank you. I'll accept that compliment on behalf of my staff. They are a splendid, highly-trained team. And I try to make sure they keep up-to-date with all the latest developments in youth care worldwide. Of course, all that costs money and we receive miserly government support.' He broke off, smiling broadly again. 'You will have spotted a sales pitch coming. And you are right. I'm always looking for ways to raise funds and I've just been struck with a marvellous idea. Every summer we hold an arts festival on behalf of the homes. It's at Chipping Sneddon in the Cotswolds. Please say you've heard of it. You have? Excellent. Well, I was wondering whether you might consider mounting an exhibition there. The festival's really becoming quite famous. Every year we attract some wonderful top per- formers. Janos Vanic is coming as our guest conductor this year. It would be a splendid showplace for some of your protégés and, of course, a tremendous boost for the festival. Do say you'll think about it.'

'Well, I . . .' Catherine found herself saying, against her better judgement. 'OK, I'll think about it.'

'Excellent!' Lord Teddy jumped to his feet with surprising alacrity. 'I'll be in touch. What is it you Americans say? "Count on it." ' Then he was gone, sidling crabwise to the next table.

After circulating for half an hour or so, the Lacys eventually came together.

Tim smiled at his wife. 'You seemed to be having a good time over dinner with your old flame.'

Catherine grimaced. 'I got an earful of campus gossip. How about you?'

'Stuck between an Oxford bluestocking and a don's wife obsessed with ladies' golf.'

'Did you get to talk to Lord Everton? Strange man. I've just been propositioned by him. I need to check him out. According to Stuart, Masquerier is cultivating him like crazy. Apparently—'

Tim coughed and frowned a warning as the Master of St Mary's House appeared behind Catherine's chair.

'Mr and Mrs Lacy, how lovely to find you together. We haven't had a proper chat yet. Young Longton has told me quite a bit about you. Not that I needed to be told about Lacy Security.' He seated himself. 'Viscount Stonor is a very good friend of mine. He was telling me how delighted he was with the job your people did at his Leicestershire place. He said he was thinking of renaming the house Fort Knox.'

Tim smiled. 'There's no such thing as perfect security but we get as close to it as we can.'

Catherine said, 'Thank you very much for inviting us, Sir Evelyn. We were very surprised to be asked.' She raised an enquiring eyebrow.

Masquerier did not respond. 'We're delighted to welcome you here. Have you had a chance to look round the college?'

'Not yet. Perhaps tomorrow morning . . .'

'That's right. Get Longton to give you a guided tour. At least I can show you the master's lodge. You're coming over for a nightcap a bit later, aren't you?'

Tim glanced at him sharply. 'Are we?'

Masquerier was caught momentarily off guard. 'Er, yes . . . At least, I asked Stuart to be sure to bring you across. I hope that's all right.'

Catherine nodded. 'It will be a lovely way to round off a delightful evening.'

'Good, good. More port?' He refilled Tim's glass from the decanter. Catherine shook her head.

Tim said. 'That tragedy last term must have shaken you all up rather badly.'

'Poor Charles Vare? Yes, it was a great shock.'

Catherine looked up quizzically. 'What was that? I don't think I heard about it.'

Masquerier drained his glass and set it down on the table with elaborate care. 'Our late Dean regrettably – and inexplicably – committed suicide just before the end of full term.'

He was on the point of changing the subject but Tim pursued it. 'According to the rather brief account in the press it was all very bizarre. I suppose that was the usual journalistic exaggeration?'

The Master covered his annoyance with a studied courtesy. 'The college was very fortunate that its domestic tragedy coincided with the Downing Street scandal and the Indian earthquake. Those events kept the tabloids occupied and we were able to put the incident firmly behind us.' He rose. 'I see that some of our guests are leaving. Will you excuse me for now?'

Catherine watched as he crossed the room briskly. 'You touched a raw nerve.'

'So it seems.'

'What were you up to?'

Tim rubbed a finger up and down the bridge of his nose. 'I don't know. Kicking out, I suppose.'

'You wouldn't care to elaborate?'

'I don't like being on appro.'

'You mean not knowing why we're here?'

'It's not just that. We've been under scrutiny all evening. Haven't you sensed it? Strange looks. Veiled remarks. Probing questions. We're being secretly vetted by a bunch of rather superior people, and I don't care for it much.'

'Perhaps all will be revealed when we go for our nightcap in the master's lodge.'

'Damn well better be!'

Half an hour later the Lacys were walking across the moonlit fellows' garden escorted by Stuart Longton. There was a light frost and the gravel path before them intersected neat rectangles of silvered lawn. Their guide had fallen uncharacteristically silent and it was Tim who spoke first.

'Were you very friendly with Dr Vare?'

'Charles? No. He not only ignored Dr Johnson's advice about keeping his friendships in constant repair, he actually went out of his way to damage them. He had too sharp a tongue. Anyone who got close to him felt the edge of it sooner or later.'

'Do you think his final act was calculated as a gigantic snub to the world in general and the college in particular?'

Catherine's frustration exploded. 'Would somebody mind telling me exactly what happened to the late Dean? I've been hearing whispered comments and half explanations all evening.'

Stuart pushed open an iron gate in the high wall and ushered his guests through into the grounds of the Master's Lodge. 'Then, since you press me, and to be as brief as woman's love, Charles Vare dosed himself up with sleeping tablets, donned his cassock and surplice, went to the chapel and there, to make assurance doubly sure, he severed the veins in both wrists.'

Catherine shivered and wished she had not asked.

Tim said, 'If that's what really happened it certainly looks as though he wanted his passing to cause the maximum distress and embarrassment to the college. There was no doubt that it was suicide?'

'Not according to the doctor who reported to the inquest. And not according to the police, who made mercifully discreet inquiries. Their evidence satisfied the coroner.'

'But not you?'

'When one is presented with the choice between two unthinkable thoughts, does it really matter which one entertains?'

They had reached the front of the lodge – a square Queen Anne house. Stuart went ahead up the short flight of steps and pressed the bell. It was opened immediately by an au pair and they entered a wide hallway. Stuart led the way up a curving staircase to the first floor, tapped briefly on an imposing double door and ushered Tim and Catherine inside.

It was a long room which, judging by the marble fire-places at each end, had once been two. A fired burned in the one on the right and the room's three occupants were seated around it.

Masquerier rose to greet them. Tall, spare and well-groomed, he looked very fit for his age. 'Mr and Mrs Lacy, thank you so much for coming over. You met my wife and Joe Zangster earlier, I'm sure.'

18

Tim and Catherine went through the formalities of refusing drinks and accepting coffee, followed by the formalities of small talk. After about ten minutes Tim saw the Master and Longton exchange glances.

Masquerier cleared his throat. 'Actually, Mr Lacy, there is a small matter of business we'd like to discuss with you, if we may. Would you mind? It will only take a few minutes.'

Tim thought, 'About bloody time.' He said, 'So I have to sing for my supper, do I?'

'Oh, nothing like that. It's just . . . Well, look, shall we go to my study?' Masquerier stood up. He smiled at his wife. 'Would you excuse us, darling? I'm sure Mrs Lacy would like to see the pictures. She's quite an expert.'

Their host led Tim and Stuart across the landing to a smaller room fitted out with expensive, modern, executive furniture. When they were seated in unyielding leather armchairs the Master explained.

'Mr Lacy, we'd be very grateful if you could undertake a professional commission for St Mary's.'

Tim crossed his legs and pinched the crease in his dress trousers. 'I'll be happy to consider it. But why all this elaborate build-up? A letter or a phone call . . .'

'I'm afraid it's not quite that simple. We're in a situation that calls for absolute discretion. We had to know that you were the sort of man who could undertake the task for us in complete secrecy.'

The two fellows looked at Tim as though expecting him to reassure them. All he said was, 'What do you want done?'

Masquerier fingered the gold fob of the watch chain stretched across his waistcoat. 'At the risk of sounding melodramatic, Mr Lacy, I must ask you not to reveal anything about this conversation – whether you decide to help us or not.'

Tim struggled to control his exasperation. 'Sir Evelyn, point number one: security is my business. That means lots of people – important people – trust me with their secrets. Point number two: it's getting very late and if these preliminaries are going to drag on much longer I doubt whether my patience will be equal to the strain.'

Masquerier nodded. 'Very well, we will give you the details. When you've heard them I think you'll understand how important this matter is to us and why we have to be so very cautious. In a nutshell, we would like you to go to Australia for us and bring back some papers that are the property of the college.'

'They must be very valuable if you're prepared to go to the expense of sending a special courier halfway round the world.'

The Master sighed and shook his head. 'They may be. Then again, they may not. Stuart, I think you're better placed to go over the salient points.'

Longton took up the story. 'A couple of months ago an old member of the college died in Sydney. His name was Sir Peregrine Whitehead-Dyer. Does the name mean anything to you?'

Tim shook his head.

'Well, I suppose there's no reason why it should. He had quite a distinguished career in the diplomatic service, most of it in the Far East, and a few years ago retired to live in Australia. Shortly before his death we had a letter from his solicitors to inform us that he would be leaving to St Mary's House an important collection of documents that had been in his family for several generations.'

'What's so special about these documents?'

'Have you heard of the Monks of Medmenham Abbey?'

Tim looked blank.

'How about the name they're popularly, though errone-ously, known by – the members of the Hellfire Club?'

'You mean that bunch of eighteenth-century bucks who indulged in orgies and shocking goings-on around High Wycombe?'

Stuart removed his glasses and polished them methodi-cally with the handkerchief from his breast pocket. 'The very same. Sir Francis Dashwood and several leading mem-bers of English society are supposed to have met frequently in Medmenham Abbey to carry out satanic rituals in the period 1745-1763. They were notorious. All sorts of stories were circulated about their activities but no one outside the Dashwood circle really knew exactly what went on at their nocturnal gatherings. One of Dashwood's hangers-on was a reprobate and poetaster by the name of Paul Whitehead. He was one of the destructive worms that wriggled in and out of London society, gnawing away at its fabric with satire and scandal-mongering. It was wholly fitting that he should end up in the service of Francis Dashwood. Among his other jobs he was made secretary of the "Franciscans" of Med-menham. He recorded their rites, kept a journal of their activities and, if the stories are true, made sketches of the members, their buxom guests and some of their lusty activities.'

'And these are the documents which are now sitting in a Sydney lawyer's office?' Tim tried to ease the commentary onto the fast track.

Dr Longton was not to be jolted out of his cautious, academic thoroughness. 'Possibly. Probably. Sir Peregrine inherited the family property in Essex several years ago. He was a bachelor. He'd already decided to retire to Australia. So he sold everything up. In the process of sorting out the contents some boxes of old documents came to light that no one had bothered with for years. Being of an antiquarian turn of mind (he got a first here in history, by the way), he delved. The result of this intellectual spadework was the discovery, as he believed, of Paul Whitehead's Medmenham memorabilia. (You will have gathered, of course, that Dashwood's gofor was Sir Peregrine's ancestor.)'

'So we're talking about the discovery of a pretty sensational cache of documents?'

Longton allowed his voice a slight timbre of excitement. 'If the Whitehead-Dyer Papers are genuine and if they go into reasonable detail then they are of enormous significance. It has become fashionable in scholarly circles to pooh-pooh all the stories about the Hellfire Club. Tales of satanic rites and the systematic deflowering of virgins are regarded as wild exaggerations. Most of our colleagues cannot stomach the idea of national leaders being involved in black masses and sexual orgies on a positively Caligulan scale. If such scepticism turns out to be unfounded . . .'

'You seem to think there's some doubt about these papers. Didn't Sir Peregrine get them vetted by experts?'

The Master grunted. 'He'd have saved everyone a lot of trouble if he had.'

Longton took up the narrative again. 'He apparently kept the discovery very much to himself. We know of only one other person he told about it. The papers went off to the

22

Antipodes with him. That was that – until we discovered that he had willed them to his old college.'

'So what's the problem?' Tim looked from one to the other of his companions. 'Why can't one of you simply pop on a plane to Sydney and pick them up?'

Masquerier shifted in his chair. 'That's where the secrecy comes in. We would rather no one outside this room got a whiff of this until Stuart here has had a chance to examine the papers thoroughly. If one of us made a sudden trip to Australia some people would put two and two together.'

Tim shook his head. 'You've lost me. I thought you said no one else knew about these documents.'

Stuart frowned. 'No, Tim. What I said was that *as far as we know* Sir Peregrine shared his secret with only one other person. But we could be mistaken. There's no telling whom he might have mentioned the papers to down under, or whom he might have corresponded with on the subject.'

'Who was the confidant you do know about? Can he be trusted to be discreet?'

There was an awkward silence, broken at last by the Master. 'I think we can count on that. The man Sir Peregrine confided in was an old friend from undergraduate days. Someone he was up at St Mary's with just after the war. Charles Vare.'

'I see.'

'They were very close friends, even though they were separated by half a planet. Sir Peregrine always came to stay here with Charles whenever he visited England and Charles made at least a couple of trips to Australia.'

After another long pause Tim said, 'My brain must be fuddled with your excellent wine. I still don't see the need for all this secrecy. Is it just a matter of keeping academic rivals at bay?'

'That's one reason, certainly. If anyone's going to work on these papers – catalogue them, evaluate them, perhaps prepare an edition for publication – then it should be someone right here, in St Mary's. It would certainly be a major coup for the college.' Stuart cleaned his spectacles again – a nervous gesture. 'But there are other reasons for caution. For one thing, we don't want to sound a premature fanfare.'

Masquerier amplified. 'We could look very silly if the papers turned out to be forgeries, or even just dull and uninteresting. Remember the "Hitler Diaries"? That resulted in a lot of egg on some very prominent faces. The academic world is in its way much more ruthless than the financial. I know; I've made the transition. In the City companies will gang up on a man to take over his business. There's not usually anything personal about it because it's the balance sheet that matters and if you let likes and dislikes influence your judgement you're very likely to come a cropper. But in the groves of academe . . .' He gave a cynical laugh. 'Here a man's only asset is his reputation and his rivals will attack that for the sheer hell of it.'

Stuart looked uncomfortable at this assault on his profession but he did not contradict the Master. 'If, as we hope and expect, the Whitehead-Dyer Papers are a major discovery the problem is hardly less acute. They will be of great interest to everyone concerned with the social and political history of the mid-eighteenth century, not to mention their importance as a unique collection of erotica. Scholars will be falling over themselves to come and study them. Other academic institutions will try to buy them. St Mary's will be under pressure to sell them or loan them to some place which has better facilities for visiting researchers. If we have to make important decisions about the collection (and that's going to be unavoidable) it's vital that we don't allow ourselves to be bounced into anything.' He looked sharply at the Master, who did not respond.

Tim said, 'I suppose this sort of material might also interest the media. Sex, scandal, satanism – it's got all the potential for a lurid story, for all that the principal actors have been dead and buried for a couple of hundred years.'

'Exactly!' Masquerier slapped the arm of his chair. 'Very adroit of you, Mr Lacy! Even in our decadent society there's a limit to the number of living politicians the gutter press can dig the dirt on. Some juicy historical revelations would do very nicely to keep circulation figures up. If we're not very careful we could have St Mary's swarming with tabloid journalists, finding out all they can and making up what they can't. It takes very little imagination to envisage the headlines: Hellfire Papers Sensation! St Mary's Sexy Secrets! That is precisely the sort of publicity we don't need.'

'And, of course, it could be worse,' Stuart added mournfully. 'By and large, we managed to keep the death of our late Dean out of the public domain. But the Grub Street scavengers would find that incident well worth the picking over, especially as poor Charles did have a – very loose – connection with Sir Peregrine's documents.'

Tim sat back. 'OK, I get the picture now. You need someone unconnected with the college to fetch these papers very quietly back to Cambridge so that you can study them and decide how best to introduce them to the academic world.'

Masquerier nodded. 'That's right, Mr Lacy. A simple commission, but one of great importance to St Mary's. Will you do it for us?'

'Yes. I'll put one of my best men on it.'

'Er . . . no. I'm afraid that won't do.' Sir Evelyn shook his head emphatically. 'I don't want to appear paranoid and I certainly have no wish to seem critical of your doubtless excellent staff, but we really can't have any more people involved than absolutely necessary. We want you to undertake this assignment personally.'

'Well, I don't know . . .'

'We appreciate, of course, that employing the top man will cost more, but what we'll be purchasing will be peace of mind. That's difficult to put a price on, wouldn't you say, Mr Lacy?'

CHAPTER 2

'Evelyn sure seems to be a workaholic,' Joe Zangster observed as the Master closed the drawing-room door behind him.

'Oh, there's no stopping him.' Deborah Masquerier shrugged nonchalantly, but Catherine detected an edge to her voice. 'I've got tired of telling him to take life easier. He seems determined to make me a merry widow.'

Catherine thought that her hostess was what would once have been called a 'handsome woman'. Her expensively-styled hair was short and businesslike yet managed at the same time to be soft and lustrous. Grey-green eyes looked candidly from strong features that were sculpted rather than moulded. Her classic silk dress could only have originated within yards of the Faubourg St Honoré. Here was a woman who knew what she wanted and probably got it.

Her smile seemed disarmingly genuine. 'Now, do you really want to traipse round Evelyn's musty old portraits?'

'It's a great collection, Catherine.' Zangster beamed at her. 'As one colonial to another, I'd say grab your chance.'

The Professor, Catherine decided, had reached the age when 'well built' was on the verge of becoming 'fat'. Why was it that large men always seemed to have personalities to match? Zangster's certainly overflowed and splashed all around him.

She said, 'Thank you, Lady Masquerier, I'd love to see them.'

The hostess rose. 'Oh for God's sake! When you see me wearing a tiara you can "Lady" me as much as you like. Otherwise it's plain Deb, OK? Now, the best ones are actually in here but we'd better start in the dining room. Tell me about your interest in art, darling.'

'My involvement is entirely with living painters and sculptors. We have an arts centre down in Wiltshire. We hold exhibitions, conferences, mini-festivals – anything to help put artists in touch with potential customers.'

Zangster held the door open for Catherine. 'Say, that's not Farrans Court, is it?'

'Yes! Surely our fame hasn't reached the States?'

'Indeed it has, Catherine. Indeed it has. You had an exhibition last year showing the work of new American artists. Am I right?'

'Yes.'

'One of our recent graduates from Princeton was lucky enough to get selected – Coreen Macdonald.'

'Ah yes, a tremendous talent. I like the intensity she achieves with a very subdued palette.'

Lady Masquerier had guided them into the dining room whose panelled walls were hung with portraits of seventeenth-century gentlemen impressively posed with hunting dogs or piles of books, and ladies in exquisitely patterned dresses. 'If it's the moderns that grab you, Catherine, you'll want to have a look at the Lucien Freud. But Evelyn keeps that in the study so you won't be able to see it until they've finished discussing those papers.'

The Professor looked at her sharply. 'Papers? Do you mean . . .?'

But Deb Masquerier was prattling on. 'Now, personally, I find this more to my taste. I reckon he was a real rogue, don't you?'

Catherine dutifully admired the painting of a sardonically smiling young courtier in part armour labelled *Portrait of an Unknown Man*: Cornelius Janssen Van Ceulen (1593–1662). She said, 'You must find Cambridge a very different world from the cut and thrust of television.'

The other woman laughed. 'Oh, darling, you mustn't be taken in by all this academic gentility. There's just as much ruthless rivalry here as in the TV world. The only difference is that in my world we stab each other in the chest, not the back.'

Without quite knowing why she asked the question, Catherine said, 'What do you suppose drove Charles Vare to suicide?'

'That's something we'd all like to know!' The answer was sharp. 'Not that he was a loss to the college – or the world.'

'You obviously didn't like him.'

'He gave me the creeps. I can say that, being on the fringe of college life. If you ask Evelyn and the others they'll all close ranks. I always felt there was something . . . what's the word? . . . unwholesome – about Charles. I'd have believed him capable of anything except . . .'

'Except what?'

'Except suicide, darling. Except suicide.'

It was almost one o'clock before the Lacys were able to extract themselves from the Masqueriers' hospitality, walk rapidly down St Mary's Lane to the riverside Granta Hotel, peel off their clothes and drop thankfully into bed.

Catherine propped herself on one elbow and looked down at the recumbent form of her husband. 'OK, what's it all about? Don't imagine I'm going to let you slip into oblivion without telling me the reason for tonight's charade.'

Tim rolled his head slowly from side to side, eyes closed. 'Sworn to secrecy. Almost had to take a Bible oath. All I can tell you is that it was Masquerier who really brought us here. He must have beavered away quite hard to discover the tenuous link between you and Stuart.'

Catherine tried another tack. 'It's all about these papers, isn't it?'

Tim's eyes flicked open. 'What do you know about the papers?'

'I'll tell you if you tell me.'

'According to Masquerier, he and Longton – and now me – are the only people who know about them.'

'Well, Lady M. is certainly in on the secret and I got the impression that Professor Zangster knew something about it, too.'

Tim stuck his hands behind his head and stared up at the ceiling. 'Curiouser and curiouser, as someone once said.'

'Alice.'

'What?'

'Never mind. Are you going to tell me?'

'OK. If people are not straight with me I don't feel any great obligation to them. How'd you like a trip to Australia?'

Tim gave his wife a potted version of the story of the Whitehead-Dyer papers.

They breakfasted next morning at a window table overlooking the hotel's frosted lawn, which stretched levelly to the river and water meadows drenched in sunlight.

Catherine sipped grapefruit juice and stared at the view. 'It's a lovely place even in the middle of winter. I wish I hadn't had all my illusions about ivory towers shattered.'

'There's rivalry, infighting, gossip and politics in every human institution.' Tim embarked with enthusiasm on his plateful of bacon, sausage, kidneys, mushrooms and tomatoes.

'Yeah, I know. It's just a shame to have to abandon the picture of inoffensive old men poring over ancient manuscripts in dusty libraries.' She tore open a croissant and applied butter and jam to its steaming interior. She gazed around the dining room. 'Did you notice that one of our fellow guests was here?'

'Finsley-Kerr? Yes.' He glanced across at the table in the centre of the room where the politician sat, accompanied by a dark-haired girl. 'That must be his daughter with him. She's a student at St Mary's.'

'They seem to be having a typical father-daughter row.'

'I suppose it's a stage of parenting we all have to go through. I can't say I'm looking forward to it with our two. Oops! We've been spotted.' Tim returned the smile and discreet wave from the other table.

'Did you get to meet him last night?'

'Only briefly. Parliamentarians, especially Tory ones, are not my favourite company.'

'Is that your working-class prejudice coming out?'

'Probably,' Tim admitted good-humouredly. 'I just hate the arrogance that goes with all establishments; the assumption that if you're not one of us you're nobody. I was never happy in an officers' mess and I get the same feel from this academic in-world. Tory politicians are the worst establishment of all because they believe that they govern by divine right. We chopped a king's head off once for that sort of arrogance. The threat of the axe might have a salutary effect on some people in Westminster.'

'Well, you'd better get ready to be nice to one of them. He's coming over. Good morning, Mr Finsley-Kerr.' Catherine smiled brightly at the newcomer who, she thought, managed to look even more aristocratic in checked shirt and well-cut sports jacket than in a DJ.

'Mr and Mrs Lacy, how do you do? I was sorry not to have a chance for a chat last night. One of the banes of public life, I'm afraid. So many people want to see me that I seldom get to meet the people I really want to meet. May I introduce my daughter? This is Emma. She's in her third year at St Mary's.'

They saw a tumble-haired young woman in jeans and denim overshirt who gave them a candid smile. Tim said, 'Won't you join us? I'll order some more coffee.'

Emma shook her head. 'Sorry. Love to but I really must fly. Bye, Daddy. Lovely to see you.' She gave her father a quick kiss, then made her escape.

Escape, Catherine thought, was precisely the right word.

Finsley-Kerr pulled up a chair. 'There goes a product of one of the most expensive educations in England,' he said ruefully.

Tim dabbed his lips with his napkin. 'She looks as though she'll survive it.'

Catherine hastily added, 'How's she getting on here?'

'Difficult to know. She's seldom at home. Always staying with friends or campaigning for something or other. Last year it was animal welfare. Now it's AIDS research. I just hope she leaves herself enough time to work for a decent degree. But what brings you here? Are you a Marian, Mr Lacy?'

'A what? Oh, you mean an old member of St Mary's House. No, we were invited by Stuart Longton.'

'I see.' The slight frown indicated that he did not see at all. 'What's your line of business?'

They engaged in small talk while the Lacys finished their meal. Then the politician stood up. 'Lovely to meet you, but I'm afraid I must drag myself away. Going to have a surreptitious word with Emma's tutor.' He offered each of them a professional handshake, then turned and made his way across the room.

Tim stared after the retreating figure. 'It seems we're still being vetted. I wonder why?'

Catherine looked at her watch. 'We're due to meet Stuart in twenty minutes for our personally guided tour.'

'That just about gives us time to pack and bring our bags down. We may as well do that. Then we'll be ready to leave as soon as we've said our goodbyes to Stuart.'

A quarter of an hour later Tim was at the check-out desk. He handed in the key and was just turning away when the clerk looked up from her computer console. 'Just a moment, Mr Lacy. There's a message for you.' She extracted an envelope from a small pile and handed it over. Tim tore it open and unfolded the single sheet of notepaper. It bore the St Mary's House crest and a short, scrawled, unsigned message. He read it a couple of times with surprise. Then, seeing Catherine approaching from the lift, he thrust it into his overcoat pocket.

Stuart Longton carried out punctiliously his duties as guide. He showed the Lacys the Old Library with its medieval chained books and seventeenth-century reading desks. He pointed out the Elizabethan splendours of Grand Court. He showed them the New Library, erected in the 1970s with a bequest from a wealthy Marian. 'The last piece of good fortune the college had,' he explained. 'We've been drawing in our horns ever since. We launched a two-million-pound appeal three years ago and managed to coincide it with the economic recession. We were lucky to struggle to half our target figure. Things were desperate. That was when we elected Masquerier.'

Tim and Catherine showed genuine interest in the architectural and historical details their host pointed out. It was when they were standing in the middle of the chapel, its ancient woodwork polychromed by the light streaming through stained-glass windows, that Tim asked, 'What became of Charles Vare's letters and diaries?'

Stuart was pointing out the organ in the west gallery. He froze, looking like the statue of a Roman orator. It was some seconds before he recovered himself. He turned to Tim. 'How do you know about that?' His voice was little more than a whisper.

'I like to know what I'm getting into. So, what happened exactly?'

'When Charles died', Stuart looked towards the Dean's stall, 'I was the first fellow to hear about it. I happened to be coming in past the porter's lodge when Emma rushed in for help.'

'Emma?'

'Emma Finsley-Kerr. She found the body.'

'Poor girl!' Catherine's imagination conjured up the scene.

'It was ghastly for her. And for me. Horrible! Quite horrible!' Stuart shook his head as though trying to dislodge the memory. 'It was obvious nothing could be done for poor Charles. I left the head porter to contact all the necessary people. Then I collected a pass key and went to Charles's rooms.'

'Why did you do that?'

'I don't know that I can give a logical answer to that question. It was obvious something was very, very wrong. It was just a reaction to see if any of his things had been tampered with.'

'And had they?'

'By God, yes! The sitting room was a shambles. His desk drawers and cupboards were open. There were papers and files everywhere. In the fireplace there was a large pile of ash.'

'Vare's letters and diaries?'

'So the forensic experts said.'

'What did you do?'

'Nothing.'

'Nothing?'

'I was thinking more clearly by then. It was obvious the police would want to examine the rooms and wouldn't want anything disturbed. So I just left and made sure the oak was firmly locked.'

'And you told the police you'd been there?'

'Yes . . . Well . . . to be honest, no. They never asked and there didn't seem to be any point in volunteering the information. I've never told anybody, so how on earth . . . Look, you won't mention this to anyone, will you?'

'I can't see that that would do any good. But, tell me, what conclusions did the police come to?'

'There was no evidence that anyone else had been in the room. They decided that Charles must have gone berserk and destroyed his personal papers before . . .'

'Poor Stuart. It must have been dreadful for you.' Catherine glowered at Tim and took her friend's arm. 'Let's get out of here.'

Ten minutes later, when the Lacys had left St Mary's and were walking back to the hotel, Catherine rounded on her husband. 'What in heaven's name was all that about? What were you trying to do to the poor man?'

Tim shrugged. 'I was following up an anonymous lead. I had no idea I was ripping the plaster off a fresh wound.' He pulled the letter from his coat pocket and gave it to her.

Catherine smoothed it out and read, 'Ask what happened to Dr Vare's letters and diaries.'

'Someone left that for me at the hotel reception this morning.'

'But who? Why?'

'Right now I'm more interested in another question – Why me? If someone's really unhappy about poor old

Vare's death why don't they direct their anonymous letters to the police?'

Neither of them could come up with an answer to that. They walked on in silence. Ten minutes later they were in their car and part of a slow column of traffic moving along Trumpington Street. They passed the forbidding façade of St Mary's House – a blank wall of ancient red brick.

Catherine shivered. 'It looks like the very embodiment of what you were talking about earlier – the establishment; closed in on itself; determined to guard its sinister secrets from probing eyes.'

'In that case I suppose we must have looked like spies who had somehow slipped in past the guards.' Tim braked as a young cyclist swerved in front of the Mercedes 500SL and stood there waiting for a gap to appear in the stream of vehicles going in the opposite direction.

'Perhaps that's it.'

'It?'

'The answer to your question, Why me? The college has had a nasty shock. There's been a grizzly death. It's taken the lid off a serpent's nest of suspicions and secrets and awkward questions. Then, the Master – who is not the most popular man for the job – invites a complete stranger along for some top-secret discussions. No wonder everyone was so curious to know why we were there.'

Someone a few cars back hooted, but at that moment the cyclist crossed to the far pavement and the convoy was released. Tim accelerated into the empty stretch of road and roared past the Fitzwilliam Museum. 'You think someone put two and two together and came up with the wrong answer?'

'Well if there are some troubled minds and guilty consciences lurking behind those walls it would be very easy for someone to assume that you've been brought in as some sort of private investigator to clear up the outstanding questions about Vare's death.'

'Hence the mysterious note.'

'Exactly.'

'That makes sense. Fortunately, it's not our problem. I've been hired to do a straightforward job which has nothing to do with suicidal deans.'

'You're going ahead with the Sydney trip?'

'Why not? To be brutally commercial, it's money for jam. And I can fit in some other jobs on the back of it. There are a couple of people I ought to see in the States. We might even manage a flying visit to your folks.'

'Mm, sounds good.' Catherine slipped a cassette into the player. She snuggled down into the soft leather. The car heated up rapidly as the engine revs increased. If she had any misgivings, the warmth, the wide, fenland landscape and the gentle strains of the César Franck violin sonata soon massaged them away.

CHAPTER 3

It was mid-February before Tim was able to fulfil his commission for St Mary's House. He and Catherine arrived in Sydney on a moist, warm Wednesday and the following morning Tim took a taxi to the offices of McDougal, Pratos and Pratos.

Harry Pratos, the late Sir Peregrine's solicitor, turned out to be a bustling, ebullient man in his mid-forties. The only evidences of Greek extraction were his very black, crinkly hair and his dark eyes. The formal business was soon concluded. Tim presented his letter of authorization from Sir Evelyn Masquerier together with his passport as proof of identity. Then the lawyer opened a wall safe and drew from it a large cardboard box. A stuck-on label bore the printed legend PAUL WHITEHEAD'S PAPERS – FOR ST MARY'S HOUSE, CAMBRIDGE, UK. He placed it on the desk, removed the lid and took out a typed sheet of paper.

'This is the list of contents, Mr Lacy. Perry was very meticulous. Would you care to check that everything is there?'

The catalogue was brief:

1. Autobiographical fragments (1 file)
2. Correspondence (2 files)
3. Journal of the Order of St Francis of Medmenham (2 folio volumes bound in contemporary full calf)
4. Drawings (1 file)
5. Notes for a biography of Paul Whitehead by P.G.F.W.-D. (2 files)

Tim counted off the eight items. Each envelope-file cover had its own neat label and, inside, a typed list of contents. 'Everything seems to be in order, Mr Pratos. I assume nothing's missing from any of the files?'

The lawyer looked pained at the suggestion. 'I had my secretary go through everything very thoroughly. Perry impressed upon me that these were very important historical documents. Not, of course, that that made any difference to our attitude. We're very conscientious here at MPP.'

He produced a receipt and Tim signed it. That concluded their business, but Pratos was in no hurry to bring the meeting to a close. He offered coffee and chattered volubly about a recent trip he had made to Europe.

'You must travel a great deal in your business, Mr Lacy.'

'Yes, but I'm afraid globe-trotting loses much of its excitement when you have to do a lot of it.'

'I see you're not based in Cambridge. You are, perhaps, also a member of Perry's old college?' The man was obviously fishing.

'No. This is purely a business arrangement.' Tim decided

to do some probing of his own. 'Did you know Sir Peregrine well?'

Pratos's smile widened – almost with relief, it seemed to Tim, as though he had been waiting for an excuse to talk about his late client. 'Oh, yes. Perry and I were . . . well, not exactly mates; he was a very solitary man who had no real friends. I reckon I got as close as anyone. Ours wasn't just a professional relationship. We shared a passion for computers. That was how we met, eight – no, it must be nine years ago. He wanted to set up his own fairly sophisticated system, so he came a couple of times to a club I helped to run – we called ourselves the Megabites.'

'Why did a retired diplomat want expensive PC equipment?'

'Oh, it was all to do with his research. He was fanatically keen on it. I suppose you could say it became almost an obsession.'

'But surely, if it was just a question of making notes and putting information on disc he wouldn't need anything terribly complicated?'

'Oh, there was much more to it than that. Perry had computer and modem links with libraries, other scholars and researchers all over the world. He collected a vast amount of information.'

Tim looked puzzled. He tapped the box. 'And it all came down to just this?'

Pratos laughed. 'Indeed, no. Perry had several irons in the fire. He had a marvellously agile brain. He was always following up some obscure line of historical enquiry.'

'So who inherited the rest of his papers?'

There was an awkward silence. Then Pratos shrugged his

shoulders and sighed. 'Ah, there's the tragedy. There were none.'

'What do you mean?'

The lawyer spoke slowly, searching for words having the right degree of caution. 'During his last few months, poor Perry was very depressed. He'd been in and out of hospital for a couple of years. That was all very wearying. When, at last, the doctors told him there was nothing more they could do . . .'

'What was it? Cancer?'

'Yes. I'm sorry, I assumed you knew. I suppose he came to the conclusion that all his efforts had been wasted. He was never going to complete his work. Anyway, he methodically destroyed all his papers and discs and erased his data banks. All he kept was what's in that box.'

'So he died convinced that he was a failure. That is sad.'

Pratos stared into space. 'He went downhill fast. The disease, of course. Wasting. Crushing. Terrible. But his soul, too, seemed to wither within him. He'd always had a mordant wit. Although he was a solitary man he did sometimes have groups of visitors to stay. He told me they met for informal seminars about religion and philosophy. Then he stopped seeing anyone. He only spoke to me in a professional capacity. He was angry, bitter. Felt that fate had cheated him. Who's to blame him for that? A distinguished public career, and it all ends in pain and despair and pointlessness.'

'Did he have no relatives at all?'

'Just a nephew in Canada. He was the sole beneficiary under the will, apart from a legacy to his Abo manservant and this box of papers. I'm sure glad to have discharged one of my responsibilities as Perry's executor. Getting rid of the house won't be so easy.'

'You've got to sell it?'

'Yes, lock, stock and barrel. The nephew hasn't even been here to look the place over.' Pratos was struck with a sudden idea. 'Say would you like to see the house?'

Tim laughed. 'What, as a prospective buyer?'

'Heck, no. Just out of curiosity. I could drive you out sometime if you're interested. I pop over once a week to make sure there are no vandals, tramps or squatters around. I'd be glad of the company and I could point out some of the local beauty spots on the way.'

Tim explained that their schedule was pretty full, but he and the lawyer managed to find a mutually free slot on Friday afternoon and arranged to meet again then. As Harry Pratos held the door open for his guest, he muttered, 'To tell you the truth I don't care to go out there alone. The house gives me the creeps. Got a pretty name, though. Perry called it "Medmenham".'

The Lacys only had a couple of days for sightseeing in Sydney and they filled them to capacity. There was little time to think or talk about Sir Peregrine and his papers, but Catherine was intrigued by Tim's report of his discussion with the lawyer. 'Positively gothic' was how she described the account of the ex-diplomat's last days. Her imagination conjured up a sinister scene; the rambling, decrepit mansion set on a storm-lashed promontory, occupied by an emaciated, dying old man and a shambling servant carrying out primitive rites in the back kitchen. It was an image that kept thrusting itself into her mind when she was not absorbed by the opera, the art galleries, the botanic gardens or bathing at Manly beach. By the time Friday arrived her curiosity about Medmenham had reached a high point.

It was a wet afternoon when Harry Pratos drove them out to Port Hacking. Rain dropped from the trees as the lawyer unpadlocked the main gate. The house was completely masked by a belt of woodland and as the car wound its way along the drive it seemed that virtually the whole of Medmenham's grounds had been given over to plantations. They came upon the house suddenly – a shambling, turn-of-the-century building, all turrets and gables. The walls were so covered with ivy and other creepers that Sir Perry's residence seemed to have grown rather than been built there.

Harry went in ahead of them, drawing curtains to let in whatever light the grey afternoon and the towering trees permitted to reach the windows. Then he led them through a wide hall into a large drawing room.

'This is lovely,' Catherine exclaimed, with some relief. The space was well proportioned, the walls were papered in a delicate pattern of greens and yellows, marred only by large discoloured rectangles indicating where pictures had once been. Tall windows looked out onto lawns and the distant sea. 'Have you stored the pictures somewhere else for safety?'

The lawyer looked at her warily and shook his head. 'No, they all went onto Sir Perry's bonfire. Leastways, I think so. We found bits of unburned, gilded frames among the huge pile of ashes over by the garden wall. Pity, I reckon he probably had some valuable stuff here.'

'You saw them?'

'Glimpsed them – once. Sir Perry never brought me into this room, but one day, as I was passing, the door was open and I saw these big oil-paintings – looked like naked gods and goddesses. Sort of thing that doesn't leave much to the imagination, know what I mean?'

They walked through other rooms, smaller and more oppressive, cluttered with dust-sheeted furniture. Catherine found the parody of an old poem learned in school days coming into her head:

> I do not love thee, Medmenham.
> To say quite why, bemused I am.
> Who knows it, I don't give a damn:
> I do not love thee, Medmenham.

She wanted to be out of this place and was annoyed with herself for being silly. The house was certainly not the Hammer Horror gothic of her imagination. Its depressing, lifeless chill was fully explained by the fact that it had been long devoid of human presence. 'Buildings do not have psychic vibrations,' she told herself and trod firmly in the lawyer's wake.

They were on the first-floor landing now and Pratos was juggling with a large bunch of keys. The door in front of him was fastened by three massive locks. 'This is the place that'll blow your mind,' he said, as he successfully located and fitted the last key.

It was dark inside and the Lacys could make out nothing until Pratos had pulled back heavy curtains from windows that they noticed were barred. A kind of bench seemed to run around three walls and was completely covered with sheeting. The lawyer whisked this away to reveal a display of very up-to-date computerized communication equipment.

Tim said 'Wow! This must have cost a packet.'

Pratos ran his fingers lovingly over video screens, consoles and tape decks. 'Yep, nothing but the best for Sir Perry. He was constantly updating his equipment. I'm supposed to be selling all this off. You've no idea what a temptation that presents.'

Tim professionally appraised the technological masterpieces. 'And you say nothing is left of all the research he was doing here?'

'Not a scrap. Every disc destroyed. Every memory bank erased.'

'Weird,' Tim commented.

'Eerie,' Catherine added.

They retraced their steps, Pratos carefully locking and covering behind them, climbed into the lawyer's sleek BMW and began the drive back into the city.

Catherine was, almost despite herself, intrigued by the enigma of Sir Peregrine Whitehead-Dyer and his clandestine researches. When she and Tim took off on their plane for San Francisco she had in her flight bag some of Sir Perry's precious papers. As the 747 headed east over the empty ocean she settled into her window seat, opened the file neatly labelled 'Autobiographical Fragments' and began to read the sheets of thick, yellowing paper, stitched down the left-hand side and covered with lines of flowing, well-spaced script.

Since stern-faced Death with fingered lips shall call
Soon for the silence of poor 'Aged Paul';
Since from the tomb no man has power to tame
The calumnies that snarl around his name;
Let these lines tell in grave-defying ink
The deeds of one who cares not what men think.

I date my birth not from the apostle's festal day in 1710 when my mother was brought to bed of her first and only surviving child in her chamber above the tailor's shop in Castle Yard, Holborn, where my father plied his honest trade but, rather, from that morning, some twenty summers later, when I was admitted to England's premier university, the Fleet prison for debtors. It was there, among bawd-masters, out-of-favour courtiers in stained silks, hucksters, suspected backgammon players,* failed tradesmen, discarded old wasps,† blockheads, boorish cits‡ railing against injustice and men brought low by their own honesty that my spirit was truly 'born'.

Up until that time I had attempted to please my father by becoming apprenticed to a mercer and, later, my mother by making a study of the law. Concluding, at last, that it was time to please myself, I essayed to make a living with my pen. For two years I trundled out poems and verse satires from a garret in Poultry, picking up gossip scraps in the taverns frequented by parliament men and court gallants to furnish my lampoons. Being ambitious for sudden fame, I

* sodomites
† prostitutes carrying the pox
‡ dull townsmen

wrote a play and felt no end flattered when Fleetwood, the theatrical manager, received it enthusiastically and undertook to produce it. The rogue promised great profits if I would only stand surety for a loan of £3000 he was taking out to finance the piece. I possessed not a hundredth part of such a sum but, dazzled by the prospect of celebrity, I willingly set my name to the bond. It was for this folly that I fetched up in the Fleet. *Dies irae, dies gloriae.* From the ashes of my humiliation sprang forth my true calling. Procuration. From that time such fortune and fame as I have achieved have come from furnishing wealthy men and women with the objects of their desires.

I was cast into the common gaol, a large chamber on the street level, and thought myself the most unhappy man on earth. The bare room was inhabited by threescore creatures – I can scarcely call them men and women – listless, emaciated, clad only in rags. As I entered, a recently-dead inmate was being carried out and four wretches were fighting over his favoured place in the far corner. All other eyes were turned on me, exploring my coat, my breeches, my shoes and hose, seeking the pocket-bulge which might indicate money, assessing the worth of buttons, braid and even the kerchief I held to my nose against the stench. I found an empty space by a wall and there crouched, wondering how I would ever dare to sleep in the company of miscreants made desperate by destitution.

So I languished, fearful and miserable till, a little after noon, a ruffian appeared in the doorway and told me I was summoned to the 'King of the Fleet'. I followed my guide across courtyards strewn with foetid pools, up shuddering staircases and along sepulchral passages devoid of all illumination save that which seeped in through grimy casements, and entered, at length, a suite of rooms which by comparison with the chamber I had just left were palatial. The withdrawing room, in which I was now left, was peopled by as motley a collection of suitors as ever graced St James's. Some were ragged, some clad in oft-repaired garments. All displayed an *hauteur* which set them apart, in their own minds at least, from the rabble without. At any other time I would have laughed out loud to see how pride of rank and name exerts itself even in the most degrading of situations. One by one they came and went through a door at the far end of the room guarded by a servant in faded blue livery that had gone many times too often to the laundry.

When my summons arrived I passed into a chamber furnished with chairs, tables and Turkey carpets. A good fire of coals glowed in the hearth and before it four gentlemen sat at a mahogany table playing loo.* They all appeared overheated with wine despite the smallness of the hour, and had laid aside coats and wigs. The host, a young man of about my years in a powder-blue brocade waistcoat and wine-stained shirt, beckoned me with a wide-armed gesture.

'So, we have a new addition to our court and a man of letters into the bargain.'

'Sir, you are well informed,' I replied. 'And there you have the advantage of me.'

'Toby Fane at your service, sir. May I present my friends, Tom Cavendish, Bubb Dodington and Signor Tampoli.'

* a card game

Tampoli, a bald wisp of a man, I knew by repute to be one of the finest fencing masters in London. The other two were unknown to me. The rotund Dodington was to feature prominently in my life over the years ahead. Cavendish was a nonentity and I can scarce now recall his appearance. Fane's name I recognized as having been mentioned in a financial scandal some months before.

'Do I have the honour of addressing the Honourable Tobias Fane, son of the Earl of Dorchester?'

He laughed, throwing back his cropped head. 'Yes, I am the son of that cantankerous old skinflint. You'll take some claret, Master Whitehead?'

I crouched by the fire with my goblet to warm myself and to mull the wine with an iron protruding from the coals.

'There's lemon and sugar on the shelf there, if you've a mind to them,' Fane said casually, then fell to concentrating on the cards.

I watched them for several minutes. They were playing the five-card version and every time a player was looed* he was obliged to double the pool. There was already a large pile of guineas and smaller coins in the centre of the table. The younger men played with sweating concentration but Bubb was casual and careless. He did not seem to mind losing, which he did with almost clockwork regularity. The climax came when Fane triumphantly spread his hand, revealing a blaze† and swept the heap of silver and gold to his own corner.

The Italian pushed his chair back. 'A thousand curses on

* failed to take a trick
† five court cards

you, Toby,' he laughed. 'I think you have Fortuna imprisoned here in the Fleet somewhere and can compel her favours. Well, you have taken enough from me for one day.' He stood up, lifted his lavender silk coat from the floor and slipped it on. Fastidiously he brushed the dust from it. 'Anyway, I have to go to Leicester House to give Prince Frederick his lesson.'

Fane was engaged in drawing the cork from a bottle with his coat of arms embossed in the black glass. 'Convey our loyal greetings to the Prince of Wales, Giorgio. Or mine, anyway. I know what it is to suffer the burden of a tyrannical and parsimonious father. Tom will pledge himself a supporter of the three feathers, too. Won't you Tom? For roly-poly Bubb, I cannot speak. He's a cautious fellow. Always backs both sides, whether it's a knuckle fight or politics. Ain't that so, Bubb?'

The large man laughed good-humouredly. 'I enjoy the confidence of Sir Robert but I forget not my duty to the heir to the throne.'

'There, what did I tell you!' Fane waved the bottle triumphantly. 'A trimmer, if ever I saw one. What about you, Master Whitehead? Are you for the King and Walpole and his damnable Whigs or for the Prince and the red-blooded new men?'

I have never espoused a political philosophy. Like politicians, I care for the public weal only as far as it serves my own. In any case, this was not a moment for nicely weighed judgement. It was an opportunity to perform and, like a precocious child or a well-trained dog, I seldom let such chances escape. My facility with verse yearned to be displayed. I stood, took a step forward, like Mr Garrick (a few years later) about to deliver a soliloquy, and declaimed, *all' improvviso*:

> 'Walpole? Who's he? A commoner raised on high.
> How came he there? Some swain left ope' the sty
> And, snorting forth, the sly, ambitious pig
> Possessed the farmer's house and donned his wig.'

The laughter and applause of my little audience were gratifyingly enthusiastic.

Fane came across and put an arm round my shoulder. 'Excellent! Excellent! What we hear of you is true. Tom, we can use a wit like this, can we not? There's several pompous bladders need deflating with such shafts as this. Master Whitehead, welcome to our little court. Now, we must find you quarters. Tom has a chamber big enough for two. It's on the better side of the building, well away from the Fleet Ditch. You'll be tolerably comfortable there. Will that suit you, do you think?'

I protested that I had not the means to pay for such accommodation. Fane waved my objection aside.

'In the brotherhood of the Fleet money is not the only currency. The sums I win from my friends on the outside enable me to maintain a certain style and to pay for all the services I need. But, as to my retainers here; they look to me, not for wages, but for such necessities and luxuries as my means can command. In return for board and lodging you shall be my court jester. Your splendid lampoons will amuse my guests and who knows but that we shall not be able to use them to dislodge some fat parrots of the court and parliament from their perches.'

So it was arranged. For three years I was a member of Toby Fane's inner circle, the Fleet élite. This young scion was one of those wastrels who, having exhausted all his substance, preferred to take up residence in a debtors' jail where no creditor could pursue him. There he lived a not disagreeable life while he waited for the inheritance which would come his way on the death of his aged sire. To him resorted friends and hangers-on who hoped, by investing acts of petty generosity, to receive a considerable return when the young nobleman came into his own. The Fleet became quite a fashionable calling place. Men and women of rank flocked thither to offer loans, gifts, or to lose at cards or dice to the man who must shortly become one of the richest grandees in England.

In this university, this *microcosmos* of humanity, I set myself to study and to profit from my labours. Many subjects fell within my syllabus. I soon graduated in satire. None of Fane's friends lacked for enemies and they paid well for lampoons which they could take away, have printed and then circulate to their foes' discomfort. It was reliably reported that not a few duels were fought and participants slain as a result of my verses. At art, too, I was an apt pupil. Daubing, like scribbling, had always come naturally to me. Some visitors were amused to have their portraits sketched. But caricature was more in fashion and I made much use of my talent with pen and brush to poke fun at rivals and opponents of my patron's circle.

The third branch of my trivium was debauchery. I graduated easily and naturally from the position of court jester to that of *major domo* of the Fane court. Boredom was always our most persistent adversary in the Fleet. It followed that diversions were at a premium. Since my benefactor and the young bucks who resorted to his chambers universally lacked imagination there was an obvious vacancy for the post of master of the revels. I readily filled it and discovered it to be lucrative in the extreme. 'Where Virtue's jewels are ne'er put forth for gold/Vice sets her stall of tawdries to be sold.' I had at my disposal an ever-changing stock of human merchandize. The destitute, the desperate, the degraded creatures admitted through the portals of the Fleet were easily recruited to provide sport for my gambling patrons. A few pennies would buy young men for bouts of fisticuffs, walking cadavers for pie-eating contests or rival whores willing to undertake feats of libidinous endurance.

It was in this area of providing for Fane's sexual satisfaction that my best hope of continued patronage – and, therefore, survival – lay. The necessary outlets for his passions were greatly restricted in the Fleet. There were many women there, to be sure, and most would do anything for silver, but Fane's fear of the French disease was so great that he shunned what lay most readily to hand. In fact, he had developed a decided preference for virgins – in the Fleet a scant commodity indeed and scarce to be found in the whole of London town. In my efforts to please him I, at first, tried him with punks and wagtails* well-schooled in the art of playing the innocent, but Fane could always tell whether a barrel had been tapped before. How to pander to my master's desires in such unpromising circumstances was a problem which constantly cudgelled my wits. I realized how much could hang upon it. If somehow I could find a

---

* prostitutes and loose women

supply of virtuous maidens there was little doubt that I could establish a permanent position in Fane's entourage – a position that would guarantee my release from prison, the settlement of my debts and entrée to England's best society for years to come. As so often happens with difficult conundrums, the solution, once stumbled upon by accident, seemed thereafter glaringly obvious.

This is how I discovered it.

CHAPTER 4

'Odious creep!' Catherine closed the file and pushed it into the rack in front of her with the sick bags and in-flight magazines.

'What have I done, now?' Tim turned to his wife, eyebrow raised.

Catherine punched him playfully. 'Not you, silly. Paul Whitehead.'

'Not a nice man?'

'A common pimp!'

'Well, his descendant thought rather better of him. I've been reading Sir Perry's "Notes for a biography".' Tim referred to the sheaf of papers he was holding. 'This is how it begins:

On a spring morning in 1775 a strange procession could have been observed making its way through the village of West Wycombe in Buckinghamshire. Six grenadiers carried a bier on which was an urn and they were followed by a little group of mourners. They left the mansion of

Francis Dashwood, Baron le Despencer, and made their way up the hill to the newly-built hexagonal mausoleum beside the church. According to a contemporary report,

> The Dead March was played by the flutes, horns and bassoons, successively with the fifes and the drums of the Bucks Militia and great guns were discharged every three-and-a-half minutes. The cortège passed three times round the inside of the mausoleum still playing Saul's Funeral March whilst a special oratorio composed by Dr Arnold was sung in the church. Its theme was 'Whitehead's soul to Heaven fled – Hallelujah'. The urn was placed in a specially-prepared niche after which the soldiers fired a salute (triple) with great exactness and precision.

The urn, so solemnly bestowed in its noble resting place bore the heart of Paul Whitehead and carried the following inscription:

> Unhallowed hands this urn forebear,
> No gems nor orient spoil
> Lie here concealed – but what's more rare
> A HEART, that knew no guile.'

Catherine sniffed. 'Well either we're talking about two different guys or Whitehead underwent a pretty thorough conversion. In his autobiography he gloats – drools would be a better word – about being a purveyor of whores to the aristocracy.'

'Sir Peregrine reckons his ancestor has been much maligned.'

'Well, I'd say the jury's still out on that.'

'How come? You haven't read all the evidence yet.'

'I don't think I want to. If this is the sort of stuff academics like to goggle at in their ivory towers, they're welcome!'

'Really? I confess I'm rather intrigued. Let me have a look at those papers, will you?'

'Men!' Catherine pulled a face and handed over the slim file.

Before Tim could settle to reading Whitehead's auto-biographical jottings a stewardess appeared with champagne and hors d'oeuvres – the opening salvo in the long bombardment of the airline's first-class lunch.

An hour and a half later he refused a second brandy, surrendered his empty coffee cup, reclined his seat and gave his attention to the narrative which Paul Whitehead had set down two and a half centuries before. Tim was a faster, less committed reader than his wife. The sort of books he liked were strong on action and wasted little space on characterization and descriptive passages. He skimmed through the first pages of the manuscript and soon passed the point at which Catherine had given up in disgust.

This is how I discovered it.

One day there was admitted to the Fleet a certain Samuel Hirsch, a member, as you will have guessed, of the tribe of Abraham. It was unusual to encounter a Jew in any debtors' prison, for that community is, by and large, assiduous in caring for its own. This Hirsch, however, was a recent immigrant who had brought his family to England to escape persecution in his own land. Arriving with virtually no resources, having little understanding of the language and customs of his adopted country, and wanting friends to advise him, he soon fell in with rogues who divested him of the little money he did have.

My first sight of Hirsch was of his feet. I had descended to the common gaol one morning to survey the latest trawl of inmates and discovered a fight in progress. Three men had a fourth pinned to the floor and were tearing off his clothes. As I entered, one of the assailants jumped up, triumphantly brandishing a pair of very serviceable shoes.

'What's afoot here?' I mildly enquired of the crone who was my principal informant among the lower orders. The jest was wasted on her.

'Don't trouble yourself with him, sir. He's only a Jew. There's many here have suffered badly at the hands of suchlike. It's a treat to have one of them at *our* mercy for a change.'

'What's his trade? Surely he cannot be a moneylender?'

'He says he's a musician.' She mimicked a flute or fife player and emitted a hideous whistling through her few remaining teeth.

'A musician?' I brought my stick down heavily across the shoulders of the nearest ruffian. 'Come off! Come off, this instant!'

I had begun to exercise not a little authority over the wretches in that inner ring of *Inferno*. They recognized me as a potential and actual benefactor whose favours were well worth cultivating. Several sprang immediately to break up the scuffle, with blows, curses and shouts of 'Mr Whitehead says to let him go!'

The unfortunate Hirsch struggled to his feet. He adjusted his clothing. He made a bow in my direction – instantly parodied by three or four members of the gathered circle. 'Zank you. Zank you, kint zir.'

He was of middle years; a small whippet of a man, lean rather than thin, clean-shaven with a good head of black hair. Despite his circumstances, he mastered a certain dignity of bearing once I had had his shoes and long brown coat returned to him.

'I understand that you are a musician,' I observed.

'Zir?' He wrinkled his brow and shrugged apologetically.

It was clear that I was going to make little progress with the man. Then I remembered 'Judge' Hampney. Hampney was a short-stay tenant – an educated man and a diplomat who had drunk his way into debt and whose friends at court and in the City were energetically raising funds on his behalf. He was known as Judge because, when under the influence of wine or spirits, he became incredibly solemn and would pontificate in profound-sounding Latin for hours together. Hampney was lodged in tolerable quarters near my own and I knew that he had command of many languages. To Hampney's chambers I conveyed my latest protégé.

We found Judge propped up in bed with a damp cloth wound, turban-like, round his head. He prised his eyelids apart and surveyed us with evident discomfort. 'Who's that? Whitehead? This is a damned uncivilized hour to call.'

I introduced Hirsch and explained the nature of our visit. Grumbling, Hampney swung his legs out of bed, wrapped himself in a brocade day gown and sat glowering at us through half-closed eyes. With Judge acting as interpreter I discovered that Hirsch was a maker of musical instruments and a violin player who, so he claimed, had performed before princes. I asked if he still had his fiddle and the little Jew assured me that it was his most treasured possession and guarded closely by his wife. I told him that if he would send for it and if he was as accomplished as he claimed I could provide him with employment that would enable him to buy some little comforts and, perhaps, go some way towards the payment of his debts.

Hirsch readily agreed. I provided pen and paper for him to write a note and gave one of the keepers twopence to convey the message to the Jew's lodgings. Then I dismissed the little Hebrew with instructions to come to my chamber that evening for a private demonstration of his ability so that I could decide whether to commend him to Toby Fane. There was a serious want of good music in my master's court. I had assembled a little choir of rough voices capable of rendering the latest roistering, bawdy songs (including some from my own pen) but there were occasions when something rather more refined was called for and I had little doubt that Samuel Hirsch would fill the bill admirably. So I congratulated myself on my new find and temporarily dismissed him from my mind.

Had it not been for a dim-witted messenger I should unwittingly have discovered a shilling and lost a guinea. An hour later the man I had despatched was back. He stood in my doorway dressed incongruously in a coat that had been well in fashion some dozen seasons before and was now grimy and buttonless. He seemed to have been struck dumb.

'Well, man,' I demanded. 'Have you completed your errand? Have you delivered Mr Hirsch's violin to him?'

He frowned, the complexity of my questions seeming to place an intolerable strain upon the inadequate mental machinery with which Nature had equipped him. 'Well, not exactly, Mr Whitehead.'

'What do you mean, not exactly? Either you've brought the fiddle or you haven't.'

'Oh, I brought it. Leastways . . .'

I thought I saw the berth to which his craft was uncertainly heading. 'If you think I am going to give you more than twopence for such a simple errand you overestimate your value and my generosity.'

'No, it's not that, Mr Whitehead. It's just that she wouldn't let me have it. She would come, too.'

'Who, man?'

'Why, the Jew's daughter, I suppose. Only I don't know for certain, for I couldn't understand a word she said. When I got to the place this girl let me in. Mrs Hirsch – I suppose it was her – was abed with a slight fever. But she was well enough to read the note and she says something to the girl and the girl fetches the violin, all wrapped up in a cloth. Only she wouldn't give it to me. She and the girl just shook their heads and jabbered in a foreign gibberish. So I come away. I hadn't gone no more than a dozen paces when I finds this girl at my elbow. Came with me all the way, she did. I didn't know what to do with her so I brought her to you.'

He stood aside and I caught my first glimpse of Hannah Hirsch.

Her hair, escaping from beneath a small cap, was glistening

and raven black. Her eyes were dark and wide. Her cheeks had the feathery softness of a finch's breast. Her lips were moist and slightly pouting. Her body, well-formed for the twelve or thirteen years I supposed her to be, was outlined in every detail by a thin dress that was slightly too small. She stood in the doorway with the tremulous, wary grace of a forest creature. She was utterly ravishing and all the more appealing because she was totally ignorant of the fact.

I beckoned her to come into the room which she did cautiously, hugging her father's precious violin to her. I signalled to her to turn around which, with a slight frown, she did. She was perfect for Fane. He would be unable to resist her. Therein lay her passport to fortune – and mine. I held out my hand for the fiddle. The girl shook her head and clasped the instrument more tightly to her. Slowly I took from my waistcoat pocket a shilling. The child's eyes widened. It was probably more money than she had ever been offered before. She looked from the coin to my face, then to the violin. I read easily the conflict taking place behind those soft brown eyes. She was weighing the family's most treasured possession against the immediate needs of her sick mother. I waited motionless, holding my breath, smiling and fixing my eyes upon that young face. Much more than she knew or I at that moment could guess rested upon her decision.

Falteringly at first, then with clear resolve, she stepped forward holding one hand palm upwards and offering the precious bundle with the other. In that instant she was unmade and made.

That night Samuel Hirsch played for Fane and his guests. Those that were sober enough to appreciate his music vowed him the finest fiddler they had heard in many a year. The Jew gathered a meagre harvest of copper coins and his gratitude to me soared to new heights. Such was his implicit trust that I easily persuaded him, with the Judge's aid, that Hannah could perform useful services for me as an errand girl – for which I would, of course, pay her well.

I need not dwell on the stages by which I won the delectable creature's confidence. I had now so far advanced myself as to be in possession of my own chamber, and in the privacy of my own domain I was, by turns, Hannah's casual employer, her English tutor, her friend and, ultimately, her instructor in the arts of Venus. It was frustrating in the extreme not to be able to bring her to her baccalaureat in that discipline but I kept in my mind at all times the ultimate purpose of my tutelage. When the moment was right I admitted my patron to the secret and aroused his eager anticipation. So successful was my stratagem that, not only did my pupil afford Toby Fane great satisfaction, she also remained his mistress for many years thereafter. In the meantime, little Hannah had begun to make playmates in the streets of Aldgate and several of them were, over succeeding months, introduced to our intimate circle. I dare say Hannah Hirsch was then the youngest madam in London. As for her father, he was by now so far dependent upon my aristocratic friend's support that, whatever his parental feelings, he raised no serious protest. I may perhaps be allowed something of a boast by way of postscript. Some years later Hannah, having abandoned her Hebrew ancestry, became the wife of a semi-lunatic duke, thus introducing talented and enterprising new blood to a failing dynasty. So I may reasonably claim to have made some mark on the pages of history.

The Shugmayers' apartment occupied the top floor of one of the taller buildings fronting the ocean. The first sight that struck Tim and Catherine as they emerged from the elevator was the sun. It rested on the horizon and seemed to be tethered there by the gold streamers which stretched across the ultramarine water. The entire spectacle, framed by the wooden surround of a wide window, gave the impression of having been painted for the exclusive enjoyment of Wayne and Gertrude Shugmayer and their favoured guests.

'Tim, great to see you. So glad you could make it!' Their host, a hundred-and-sixty pounds of tanned, light-suited energy, pounced on them immediately. 'Honey, this is Tim Lacy, another visitor from England.'

Introductions were made and Catherine shook hands with Gertrude ('Call me Gerty') Shugmayer, the more sedate (dominated, Catherine guessed) member of the partnership. Catherine appraised and approved the floral silk suit. Gerty, unlike her husband, was content to look her age and did not try to behave like someone twenty years younger.

'*Another* visitor from England?' Catherine enquired.

'Why, yes. We have a very dear friend staying with us. He arrived this morning. Such a lovely surprise. We hadn't seen him in five years, and suddenly we had this call from the airport. Now, let me see if I can find him and introduce you.'

She led the latest arrivals through three interconnecting rooms lightly sprinkled with little clusters of guests. 'Ah, there he is.' Mrs Shugmayer viewed her quarry in a far corner. She advanced on the backview of a stocky figure in an alpaca jacket. She called out 'Teddy' and added *sotto voce* to the Lacys, 'He's really a lord but he doesn't like friends using his title. Teddy, I want you to meet some other visitors from England.'

'Lord Everton!' Catherine exclaimed.

The flabby features arranged themselves in a wide smile. 'Mr and Mrs Lacy! Good heavens! Small world. Small world.'

'You know each other? How lovely.' Their hostess beamed, then excused herself as Wayne Shugmayer's 'Honey!' boomed from the next room.

'So,' the peer grasped their hands in turn and leaned forward to kiss Catherine's cheek. 'What brings you to California? By the way,' he added softly, 'it's just Teddy Everton out here. Some of these ex-colonials can get a bit touchy about titles.'

'Just a flying business trip,' Tim explained. 'Wayne wants to discuss the security for the extension he's donating to the museum.'

'Ah yes, he was showing me the plans earlier. Very impressive. Wayne and Gerty are generous patrons. Mind you, it's largely a tax dodge, isn't it?'

Tim took two glasses of white wine from a passing waitress and handed one to his wife. 'Yes, they get total exemption from state tax on the amount of their donation. It seems like a good idea to me. If we had something similar in Britain perhaps the arts wouldn't have such a hand-to-mouth existence. What's the reason for your visit, Teddy?'

'Project Anson,' the peer responded promptly. Then,

when the name drew no response, he went on to explain. 'One of my youth charities. We have a sail training ship, the *Admiral Anson*. She makes regular cruises all over the world with crews of underprivileged kids – actual or potential delinquents. They spend about three months aboard getting an invaluable experience of adventure, discipline and teamwork.'

Catherine sipped the chilled wine. 'Sounds like a good idea. It must be a very expensive scheme to run.'

'Quite right, my dear. We need to raise two hundred thousand a year, just to keep the *Anson* afloat. That explains why I'm here.'

'Fund raising from wealthy Americans,' Tim suggested.

'Just so, just so. Wherever the *Anson* docks we try to organize special events – civic receptions, displays, lectures. We try to point out the advantages of our corrective system. Putting a young thug on the *Anson* for three months costs a fraction of shutting him up in a detention centre for the same amount of time and is seventy-five per cent more effective in terms of keeping him away from a criminal career.'

Catherine gazed out at the setting sun, half-buried now in the ocean's rim. 'So your ship is here, in San Francisco?'

'Yes, she came in a few days ago for a crew changeover. A dozen American boys and girls will be replacing some of the youngsters who brought her across the Pacific. It gives us a good opportunity to unzip some of the fat West-Coast wallets. We're having a big charity dinner on Wednesday. You must come.'

Tim shook his head. 'I'm afraid we have to leave Wednesday morning. We're flying across to Maine for a couple of days with Catherine's parents. Then it's back to Wiltshire and, probably, a mountain of correspondence.'

'That's a pity.' Everton looked genuinely sorry. He brightened quickly. 'Talking about fund raising may I pester you further, Catherine, about our little festival at Chipping Sneddon? You did get my letter?'

'Er . . . yes. Thank you.' Catherine was embarrassed. A couple of weeks after her last chat with Lord Teddy the post had brought her a thick envelope containing glossy brochures about the Downham Homes and the Chipping Sneddon festival. It was still in her pending tray. 'I'm so sorry not to have gotten back to you before this . . .'

The fat peer raised a hand. 'No apology necessary, my dear. By way of expiation just say you'll help us by putting on one of your stunning exhibitions.'

Catherine found herself saying, with an enthusiasm she did not feel, 'Yes, of course, I'd love to.'

He beamed. 'Excellent! That's settled then. Now, look here, while you're in San Francisco you must at least fit in a visit to the *Anson*. She's a beautiful ship. How about lunch tomorrow?'

Tim looked doubtful. 'We've got a pretty tight schedule . . .'

'I won't entertain a refusal. Look here, one of our local committee members has access to a company helicopter and there's a pad on the roof of this very building. We can be over at the *Anson*'s berth in Oakland in a matter of minutes. And you'll have a fabulous view of San Francisco Bay from the air. Come on, now. What do you say?'

In the cab on the way back to their hotel Catherine said,

'That was an incredible coincidence meeting up with Lord Everton this far from home.'

Tim sat in the corner of the seat, running a thumb up and down the bridge of his nose. 'Perhaps incredible is the right word.'

'Whatever do you mean?'

'I don't know. Just an uneasy feeling. It seems a bit odd, that's all.'

'Stranger things happen.'

'Sure. I suppose I'm a bit nervous about these Hellfire Papers. Masquerier and Longton as good as told me they were afraid someone else would try to grab them. Then, when we're halfway home with them, this do-gooding peer of the realm whom we happen to have met for the first time at St Mary's House, turns up unexpectedly. Even his friends were surprised by his arrival.'

'But what interest can someone like Everton possibly have in a bundle of eighteenth-century memoirs? He's not an academic.'

Tim shrugged. 'I expect you're right. I'm just overreacting. Of course, there could be a different explanation.'

'Oh?'

'He's probably pursued you ruthlessly round the world to get you to agree to do that charity exhibition for him.'

Back at the hotel, Tim collected some of the files from the strongroom and sat up late delving further into the Whitehead story. There was a gap of several years in the rake's autobiographical material and Tim had to turn to his descendant's racy commentary to discover how Whitehead extricated himself from the Fleet prison and what happened to him over the next few years.

★ ★ ★

Lord Dorchester was gathered to his forefathers in April 1735. Determined to the last, he refused to allow his heir a foretaste of his patrimony. However, the strong dynastic principle to which ancient families are frequently enslaved prevented him disinheriting his ne'er-do-well son and young Toby became the owner of a fine Dorset mansion, an extensive estate, well-managed and unencumbered by mortgages, and a splendid town house in Pall Mall.

On the eve of his departure from the Fleet the new Earl of Dorchester threw a party, the like of which that austere building had never seen. It was the talk of London for weeks afterwards. And of course it was Paul Whitehead who organized it. The elaborate arrangements took several days and Paul insisted on his instructions being carried out to the letter. This was to be his moment of glory and he was going to make the most of it. He commandeered all the rooms on the first floor. He ordered bolts of blue and gold cloth to drape the grimed walls. At his behest, a procession of carriages and carts trundled between Pall Mall and Fleet Lane bearing barrels of wine, silver plate, candelabra, carpets, chairs and tables. Paul sent to the City poulterers, butchers, fishmongers and mercers for the very best produce to be delivered either direct to the prison or to the kitchens of Fane House for preparation. Note after note was sent off by the Earl's master of ceremonies to his patron's household servants, to his patron's tailor, and to the 'Abbess of Santa Carlotta'. This last was Charlotte Hayes, keeper of the most fashionable bagnio in London (Paul was careful to keep Hannah and her companions away from the company of common doxies). The invitations, despatched to many of the most prestigious addresses in the capital, respectfully requested the attendance of the recipients at 'a Solemn Ceremony to Mark the Disbanding of the August Brotherhood of the Fleet'.

When the guests arrived on the evening of the party they ascended a covered staircase erected outside the building which brought them to a casement on the first floor from which glass and frame had been removed. Within, a glittering scene welcomed them. A thousand candles flickered from stands and sconces. Liveried servants stood sentinel round walls gleaming with colour. Paul Whitehead was at the elbow of the host, who, resplendent in a coat of midnight blue over waistcoat and breeches of palest yellow, received his guests and gestured them towards the delights beyond. There his lordship's friends discovered chambers dedicated to all the pleasures. In one a banqueting table sagged beneath delicacies of every description. Another was sprinkled with card tables. In a third musicians played for dancing. A fourth had been divided into curtained and cushioned alcoves whither the gentlemen could resort with the nuns of Santa Carlotta, or other companions of their choosing.

Shortly before midnight servants circulated the rooms to gather all the revellers into the main salon for the 'ceremony'. Some of the gentlemen were by now staggering drunk. Other guests grumbled at being torn away from their diversions. But everyone duly assembled. Each, on entering the room, was presented with a long cloak of blue silk embroidered with a gold chain, the badge of the 'Brotherhood of the Fleet'. A similar covering had been spread over a table at one end of the chamber to transform it into an altar. On this a row of candles glinted in gilt holders. All other lights had been extinguished. In the gloom the congregation stood or lolled, amused and expectant. Though there was a deal of giggling and ribald comment, it was all in whispers. The master of ceremonies had succeeded in creating a church-like atmosphere.

At midnight precisely, three loud knocks shook the chamber door. A woman screamed at the sudden noise. Others laughed – some rather nervously. The door was thrown open to admit a little procession of white-robed figures, Fane's closest cronies. They slowly paced the length of the room, unmusically intoning a poor imitation of ecclesiastical chant. They carried a long chain, leading by it the head of their 'order' – a sombre-faced Toby Fane, robed now in a gold cope and mitre. Paul Whitehead brought up the rear in a cowled blue vestment and reverently carrying a large book.

When the group had arranged themselves before the altar, Whitehead turned to face the congregation and embarked on a solemn litany.

'Let us pray,' he chanted, in a high, quavering voice that drew snorts of laughter from the assembly. 'O spirit of the Fleet, hear us, we beseech thee.'

'Amen,' the brothers croakily responded.

'For those hours within these walls in which we have not dedicated ourselves to pleasure.'

'Forgive us, great spirit.'

'For days passed in soberness.'

'Forgive us, great spirit.'

'For maidens who have entered these precincts and departed in the same state.'

The congregation now began to fall in with the charade and joined the response. 'Forgive us, great spirit.'

'For nights when we have used our beds only for slumber.'

'Never!' someone shouted, to a chorus of laughter which drowned the response.

The 'high priest' raised his arms aloft and the room fell silent once more. 'O great spirit, since it hath pleased thee to release into the world thy faithful servant, Tobias, mercifully grant that he forget not those truths thou hast taught him in this place. Grant him long life and vigour to dedicate himself to the service of gut, tackle and baize.* World without end.'

A gusty 'Amen!' thundered from all throats.

Whitehead then turned to Lord Dorchester and, pointing with a bony forefinger, he commanded, '*Karxes meganoite.*'

Two of Fane's attendants released the chains, which fell with a clatter to the floor. The guests cheered. Whitehead took his patron's hand and led him slowly the length of the room. The crowd fell back on either side, the men bowing, the ladies deeply curtseying. The Earl passed into the neighbouring chamber, where the musicians struck up a martial air, and so to the opened casement. There he turned, held up a hand in brief benediction, then stepped out onto the improvized staircase. He descended to his carriage. The coachman cracked his whip and the freed man's equipage clattered away into the night.

Within hours someone, perhaps Whitehead himself, had written an account of these irreverent revelries, and rushed them to a press at the Sign of the Anchor in St Botolph's

---

* belly, genitals and the gambling table

Lane. Soon they were being sold on street corners all over the City.

Whitehead, literally, shared his patron's good fortune. Lord Dorchester found his Fleet companion too valuable to part with. He therefore settled Paul's debts and took him into his entourage. Thus was my outrageous ancestor well and truly launched into the very highest society. Dorchester and Bubb Dodington were firm favourites of the Prince of Wales who had by now established, at his house in Leicester Square, a rival court to that of his hated father, the King. The Prince's establishment was a honeypot to which were drawn wits, Tory politicians, malcontents and those who had fallen out with Walpole's regime. Whitehead luxuriated in the praise and generous support of several new patrons. But there was only one man in this glittering throng who was destined to change the course of Whitehead's life. Indeed, were it not for this one man my ancestor would have remained nothing but an insignificant royal hanger-on. That man was Sir Francis Dashwood.

Four bronzed young men in jeans and navy blue jumpers bearing the word ANSON in white letters, hauled powerfully and smoothly on the oars. With each stroke Tim and Catherine felt the boat surge across the surface of Oakland's inner harbour. As they sat in the stern with Lord Everton they had an excellent view of the *Admiral Anson*. She was moored in the centre of the bay against the backdrop of the massive San Francisco-Oakland bridge. The two objects made a dramatic contrast. The double-decker bridge was a considerable engineering feat but the *Anson* made it look cumbersome, heavy, crassly utilitarian. She rode serenely in the water, her white paintwork reflected in the still surface. The sails were tightly furled to the spars of her three masts. The ship was dressed overall with flags which twitched occasionally in the light breeze.

'Do you know what message the flags are giving?' Catherine asked the corpulent figure beside her.

Everton shook his head and repeated the question to one of the rowers, a slender lad with a thin face accentuated by his hairstyle – stubbly furrows ploughed between spiky black ridges. Without looking over his shoulder the boy responded, '*Anson* welcomes her honoured guests.' Having delivered himself of this concise reply, he returned to concentrating completely on the work in hand.

'She's certainly beautiful, isn't she, Tim?' Catherine gazed admiringly at the *Anson*'s graceful lines. 'She reminds me of some Masefield I learned in school:

> Those splendid ships, each with her grace, her glory,
> Her memory of old song or comrade's story,
> Still in my mind the image of life's need,
> Beauty in hard action, beauty indeed.'

Tim adjusted his sunglasses. 'Is there much that doesn't remind you of English Literature?' He turned pointedly to their host. 'How old is she, Teddy?'

The peer clapped a hand to his panama hat as a sudden gust threatened to snatch it off. 'Not as old as she looks, I'm afraid. She was purpose-built for another sail-training outfit about twenty-five years ago. When the owners went bust we got her for a song, did a refit and changed the name. I believe she's modelled on one of the great tea clippers, but the man you'll have to ask about all things nautical is Captain Stow. He has a great passion for everything to do with square-riggers and a knowledge to match.'

The boat almost imperceptibly nuzzled *Anson*'s companionway. As the guests climbed to the deck a bosun's pipe sounded. Six crew members were drawn up in two lines, beyond which stood a tall man with a weatherbeaten face completely fringed by dark hair. Captain Stow displayed what was probably a well-practised bonhomie as he gripped the visitors' hands in turn and, Catherine noted, favoured her with an unashamed, approving scrutiny.

'Friends are always welcome aboard Old Annie; friends from home doubly so. I'm so glad you could find time to give us the once-over.'

Tim glanced around at the youngsters, who were dispersing about their duties. He judged that they ranged in age between about fifteen and twenty. 'This isn't all your crew, surely?'

'No, Annie carries a complement of thirty-six. I've given most of them shore leave today. A sort of reward in advance. We've a round of social events coming up. That means best bib and tucker and best behaviour for the kids.'

Catherine grinned. 'I guess they don't care for that too much.'

'I see you understand youngsters perfectly, Catherine – I may call you Catherine?' Again the frank stare that flattered more than flowery compliments. 'They'd rather be pushing Annie through a force eight than handing round canapés and making small talk with rich old farts who can't tell a binnacle from a barnacle. Now, let me show you round.' Stow led the way along the deck.

77

Catherine fell back out of earshot and whispered to Tim, 'What's the difference between a binnacle and a barnacle?'

Tim squeezed his wife's hand. 'I don't know. But don't you dare ask old letch-eyes – unless, of course, you want a very *private* lesson in seamanship.'

Catherine giggled. 'Well, now, he *is* very sexy. What a pity I'm bespoke.'

'Don't you forget it,' Tim growled.

The tour of the *Admiral Anson* was exhaustively thorough and the guide was enthusiastic. Stow had a well-practised patter. In between pointing out the modern mechanism for hoisting sail, the ship's radar and navigation equipment, the crew's quarters, the well-equipped galley and the rows of leather-bound logbooks, he detailed the virtues of Project Anson.

'We've had thousands of kids through our hands over the years. All of 'em had question marks over them when they came to us. Most of 'em are now solid citizens. That's a record that speaks for itself.'

Tim was sceptical but kept his questions polite. 'What's your secret – a dose of tough naval discipline?'

The word 'discipline' clicked the Captain's mind to another track of his standard commentary. 'What I aim at is discipline with a purpose. Most kids will do what they're told if they can see why they're being told to do it. That's the basic mistake that most conventional corrective institutions make. Well, the "why" is pretty obvious on a working ship. If ropes are left snaking around all over the deck; if a sail isn't properly furled; if someone skives when he should be on watch, the results could be disastrous. That's obvious to all but the dimmest landsman. So when someone gets hauled over the coals for sloppiness or disobedience he may not like it but he can see the justice in it.'

'And just what does "hauling over the coals" entail?' Catherine wanted to know.

The Captain put an arm round her shoulders and muttered conspiratorially. 'A touch o' the cat, my dear, or maybe a keel-hauling or – if I'm feeling particularly jovial – a hanging at the masthead.' He roared with laughter. 'Just my joke, Catherine. Most punishments involve loss of privileges, especially shore leave. You can imagine how important it is to be able to get away from the ship for a few hours after several weeks at sea. I keep that for serious or persistent offences. On a day-to-day basis most punishments are carried out by a boy or girl's team mates. We have two watches, port and starboard, and we deliberately foster competition between them. Someone gets a black mark? It's also a black mark against his watch. He can best expiate it by being punished by the other members. They might make him run the gauntlet or send him to Coventry for a few hours. By and large that hurts 'em more than anything I can do to 'em.'

Catherine frowned. 'Isn't that legalized bullying?'

'I prefer to call it getting the peer pressure on my side. Most adult authority – parents, teachers, probation officers – breaks down because it has to compete with peer pressure. If you can get that force *behind* your authority you've got a chance to achieve something. Now, this is the chart and radio cabin. I'm particularly proud of the chart chest. I designed it myself.'

Lunch around the single table in the officers' mess was a surprisingly sumptuous repast – lobster Newburg followed by strawberry profiteroles. Stow offered his guests wine but drank lager himself.

'This isn't standard fare,' he explained, 'but neither is ship's biscuit. We all eat well. It's important both for health and morale.'

During the meal the conversation came back to the young people for whom Project Anson ostensibly existed. Tim wanted to know how crew members were selected.

Lord Everton explained. 'Every country has its own system for dealing with juvenile delinquents. In Britain we get referrals from the social services: youngsters who don't fit in well in a children's home or are too troublesome to be successfully fostered. Sometimes it's just a social worker's hunch that's responsible for sending a boy or girl to us. Others come from our Downham Homes.'

'So you don't go in for really hard cases?' Tim asked.

Stow beckoned to the girl who was serving them, a coquettish youngster of about sixteen with red hair and freckles. 'You can clear now, Charlie.' As she circled the table collecting plates, the Captain said, 'Personally, I'd love to get some of the self-appointed "toughies" aboard Old Annie. They'd soon discover that their street cred doesn't count for much when you're battling across Biscay or wallowing through mountainous seas in the Roaring Forties. Unfortunately, I have to recognize the limitations of the system. Too many rotten apples in a small barrel . . .'

'Could lead to mutiny?'

'Something like that.'

By the time the Lacys had returned by helicopter, delivered

Lord Everton to the Shugmayers, stayed for tea and small talk and ridden a cab back to their hotel, it was about 5.30. Catherine immediately took a shower.

'So, what did you think of the gallant Captain?' she called out over the hissing of the water. 'Or perhaps you could only see him through a green haze?'

Tim replied from the depths of an armchair by a large window looking out over Golden Gate Park. 'I thought he was a lecherous, self-opinionated sadist with the intelligence and morals of a caged Rottweiler. Otherwise, a thoroughly nice chap.'

Catherine giggled. 'That's your honest, unbiased opinion? Wouldn't you say he's doing a good job with those kids?'

'Let's just say I have an open mind on the subject.'

'Isn't that a bit mean?'

'I've seen these outfits before. They all work on the theory that someone with criminal tendencies can be converted into a model middle-class citizen by a short, sharp exposure to adventure, team-work and discipline. I've yet to be convinced.'

'The statistics Teddy Everton quoted were pretty impressive.'

'Well, you know what they say about statistics.'

'That's a cop-out.' Catherine came through from the bathroom enveloped in a large blue robe and sat in front of the dressing mirror to brush her hair.

'OK, let's be objective.' Tim turned from the window. 'All the kids who go on *Anson* cruises are hand-picked. By his own admission Stow doesn't deal with hard cases. So we're not looking here at any serious attempt to help junkies, persistent offenders or real no-hopers. Stow's clients are very much the borderline cases. Now, despite what we read in the right-wing press, most kids from deprived backgrounds don't turn out too badly. Sooner or later they manage to get themselves together. For most, it's a long process. It took me ten years of army life to discover who I was and what I wanted to be. Settling down has got more to do with finding a meaningful role in life than spending a few boisterous weeks aboard "Old Annie".'

'What you're saying is that Project Anson makes little difference to youngsters one way or the other?'

'I'm prepared to concede that for a few it might be a significant part of the growing-up process.'

'Isn't that justification enough?'

'Well, it's an expensive way of doing not very much towards solving a major social problem. And I suspect it has more to do with keeping immature mavericks in congenial employment.'

Catherine turned with a reproving frown. 'I guess we're back to your favourite sea-dog again.'

'I've seen lots of Captain Stows in my time. The army is full of them, or used to be. Life's just a big giggle for them. They never grow up. In a service environment they can play their macho games and never have a serious thought about anything. As officers they're damned useless. They get passed over for promotion and don't know what to do with themselves. Some of them end up in "adventure training". They'll tell you that getting youngsters involved in sailing, scuba-diving, mountaineering or what have you is a way of "building character". All they're really doing is preserving their own adolescence as far as possible into middle age.'

The telephone rang. Tim stepped across to the bedside table to answer it. 'If you're going to build character in others, you have to have some of your own to start with.'

He picked up the receiver. 'Hello . . . Yes, this is Mr Lacy speaking.' He gazed around the room. 'Yes, fine thanks. Why do you ask? . . . Sure. Come right up.' He replaced the handset.

Catherine raised a questioning eyebrow.

'Hotel manager,' Tim responded. 'Is everything all right? Are we quite sure? Can he come up and have a word with us?'

'I wonder what that's all about? If we're expecting visitors I'd better make myself respectable.'

By the time there was a knock at the door a few minutes later Catherine had donned pale slacks and a blue silk shirt. She opened the door to admit a young bespectacled man in a dark suit. His name was printed on his lapel badge: Ed Backus.

He stood in the middle of the room slightly awkwardly. 'Mr and Mrs Lacy, are you sure everything's OK?'

Tim looked at him warily. 'Yes. Shouldn't it be?'

'There's nothing . . . er . . . missing?'

'I don't think so. Why?'

'Well it's just that early this afternoon a couple of men jumped one of our chambermaids, pushed her into a closet and grabbed her pass key. She managed to get out and as she did so she saw the men come out of your room and take off down the hallway.'

CHAPTER 5

Tim and Catherine exchanged glances.

Ed Backus said, 'I'm very sorry about this. It would sure set my mind at rest if you wouldn't mind checking to make quite sure nothing is missing.'

Tim went straight to his briefcase which was standing by the window. He had left it shut. It was now open. He glanced through the contents – a file of letters, a couple of magazines and a paperback novel. 'Nothing missing here.'

Catherine went quickly through the dressing-table drawers. 'I don't think we have anything that would interest a casual thief. We always carry our money and credit cards. Our passports and anything else of value are in your strong room, Mr Backus.'

'I'm sure relieved to hear that, ma'am. I hope you don't think we have this sort of problem often. In fact, I don't recall . . .'

Tim was suddenly alert, businesslike. 'Did your chambermaid get a good look at the thieves?'

'All she could say was that they were white and young – probably under twenty.'

'Did you call the police in?'

The manager looked uncomfortable. 'There didn't seem much point. Whoever those guys were they'd gotten clean away. I didn't want to alarm other guests unnecessarily.'

'What about fingerprints?'

'I . . . I thought it best to wait till I'd spoken with you. They hadn't broken anything and if they haven't stolen anything either . . . Of course, you're absolutely within your rights to insist on sending for the police, but . . .' He shrugged.

Tim nodded. 'You're right. There's not really much point and there's no harm done.'

Ed Backus became voluble in his relief. 'Well, that's really understanding of you, Mr Lacy. I sure appreciate it. Thank you, thank you. Let me assure you again, this sort of thing really doesn't happen. Of course, the hotel will take care of your bill. Perhaps you'd like to change your room? I hope you'll be able to forget this little unpleasantness. We get lots of visitors from England. I wouldn't want to think . . . If there's anything I can do for you . . . anything at all . . .'

Catherine smiled. 'How about a bottle of champagne – your best.'

'Of course, of course. I'll get one sent up right away.' Ed Backus almost bowed himself out of the room.

For some seconds the Lacys stared in silence at the closed door. Then Catherine said, 'Are you thinking what I'm thinking?'

'I'm thinking that your Cambridge chums have got some explaining to do.'

'But surely . . .'

'There are just too many coincidences to swallow. Masquerier and Co got me to go to Sydney to pick up these mysterious papers because they were too scared. They knew something they weren't letting on about. We arrive here – the first stop on our homeward journey – and who should pitch up but our fat friend, plus a boatload of juvenile delinquents. Then, when we happen to be conveniently away from the hotel all afternoon, two "young men" break in. They're not common-or-garden burglars. They don't make a mess. They don't take anything. If they hadn't been seen leaving probably no one would know they'd been in this room.'

'You think our visitors came from the *Admiral Anson*?'

'Don't you?'

'I can't imagine the ship being sailed halfway round the world just to coincide with our visit. Anyway, who knew our itinerary?'

'Masquerier, for one. He insisted on getting the tickets personally. He said he had a special deal with a travel company.'

'But it's crazy to imagine that he would steal the Hellfire Papers. He's gone to a lot of trouble to get them safely back to Cambridge.'

'Is it so crazy? It would be a very good cover. If, for some reason, Masquerier *did* want to get hold of the papers himself, having them pinched thousands of miles away from England would be a perfect way of going about it. No one could possibly suspect him.'

'It wouldn't do Lacy Security's image much good.'

'Exactly. That's what makes me so hopping mad. I've

been set up so that some pseudo-academic fat cat can make a killing.'

'Hey, hold on there, Buster. You don't know that. You're just guessing.'

Tim slumped in an armchair, thoughtful. 'OK, I agree, I'm guessing. But something in this whole set-up has a decided odour of Billingsgate. I've thought so from the start.'

Catherine curled herself into the chair opposite and gazed out across the city. 'How much are the Hellfire Papers worth?'

Tim shrugged. 'At Masquerier's suggestion, I've insured them for five hundred thousand in transit. Whether that represents their real value I guess nobody knows.'

'That certainly makes them worth stealing, but I can't see someone like Masquerier being involved. I agree that there's something screwy about this business but we ought to keep an open mind. What about the gruesome death of the Dean of St Mary's? Where does that fit into your theory?'

'I hope very much that it doesn't fit in at all.'

'But surely it's just another unlikely coincidence? You can't write it out of the script because it's too bloody. Supposing Charles Vare discovered something that made it imperative for him to "disappear". That would explain his death and also why all his papers were burned.'

'Now who's guessing?'

Catherine pulled a face. The room waiter arrived with a trolley bearing not one but two bottles of Krug in ice buckets, and a tray of canapés.

'Young Mr Backus certainly seems worried.' Tim silently

uncorked a bottle, poured the wine and carried a glass to his wife.

Catherine held the flute aloft. 'Well, here's to him – "Plumpy Backus with pink eyne".'

'What?'

'Sorry. Shakespeare – *Antony and Cleopatra*.'

'Oh.'

Catherine metaphorically kicked herself. Tim bitterly resented his lack of a literary education. Mysterious allusions to the poets always annoyed him and put up barriers between them. She smiled provocatively. 'Looks like we're in for a wild evening.'

Tim sipped his champagne abstractedly. Catherine went across and sat on his lap. 'Take me. I'm yours. Or would you prefer me to play hard to get?'

He kissed her – but still seemed preoccupied. 'I was just thinking that we'll have to change all our plans.'

'Why?' Catherine loosened his shirt buttons and slipped her hand inside.

Tim grinned. 'Stop it, honey. I need to think. If someone has tried to get hold of the Hellfire Papers and failed, the chances are they'll try again. It seems safe to assume they know our itinerary. So the sensible thing to do is change it. I think we should leave tomorrow instead of Wednesday.'

Catherine pouted. 'What? Just when we've got the hotel eating out of our hands?'

'Be serious. Whoever these would-be thieves are, they may play much rougher next time. I want to avoid trouble. I also want to see Masquerier's face when I deliver his little package five days early.'

'Do you mean we're going straight back? What about our visit to Maine?'

'There's no reason why you shouldn't stay with your folks as planned – as long as you change your return-flight ticket. I'll get the first available London plane after I've seen you onto your connection.'

'Oh, Tim, is that really necessary? Mom and Dad will be terribly disappointed. Aren't you making a mountain out of a molehill?' Catherine stood up to refill her glass, the relaxed, intimate atmosphere spoiled.

'If I am, it's in order to keep you out of possible danger. And now,' he heaved himself out of the chair, 'I have a date with the Hellfire Papers.'

'They'll be safe enough in the strong room.'

'Yes, but this may be our last chance to have a really good look at them.'

'You want a final wallow in eighteenth-century erotica?'

Tim put his arms round his wife and kissed her neck. 'Could make an excellent accompaniment to all this champagne.'

'You poor old man. Do you really need a stimulus nowadays?'

Tim crossed to the door. 'As a matter of fact, I'm intrigued to know what it is that makes these pornographic memoirs important enough to steal – perhaps even to kill for.'

When Tim brought back the suitcase containing the documents he spread the contents over the bed. Together he and Catherine looked at the sheaf of drawings in age-browned ink on thick paper. They laughed at buxom nude women in provocative poses and men in various states of

debauched undress. They puzzled over the grotesque carica-
tures that had once outraged or amused Whitehead's circle
of roués but had lost their significance with the passing of
the years. They flipped through the two bound volumes,
neatly labelled 'Minutes of the Order of St Francis of
Medmenham'. The now-familiar sloping handwriting
recorded dates of meetings of the chapter, names of members present and quantities of wine ordered up from the
cellars to lubricate the rites. There were bawdy anecdotes
and rhymes that had been invented by various 'monks' and
cryptic comments about the entertainments they had offered
their 'nuns'. Obviously, Whitehead's well-prepared volumes
would provide scholars with much information about the
behaviour of some of England's ruling élite in the reigns of
George II and George III, but there was little that a
non-specialist could glean from a cursory examination of
these pages of closely-written text. The Lacys, therefore,
returned their attention to the more straightforward notes
written by Whitehead and his descendant.

Within days of my enlargement from the Fleet I was
summoned to Leicester House to do allegiance to the Prince
of Wales. This advancement was effected by Bubb Dodington, whom I must now introduce more fulsomely to the
reader. 'Fulsome' is for sure the word best suited to describe
this waddling tun of a man whose weskits and breeches ever
threatened to burst asunder (and not infrequently made
good the threat, to the vast amusement of those in his
company). He was born, some ten years before the present
century, as plain George Bubb. As a young man he came
into an immense property from a distant relative on the

understanding that he assumed the name Dodington, a condition he made great haste to fulfil. Like many fat men, he was a well-natured buffoon. Men liked him for his good humour and his generosity; he could never abide to see a friend in want. Women liked him . . . well it is difficult to fathom why women liked him, for he was beyond doubt the ugliest satyr ever to lift a skirt. Several years later our friend, Charles Churchill, described him thus: 'Bubb is his name and bubbies doth he chase,/This swollen bullfrog with lascivious face.'

Dodington, whose father had been a mere Irish adventurer, determined to play the part of gentleman to the full. He had Vanbrugh build him a great house in Dorsetshire and he bought himself the parliamentary seat of Winchelsea. As much a stranger to principle as he was a boon companion to intrigue, he found that politics suited him well. Since all power and patronage lay with Walpole, Dodington became a devout Whig and was rewarded with various posts and sinecures.

Yet fine-feathered social birds, such as Dodington liked to consider himself, need an aviary in which to preen themselves. Walpole's entourage was almost duller than the court of our little captain, George II, who never indulged anything more exciting than a game of cards and imposed a clockwork regime on himself and his household. Our Bubb was irresistibly drawn to Leicester House, caring not that intimacy with the Prince must distance him from the King and his first minister. Men marvelled that such a man as Dodington was not only admitted to Frederick Louis's inner circle but came to dominate it. The answer is simple: our fat friend had a plentiful supply of that commodity of which the Prince was starved by his niggardly father – money.

It was during the height of the 1736 season at a supper given by Bubb in honour of the Prince that I met Sir Francis Dashwood. I had, of course, heard of this hellraker – who had not? He had come into an enormous fortune before reaching his majority, swiftly divested himself of his solemn tutors and embarked upon his own education. This had largely involved extensive foreign tours in the company of selected friends, to learn the customs of other peoples – and to ridicule them mercilessly.

We were seated, a dozen of us, round the long table in the house Dodington had acquired in Pall Mall, conveniently adjacent to the Prince's own Carlton House, whither His Royal Highness came to relax and escape the more formal atmosphere of Leicester House. We had reached the stage when waistcoats are unbuttoned and the servants, instead of industriously replenishing empty glasses, leave small groves of bottles on the mahogany and withdraw. The hour was late. The copses of port and claret were being systematically felled. The conversation sought to match the brilliance of the surroundings (Bubb's taste was exuberant rather than elegant: his dining room glittered with the lights of vast crystal chandeliers reflected in rococo-framed mirrors reaching to the high ceiling). Our talk flowed freely back and forth, lapping the shores of politics, gossip, art and venery, each speaker determined to outdo his predecessor in knowledge, wit or outrageous bawdry.

Snatches of that evening, like holes of brilliant blue in a dome of cloud, remain vivid in my memory. We talked at one point of the prevailing fashion among certain 'liberated' ladies of donning man's attire. A song sprang, fully-formed to my head. I gave voice and the assembly readily took up the refrain:

> Ye belles and ye flirts and ye pert little things,
> Who trip in this frolicsome round,
> Prithee tell me from whence this indecency springs,
> The sexes at once to confound?
> What means the cocked hat and the masculine air,
> With each motion designed to perplex?
> Bright eyes were intended to languish, not stare,
> And softness the test of your sex,
> *Refrain*: Dear girls, and softness the test of your sex.

I was applauded warmly for this impromptu trifle and I noticed Sir Francis looking at me keenly from the other end of the table. He was a fresh-complexioned man, still on the light side of thirty, who affected a languid air. He was, as I subsequently had considerable opportunity to discover, a committed observer of the human scene and a ruthless exposer of its inconsistencies and hypocrisies. Someone asked him for the true version of his famous exploits in Rome, which had become much coloured in the telling and retelling.

He leaned back in his chair drawling out his narrative like a soliloquizing actor determined to have the audience hanging on his every cadence.

'Well, d'ye see, it was the shame of it all that turned my stomach. There's this magnificent Sistine Chapel and Michaelangelo's superb *Last Judgement*. God what an imagination! I defy any man of sensibility not to be moved by it. Now, while we were standing there in awe of that great masterpiece in creeps this rabble of papist penitents – pilgrims come to have their purses purged by Vatican quack-salvers.* They were there to contemplate heaven and hell and lament their sins. All very proper; your average papist has more to lament than most. So, what happens? Up comes a little black priest with a pile of little whips which he sells to visitors. I swear they were no longer than a foot rule. Then, off they set round the chapel tapping themselves with their whips and wailing a dirge. What a mockery! I thought of Michaelangelo, year in and year out grappling with the themes of sin and death and judgement and forgiveness. And I thought, "What do these priests and their gullible tribe know about these things?" In that instant, I resolved that if they were intent on flagellation they should do it properly. Next day my friends and I were back with horse-whips under our cloaks. When the next mob of malingering craw thumpers† began their dismal chant we laid about them. By God! You should have seen 'em run and jump. It was better than letting a cur loose in a henhouse!'

When the laughter had died down the Prince observed seriously, "Tis a pity, Sir Francis, you don't go into parliament and give Walpole's followers a lashing with your tongue.'

'Not I, Your Highness!' Dashwood laughed but was serious. 'I wait for better times. As long as Walpole crows atop it, Westminster's naught but a dungheap of jolter-heads, placemen and gentlemen cloyes.‡ I'll none of it. One

* mountebank sellers of patent medicines
† breast-beaters
‡ idiots, time servers and upper-class thieves

day the whole stinking lot will come down. Then some of us who've kept our hands clean will be on call.'

Bubb had been scribbling with a pencil while Dashwood spoke. Now he called for silence and read:

> Love thy country, wish it well–
> Not with too intense a care;
> 'Tis enough that when it fall,
> Thou its ruin did not share.

We all murmured agreement, assuring the Prince that we were men who looked to the future when he would be King, and Whiggery and corruption things of the past.

For some time talk inevitably ran on the iniquities of the government – of an all-powerful Walpole, secure in the King's favour, handing out lucrative offices to relatives and supporters and devising new taxes to pay for his profligacy. Someone reported that a mob had been hired to smash Alexander Pope's windows and that that great scourge of the Whig administration had been intimidated into silence. All agreed that affairs of state had deteriorated further since the great John Gay had lampooned politicians and, in his *Beggar's Opera*, made a hero of Jonathan Wild, the felon hung at Tyburn. I recall that I was able to cap the argument in verse:

> Guilt still is guilt to me in slave or king,
> Fettered in cells or garter'd in the ring:
> And yet behold how various the reward,
> Wild falls a felon, Walpole mounts a lord.

Yet we were not all of one mind at that cheerful board. And

not all friends. Someone, I think too far gone in wine, called out, 'Whitehead's nothing but an old hypocrite. Why the man's a ranting recub – recup – republican. Ain't it so, Whitehead?'

'You mistake, sir.' I looked anxiously at the Prince, who was eyeing me quizzically.

'Mistake? No, sir! You're one of those who'd see old Noll Cromwell back and be glad of it.' With difficulty, he fished a pamphlet from his pocket. 'This is what you wrote and had printed not ten days since.' He cleared his throat and declaimed:

> Well, of all plagues which make mankind their sport,
> Guard me, ye heav'ns, from that worst place, a court.
> Midst the mad mansions of Moorfields, I'd be
> A straw-crowned monarch in mock-majesty,
> Cursed with the follies and the farce of state
> Than lick the crumbs from a tyrant's plate.

I looked up to see eleven pairs of eyes fixed upon me.

Tim arrived at Heathrow in mid-afternoon. He spent the night in the small flat in Westminster that he had kept since his bachelor days and planned his visit to St Mary's House. Someone was playing games with him. Well, they would learn that he could be devious, too. He drove straight to Cambridge the following morning.

At St Mary's Master's Lodge the au pair informed him that Sir Evelyn was away for the day but that Lady Masquerier was at home.

'What a pleasant surprise.' Deb Masquerier rose to greet

him from a sofa in the long drawing room. She was dressed for comfort in a black velvet jumpsuit and had been working on papers scattered over a long coffee table. 'I'm afraid Evelyn won't be back till this evening, but if there's anything I can do . . .' She waved Tim to a chair.

She seemed completely relaxed but Tim set little store by that. Since his arrival had been announced by the servant he had lost whatever element of surprise his arrival might have given him. 'I just called in to deliver something to your husband.' Tim watched for a reaction but Lady Masquerier's face gave nothing away.

'Oh dear. Was he expecting you? It's most unlike—'

'Oh, no. He wasn't expecting me for a few days. It's just that I was able to get the job done earlier than I thought. Since the package was rather valuable I wanted to get it to its destination a.s.a.p.'

'Well, you can leave it with me. I'll see that Evelyn has it as soon as he gets in.' A little too eager?

He smiled what he hoped was a disarming smile. 'Unfortunately, that's a bit difficult. The Master was very insistent that I deliver it into his hands personally. What time do you expect him back?'

'He has a Senate meeting. They always go on all day. He may come back to change around six or he may not. He's due to dine at Magdalene. He'll go straight there if he's running late. In that case it could be ten o'clock before he gets home.'

'Then I suppose I'll just have to wait and hope to catch him later.'

'That seems an awful waste of your time. Are you sure I can't relieve you of your responsibility?'

'Thanks, but I need to talk with him anyway.'

Deb Masquerier reached out to touch a button on the wall behind her. 'Well, if you're determined on a vigil the least I can do is make it as comfortable as possible. I'll get Gerda to fix some lunch for you.'

Tim shook his head firmly. 'That's very kind of you, Deb, but I'm afraid I already have a lunch appointment.' He hoped the lie sounded convincing. 'Anyway, I can see that you're busy. I mustn't hold you up any longer.'

'In fact, I must get back to town this afternoon. I shouldn't really be here at all; I'm not usually in in the middle of the week. But we're considering a proposal for a big new series. It's a nail-biting decision whether to take it on or not. It would mean megabucks and touting for co-production money, etc., etc., etc. So I needed a bit of peace and quiet to go over it really carefully.'

'Sounds exciting. What's it about?'

'Promise me you're not spying for Granada or Channel 4.' Deb laughed.

'I promise.'

'It's a history of sexual attitudes from ancient cult prostitution to modern laissez-faire promiscuity. It's either a goldmine or a minefield. I have to decide which.'

'Well, they say nothing sells like sex.' Tim stood up as the au pair appeared in the doorway.

Deb Masquerier walked across the room with him. 'I'm sorry I couldn't be more help. I'll certainly leave a note for Evelyn and let him know you'll be calling later.' She shook Tim's hand.

'Thanks. Oh, by the way, where's the best place to park in Cambridge? I'm on a meter at the moment.'

Deb put a hand to her head. 'Parking in Cambridge? What a joke! We don't even have our own garage here at the lodge. Soon after we arrived we applied for planning permission. My God, the fuss! You'd have thought we were asking to pull down King's Chapel! Your best bet, Tim, is to use the fellows' car park. I'll phone through to the porter's lodge. They'll send someone to let you in.'

Tim eased the Mercedes into one of three remaining places in the car park behind St Mary's, checked that the car alarm was off and turned to walk through the college.

'Mr Lacy?'

Tim turned and found himself looking into an earnest young face that he knew he should recognize. It came to him suddenly. 'Miss Finsley-Kerr. We met briefly over breakfast a few weeks ago. Forgive me for not recognizing you immediately. How are you?'

'My name's Emma. And I don't use the Finsley bit of my name. It's an affectation of my father's. Since I'm not an aspiring politician I don't need to impress people. May I introduce you to Gavin Turner? He's a second year student here at St Mary's.'

Tim shook hands with a thin, very pale, bespectacled young man who seemed to be wearing at least four layers of woollen jumpers beneath a heavy overcoat.

In a surprisingly olde worlde gesture Gavin touched the cap which was pulled well forward over his forehead. 'Good morning, Mr Lacy. I hope you enjoy your visit to Cambridge. I'd love to stay and chat but I'm supposed to be with my supervisor as of now.' He turned and walked towards a nearby staircase.

Emma said, 'May I walk with you? I'd like to talk.'

'Of course. I'd enjoy that. And my name's Tim.' He appraised the girl's unsmiling features, practical clothes and disinclination for small talk. He decided that Emma was a young woman who knew her own mind.

She fell into step beside him, carrying a canvas bag slung over her shoulder.

Now she did concede a half smile. 'Hello, Tim. How's the investigation going?'

'Investigation?'

'Come off it. We all know why you're here.'

'Really. Then perhaps you'd better tell me, because I don't seem to be in on the secret.'

Emma sighed impatiently. 'I suppose you have to keep up a pretence. But really there's no point. Your cover's been blown.'

As they emerged into Grand Court Tim stopped. He stared hard at the young girl who, if she gave herself half a chance, would be very pretty. 'Look, this conversation seems to be travelling on different tracks. Suppose we go back to the junction and try again. Just what is it that you think I've come to Cambridge for?'

Emma looked wary. 'Are you telling me that you're not a private detective?'

'I am not a private detective.'

'Then you're not here to investigate the death of Dr Vare?'

'Good heavens, no!'

'Really?'

'Really.'

'Oops!' She frowned though Tim could not work out whether she was registering disappointment or annoyance.

'I thought . . . we all thought that Moneybags had brought you in to do some private snooping.'

'Moneybags?'

'Masquerier, our unrevered Master.'

'Sir Evelyn did invite me here to do a job for him but it has nothing to do with Dr Vare's death – at least, I don't think so. I'm a security expert. He wanted me to collect something for him. I've come to deliver.'

Comprehension glowed on Emma's face like the sun emerging from behind a cloud. 'Oh, that must be the papers.'

Now it was Tim's turn to be bewildered. 'You know about them?'

'Yes . . . well, not exactly. Oh, hell! It's all such a mess.' She stood silent for several moments. A young man hurrying along the far side of the large square of shaven lawn called out to her but she made no response. 'God, I wish I knew what to do.'

'Would it help to talk?'

She looked up at him. Doubtful. 'Can I trust you?'

'Confidentiality is my middle name. How about some lunch in, say, half an hour?'

Emma made up her mind suddenly. 'OK. Back here at twelve fifteen.' She turned and strode through an archway leading to the screens passage.

Tim walked on thoughtfully. At the porter's lodge he enquired whether Stuart Longton was available. The young man across the counter turned briefly to the clock on the wall behind him. 'Let's see, sir; ten to twelve on a Thursday morning? Dr Longton should be back in about a quarter of an hour.'

Tim smiled. 'Do you know the movements of all the fellows off by heart?'

'Not quite all, sir. But Dr Longton is one of our more predictable members. He has an eleven o'clock lecture on Thursdays and always cycles straight back to college.'

Tim stepped out onto the pavement, turned to the left and strolled slowly towards the town centre. Thinking. It was a bright, tingling day, cold as only Cambridge can be. He thrust his hands deep into his overcoat pockets and bent his head against the scouring wind. Nice town. Tim approved the way that it was a genuine centre of learning, unlike other places where universities had been imposed on an existing population centre. Take away the lawned courtyards, the impressive façades of brick and stone, the researchers beavering away in libraries and laboratories and the scurrying youngsters on bicycles who gave every appearance of being perpetually interested in pastimes much more important than work – and what would be left? He looked along the gothic arcade fronting King's. Perhaps if he had been born into a different family, a different social stratum in a different part of England . . . Oh well, no use eating your heart out over what might have been. Anyway, as the St Mary's situation indicated, Cambridge life was far from being all about scholarly reflection in elegant surroundings.

What the hell was going on in that introverted, bitchy little community? Secret papers that everyone knew about. A death that everyone knew about which involved a dark secret. Self-assured men and women who looked out through wary, fearful eyes. Devotees of learning who told infantile lies. A bright young student carrying a burden of anger and suspicion. There was something seriously out of kilter, distorted, dislocated in the common life of St Mary's House.

Tim struggled to discover an image that would fit the vague but strong feelings he had about Sir Evelyn Masquerier's college. Somewhere in his past there was a ghastly episode which paralleled the situation he now confronted. It emerged, at last, from the closet of deliberately discarded memories. A shop. A toyshop on a busy Belfast street . . . how long ago? Thirteen years. Large windows bright with a Christmas display of board games, dolls, plastic space warriors and battery-operated trucks, scattered with imitation snow. Parents and eager children going in and out. And, now and then, others. Known men. Tim remembered a young Captain Lacy organizing surveillance on the premises and being fairly sure that there was an IRA bomb factory in the basement; fairly sure that semtex and timing devices were arriving under the noses of the security forces in boxes labelled as computer games and construction kits. Fairly sure. Not sure enough to recommend a raid to his superiors. Hanging on for the vital bit of evidence that would prove his suspicions, justify his actions. The evidence turned up; with a vengeance. One day – 22nd December, a date Tim would never forget – some inexperienced or half-drunk terrorist got careless. The explosion killed seventeen people and maimed twenty. A dozen of them were children. Tim had the same sense at St Mary's of a tragedy waiting to happen.

He checked his watch and turned back along King's Parade. One half of his brain said, 'Whatever academic shenanigans are going on here are nothing to do with you. Deliver the papers, take the money – and run.' The other half did not reply in words. It just projected a vivid image of a pile of debris strewn with broken toys and fragmented bodies. Tim threw the mantle of logic over both arguments. 'Of course I'm involved. Masquerier and Longton wrote me into their script without giving me a copy. I'm going to find out what they've got me into. That's all. Explanation. Apology. Cheque. Then goodbye.'

With the wind at his back Tim soon found himself once more approaching St Mary's. Stuart Longton arrived at the same moment. He ran his bike onto the pavement, dismounted and was about to wheel it past the porter's lodge when Tim came up behind him.

'Hello, Stuart.'

Longton turned. His eyes peered hard from behind thick lenses. Then he took a step back and would have fallen over his bicycle if Tim hadn't thrust out a hand to steady him.

'Lacy?' It came out in little more than a gasp but to Tim it spoke loudly of the man's genuine shock. Longton recovered quickly. 'Sorry. It was the surprise of seeing you. We didn't expect you back quite . . .'

'Change of plan.' Tim shrugged.

Longton set his bike in one of the stands beside the college's front wall. 'Did you manage . . . Have you brought the papers back safely?'

They walked together along one side of Grand Court.

'Safely?' Tim affected surprise at the word. 'Have you any reason to suppose they might have been in danger?'

'No, of course not.' Longton had completely regained his poise now. 'I chose my words carelessly. You were right to pick me up on them. We'll make a scholarly pedant of you yet. What I should have said was, I trust you had an enjoyable journey and that your mission did not prove onerous.'

Tim smiled. 'Unfortunately I had to trim my schedule, but apart from that everything went fine.'

'So you've delivered the package to Sir Evelyn?'

'Not yet. The Master was out when I called earlier. But don't worry, your Hellfire Papers, or whatever you call them, are quite safely locked in the boot of my car and my car is in the fellows' parking area.'

'Good, good.' After a thoughtful pause Longton added, 'Now, how about some lunch? We must look after you since you've rendered us such a great service.'

'Thanks, Stuart, but I already have a date. Ah, and there she is waiting for me.' Tim pointed at the figure standing beneath the oriel window of the hall.

Longton peered. 'Anyone I know? I'm afraid I'm not very good with faces at a distance.'

'Emma Finsley-Kerr – or Emma Kerr, as I gather she prefers to be known.' Tim watched for any reaction as he spoke.

A frown which might have signified annoyance or disapproval hovered over the scholar's face, then was gone. 'Well, then, *bon appetit*. I mustn't keep you from the young lady. Perhaps we can chat later. Dinner? I should be delighted to have you as my guest in hall.'

'Thanks. I'd like that.'

Half an hour later Tim and Emma were wedged into a corner table of a wine bar rapidly filling with young people.

Tim watched his guest hungrily attack her salmon mousse. 'I'm glad to see you're not a vegetarian. So many of your contemporaries seem to have an abhorrence of anything that doesn't actually grow out of the ground.'

'I can't stand philosophical fashions,' Emma explained between mouthfuls. 'If anybody tells me what to think I automatically think the opposite.'

Tim laughed. 'Good for you. What are you reading?'

'Classics.' She laid down her fork suddenly and looked up with a slight frown. 'Look, we'd better get straight to the point, hadn't we? Dr Vare didn't take his own life.'

'Presumably that's not the decision the police and the coroner came to.'

'Police? Huh! They were just part of an establishment conspiracy to hush everything up.' Emma's glare defied him to contradict her.

Tim did not contradict. 'What makes you so sure they got it wrong – deliberately or otherwise?'

'It's just not the sort of thing he'd do. And don't tell me that most suicides are committed out of character. Gavin's spent weeks trying to din that idea into me.'

'Gavin? Boyfriend?'

'Boy, yes. Friend, yes. Boyfriend – no. Gavin is . . . Never mind, he's nothing to do with it.'

'Did you really know Dr Vare well enough to be sure that he couldn't have done what it's claimed he did?'

'I think so.' She sipped her mineral water, thoughtfully. 'Yes, I really think I did. I've asked myself the same question lots of times and I always come up with the same answer. I'm sure I would have known if he'd been contemplating anything like . . . like that.' She turned her attention back to her food.

'You were fond of him?'

She did not answer for several seconds. 'I suppose I'd better try to explain. Until a year ago the Dean of St Mary's was scarcely aware of my existence. Then we had a flaming row.'

'What about?'

'I organized a demonstration in the college. One of the undergraduates contracted AIDS. They wanted to send him down. I thought that was monstrous. I got up a petition. Eighty per cent of the college signed it, including a couple of fellows. One night some of us stuck up posters all over Grand Court.'

'Not smart!'

'No, well, in retrospect I have to agree. Anyway, it got me carpeted before the Dean. He told me, in his most sarcastic vein, that if I was determined to devote myself to social issues I ought to choose something more worthy of my obvious intelligence. He said that contracting and spreading a sexually-transmitted disease was ethically indefensible and that by condoning such action I was calling my own morals into question. I'm sure he expected me to wilt under the onslaught of his wit and logic. Everyone else did.'

'But Emma Kerr is not the wilting kind?'

'Well, I certainly hit back. Not very subtly, I'm afraid. I told him he was a hypocritical, randy old queen.'

'That must have shaken him.'

Emma grinned. 'I can see him now, standing in the middle of his room with his mouth wide open. I remember thinking, "Oh, God, I've done it this time. Here endeth a promising university career." Then he burst out laughing. From that moment on we were friends. He took a close interest in my work. He gave me a lot of help with my finals dissertation.'

'Vare wasn't a classicist, was he?'

'No, early church history was his scene. But my subject was "Latin style in the last days of the Roman Empire". He was a brilliant Latin scholar and had lots of very stimulating ideas. Sometimes we sat for hours discussing them.'

'It sounds as though he became some sort of father figure.'

Emma was half-amused, half-shocked. 'Oh, no, nothing like that. Dr Vare always kept his distance. For instance we never got anywhere near first-name terms. He was a man who found any kind of emotion difficult . . . impossible . . . to handle. What we had was, I think, an immense respect for each other. From my side there was always an element of fear.'

'Fear? You don't look to me like the sort of woman who scares easily.'

Emma gulped down the last mouthful of food. She closed her eyes and sculpted air with her hands trying to give shape to her thoughts. 'Not really *fear*. Oh God, how do you describe a relationship? Talking with him was like a game of cat-and-mouse; exhilarating but exhausting. He kept you up to the mark mentally. The moment you said something not properly thought out – wham! Out came the claws and your argument was cut to ribbons. He was the best teacher I've ever had or am ever likely to have.'

They sat in silence while Tim finished his hot game pie. At last he pushed his plate away. 'Coffee?'

'Mm, yes please – cappuccino. You have to go up to the bar for it.'

When Tim had negotiated his way through the closely-packed tables and set down the cups, he said, 'I can understand your not wanting to accept that Dr Vare could ever bring himself to commit suicide . . .'

'You're going to join the "There, there" brigade, are you?'

'I don't quite—'

'It's what everyone says; "There, there, my dear. You're upset, of course, but you'll get over it." Look, Tim, it's not just how I feel. Something else happened that night. Something that no one is prepared to take seriously.'

'I'm listening.'

'After I discovered the body I went to the porter's lodge. God, it was a foul night – bucketing with rain. I bumped into Dr Longton and babbled something to him and he came to the chapel and took charge. The little creep was really quite impressive in a crisis. He organized someone to phone for the police and someone else to run to the Master's Lodge. He realized I was probably going to get hit with delayed shock and he told me to go to my room and get a friend to come and hold my hand. I was beginning to feel a bit weak at the knees, so I did just that. My room is on the next landing up from the Dean's suite. As I was passing his door I thought I heard a noise inside. I stopped and went over to listen. At that moment the door opened suddenly and someone rushed out. Whoever it was sent me sprawling on the floor. I don't know whether I hit my head or succumbed to a touch of the vapours. Anyway, I blacked out. It wasn't for long; probably no more than a minute. When I came to, Jane – that's Jane Ironbridge; she has the room opposite mine – was bending over me. She got me upstairs and plied me with strong, sweet tea.'

'You've no idea who . . .?'

'Not the foggiest. Not that it matters much. The police are convinced that I imagined the whole thing.'

'Even when they went into Vare's rooms and found them in a mess and his personal papers reduced to ashes in the grate?'

Emma's eyes lit up. 'You found out about that, then?'

'Yes. It was you who left me that note at the hotel, wasn't it?'

'That's right. I thought if you were investigating Dr Vare's murder you ought to get straight to the heart of the matter.'

'But what gave you the impression that I was a private eye? Do I look like one?'

Emma sat back and surveyed him appraisingly. She grinned. 'No, not really. You're not nondescript enough. Proper detectives are supposed to melt into the background, aren't they?'

'Then?'

'I don't know how the rumour started. I suppose it was because Moneybags changed tack.'

'What do you mean?'

'Well, first off he went into a blue funk. Bloody death doesn't help the "ancient seat of learning" image he's been projecting for his fund-raising efforts. The only thing that mattered was keeping Dr Vare's demise hushed up. He called a meeting of the whole college, gave out the bare facts, and read the riot act about not talking to the press, etc. He had me in to tea the day after the incident and came over all avuncular. Was I feeling all right? Should he telephone my parents and explain? What he really wanted was to find out what I thought about the Dean's death and what I had told the police. Everyone reckoned that Moneybags put pressure on the local constabulary to tie the case up quickly – which is exactly what they did. By the time I came back for the inquest in the middle of the Christmas vac they had it all neatly packaged. The police surgeon gave it as his opinion that Dr Vare had died by his own hand and that was that. Damage-limitation exercise complete.'

'That all sounds very satisfactory – from the college's point of view. What makes you think Sir Evelyn subsequently changed his mind?'

'I got back a couple of days early at the beginning of term and within hours I had an invitation to dine with the Masqueriers. God, what an ordeal that was!'

'Why?'

'It was like attending a selection conference. There were just Moneybags, Lady Moneybags and Dr Longton and they were all firing questions at me. Had Dr Vare seemed upset in the weeks before his death? Was I sure I'd seen someone coming out of his room on the night of the tragedy? Could I remember anything – anything at all – about the intruder? Had I noticed any guests calling on him recently? Had the Dean made any mention of receiving some papers from an old friend living in Australia?'

'Sir Peregrine Whitehead-Dyer?'

'That's right. What do you know about him?'

Tim ignored the question. 'And *had* Dr Vare made any mention of this double-barrelled Oz?'

Emma shrugged. 'Well, only obliquely. I went to see him a week or so before he died and he was reading a long airmail letter. He didn't look very pleased about it. When he'd finished he tossed it aside and muttered, "Exodus twenty, verse five". Then we got on with some work. It was while we were looking at a text of St Augustine's that I happened to notice the addressee's name on the envelope. It was Sir Peregrine Whatsisname.'

'And you've no idea what he meant by "Exodus twenty, verse five"?'

'No. I did look it up out of curiosity. It's one of the ten commandments. All about not worshipping graven idols. Hey! What's all this questioning about? You're as bad as the Moneybags gang. Are you *sure* you're not a private tec?'

Tim held up his hands. 'Sorry. I didn't mean to pry. You said you wanted to confide in me. I was just trying to get a clear picture. You told Sir Evelyn and the others about the Australian letter and Dr Vare's reaction, I suppose?'

'Did I, hell! By that time I'd had it up to here with their interrogation. Especially as they wouldn't answer any of my questions. When I asked them what all this was about all I got was a load of bullshit. Certain aspersions had been cast on the late dean and the fellows were anxious to clear his name. Honestly! They expect me to go all out for a first in the Tripos and at the same time they treat me like a complete idiot.'

'Well they've certainly made a mistake there. Shall we go?'

As they emerged onto a sunlit and less windy Trinity Street, Tim said, 'So what do you make of it all, Emma?'

'Oh, I don't know. It's like trying to make sense of some swine of a Latin unseen when you don't recognize half of the words. I think someone killed Charles Vare and burned his papers, but who or why is anyone's guess. The college is very upset about the whole business. Poor old Vare wasn't terribly popular but there are lots of people who think there's something fishy about his death. There's lots of talk about a cover-up. They think you've been brought in to help Moneybags dig up the truth so that he can re-inter it.'

'Well, I hope you'll be able to scotch these rumours as far as I'm concerned. I'm just a humble security man doing a delivery job.'

'You've brought these mysterious documents from Australia? What are they exactly?'

Tim was deliberately vague. 'Some historical papers hundreds of years old. Sir Peregrine Whatsisname bequeathed them to St Mary's. It's difficult to see them having any connection with your defunct Dean's gruesome death.'

Emma stopped and held out her hand. 'This is where I have to leave you. I need to spend a couple of hours in the University Library. Thanks for lunch and thanks for the chat. It's been a help to talk it all through with someone outside the claustrophobic atmosphere of St Mary's.'

Tim gave her his card. 'It's been my pleasure. If you need the services of a discreet confidant again, give me a ring.'

He returned to St Mary's House and made two discoveries. The first was in the chapel. He spent a few minutes there, trying to picture the scene on the night of Charles Vare's death. He looked at the dean's stall beside the door. Suicide or murder? He had said nothing to contradict Emma but try as he might he could not see how anyone could have got a drugged man into his surplice, then carried or dragged him to the chapel and propped him in his place, before cutting his wrists. It was as risky as it was difficult. There would have been people walking through the court, not to mention others who might have been at the windows that overlooked it.

He turned and crossed to the reading desk. The large Bible lay in its place. Tim turned to its second book and to the twentieth chapter of that book. In the empty chapel he read aloud verse five: 'You shall not bow down to them or serve them; for I the Lord your God am a jealous God, visiting the iniquity of the fathers upon the children to the third and fourth generation of those who hate me.'

In the fellows' car park he discovered that the boot of the Mercedes had been forced open.

CHAPTER 6

'So, Mr Whitehead, would you lop off all crowns and the heads with 'em?' It was the Prince of Wales who asked the question. The atmosphere in the room was now drained of all levity. An English gentleman may despise corruption in the governing class but he has a greater fear of revolt among the governed. It was, then, less than a century since the people had cut off one king's head and scarce half a century since they had chased his son into a French exile, whence the Stuarts still plotted the overthrow of our German rulers. The satire just quoted had certainly come from my pen and I could not, nor would I, disown it, for it expressed a deep conviction. But it had put me in a damned difficult position.

It was my fixed opinion – and remains so – that when a monarch is the fount of all patronage, his court becomes a spring of every kind of vice. Sycophants and back-stabbers jostle for favours. Offices, lands, titles and political power are distributed not to the worthy, but to those who can flatter or bribe their way into the trust of the king. I gazed at my companions. When Frederick Louis was seated upon his father's throne and those around this table held offices of state would they be any the less susceptible to corruption? I could not believe so. If I looked into the future at all, I knew that my pen would be turned against arrogance and injustice under Frederick I just as it was in the days of George II.

But that was no reason, in the interim, to lose convivial companions and intelligent friends. Principles may be firmly held without being lustily maintained at all times. Thus, while my face flushed not only with wine, I scrabbled around in my empty brain for some quip or jest which would restore the party to good humour and discourage closer scrutiny of my political philosophy.

It was Dashwood who came to my rescue. He threw back his head in a great roar of laughter. 'Damn me if that ain't the very truth, Whitehead! When I was in Petersburg the whole city was choked with aristocrats, come in from the country by the coachload. The Tsarina didn't know what to do with 'em but she couldn't trust 'em to stay on their estates and plan revolt. They had nothing better to do than vie with each other for favours and see who could throw the most extravagant parties. You've never seen such an aviary of useless, twittering parakeets. The Russian women, though, they're like Petersburg houses in winter – ice outside and red-hot stoves within. There was a girl I saw at a soirée in the summer palace. She was no more than eighteen and so serene she might have been carved from snow. Now, in my creed, snow maidens are for the melting. So . . .' and he set forth on yet another bawdy tale.

I had no opportunity to thank Sir Francis that night, but two days later he sent for me to dine with him privately. We talked of things indifferent until after the meal, when he led me to a small salon where bottles and glasses and a good fire awaited us.

When we were set in winged chairs either side the hearth, Sir Francis said, 'Now then, Whitehead, just what are your politics?'

'I am of no party,' I responded cautiously.

'That's as much as to say, "I'm a cynic standing on a wall and pissing on both sides".'

I was stung into a retort. 'Ain't that better than pissing in foreign courts, Sir Francis?'

He roared with laughter but then, as was his wont, fell suddenly serious. 'It may be we're both in the wrong. You rail on the crimes and stupidities of our masters. I turn my back on 'em. By set of sun neither of us has ploughed an honest furrow. Now, I've a mind that together we might make a programme for reform which would find support among many in the Commons and the Lords. What would be top of your agenda for such a programme?'

'Why, to be rid of Cock Robin.'

He shook his head impatiently. 'And after Walpole, what then? Some other royal creature with a wagonload of impecunious relatives and hangers-on. As long as the King chooses his ministers we shall have corruption. You've said as much in your verses. They go to the heart of things, which is why people don't like 'em. You saw the Prince's reaction the other night and you know what he was afraid of. All he can see is: "No minister means no king and no king means revolution and revolution means mob rule and anarchy." For all that Frederick Louis hates his father, he is but another monarch in the making. Once in power, he'll expect to rule and choose his own officers of state. This is where I part company with that schemer, Bubb Dodington. He looks to form an opposition party around Frederick Louis. I am for principles, not princes.'

'And I for neither princes nor parties.'

'But do you not see, man, party there must be. Why has Walpole been twenty years in power? Because he's only opposed by factions and alliances, forever dividing and squabbling amongst themselves.'

'You'd never get enough men to unite around a common programme.'

'Damme, man, but you make difficulties!' Sir Francis angrily flung his glass into the fire, where it splintered against the blazing logs. 'I ask you what your politics are and you tell me what they ain't!'

I watched the stem of the broken wineglass roll across the stone hearth, its enclosed spirals of yellow enamel twirling like a corkscrew.

Dashwood glared at me intently. His youthful features were already fleshing out. He looked what all the world took him for, a rake bent on nothing but the dissipation of his inheritance. Clearly, the world was wrong. 'Look here, Whitehead, I took you for something more than a gybing hackney.* Was I wrong?'

I was determined not to be cowed. 'Poor men can scarce afford the luxury of principles.'

He waved away my argument. 'And rich men may afford to change 'em at a whim. That's not to the point. Come, tell me what may we do to make a better land?'

'Stop rich men buying votes to control parliament.'

---

* writer of hack lampoons

'Agreed, but it's difficult to break long habits. Yet I have a plan that might curb the hustings paymasters. Suppose elections were every year instead of every seven. Buying votes would become a deuced expensive business.'

'And who would put his own seat at risk by voting for such a reform?'

'Aye, but think, man.' Dashwood's eyes glowed with an intensity I had never seen before. 'A parliament elected by the people and answerable to them every year – or maybe every three years. Ministers chosen by that parliament rather than by the king. Could there be any better – any other – guarantee of common freedoms?'

'Freedom's the watchword,' said I, catching my host's enthusiasm.

'Aye, freedom.' Dashwood sat gazing into the fire as though stupefied by its flames. 'An excellent slogan but the devil of a principle. What does it mean? Liberty to do as a man likes?'

'Why, it's freedom under law, surely.'

'As long as law is made by the people, not by tyrants or favourites.' His speech had slowed. 'Much to be thought on there, Whitehead, much to be thought on.' He sat back in his chair, the passion that had flared so quickly as rapidly dwindling to a mere ember. Sir Francis Dashwood, as I had much cause to know later, was a man by turns vigorous and lethargic, brilliant and dull, readily given to enthusiasm and boredom. Now he closed the debate by saying, 'We must discuss this more on my return.'

'Return?'

'Aye, I've a fancy to see the Mohammedan world for myself. Next month I've a ship taking a few of us to

Constantinople and Cairo, the ruins at Ephesus and the pyramids of Gaza. D'ye know, Whitehead, the Grand Sultan has a seraglio of three hundred wives, kept for his exclusive use. Now there's a remedy for the pox, eh!'

I thought to hear little of such matters again but when Dashwood returned, towards the end of 1740, I was among the first to be summoned to his house. I entered a scene of confused activity. Several carts were drawn up outside and were being unloaded under the orders of Lancet, Sir Francis's major domo. In the wide hall stood the traveller himself surrounded by boxes, baskets and bales of silk. Behind him, leaning against the staircase, was something resembling an immense chrysalis bound in time-blackened strips of cloth which, Dashwood subsequently told me, was the mummified cadaver of an ancient pharaoh. The marble floor was strewn with fragments of stone, bearing antique picture writing, paintings, pots of bizarre shape and items of oriental clothing.

As I entered, he grabbed up a flowing garment of several vivid hues and wrapped it around himself. He clapped a wide turban on his head and made a low bow. 'Dashwood Pasha welcomes you to his humble home, O Whitehead Effendi. How do you like this? It is the height of fashion in Constantinople. We are to have a new club. I'm calling it the Divan and this shall be the uniform. And we shall solemnly discuss Mohammedan art and keep a harem and take our pleasures in silken bowers. But now,' he threw off the strange clothing and left it where it fell, 'Whitehead, my friend, have you brought our manifesto?'

I tried not to show my bewilderment, but he did not notice for he was already hurrying on, revealing his plans as eagerly as he was unpacking his treasures. He took me by the arm and led me into a small room into which the flood of souvenirs had not yet seeped.

'Now that Cock Robin is knocked off his perch we may hope to change things,' he declared.

There was truth in what Dashwood said. Walpole's unpopularity had at last penetrated the walls of St James's and reached the King's ears. The minister still clung to power but was forced to share it with men of different temper and ideas. Now, he and his understrappers could scarce go abroad without attracting a mob hurling abuse or garbage.

'The Whigs are for a drubbing at next year's election and I mean to be dealt a hand in the new game. I'll stand in my borough at Romney and you'll write my speeches. It'll be the first test of our new programme.'

It was clear that my patron was in one of his enthusiastic phases. How long it would last there was no telling, but it was obviously in my interest to encourage his newfound political activism.

In fact, over the next few months Sir Francis indulged in a veritable frenzy of activities. He was much in demand socially, all London wanted to hear of his exploits in the lands of the infidel. He joined many clubs and formed others. The Divan partway satisfied his desire for the exotic. The Dilettanti gave an outlet for his more scholarly interests. Its members were mostly young men who, returned from the Grand Tour, were intent on pursuing their studies of classical and Renaissance art and thought. It was my first sight of the portrait he had painted to grace the walls of the club's premises in Cavendish Square that planted in my mind the mustard seed of a grandiose plan. The dress espoused by members of the Dilettanti was a toga in the Roman style, but Dashwood chose to be painted in a friar's habit as 'San Francisco di Wycombe', grasping not a pilgrim's staff, but a wineglass and raising his eyes in veneration not to a holy relic, but to a statue of Venus.

The picture expressed well Dashwood's contempt for all outward trappings of religion in general and of Roman Catholicism in particular. I was present for its unveiling and as I contemplated its celebration of the outrageous, the arcane and the libertine, I realized that Mr Knapton, the artist, had expressed something of the soul of Sir Francis. Dashwood was, essentially, a religious man but his mind and passions would never be contained within the conventional tenets of Christianity. His mercurial, restless spirit sought obscure fragments of truth amidst Roman ruins and Egyptian tombs, in Mohammedan mosques and the writings of necromancers. He was a man emerging with difficulty from the dissipations of youth and casting round for purpose and fulfilment in philosophy and public service. Hence the clubs, most of which he tired of after a few months. For all I knew then, he would as quickly become bored with active politics. What if some means could be found of engaging his many interests, his need for both roisterous and intelligent company? The motto of Rabelais came unbidden to my mind – '*Fay ce que voudras*' ('Do as you please').

[There is a break in the narrative here]

We drove down to new Romney for the election in Sir Francis's coach and four. Other supporters had gone on ahead to canvass the local freeholders, plaster every wall with posters, distribute pamphlets and spread round ale-houses and market stalls the lampoons I had written against our enemy, but Dashwood wanted to spend the journey rehearsing the speech he was to deliver on the hustings.

'Dashwood for Freedom!' was to be our slogan. As we jolted our way across Kent we agreed on the most telling phrases and Sir Francis declaimed them. 'Down with the new excise, say I!' 'Why should a man not be free to do as he chooses with his own property?' 'Elect an independent man! Elect a man who cannot be bought with royal guineas! Elect a man who goes to Westminster to do your bidding and not follow his own whims! Elect Dashwood.' 'Make parliament the servant of the people not the lackey of the King!' 'Dashwood for better roads!' 'Dashwood for a county militia!' 'Dashwood for lower land tax!' 'Dashwood for Freedom!'

Much of my endeavour was concentrated on setting the candidate's mind at rest. He was remarkably nervous about exposing himself to the assembled electors and the paid hecklers of his adversary. He had frequent recourse to the brandy bottle during our ten-hour journey. I assured him that he had nothing to fear, which was no less than the truth. Dashwood was a considerable landowner in the area and could count on the support of most of the leading gentle-men. Gold judiciously distributed among the Romney busi-ness community had elicited promises of more support. But mostly in his favour was the unpopularity of the Robinoc-racy. Walpole's main supporter in East Kent was Lord Tregarth and he had put up one of his cronies, Jack Scrope (our pamphlets made much play with the name: 'A scrope*

* slang for a farthing

is all he's worth'. Our local agents reckoned that the Tregarth interest could count on barely two hundred of the 1053 eligible voters. Scrope's mobs had been out smashing windows, burning ricks and menacing some of our more timid supporters. These, as I assured Dashwood, were the tactics of desperation. There was nothing the opposition could do to avoid defeat.

I was wrong.

We were negotiating a belt of woodland within ten miles of our journey's end. The road had been shamefully neglected by the parish responsible for it so that ferns, gorse and scrub grew to within a few feet of the carriageway. Our driver, knowing the reputation for highwaymen enjoyed by the area, was making the best speed the ruts and potholes would allow.

Suddenly, he reined in his team with a jolt that sent Sir Francis and me to the floor in a heap. We extricated ourselves, aware of a tumult of shouting, angry voices. Thrusting our heads out of the windows on either side, we espied a crowd of ruffians armed with axes, pitchforks and cudgels. They were some twenty paces off and advancing slowly. There could be no doubting their purpose.

Dashwood turned to me, his face reddened with fury. 'Tregarth's mob come to keep me from the poll. Well, let's test their mettle.'

He grabbed up a box from the seat beside him. Out of it he drew a pair of neatly nestling pistols. They were primed and loaded, ready for just such an emergency. Dashwood cocked them and thrust one into my hand. 'Can you use these things, Whitehead? Only fire if you have to – but if you have to, make sure you kill.'

★ ★ ★

'Gotcha!' Tim surveyed the bent metal and broken lock of his car boot with a smile of satisfaction. It was a hamfisted job, probably done with a jemmy. He lifted the boot lid. The parcel he had placed inside, firmly secured with string and sellotape, was, of course, missing. He opened the driver's door, tilted the seat and reached behind it. He unfastened the rear bench seat. The two smaller packages were still there in the space beneath. He removed them and placed them in the canvas bag which had shared their hiding place. It would be foolish to leave the Hellfire Papers in the car. When the thief discovered his mistake he just might risk a second attempt. Tim took a roll of twine from the boot and lashed the cover down. The damage was annoying but the cost would be added to Masquerier's bill – and some. He shouldered the bag and sauntered off to spend the afternoon on a private sightseeing tour.

He wandered happily through the compact display of every style of architecture from high gothic to Victorian gothic. He luxuriated in evensong in King's Chapel. He strolled along the Backs where the first daffodils raised their heads defiantly by the slow-moving river. He browsed in antique shops and paid more than he should have done for an early Bristol delft charger. He spent a pleasant hour in the Fitzwilliam Museum which was hosting a travelling exhibition, 'Gainsborough's Contemporaries'. His itinerary ended in a backstreet pub where he was able to linger quietly over a pint of Greene King before the undergraduate influx began.

During the afternoon Tim's thoughts hovered back and forth between two problems; problems he tried hard to keep in separate containers, though with steadily decreasing conviction. First there were the two attempts to steal the Hellfire Papers. Tim had always been convinced that someone at St Mary's was responsible. That was why he had baited the trap. The bait had been taken. That could only have been at the instigation of one of the three people who knew the documents were in his car: Stuart Longton, Deb Masquerier and Sir Evelyn (his wife could easily have passed on the information, despite her insistence that he was unreachable). Perhaps they were all in cahoots. Well, whoever was responsible knew that he (or she) had bungled – *and* knew that Tim knew. Perhaps, as he had first suspected, Masquerier was bent on some private deal, but the more he thought about it the more Tim realized that that solution had a flaw in it. There was, however, another obvious explanation and Tim intended to put it to the Master of St Mary's House – straight! That would make for a very interesting bout of intellectual sparring. Tim was looking forward to his next encounter with Sir Evelyn Masquerier.

But Tim's theory took no account of the other business. Two men – two old friends – had died on opposite sides of the world. Both deaths were unpleasant but not necessarily suspicious. Their personal papers had all been destroyed – probably by themselves but possibly not. The only tangible link between Vare and Whitehead-Dyer was the one in the canvas bag at his feet. And someone was desperate to get hold of it. Why? Why? Why? What harm could a bundle of two-hundred-year-old erotica possibly do anyone? The Masqueriers and Longton were worried enough to quiz Emma extensively. Then there was Teddy

Everton. Tim was still not convinced that the peer had turned up unexpectedly in San Francisco purely by chance. But most unnerving of all was Emma's recollection of Charles Vare's misgivings. 'I, the Lord your God, am a jealous God, visiting the iniquities of the fathers upon the children to the third and fourth generations of them that hate me.' Was there some kind of dark retribution in train, divine or otherwise? And if so, who was its agent?

These questions were still dogging his heels when Tim made his way back to St Mary's House, left his bag at the porter's lodge for safe keeping and climbed to Dr Longton's rooms at the top of A staircase.

Stuart welcomed him warmly and poured him a sherry.

'Well, I'm delighted your trip went so smoothly. It's very exciting to have these mysterious papers actually here. I must say I'm longing to examine them.'

Tim watched his host carefully. He detected no sign of nervousness but, then, he did not expect to. If Longton knew about the attempted thefts he would have to make a pretence of relaxed ignorance. The only question was how long he could sustain it under pressure.

Tim propped himself against the desk. He spoke casually but kept his eyes on the academic. 'I wouldn't say it was a totally uneventful journey. Someone tried to steal your precious papers in San Francisco.'

Longton's eyes opened wide. 'Good Lord! Who on earth—? How? Did you . . . did the police catch whoever was responsible?'

'No, but I think I know who was behind it.'

'You do? Who?' A little too eager?

Tim drained his glass languidly. 'Excellent sherry, Stuart. Dry Oloroso?'

'Yes. It's bottled specially for the college. But you were saying, about the Whitehead-Dyer Papers?' He could not contain his anxiety now. 'I mean, they didn't come to any harm? You said earlier today that you had them with you.'

Tim put his empty glass down on the desk. He spoke slowly, deliberately keeping any trace of emotion out of his voice. 'When we met this morning they were in my car, in your private car park. During the early afternoon my car was broken into.'

That did shake Stuart Longton. He stared, open-mouthed. 'You mean the papers were stolen? Here? In Cambridge? Right under our noses? This is terrible, terrible.'

Tim thought that if the man was faking shock he was doing it remarkably well. He said nothing.

Another thought struck Longton. He took a couple of steps forward. He stared at Tim shortsightedly. 'You've been to the police?'

Tim shook his head slowly. 'No. I didn't know how the college would feel about the publicity.'

'Good, good.' Longton sighed his relief. 'We must tell the Master.' He moved towards the phone. 'This is terrible, terrible. You're quite sure? No, that's a silly question. Of course you're sure.'

'I think you'll find that the Master is out until later this evening. Dining in Magdalene, I believe. And talking of dining, is it time we went down? I'm starving.'

Stuart peered closely at his watch. 'Yes, I suppose . . .' He grabbed his gown from a hook on the door. 'I must say you're taking all this remarkably calmly.'

'Oh, we shan't solve this nasty business by getting excited.' Tim preceded his host out to the staircase. 'And there's much more involved than some missing old papers, isn't there, Stuart?'

Tim enjoyed the meal. Longton did not. While his guest chatted with the four other fellows who were 'dining in', he played with his food and conversed in monosyllables.

When the company had retired to the blazing fire in the combination room and the senior tutor was pouring coffee, Longton excused himself. He called Tim aside and spoke *sotto voce*. 'Look, I'm going to grab a taxi and get over to Magdalene to collect Sir Evelyn. Could you meet us in the Master's Lodge in half an hour?' He strode the length of the room, gown billowing behind him.

It was fifty minutes later that Tim ascended the steps of the Masquerier residence and pressed the bell. It would do these devious, arrogant establishment men no harm to sweat for a bit. The ever-vigilant Gerda let him in and offered to take his bag. Tim smiled and shook his head.

Sir Evelyn was already descending the wide staircase. 'Mr Lacy, what a delightful surprise.'

Tim briefly shook the proffered hand. 'Is it?'

Masquerier looked puzzled. 'I beg your pardon?'

'I was just wondering whether you found my appearance either pleasant or a surprise.'

Sir Evelyn led the way up to his study without comment. Longton was there, perched nervously on an upright chair. Tim accepted a glass of armagnac and settled himself on the leather chesterfield.

Masquerier sat down opposite. 'Stuart has been telling me

about your misadventures. I was appalled to hear of the trouble you've had and about the theft of the papers. I need hardly tell you what a terrible shock this is.'

Tim raised an eyebrow. 'Theft? I don't recall saying anything about a theft.'

Longton almost choked on the whisky he was sipping. 'But you told me your car—'

'That my car had been broken into. That's right. But I'm not so foolish as to leave valuable documents where an opportunist thief can find them.' Tim unzipped the canvas bag and placed the two packages on the seat beside him. 'Here, Sir Evelyn, are the Whitehead-Dyer Papers. Safe and sound.' Tim looked for anger or confusion on Masquerier's face.

What he saw was a broad smile of pleasure and relief. 'But that's wonderful, Mr Lacy. I see, now, that you've been playing a little game with us. Well, you caught us out fair and square. Poor Stuart here was on the verge of cardiac arrest. But if you've brought the papers – I trust these *are* the papers – I'm sure he'll readily forgive you.'

Tim put a hand possessively on the packages. 'Before I hand these over there are one or two matters to be cleared up. You mentioned games, Sir Evelyn. OK, let's talk about games. Who's been playing hare and hounds with me, and why? I was sent halfway round the world to collect some papers. Then someone came after me to grab those papers. They failed in San Francisco so they tried again here – a last ditch attempt. Now, I strongly object to being messed about. So I want to know who is responsible for these ham-fisted attempts and exactly what's behind them.'

Masquerier shrugged. 'My dear Mr Lacy, why are you

asking us these questions? We're the ones who engaged you to fetch the papers. We agreed a not inconsiderable fee. I assure you that the college can't afford to throw that sort of money away.'

Tim's annoyance broke free. 'Don't take me for a fool, Masquerier. I may not have an Oxbridge degree but I'm not stupid enough to fall for what was really a rather pathetic fraud. I honestly expected something better from you. In fact, you bungled it from the start. A few weeks ago when we sat in this room you solemnly impressed upon me the secrecy of my mission. You personally arranged my itinerary so that no one else would know where I and the papers were at any given time. What you were doing was backing yourself into a corner. If only you knew my whereabouts, then only you could have set up the hotel break-in in San Francisco.'

'But, Mr Lacy, I assure you—'

'I haven't finished. This morning I left a dummy package in my car boot and my car was broken into. Now I told only two people where the fake papers were: Lady Masquerier and Stuart Longton. Wouldn't you say that that very considerably narrows the field of suspects?'

'But I knew nothing about your car. I didn't even know that you were in Cambridge until Stuart interrupted a very agreeable social gathering an hour ago.'

'Do you seriously expect me to believe that your wife didn't call you as soon as I left here this morning?'

Masquerier was beginning to show his annoyance. 'Mr Lacy, you may believe whatever you choose to believe. I fully appreciate that this assignment has involved certain unforeseen unpleasantness for you. I regret that, but I must protest at these unsubstantiated allegations. What could I possibly have to gain from these criminal acts you accuse me of?'

Tim stuck to his guns. One more burst and the man would surely run up the white flag. 'I puzzled over that for quite some time. Then I realized the answer was glaringly simple – especially for a financial expert. St Mary's receives a legacy of some important and valuable papers. Very nice, but what the college needs right now is not historical documents but cash. How to turn the one into the other? Employ some unsuspecting security firm to collect the papers and bring them back to England. They will, of course, be covered by the company's own insurance. So, when the documents are unfortunately stolen thousands of miles away from Cambridge the loss will be made good and no one can possibly suspect anyone at St Mary's of fraud.'

Longton protested, 'What an unnecessarily complicated plot. If we wanted to realize the value of Whitehead-Dyer's papers it would be far easier to sell them.'

Tim nodded. 'Yes, I stumbled over that objection. Then I remembered something else that the Master said in this room. You pointed out, Sir Evelyn, that no one would know how important – and therefore valuable – the papers were until they'd been examined. If they turned out to be forgeries they would be worthless. No, waiting and hoping was far too risky. The papers had to disappear before anyone could vet them.'

Masquerier had recovered his composure. He smiled as though mildly amused by an intriguing story. 'A bit risky, though, stealing them in our backyard, wasn't it?'

'I gambled on your being desperate – and piqued because

I'd outwitted you. I thought that if I gave you one more chance, you just might grab at it. I was right.'

Masquerier sighed. 'As it happens, Mr Lacy, you were wrong, but I can see we shan't be able to convince you of that. Well, if it amuses you to believe that you have outsmarted us, so be it. It's all academic now, anyway. You have safely delivered our property. Now, may we see it, please?'

The two Cambridge men carefully unwrapped the parcels and laid out the contents on Masquerier's desk. Longton fell to examining them eagerly.

Masquerier held out an envelope. 'While I was waiting I made out your cheque. I took the liberty of adding a premium to compensate you for your extra trouble. I hope you will find that satisfactory.'

Tim produced a slip of paper from his pocket. 'Thank you, Sir Evelyn. Now, if you wouldn't mind signing this receipt that will conclude our business.'

Masquerier smiled. 'Certainly. I see you leave absolutely nothing to chance, Mr Lacy.' He returned the receipt. 'That discharges you of all responsibility. Now this troublesome inheritance is our problem. Let us hope that we can keep the papers safe from any further burglarious attempts.'

Tim thought, 'He's maintaining the act to the last,' but a twinge of doubt tweaked his self-congratulation.

Longton, meanwhile, was leafing through the files with growing excitement. 'All this stuff certainly looks genuine. And Sir Peregrine appears to have made a very good fist of sorting it. That will save a lot of time when we come to examine it thoroughly.'

Masquerier said, 'I think we'd better go across to the college and see it locked away in the safe. Perhaps we should even consider depositing it in the bank. If what poor Charles said is true, and Mr Lacy's experiences seem to bear that out, we'll have to take every possible precaution.'

Tim was not prepared to be ignored, dismissed as no longer relevant. 'Where exactly does the late Dr Vare fit into all this?'

'I thought you had everything worked out to your satisfaction.' Masquerier made no attempt to conceal his disdain.

Tim thought, 'Smug bastard!' He said, 'I'm prepared to listen to alternative hypotheses.'

Stuart looked up from re-wrapping the files. 'I think, perhaps, we do owe Mr Lacy an explanation, Master.'

Sir Evelyn looked only partially convinced. 'I'm afraid he won't find it very enlightening to have his certainties replaced by our doubts.'

'If we had passed on Charles's warning Mr Lacy probably wouldn't have got hold of the wrong end of the stick.'

'Very well.' Masquerier shrugged and turned to Tim. 'When you came to see us in January, Mr Lacy, and accepted the commission, we were not a hundred per cent frank with you. What we told you was the truth but not the whole truth. More brandy?'

He took Tim's glass, refilled it and returned to his armchair. 'We heard about Whitehead-Dyer's bequest last September. His solicitor wrote to us on his instructions. He gave a very brief description of the documents and intimated that his client's state of health suggested that it might not be long before they passed to the college's ownership. Naturally, I mentioned it to Charles Vare. He seemed surprised and somewhat put out that his old friend had made no mention of the legacy to him. But then, Charles was given to moods, so I thought no more about it. In fact, I put the whole thing out of my mind.'

'You didn't tell anyone else?'

'Dr Longton and a couple of our colleagues. I certainly didn't make a big thing of it. No sense in counting one's chickens. It was about a month later that Charles came to see me in some agitation. He was uncharacteristically incoherent. All he would say was that there would be other people "desperate" – that was his word – desperate to get their hands on the papers. The college might find Sir Peregrine's bequest something of a poisoned chalice. Then, off he went.'

'You didn't press him for an explanation?'

Stuart intervened. 'If you'd known Charles Vare you wouldn't have asked that question, Tim.'

Masquerier continued. 'Another three weeks passed. Then I received a fax from the Sydney lawyer informing me that Sir Peregrine had passed away, that he expected no difficulty with the probate and that he was looking forward to receiving my instructions regarding the papers. I decided it was time for another chat with Vare. I put it off for a couple of days. That proved to be a mistake.'

'He was dead by then?'

The Master nodded. 'What were we to do? We obviously had to take Charles's warning seriously but we had no way of assessing the risk. The wisest plan seemed to be to hire the best professional we could find. Someone experienced, tough and discreet.'

'It didn't occur to you that by not being up front with me

you were sending me out with one hand tied behind my back?'

'With hindsight it would have been wiser . . . But Vare's warning was so vague as to be of no practical use to you. And it might have put you off completely.'

Tim sat for some moments in thoughtful silence. At last he said, 'Vare's "vague" warnings didn't dissuade you from grilling Emma Kerr.'

'Ah, you heard about that. Stuart mentioned that you seemed to know the girl.'

'You obviously took her story of an intruder in Vare's rooms seriously. Why didn't you convince the police there was something in it?'

Longton blurted out, 'Emma is a very excitable girl; bright but highly strung.'

Masquerier shook his head. 'I don't altogether agree with that. I'd prefer to call her spirited, headstrong. She gave us quite a lot of trouble last year but I respect her for that. She's got the determination and the brains to go a long way.'

'And the contacts?'

'Well, it certainly helps if your father's in the government.'

'I presume you believe her story?'

'Yes, despite what Stuart says, I think she saw someone come out of Charles's room. But who it was and why he was there, whether it has any connection with Charles's forebodings . . .' Masquerier shrugged.

'It seems that your late Dean had a secret life.' Tim happened to be looking at Longton as he spoke and noticed the startled expression which passed rapidly across his face.

He stood up. 'Well, I have to set out for London. I'll bid you gentlemen goodnight.'

The Master preceded him to the door. 'We're very grateful to you for all you've done, Mr Lacy, and I hope you don't think too badly of us.'

Tim left the implied question unanswered as he descended the staircase with his host. 'I hope your problems are over, Sir Evelyn.'

They said goodbye at the door. Tim strode thoughtfully through the fellows' garden. At the porter's lodge he obtained a token to open the car park gate, collected the 500SL and headed for the M11 and London. He hoped his involvement with St Mary's and its legacy was at an end. But somehow . . .

CHAPTER 7

Dashwood jumped down from the coach, motioning me to follow. 'Stay close,' he whispered. 'Make sure they see your pistol. There's powder and shot in the box. Keep it handy so that we can reload.'

He stepped forward and called out to the twenty or so scoundrels, 'That's far enough. If any man takes another step I'll save Ketch a job.'*

The mob shuffled forward, but more slowly, all men looking uncertainly to one of their number, a burly fellow in a battered tricorne and a dusty coat over his working apron. This captain huff† brandished a hand axe at us. 'We want no Dashwoods here. Get ye back to London or it'll be the worse for ye.'

Sir Francis raised his weapon and pointed it at the villain's head. 'Stop littering the King's highway with trash and let us pass.'

* save the hangman a customer
† swaggering ringleader

The two players glowered at each other, neither prepared to lose face; neither ready to call the other's hand. Silent seconds passed and my heartbeat marked every one.

Suddenly, the ruffians' leader shouted, 'Right, Tom, take 'em in the rear!'

It was an old trick but we both spun round to stare at the empty road beside us. As we did the crowd ran forward, screaming and hullowing. We turned to face them. Dashwood raised his pistol. He had no time to aim. The explosion was deafening. There was a scream of pain. Looking past Dashwood I saw a red-haired man, little more than a boy, writhing on the ground clutching his leg. His fall had brought down others who now scrambled to their feet in confusion. The charge was halted – for the moment.

Sir Francis pushed the still-smoking pistol into my hand and grabbed the other from me. 'Reload!' he whispered.

I turned back to the carriage. While my trembling hands fumbled with the powder horn Dashwood called out, 'Who's next for a dose of leaden physic?'

The ringleader remained defiant. 'Our orders are not to let you pass.'

'And you're to be paid by results, I'll be bound. Well it'll be my pleasure to save Lord Tregarth his money.'

As I returned to Dashwood's side with the primed pistol, I saw the mob fall back, two of them supporting their wounded comrade.

Sir Francis scowled. 'They'll not give in that easy.' He pointed to the knot of men gathered round their general in a council of war. 'Unless they're very stupid, they'll soon see the best plan is to take us from the front and sides at once. Ah, yes, as I thought.'

A group of men were dragging a fallen tree stem across the road.

I pointed to the obstruction. 'We'll not get the coach through there.'

'The coach – no. Dickon, Tam!' He called the driver and footman down from the box. He whispered something to them which I did not hear. Then he added, 'Not till I say, mind!'

Moments later our assailants dispersed into the woods on either side leaving their barrier guarded by six of their number.

As soon as most of the mob were out of sight, Dashwood called softly, 'Now, lads!'

Quickly and efficiently the servants loosened the traces on the lead horses. They drew them clear of their companions. Dashwood leaped nimbly onto the back of a restless bay while Dickon held his head.

'Come on, Whitehead!' He reached down and half pulled me up behind him. Then, with a shout, he kicked the beast into a canter. We leaped forward, I clinging to Dashwood's coat with rigid, white fingers. The keepers of the barrier fell back as we charged at them, bounded over the tree and careered down the road with Dickon and Tam following on the other horse.

Thus did the independent candidate and his retinue arrive in New Romney and the devil of a stir did we make as we clattered into the square with curs and small boys running alongside as though we were messengers bringing news of some great victory.

A great victory there was, indeed. The next day Sir Francis Dashwood was elected as the member for New

Romney with a majority of over nine hundred.

Our friends were all cock-a-hoop at the turn of the political wheel. With no majority in the Commons, Walpole was forced to resign. His enemies could not rest content with that. They clamoured for impeachment on charges of corruption. But their rejoicing was premature and their expectations unfulfilled. The King protected his old friend from prosecution and Robin continued to exercise influence behind the scenes. This was evident in the choice of ministers who succeeded him. Within a few years the pack was shuffled and reshuffled but always it consisted only of court cards – men agreeable to the King and pledged to continue the old policies. At last it was the Clan Pelham which succeeded to the offices and perquisites of the Tribe Walpole. Henry Pelham became first minister. His elder brother Thomas, Duke of Newcastle, as secretary of state, was his mentor. Affairs political went on much as before. It was not the radical change in the nation's fortunes our friends had looked for. Sir Francis was offered a government post and declined, determined as an independent to harry the administration. Bubb Dodington, however, judging the time appropriate for another shift of allegiance did take office under the Pelhams.

[The narrative breaks off at this point]

I was at the Sign of the Bible in Covent Garden when panic struck the city. Emile Coustance – a dark, twisted little fellow with fat blubbering lips and shifting eyes – operated, beneath the pious sign of holy writ, a trade in books old and new that was perfectly respectable to the casual browser.

Only in the rear of his premises were the cognoscenti admitted to peruse volumes devoted to subjects not fit for all eyes.

I had long known Coustance and his predecessor, Edmund Curll, and amused myself by purchasing manuals on the arts of love translated out of Arabic and Persian, novels printed in limited editions for very private circulation and the newly Englished memoirs of certain French courtesans. I had become particularly curious about the chameleon relationship between religion and the pleasures of the flesh. For seventeen centuries the Church, largely following the dualism of Plato and the Greeks, had set barriers between body and spirit, heaven and earth. Believers had been taught to loathe fleshly lusts, to pursue virginity and the ascetic path. Such aspirations were far beyond the reach of ordinary mortals and, indeed, of most clergy, as Boccaccio, Chaucer, Rabelais and other irreverent authors had delighted to point out. In this desultory study I had come upon the descriptions of certain medieval Adamite sects. These bands of men and women, sometimes known as the Brothers and Sisters of the Free Spirit, resolved the tension between natural passions and the call of holiness by claiming to have reached a state of grace in which they were no longer capable of sin. It became their practice in their communes to go about completely naked, save for wooden crosses worn on chains round their necks, and to follow there their passions without shame. Many avoided the charge of shallow libertinism by being prepared to die at the stake for their faith.

Coustance was also something of a martyr to the cause of freedom. He was frequently attacked from city pulpits and had twice been placed in the pillory for 'publishing obscene and immodest books'. This, you may well imagine, only added to the attraction his establishment held for what he called his 'discerning clientele'. However, several of the more prominent members of that band chose not to be seen personally at the Sign of the Bible, preferring to hide private vice behind public virtue. Somewhat to my surprise, Sir Francis Dashwood, after his election to parliament, employed me to acquire his reading matter from Coustance.

This placed me in the position of being able to encourage my patron's interests in certain directions, a task made easier by Dashwood's commitment to free thought and speculation. He devoured with equal appetite the treatises of Rousseau and Voltaire, the works of Apuleius and *The Arabian Nights*, accounts of cabalistic and Rosicrucian practices, romances about the exploits of Renaissance libertines and studies of the black arts. He was something of a latterday Faustus, torn between the allurements of competing arcane temptresses. Often we sat late in his library at Wycombe or in Hanover Square discussing the fruits of our reading. I must not, however, give the impression that Sir Francis was a gullible wool-gatherer, stuffing into his noddle every new idea upon which he chanced. Much of what he read he classed as 'fascinating but absurd'. His quest for leaves of truth among the groves of the exotic, the enigmatic and the mystic was more by nature of being a diversion from the duties of his estates and his parliamentary responsibilities. As a result of our reflections and our gleanings from Mr Coustance's literary store the shape of the Brotherhood of St Francis assumed more precise definition in my mind, though as yet I made no mention of it to Dashwood.

On a morning in December 1745 I was just emerging –
empty-handed on this occasion – from Coustance's back
room when I heard a commotion in the street. The book-
seller was standing in his doorway looking out at people who
were running past screaming and calling out to one another.

'What's the hubbub?' I enquired.

The little man shrugged but looked worried. 'I can get no
sense from 'em. They all say the Scots are on the road –
though where, no two people can agree. Some say St
Albans, some Potter's Bar. One woman has just told me the
Highlanders are camped at Bunhill Fields. What's a man to
believe, Mr Whitehead? They're all terrified that the
Pretender and his men mean to plunder and fire the city.'

'It's nothing but foolish, needless panic, Mr Coustance.
The Duke of Cumberland has the Jacobites' measure,
depend upon it.'

'I do, sir. I do. Nevertheless, I think I'll put up my
shutters.'

Coustance busied himself securing his premises. I made
my way as fast as I could through the jostling crowds to
White's. At the club I found threescore anxious men sitting
or standing in twos and threes, talking agitatedly or scanning
the latest newsheets. I espied the bulky figure of Dodington
through the throng and made my way to him. He was talking
animatedly with a man who, in dress and deportment, was
his very antithesis – tall, thin, haughty of countenance and
impeccably attired in full-dress coat and tie wig. I knew him
instantly and, for my part, Bubb's formal introduction was
scarcely necessary.

'Mr Pitt, may I present Mr Paul Whitehead, a poet of no
mean stature.'

'Indeed, indeed,' the other responded civilly. 'I've read many of your satires, Mr Whitehead, and your poem "On Honour".'

'And I, sir, have read your speeches. It's a privilege to make your acquaintance.' It was no empty flattery. William Pitt had a reputation which spread well beyond the Commons chamber. Still in his thirties, he was already acknowledged parliament's best orator and the government's most dangerous critic. He was often to be seen in the Prince of Wales's suite. I had myself observed him a few times at Leicester House but we had never spoken. 'Now, gentlemen, what's the truth in all this to-do about the Jacobites?'

'The truth is', Dodington blustered, 'that Charles Edward Stuart and his Scotch rabble have had a damned sight more success than they should.'

Pitt agreed. 'If our pitiable army hadn't been in the Low Countries propping up foreign regimes and if the counties had properly trained bands of militia this Jacobite rebellion would have been crushed even quicker than its predecessor, thirty years ago. As it is . . .'

'But what is the military situation?' I persisted. 'On the streets folk are saying that London is at the mercy of the Scots.'

'Not yet,' Bubb explained, 'though the devils come on at some pace.'

Pitt added, 'Our latest intelligence is that the rebels have taken Derby and that Stuart is determined to press on to the capital. He means to make our Hanoverian master fight or fly this side of winter.'

'But where is Cumberland?'

Bubb sneered. 'There's many of us calling for the answer

to that question. For all our royal Duke's girth the mantle of command sits loose upon him. Our last report was that he was following the Pretender's army – at a safe distance. Meanwhile, the savages from over the border hold towns and villages to ransom without let or hindrance.'

'Aye, and the French stand ready to bring reinforcements of men and treasure across the Channel,' Pitt observed gloomily.

'But it cannot be believed that Cumberland will let the rebels come much farther south.'

'He has been ordered to offer battle but always his complaint is that the government keeps him starved of troops.'

'And there's truth in that,' Bubb agreed. 'I have argued for more levies but the Pelhams will not have it. The King wants to bring over more German mercenaries and everyone mislikes that. Some call on the sovereign to disengage our armies on the continent but he'll none of it. The Commons almost to a man want Mr Pitt brought into the administration, preferably as Secretary at War, but the merest suggestion of that puts royal George in a pet. And so the arguments chase about hither and yon like coursers and hares, and nothing done.'

All the time we were speaking men were rushing in with tit-bits of news and gossip – little of it good. I retired to my Strand lodgings in some agitation.

On the warmest day of an indifferent early summer the Lacys were enjoying a rare hour *en famille* on their private lawn at Farrans Court. Three years' work on the old walled vegetable garden was beginning to produce results. The shrubs had grown to fill in most of the spaces between them and the grass extended smooth and level from a small terrace to the dozen fruit trees Tim rather grandly called the orchard. Here the proprietors of Lacy Enterprises could escape from the staff, guests and business associates who were free to enjoy the rest of the grounds. It was an infrequent indulgence. Tim was often away visiting clients or supervising the installation of security systems. Catherine was kept busy arranging new exhibitions, attending to artists, dealers, collectors and members of the public who came to Farrans for views, seminars and conferences. They were both aware that they did not see enough of each other and the boys.

They were, therefore, very self-consciously enjoying these stolen moments away from their desks. They had collected the children from their nanny, hastily made some sandwiches, grabbed a bottle of wine from the cellar and rushed almost furtively from the house before secretaries waving papers and telephones could stop them.

Lunch had been as leisurely as the presence of two lively infants would permit. Afterwards they played catch with the boys. Timothy (always known as 'Toot') was slim and fair like his mother. He rushed around with all the semi-co-ordinated, seemingly inexhaustible energy of a three-year-old. At eighteen months, Rupert ('Root'), dark and square-built, after the pattern of his father, was at the stage of trying to copy his brother in everything. He threw the ball with windmill-like gestures, then rushed after it for half a dozen paces before tumbling over with obvious glee. The game went on for ages, neither child tiring of its simple appeal. Then, suddenly, Root spreadeagled himself on a plaid rug and fell asleep. Toot demanded to be read to, and after a couple of pages of his favourite story book, he too succumbed to the somnolent warmth of the afternoon.

Catherine stretched out on a recliner. 'Gee, I thought children were supposed to keep you young. I feel about ninety.'

'Well, you don't look it.' Tim bent over and gave his wife a quick kiss before perching on the edge of the terrace.

Catherine sighed a long, contented sigh. 'This sun is great.' She pulled her skirt up well above her knees. 'I could lie here all afternoon. Tim, why do we spend so much time rushing around?'

Tim chuckled. 'I suppose so that we can keep up a beautiful home that we never have the leisure to enjoy.'

'Seems crazy, doesn't it. Will we ever be able to afford to stop?'

'It's a bit early to be thinking of retirement.'

'You know darn well I'm not talking about retirement. There must be some expenses we can cut down on, some savings we can make, so that we wouldn't have to work quite so hard.' She sat up and gazed fondly at her recumbent sons. 'Childhood's so short. Another ten years and we'll all fall into the generation gap – teenage traumas, rebellion and all that. It would be good to get some quality family time in before then.'

Tim watched swallows swooping and soaring over the giant cedars beyond the wall. 'Yes. I wish I could see some way of easing back.'

'You could take a partner.' Catherine watched for the reaction.

It came in a toss of the head and a dismissive snort. 'You

mean let someone else share a quarter of the work and half the profits?'

'No.' Catherine responded levelly. 'I mean find someone with his own contacts and some capital. Someone who could help the business grow and take some of the load off your shoulders.'

'I can't see that working.'

'Look, Buster, I know Lacy Security is your baby and you think nobody else could possibly operate it. Well, that ain't necessary so. You're damned good, Tim, but you're not unique.'

Tim stared moodily down the lawn. 'Why do I feel it suddenly getting chilly?'

'OK, be stubborn, but at least think about it.'

At that moment there was a discreet cough from the gateway behind them. Catherine turned to see Tim's secretary standing there awkwardly and groaned inwardly as she noticed the telephone in her hand. 'What is it, Sally?'

The young brunette advanced into the garden. 'I'm terribly sorry, Catherine. I've got a Dr Longton on the line for Tim. He says it's urgent. This is the third time he's called in the last hour. I didn't think I could put him off any longer.'

Tim jumped up and took the receiver from her. He grimaced his disapproval and said brightly into the machine, 'Hello, Stuart. This is a surprise. How are you?'

The voice at the other end of the line was excited. 'Tim? Thank goodness I've got hold of you. Look, I've a big favour to ask of you.'

'Go ahead.'

'What you were saying when you came to deliver the

Whitehead-Dyer Papers set me thinking. I've been doing a great deal of thinking . . . And I've been going through the papers . . .' The voice trailed away.

'Yes,' Tim prompted.

'There's something odd about them . . . things about the whole business that smell . . .' Again Longton broke off.

'So, how can I help?'

'Well, it's a bit of a cheek, but I wonder if I could possibly come down to your place to discuss things with you and to complete the work on the papers?'

'You want to come to Farrans?'

'Look, if it's inconvenient . . . I mean, I'm not expecting you to put me up. If you've just got a corner somewhere where I could read without being in the way?'

'Sure, that's no problem. But what's—'

'Oh, thanks. That would be really wonderful. I've actually taken the liberty of sending the papers on ahead – recorded delivery, for safety.' The relief was almost tangible.

'Stuart, you sound as though you're in a bit of a state. What's the matter?'

There was a long pause. Then, 'It's very complicated, Tim, and rather nasty. I need a few more days to be sure about it and work out all the details. The papers are marvellous. They tell us a lot about several of the leading eighteenth-century figures. Only, you see, they're totally wrong about Jenkinson, and probably others . . .'

'Stuart, you're not making very much sense.'

'No . . . no, I suppose not. Well, look, if you're sure it's OK for me to come.' He stopped abruptly. 'Sorry, Tim. Someone at the door. I'll call again later.'

He did not call. The following day, Wednesday, the

Hellfire Papers arrived at Farrans Court in the first post.

Tim left home mid-morning to catch a train to London where he had a lunch appointment. He settled himself in a corner seat and spread out *The Times* on the table. Almost immediately a headline on the second page caught his eye. Quickly, he read the short report.

MYSTERY DEATH OF CAMBRIDGE DON

Police were called to St Mary's House, Cambridge, last night after the body of one of the fellows was discovered. Dr Stuart Longton (35), a member of the university's history faculty, was found hanged in his rooms. Detective Inspector Tibbs of Cambridge CID, who is in charge of the investigation, said that it was too early to know the details about the tragedy. At this stage the police could not rule out foul play. The Inspector added that he hoped this would not be taken as an invitation to media speculation.

It is less than seven months since the college experienced another sudden death. In December the Dean, the Revd Dr Charles Vare, died in the chapel at St Mary's. The coroner delivered a verdict of suicide on Dr Vare.

The Master, Sir Evelyn Masquerier, was not available for comment last night. A spokesman for St Mary's said that there was no reason to link the two deaths.

II

NIGHT

Then say how hope and fear, desire and hate,
O'erspread with snares the clouded maze of fate,
Where wav'ring man betrayed by vent'rous pride
To tread the weary paths without a guide,
As treach'rous phantoms in the mist delude,
Shuns fancied ills, or chases airy good.

– Samuel Johnson, *The Vanity of Human Wishes*

CHAPTER 8

Tim sat back, stunned. He had spoken to Longton not twenty-four hours before. And now . . . He read the report again. 'Found hanged in his rooms.' Suicide then? Stuart had certainly seemed very upset. But he had spoken of a visit to Farrans. 'The police could not rule out foul play.' That meant they had a damned good reason to suspect foul play. Murder then? But if so . . .

Tim's mobile phone buzzed. He took it out of his brief-case.

'Hello.'

'Tim!' It was Sally. 'I've got a very agitated woman on the other line. Her name's Emma Kerr and she says she must speak to you urgently. Do you want me to put her on?'

He sighed. 'Yes, I suppose you'd better.'

If he expected to have a hysterical female to deal with, Emma's first words forced a quick rethink. 'Tim? Good. You've got to do something! Everyone here's being thoroughly stupid!'

Tim realized that he would have to try to calm the anger

and the anxiety that lay behind it. 'What precisely do you mean, Emma?'

'That ratbag Longton's been killed.'

'Yes, I've just read about that.'

'Best thing that could have happened!'

'I didn't realize you felt so strongly about him.'

'Well,' grudgingly, 'perhaps I was a bit OTT, but I have my reasons.'

'Since there was obviously no love lost between you and Stuart Longton, why is his death bothering you?'

'Because the dumb local plod have arrested Gavin!' Emma shouted her indignation.

Tim held the receiver momentarily away from his ear. 'That's Gavin, your non-boyfriend?'

'Yes, of course!'

'And why would the police want to do that?'

A pause. Tim could almost hear the girl's frustration. Then, 'Oh, it's too complicated to discuss on the phone. Can I come and see you?'

'I really don't know that there's anything I can possibly—'

'Please!' Now the voice was approaching hysteria. 'There's no one here I can talk to – at least, no one who'll listen.'

'Well, if it's just a sympathetic ear you want . . .'

'Thanks, Tim. How do I find you?'

'I'm on my way into London.'

'Great, I can grab a train and be with you in a couple of hours.'

'Hang on, I do have some business to attend to. I could meet you about four o'clock.'

'Right. Where?'

Tim gave her the address of the flat and she rang off abruptly.

Preparing himself for, and then undergoing, a long and complicated business lunch put the trouble at St Mary's House out of Tim's mind for the next few hours. He arrived at his apartment only minutes ahead of his guest, who was prompt. Emma Kerr strode in – jeans, tee shirt and high resolve. Tim settled her in an armchair and made tea.

'This is nice,' Emma observed, glancing round the living room, as her host set down the tray on a low table. 'Very bachelor. I guess your wife doesn't exercise much influence in this cosy male pad.'

'It's much as it was before we were married,' Tim conceded. 'But you haven't come here to advise me on decor.'

Emma frowned. 'No. It's Gavin. Someone's got to do something for him. It's so unfair the way everyone picks on him just because—' She stopped abruptly.

'Just because he's got AIDS?'

She nodded. 'How did you know?'

'I've seen others. When you told me you'd been campaigning on behalf of a fellow student with AIDS I put two and two together. People usually have personal reasons for espousing a cause as you did.'

'Someone had to stand up for him. Bloody hell! He is dying. The last thing he needs is all this harassment.'

'Why have the police arrested him? It can't be just because they disapprove of his lifestyle.'

Emma clenched her eyes and shook her head violently. 'It's all circumstantial. They've got nothing, absolutely nothing, that would stand up in court.'

'Just what have they got?'

'Gavin was, apparently, the last person to see Longton alive. He went up to his rooms after hall last night. Gavin admitted as much. He was absolutely open about it.'

'And that's the only reason he's been taken into custody?'

Emma's head dropped. 'No. Somehow, the police have found out that Longton was responsible for Gavin contracting AIDS.'

It was the euphoria of the populace in general and our political friends in particular at the rout of the Jacobites that provided the opportunity I had patiently awaited to acquaint Dashwood with my ideas for his new club. No sooner had Butcher Cumberland returned triumphant from Culloden and the merciless harrying of the Highlands than all London society was intent on a seemingly endless round of wild celebrations. The Dashwoods and all their friends spent night after night at parties and balls but Sir Francis, as ever, wanted to cap the endeavours of his peers with something, as he confided in me, *different*. That was when I invited him to sup with me privately at the George and Vulture in Lombard Street, an inn which retained something of the reputation it had acquired when the roistering boys of the Hellfire Club had met there a generation before.

It was a foul, tail-end-of-winter night, raining and sleeting by turns, when the carriage drew up outside the George and Vulture. The landlord met us in the doorway with many obsequious gestures as we stepped quickly over the mud and puddles. Well he might, for I had promised him excellent business if his premises pleased my patron. Sir Francis and I shed our hats and topcoats and followed him down freshly-swept stone steps to a veritable cavern of a cellar. The place reeked of mould, despite our host's recent efforts at renovation, for it had been little used in years. However, at the far end an old fireplace had been unbricked at my instruction and a bank of coals glowed invitingly. Our supper table had been set before the hearth and we were soon settled there with the landlord in person attending to our needs.

'Well, Whitehead, why have you brought me to this hell-hole?' Dashwood demanded.

'Hell-hole's the word. You'll know, I'm sure, that the satan-worshippers met here in years gone by?'

'I had heard it. They were closed down by law, were they not?'

'As to that, our host can tell you more. Come, landlord, what's the story?'

The landlord paused in setting bottles and pipes for us by the fire. 'All that was in my father's time. I was told to keep well away from the cellar when the gentlemen were assembled and I needed no second bidding. Their chantings were enough to chill a young boy's heart. In the morning after their rites there was always blood to be wiped from the floor and from a stone slab they had for their altar, over there beneath the lamp.'

Dashwood gazed at the curious article, a glass globe encircled by a gilded serpent. 'The devil's own emblem, I see, and pretty ancient, unless I mistake me.'

'There was something very similar used by the Rosicrucians years ago,' I said. 'You may remember a sketch in a book we were looking at a few months back.'

'Now you mention it, I do recall something of the sort. But what happened to these hellfireans, landlord?'

'Disbanded by order of the Lord Chancellor, Lord Macclesfield. He was no saint, himself. Sent to the Tower he was, not long after, for bribery, embezzlement and I know not what.'

The host departed about his duties and we fell to our victuals.

'A queer place this, then, in both senses of the word,'* Dashwood suggested.

'And just the place for a new club, convened in honour of the Jacobite defeat. Think of it, while all the society hostesses and nobs are giving their elegant dinners and balls, what does Sir Francis do? Why, he gathers all his friends together in a cellar to drink confusion on Charles Edward and all his scapegallows crew. It will be the talk of the town.'

I could see the idea appealed to him, though he still looked puzzled. 'You ain't suggesting we set up the Hellfire Club again? By all reckoning they were rank atheists and ruffians who believed in conjuring up demons and hobgoblins.'

'Rather the contrary. I think the Brotherhood of St Francis of Wycombe should have its own creed and cry a plague on all heresies from satanism to papistry. It will perform its own rites, but only in jest at the mumbling mumbo-jumbo of all over-formal religion.'

'And what shall be the creed?'

'Why Freedom! And *Fay ce que voudras* our motto. It shall be a philosophy without boundaries and have a moral code which makes no condemnations. The only penance shall be on any brother who transgresses the liberty of another. Whatever ghosts or devils haunt this place, we'll put them to rout with our laughter.'

Dashwood caught the infection of my enthusiasm. After supper we sat long over our pipes and mulled wine. The glory

---

* 'queer' meant both 'odd' and 'roguish'

of the Brotherhood, we agreed, would be its absence of rules and regulations. Apart from formal chapter meetings, where mock solemnity should rule, brethren would be free to take their pleasures as they pleased – whether of the intellect, the table or the couch. We discussed dress and forms of address, and officers and the terms upon which women – 'nuns' – should be admitted to our revels. It was agreed that the Brotherhood would be inaugurated in three weeks' time with a 'solemn mass' followed by a banquet in the 'refectory' at the George and Vulture. To keep our activities secret, to ensure the club's exclusivity, and also out of pure drollery, we agreed to limit membership to twelve. The landlord furnished paper and ink and quantities of both were consumed before our apostolate was agreed and complete.

The following printed notice is pasted into Whitehead's memoir at this point. The text is headed by the emblem of a female nude holding aloft a chalice with the legend beneath, *Fay ce que voudras*. It reads:

By Order of Abbot Francis of Wycombe

You are commanded to present yourself
at the Conventual Buildings under the sign of
St George and the Vulture
in Lombard Street

Thursday 12 May at 7 o'clock

Toasts: The King, St William of Cumberland,
St Francis of Wycombe, The Brotherhood

The group which assembled expectantly on the inaugural evening was as diverse as was compatible with conviviality. It would be tedious to rehearse all their names. Each was a man of independent mind, of standing in his own field and, above all, of character. Arthur Vansittart represented the world of commerce. His vast wealth had come from overseas trade and he was a director of the Russia and East India Companies. Like Dashwood, he was much travelled and since his country estate was at Shottesbrook, near Reading, he and Sir Francis were often in each other's company. My especial friend, William Hogarth, we had to have to speak for the graphic arts. No man more fearlessly held up a glass to contemporary society.

'Load, load the pallet, boy! Hark!' Hogarth cries,
'Fast as I paint, fresh swarms of fools arise!'

The law was represented in Thomas Potter, member of the Middle Temple and son of the Archbishop of Canterbury. Neither connection dulled the wits or tamed the passions of this handsome young man. He was well known in all the stews and gambling houses of the city and, doubtless as a result of his proximity to things ecclesiastical, he shared to the full Dashwood's contempt for the fripperies of organized religion.

To speak for the Church we chose the Revd Edmund Duffield, Rector of Medmenham on Thames, from where he also administered the family estates. He was a troubled man with a weak constitution and I draw attention to him only because of the singular events surrounding his death (to which I shall return) and his connection with Medmenham.

For medicine, we had surely the greatest eccentric of the day – a man of singular and pronounced opinions. Though a physician to Frederick Louis and often seen about the Prince's court, anyone who did not know him would have taken Dr Thomas Thompson for a down-at-heel vagrant. Money spent on dress he accounted vanity and replaced coat, shirt or shoes only when they would no longer serve. I recall Dodington neatly riposting to one of Thompson's thrusts across his breakfast table. The good doctor had an aversion to muffins. Spying the muffineer, he ordered its immediate removal. Our host quickly replied, 'Doctor, I've an utter aversion to muffins – and ragamuffins!' Thompson was often to be found – except by his patients, who frequently could not find him when they wanted him – airing his views and telling outrageous stories to anyone who would listen in coffee houses, cider cellars and hedge ale houses.*

Dodington, of course, was of our number, as were several parliament men. The one name over which Dashwood and I disagreed was that of John Montague, Earl of Sandwich. I found the young man, besides being ugly and shambling of gait, to give much evidence of being a false friend – which later proved true, as all the world now knows. Yet he had, I allow, a certain grace of manner (though no wit!). For that, for his political alliance with Sir Francis and his fellowship with Dodington as colleagues at the Admiralty, my patron would have him included. Would that I had been able to persuade him otherwise!

All who were present talked long after about the first

---

* small, insignificant hostelries

meeting of the Brotherhood. Each arrival was handed a white hooded robe and conveyed down to the cellar, dimly lit by candles in embrasures. The trestles had been set back against the wall. The long room was bare, save for three rows of prayer desks facing an altar at the far end. Embroidered across its frontal in fiery red were the words *Fay ce que voudras*. Above it was suspended the Rosicrucians' lamp. From my vantage point in a side 'vestry' I was delighted to see the impact made by the atmosphere. As the members took their places they fell to conversing with each other in hushed, giggling whispers. At the appropriate moment our little band of concealed musicians struck up a solemn dirge and my 'choir' preceded me into the 'chapel'.

Our group of 'nuns' had been assembled by Hannah Hirsch, whom I had early brought into the conspiracy. They were clad, like the brothers, in white robes, though theirs were of wool – a necessity, for they wore but little beneath. Hannah herself, now a woman in the full flush of her beauty, headed the procession swinging a censer. The choir intoned a chant composed entirely of a meaningless jumble of Latin words and phrases. I followed and the procession culminated in 'Abbot' Francis, whose simple garments were incongruously crowned by a red, wide-brimmed cardinal's hat. We took our places either side of the altar. The 'Abbot' halted centrally, removed his hat, turned to face the congregation and intoned the following:

'Brothers, we greet you in the name of Liberty, our great divinity. In her name we call upon you to make your solemn vows as members of the sacred Brotherhood of St Francis of Wycombe. Do you solemnly promise to obey Liberty, and her alone?'

Prompted by the choir, the assembly responded, 'We do.'

'Do you acknowledge only one rule of life – *Fay ce que voudras*?'

'We do.'

'Will you be diligent in your attendance at chapter meetings?'

'We will.'

'Will you serve the Brotherhood and help one another to enter into the fullness of Liberty?'

'We will.'

'Will you speak your mind truthfully on all matters proposed by the Abbot or anyone appointed by him?'

'We will.'

'Will you maintain the secrets of the Brotherhood?'

'We will.'

'Will you conceal from all unbelievers the identities of your brethren and all who shall from time to time be admitted to our rites?'

'We will.'

'Then I embrace you as honoured brothers. *Fay ce que voudras*!'

'*Fay ce que voudras*!' the congregation roared back.

At this point I proffered a flagon of wine to Dashwood. Each of the ladies produced a silver chalice from beneath her robe and came forward in turn for 'St Francis' to fill it. The full cups were taken to the members of the congregation. As each nun proffered her goblet to her selected brother she whispered, '*Fay ce que voudras*'. What fumblings went on during the administration, what gave rise to the gasps, laughter and rustlings, the meagre light did not permit of great elucidation.

The ladies withdrew. Servants set up the tables and spread them with food and wine and we fell to our supper. It was a good feast. The bill of fare promised such delicacies as Soup Libertas, Jacobite Haunch with Cumberland Sauce, Culloden Pie, Mounds of Venus, Maiden's Milk and Rabelais Ragoût. The mood had been well set and I swear that more sparkling and witty conversation never flowed across any board. Later, there was much singing of bawdy songs accompanied by our band. As the night wore on some brothers stayed to talk and laugh together. Others sought out the company of our nuns, for which purpose the landlord had provided chambers above.

The first meeting of the Brotherhood was voted a vast success. Within days it was the talk of the capital – the more so because the members either refused to divulge what had passed or, in response to urgent enquiry, gave outrageous and exaggerated accounts of our proceedings. Soon the Brotherhood became the most exclusive club in London. Men of wealth, fashion and influence were clamouring to join.

Would that those first days of heady innocence could have continued!

Emma finished her tea with a gulp. 'I suppose I'd better start at the beginning.'

'I suppose you had.' Tim replenished her cup.

'The cruel thing is, I don't think Gavin was gay before he came to Cambridge. Not really. Not, you know . . . congenitally. He was just a state school kid who happened to be bright and sensitive and not very macho. He suffered from over-ambitious parents and teachers. God! Don't we all!

When they realized he was potential university material they pushed him for all they were worth. He spent every waking hour working. His social life was virtually zero. When his friends were out experimenting with sex, Gavin was at home with his nose in a book. Of course that didn't mean he was devoid of sexual urges, and one of his teachers took advantage of that. Gavin used to go to the chap for extra tuition. They got friendly. Friendship led to fondling and fondling led to groping and, well . . .'

'I get the picture.'

'This teacher knew Stuart Longton. They'd met through some very discreet homosexual club, I gather.'

'Longton was gay?'

'Oh yes. He stayed in the closet. He even made occasional passes at women students, but he was definitely gay; not even bisexual. Well, this teacher pointed Gavin out to Longton as a likely lad and Longton introduced him to this club that meets in London. Gavin didn't like it but Longton put pressure on him. Told him that his university career depended on his pleasing the right people.'

'Gavin told you all this?'

'Not until afterwards. Not until he got sick. Not until the college tried to get rid of him. We launched our campaign on his behalf. Some of us came pretty damned close to being sent down. It didn't do much good. It wasn't till Gavin poured it all out to me in private one evening that I realized we had a real weapon. We went to Longton the next morning and told him that if the college took any action against Gavin we'd go straight to Fleet Street and sell his story to the highest bidder.'

'That must have shaken him.'

Emma gave a bitter laugh. 'He went berserk. I've never seen anyone so angry and so scared all at the same time. We had it in our power to ruin him and he knew it. He said he couldn't get the governing body to change their minds. But, of course, he did.'

'So what happened last night?'

Emma stared gloomily into her teacup. 'I don't know.'

'What!'

'I mean, I know Gavin went up to Longton's rooms around eight thirty. But I don't know why he went.'

'So that's it? That's your proof of Gavin's innocence?'

'No, of course not! Look, Longton's death was all round college by midnight.'

'When was he found?'

'About ten thirty. As soon as I heard I went to find Gavin. He was working in the library. When I told him he was absolutely shattered. He said, "But I saw him only a couple of hours ago." And this morning, when the police were asking if anyone had any information, Gavin immediately volunteered. The next I knew he was being pushed into a car and rushed off to the police station.'

'I expect he was only being taken to make a statement.'

Emma glared at him. 'They put him in a cell! I went to see what was going on and all they would say was that Gavin was helping them with their enquiries. I made a fuss but it didn't do any good. That's when I phoned you.'

'And just what is it you think I can do?'

'Help me to convince the police that Gavin is innocent. Can I have some more tea please?'

Tim added hot water to the pot and stirred it.

'Your confidence in me is very flattering.'

Emma looked up at him appealingly. 'Tim, don't put me off. You're the only person who has listened to me about that other business.'

'So?'

'There just has to be a connection. Look, if Gavin didn't kill Longton, someone else did.'

'Why are the police so sure it wasn't suicide?'

'Oh that's easy. He was found by Kenton, the junior porter. After the police had finished with him in the small hours some of us grabbed hold of him, plied him with strong drink and got him to talk. Not that that was difficult. He's quite a ghoulish young man and he loves an audience. He says that when he got over the shock of seeing Longton swinging in the middle of the room, he had a good look round. The first thing he noticed was that there was no way Longton could have done it. I mean, the usual method is to stand on a chair or a stool and kick it over. According to Kenton there wasn't a piece of furniture near enough that Longton could have used. Then he looked at the body and saw that there was blood on the face from a cut on the temple.'

'Did he mention whether the room was disturbed?'

Emma's eyes gleamed. 'Ah, I see you're thinking the same as me. I asked Kenton that and he said the room was in a bit of a mess. He reckoned there'd been a scuffle. I think it's more likely that the place was disturbed by somebody searching for something.'

'That's a big logical jump.'

'True, but if it wasn't Gavin who did the wimp in – *and it wasn't* – ' she stared at Tim defying contradiction – 'then there must be a connection with Dr Vare's death. Of course,

171

the police don't want to open up that case again. Much simpler to find someone to pin Longton's death on. Poor Gavin fits the bill perfectly. He admits to being in Longton's rooms. He had plenty of motive and no alibi. They'll pin it on him for sure.'

Tim stole a glance at the bracket clock on a corner table and wondered if he stood any chance of catching the 5.35 from Paddington. 'I think you're being unduly cynical. The fact that they've pulled in your friend as a suspect doesn't mean that they'll fasten the murder on him come what may. I know this is all very distressing for you, especially coming on top of that business last winter, but I don't think you really need worry. The police are sure to be following up other leads. Without good evidence they won't be able to hold Gavin long. I should try to get down to work again if I were you.'

'Fortunately that's one problem I don't have. I did my final exam last week. I'm a free woman. All set to climb the unemployment heap.' She stood up. 'Well, it was good of you to listen. I expect you think I'm a neurotic female.' Before he could politely deny any such opinion, she went on. 'But don't you think there *has* to be some connection between these two deaths?'

Tim thought of the Hellfire Papers in his safe. He said, 'Coincidences do happen. It's tough on St Mary's though, and an unhappy ending to your three years. When do you actually – what's the expression? – "go down"?'

'I was going to stick around for a couple of May balls. Last fling and all that. But now . . .'

'Well, take my advice. Stick around. Go to the balls. Have fun. Go out with a bang.' He opened the door for her.

'As for this other business, I'll tell you what I'll do. If Gavin hasn't been released in a couple of days, call me and I'll have a word with the police.'

She smiled broadly and stepped quickly forward. She gave him a quick hug. 'Thanks, Tim. It's good of you to care. It's a pity you're married.'

Tim laughed. 'Not to mention being nearly old enough to be your father.'

Emma crossed the landing and ran down the stairs, like a young woman without a care in the world.

It was Tim who was worried now.

CHAPTER 9

'You're sure you heard the name right?' Catherine sat in the middle of the emperor-size bed with pages of Sir Peregrine's print-out strewn over the coverlet.

Tim, sprawled in the bedroom's single armchair, lowered Whitehead's eighteenth-century script. 'I could have got it wrong. Longton was very agitated. But I've tried every possibility I can think of – Jenkinson, Jenkins, Jamieson, even Blenkinsop. There's simply no mention of any name remotely like whatever it was that puzzled Longton.'

Tim had not waited to see if there were any further developments in Cambridge. He knew that something was very wrong, and that whatever it was the Hellfire Papers were at the heart of it. As soon as he had returned to Farrans he had reported to Catherine on his meeting with Emma Kerr. She knew better than to try to talk him out of his anxiety. When something bothered Tim he had to worry it until he made sense of it. So she had joined him in the quest for the only clue they seemed to have. The two of them had devoted most of their spare time to going through

175

all the Whitehead-Dyer files, with eye-aching intensity.

Stuart Longton had said there was something very wrong about the Hellfire Papers. He had been sufficiently troubled about whatever he had discovered to send the documents to Farrans and to arrange to continue his research there. That could only mean that he did not want them to fall into the hands of someone at St Mary's House. That, of course, tied up with all that had gone before – Dr Vare's cryptic warnings, the unknown person in his rooms, the attempts to steal the papers and now, presumably, Longton's murder. And according to Stuart, the chink of light he had discerned had to do with a reference in the papers to someone called Jenkinson. Only there was no one called Jenkinson.

Catherine yawned and stretched. 'It's getting late and I'm bushed. We're getting nowhere. I guess the only thing we can do is hand all this stuff over to the police.'

'Mm,' Tim's grunt was non-committal. 'The Hellfire Papers are the property of St Mary's. The only honest thing to do is to return them to the college.'

Catherine drew her legs up beneath her. 'Why do I get the distinct impression that you're not going to do the honest thing?'

'Because that must be exactly what the murderer wants. Longton was on to something – some *person*, perhaps. He certainly knew that all this stuff wasn't safe in Cambridge. That means he suspected that someone there was still trying to get his hands on it. If we calmly take the papers back, what's to stop whoever wants them trying again?'

Catherine was gathering the sheets of typescript together. Suddenly she stopped. 'Hey, I've just thought of something.

We're agreed that someone wants these papers very badly, right?'

Tim nodded.

'So badly that he's prepared to kill for them.'

'I don't see any other explanation for Longton's murder.'

'Then I'd say we had a pretty good reason for getting this little lot back to Cambridge pdq.'

'On the grounds that whoever did Longton in must have got him to tell them what he'd done with the papers?'

'That's a reasonable assumption, isn't it?'

'Maybe.'

Catherine scowled. 'Well, maybe's not good enough for me. I don't want all this archaic erotica acting like a honeypot for thieves and assassins. I have the boys to think of. So do you. Dammit, Tim, it's really nothing to do with us now. When you were responsible for these wretched papers and someone was trying to steal them, OK. That was your job. Now things are different.'

Tim stood up and began peeling off his clothes. 'Darling, I wish that were true. I don't want to be mixed up in this business any more than you do. Frankly, I never cared much for the St Mary's crowd. Whatever sordid games they're playing I couldn't care less. But don't you see, the moment Longton sent the papers down here he involved me again. He bequeathed me one hell of a moral dilemma. On the one hand I can return the papers and walk away. As I see it that would make life easier for the murderer, and do nothing at all to help young Gavin and his family.' He sat down to remove his shoes and socks. 'What do you reckon life's like for them?'

'I guess they're going through seven kinds of hell. They

must have been awfully proud when Gavin got into Cambridge. Then they discovered that he was homosexual. That must have been hard.'

'Especially for a "respectable" suburban family. I gather his father's a civil servant and something big in the local Baptist chapel.'

'When he told them he had AIDS that must have been just about the end of everything. Certainly the end of all their hopes and ambitions for their clever son. Then, to cap it all, they see his name splashed all over the papers in connection with a murder enquiry.'

'If there's anything I can do to minimize their anguish and get their son out of jail I ought to do it.'

'But surely the police can't hold Gavin for long? They haven't really got a case that'll stand up in court.'

'That's what I told Emma, and I hope she believed me. In reality . . .' He shrugged. 'This is a high-profile affair. The police have to be seen to be doing something. My guess is that they'll charge him and hope he cracks. If Gavin was a healthy, resilient young man that wouldn't matter so much, but in his condition every twenty-four hours in a cell knocks weeks off whatever time he has left.'

Catherine nodded. 'OK, I see that's one horn of the dilemma. The other is that by hanging on to the papers you may attract a gang of armed thugs down to Farrans.'

'Exactly. Damn Longton! I could cheerfully murder him myself if someone hadn't beaten me to it. I hoped we could get out of the problem by making some sense of this Jenkinson business and giving the police another lead to follow up.'

'Then I guess we'd better hand the papers over to them and let them puzzle it out.'

Tim shook his head wearily. 'Can you really see the local CID, overworked and understaffed as they probably are, spending expensive man hours poring over two-hundred-year-old documents just because I suggest they have a bearing on the case?'

Catherine turned down the coverlet and slipped into bed. 'So what are you going to do? Say nothing and wait for Mr X to come here threatening your nearest and dearest with a gun? That still strikes me as being pretty dumb.'

Tim slipped on a dressing gown. He walked over to the bed and sat beside his wife, an arm round her shoulder. 'I don't think it'll come to that. For one thing we don't know that Mr X knows where the Hellfire Papers are.'

'But we have to act on the assumption that he does.' Catherine lay propped against the pillows, stiff and unyielding.

'Right. And if that's the case he has a real problem. He can't afford another failure. If he tries to get the papers from Farrans – and with our security system that's a pretty tall order – and something goes wrong he knows he'll be linked directly to Longton's murder.'

Catherine was not convinced. 'He's shown himself to be pretty persistent so far. He's been prepared to chase these papers round the world.'

'True. But he's also shown himself to be an amateur, and a pretty bungling amateur at that. Look at that pathetic attempt at burglary in California. And then breaking into the Mercedes – any self-respecting car thief would have picked the lock. I get the distinct impression that our Mr X is an opportunist who hasn't the brains or the know-how to plan a crime intelligently. Now that the stakes have risen my guess is that he'll sit tight – for a while, at least.'

Catherine looked up at him. 'But that's only a guess. What are we supposed to do meanwhile? Go around in bullet-proof vests?'

'I have got one idea, but I'll only follow it up if you agree.' Tim slipped between the sheets on Catherine's side of the bed.

Catherine edged away from him. 'Don't think you'll get round me like that. I feel a distinct headache coming on.'

'I'd like to have another set of brains working on the Hellfire Papers. Longton spotted something, presumably because he's a historian, a specialist in the period. What was obvious to him should be obvious to another expert.'

'Who have you in mind?'

'What was the name of that Oxford woman we met at the St Mary's dinner back in January?'

'Oh, you mean the sallow-faced, serious-looking creature with a funny name. I remember thinking it reminded me of something out of Wagner. Brünhilde . . . something like that.' Catherine wrinkled her brow in concentration, then smiled triumphantly. 'Got it! Brunhill – Dr Ingrid Brunhill. Are you thinking of sending the papers to her?'

'No, I daren't let them out of my sight. I was hoping I might lure her down here for a few days. It's a long shot, but with any luck her scholar's curiosity will get the better of her.'

Catherine still looked dubious. 'And if she turns up nothing?'

'Then I promise I'll take the papers back to Cambridge

and forget about the whole thing. What do you say?' He drew her close. 'How's the headache?'

She nestled against him. 'What headache?'

A visit to Drury Lane early in 1749 is worthy of record, not for the play but for what transpired during it. Garrick had recently taken over the management, made several changes to the company and was set on trying new works. So it was that he presented the tragedy of *Irene*, written by Samuel Johnson, an old friend who was then compiling his famous dictionary and was, thereafter, much courted in society. The world now knows Johnson for a fine lexicographer, a wit and a poet of no mean repute, but he is no dramatist, as *Irene* proved. Even the great Garrick's efforts and those of Mrs Pritchard, his leading lady, could not transform the piece into any more than a series of tedious philosophical dialogues between the Turkish emperor and various Greek captives. The costumiers and scene painters created a lavish spectacle in an effort to commend the piece to the pit, but the rabble received it ill and those the management had brought in to cheer were shouted down.

I was of Sir Francis and Lady Dashwood's company and was sitting in their box, fairly well bored, when in pants Dodington, in a sweat of excitement.

'Hail, Brother George.' Dashwood greeted him by his title in our Order. Such had become our custom, and it heightened the sense of the Brotherhood's exclusivity.

Our fat friend made his obeisance to the ladies and lowered his bulk onto a well-padded chair at the back of the box. He searched for a kerchief in the deep pockets of his lilac coat and, failing to find one, dabbed his forehead with a lace cuff. 'Your people said you were here, Lord Abbot, and I've news that'll not wait the telling.'

Sir Francis turned his chair away from the stage. 'Say on, O huge one. I trust your soliloquy will be more interesting than the Turkish pasha's.' He leaned forward as Dodington beckoned, an unnecessary precaution since Bubb's attempt at a whisper could be heard by the rest us in the velvet-draped enclosure.

'I was with the Prince of Wales this afternoon. He summoned me for dinner at Carlton House.'

It was inevitable that our friend's urgent intelligence should concern politics. We had known for some time that he was out of sorts with his government masters. It seemed that the frog was jumping back once more to his old lily pad.

'The Prince sent for me especially.'

I could scarce suppress a laugh. Our gundiguts* was always hovering around Frederick William's entourage, and his toady, the scribbler James Ralph, had worked assiduously on his behalf at Leicester House. Though he had transferred his allegiance to the King's party, he yet contrived to maintain good relations with those close to the King's hated elder son. I never saw such an adept as Dodington for dining at one table while keeping his feet under another.

'The long and the short of it is His Highness wants me back in his service – at any price. He said if I stood by him, as soon as he is King I shall be Secretary of State with a peerage and the management of the upper house.'

Dashwood was sceptical, as well he might be. 'The Prince truly said as much?'

* fat fellow

'Truly. Yet there's more. He gave me leave to promise high offices to my friends. Mr Furnese is to have the Treasury, Mr Henley shall be Solicitor General – and Sir Francis Dashwood is to fill my room as Treasurer to the Navy, if he will have it.'

There was a long pause and then Sir Francis asked, 'Has the King been took ill?'

A similar question had been forming in my own mind. If Frederick Louis was really preparing a cabal ready to take office it must be that his father had been struck down and a new reign was in the offing.

'No, but he approaches threescore years and ten and the Prince grows impatient. Francis, the prize really is within our grasp now. We can actually work towards an administration that represents the people. We can put our ideas for reform on the agenda.'

Dashwood made no reply but I could tell what was passing through his mind, for it was a subject we had often discussed. Can a group of idealists change government by faction by forming another faction? It was a question the republicans – and they were growing in number – answered very firmly in the negative. For them the crown and all who depended on it must be swept aside – by revolution if necessary. There was not a political man in England, whether of the old money or the new, who did not shudder at the very thought. Those who sought to change the balance of power wished to achieve it from within; 'evolution not revolution', as Sir Francis frequently said. His immediate target was the transformation of parliament by the introduction of more independent members.

Bubb resented his friend's silence. 'Damme man, this is

the only way it can be done!' The words blared out like a clarion call, causing several of the audience and some on stage to look in our direction. Dodington lowered his voice. 'The Prince lends a willing ear to our views, as you know.'

'Ay, but will he when he's king? For all that he loathes his father, he is still his father's son. Look how he attacks his brother with viperous venom.'

The charge was just. For no better reason than reasonless jealousy, Frederick Louis had, for months past, poured scorn on Cumberland's achievements. James Ralph had done his master good service here. Through *The Remembrancer*, the weekly organ of Leicester House, so much clever ridicule was heaped on the hero of Culloden that 'Butcher Cumberland' or 'Stinking Billy' became an object of derision. He seldom showed his face in London but kept court at Windsor where he became a magnet for malcontents who constituted yet another royal faction.

Dodington persisted in his argument. 'If we lose this chance to bind ourselves to the Prince and him to us, others will grasp it. Then we can say farewell to power for good and all. The Prince needs allies now and is of a mind to be magnanimous. It behoves us to respond in kind. I thought we might admit him to our Brotherhood. More than once he has hinted—'

'No!'

I turned to see Dashwood flushed with sudden anger.

'I'll not have the Order polluted with politics. That would lead to quarrels and bring everything down about our ears.' His voice softened rapidly for he could never be long out of humour. 'We are a happy fellowship, Bubb. Let us keep it so.'

★ ★ ★

I had cause to recall Dashwood's words not two weeks later. The Brotherhood, or the Order of St Francis as we now called our club, had assembled for the spring chapter. Our traditions were deliberately flexible. Our members had increased. The original twelve 'apostles' still formed the inner ring or 'council' but such had been the clamour from our wide circle of friends that we had instituted the ranks of 'disciple' and 'novice'. This increased our need for 'nuns'. Rather than obtain them from 'sororities' of Covent Garden, with the attendant risks that involved, we allowed – nay, we encouraged – brothers to bring female companions to some of our gatherings. Many a dell* was thus introduced to our mysteries. They came from all ranks: servants, tradesmen's daughters, the quality. They came always hooded and masked, after one incident when one of our lady guests was brought suddenly face to face with her husband. That matter ended almost in a duel and it became imperative for our nuns to remain incognito so that they could withdraw if they recognized anyone likely to compromise them.

Inevitably, however, our rituals on more formal occasions had developed a pattern; 'worship', initiation of new members, supper and *ce que voudras*. The liturgy was concocted for each chapter meeting by Potter and myself. Usually it was a parody of Roman Catholic ritual but we did not restrict our satirical palette. We took the bizarre pigments from all over-ornate and meaningless ceremonial. Thus, members found amusing reference in our lampoons to

* willing woman, ready for sexual activity

Anglicanism, freemasonry and satanism. On one occasion, Potter (Brother Thomas) did an excellent imitation of Mr Wesley's preaching.

On the evening to which I refer Potter and I had not, I own, been greatly inspired. The focus of our devotions was The Psalms of David, number 151, intoned alternately by Brother Thomas and Brother William* in the cellar's sepulchral gloom. The religious poem was, of course, directed to Venus and was very particular in petitioning the goddess to grant specific favours to various of her devotees. Both cantors performed splendidly, pausing theatrically with feigned dismay every time their libretto brought forth gusts of laughter from the congregation.

They had almost concluded when there was a sudden scream of 'Stop' from the semi-darkness. From my stall close to the altar I peered at the assembly, expecting some prank by one of the brothers. A white cowled figure towards the back leaped to his feet, still shouting, 'Stop! Stop! This is blasphemy!' Several people giggled. All eyes turned upon the protester who was pushing his way to the front.

He arrived at the altar, pulling off his habit. It was Brother Edmund – the Reverend Edmund Duffield -- and I realized with sudden shock that he was in earnest.

He stared round at Dashwood, myself and the performers. 'An end to this profane mockery! This is devilish! Stop it at once!'

Sir Francis hurried across to him. 'Come, Brother Edmund. You must not take amiss our innocent—'

'Innocent! You call it innocent to mock holy things!'

* Hogarth

Duffield was staring like a creature from Bedlam, eyes wide, saliva dribbling down his chin. 'Stop at once, I say, or feel the wrath of God!'

Thomas and William had now recovered from their surprise. They stepped forward and took Duffield's arms.

He shook them off. 'No, I'll not be silenced! Too long I have shared in this obscene mockery of Heaven! No more!'

He leaped upon the altar and kicked out with his feet at the candlesticks, chalices and books upon it. He grasped the small marble statue of Venus and hurled it against the wall.

A woman screamed. All the brothers were now on their feet. Yet no one moved. We were all mesmerized by the demented cleric who was staring around to see what further havoc he could wreak.

He reached up, grasped the Rosicrucian lamp glowing above his head and wrenched it from its chain. He hurled it to the ground before him. The darkness intensified as the glass globe shattered, but immediately lessened again as rivulets of flaming oil snaked across the rush-strewn flagstones. Some found Duffield's discarded habit, others the altar cloth. One flame seized Hogarth's gown and rapidly began to climb. Yelling he beat it. He struggled with the girdle. Only with the aid of two other brothers did he manage to scramble out of the burning cloth.

By now there was panic. Women screamed. Men shouted. Chairs were thrust aside. Everyone rushed for the door at the back of the cellar. Dashwood called for calm but no one heeded. Smoke and flames were spreading. Like everyone else, I thought of nothing but escape.

I was one of the last to reach the staircase and force my way up. The landlord and other men were trying to get down to see what was amiss but they could not reach the cellar until every one of the guests had vacated it. By then the chamber was filled with clouds of smoke, glowing yellow and scarlet.

That night the George and Vulture was burned to the ground.

Within hours, broadsheets were on the streets describing the conflagration and blaming it upon the bizarre proceedings of 'Dashwood's Diabolical Disciples'. Several members of the Order were named as being among 'Satan's revellers'. So were a number of gentlemen and ladies who had never had any association with us. On the following Sunday churches resounded with denunciations of the profanity and ungodliness which had attracted such dramatic divine retribution. Some preachers proclaimed that God had struck down seven or seventeen (one claimed as many as seventy fatalities) evildoers in the midst of their atheistic ceremonies. The truth is that no one perished in the fire. The only member not accounted for was Duffield. Some swore that they had seen him among the flames, still declaiming like a madman. Others were equally insistent that he had escaped with everyone else and had last been observed running along Poultry and West Cheap screaming and laughing by turns.

Those were critical days for the Order. At a meeting of the Apostles three days after the blaze, four of our number argued for quiet disbandment. It was the very ferocity of the attacks made upon us that decided the majority against this course. Some of the most libellous assaults had come from those who had tried unsuccessfully to gain admittance to the Order and were determined to destroy what they could not have. Others were paid government hacks who trumpeted Dodington's 'betrayal' of the administration and denounced him and his friends as unworthy of trust among Christian men.

'Damme, I'll not be hounded out of public life!' Dashwood declared as we all sat around Bubb's supper table.

Our host responded without his usual ebullient self-confidence. 'The Prince is much embarrassed by all this talk.'

Hogarth said, 'If the Prince wants his friends to stand by him he must learn to stand by his friends.'

Sandwich uttered a string of profanities to the general effect that Frederick Louis was not a man to be relied on and that those who sought to form an opposition party around him were fools.

That prodded Bubb into a counter-attack. 'His Highness is more constant than the Pelhams, my lord, as you may soon discover unless you watch your back more carefully.'

Sandwich's face assumed its habitual sneer. 'And what, pray, d'ye mean by that? The comment comes ill from someone who has turned his coat so often that he can no longer find the buttons!'

'Brothers, enough!' Dashwood's shouted command cut short the argument. 'You forget why we are here. I propose that the Order continues to meet – though perhaps more discreetly.'

'But where?' Someone asked the obvious question.

'As to that, I have some plans that I think brothers will find amusing, though for the present they must remain secret.'

At that point one of Dodington's servants entered bearing

a letter on a silver tray. He spoke briefly to his master, who nodded, took the message and passed it to Sir Francis. 'For you, Dashwood. An urgent note come from your house at Wycombe.'

We all watched, as our abbot broke the seal and read the letter with a grave demeanour.

He sat back with a deep sigh. He looked around the table. 'They have found poor Duffield. His body was this morning taken from the Thames at Newlock.'

Weekends for the Lacys were seldom relaxing interludes in a busy life. Especially during the summer, Saturdays and Sundays brought hundreds of visitors to the gallery. After four years Farrans Court was becoming widely known to the general public. Some came because it was the only 'stately home' to which entrance was free. Although the Lacys had firmly resisted all temptations to make their home-cum-business centre a tourist attraction, they had deliberately created a relaxing ambience for the casual caller. Visitors could wander unhindered through the main ground-floor rooms which had been converted to galleries, stroll in the grounds, where larger items of sculpture were frequently on display, and enjoy tea, coffee or light meals in the panelled dining room. Some callers – an increasing number – came to see the exhibits. Catherine frequently changed the displays and had a growing list of painters, sculptors, carvers, engravers and potters who wanted to be 'shown' at Farrans. It was the basic objective of the Laportaire Memorial Arts Centre – the official title of Catherine's business – to bring ordinary people into contact with living artists and their work in an atmosphere as far removed as possible from the pretentious exclusivity of 'fashionable' galleries. Non-specialist visitors to Farrans could latch onto gallery tours and learn about the items on display and their creators. Sometimes they could meet the artists themselves. During the summer months Catherine made a point of including a large number of modestly priced student works in the exhibition, and took more pleasure from seeing a painting by a promising newcomer placed carefully on the back seat of a family saloon next to Grandma than in any four-or five-figure sale made at one of Farrans' prestigious autumn or spring exhibitions. Weekends were, therefore, busy times for the Lacys' small staff and Tim and Catherine might find themselves involved in any activity from explaining the principles of post-modernist art to cutting sandwiches in a frenetically busy kitchen.

On this particular Saturday, however – the second Saturday in June – Catherine had left Farrans in its hidden hollow south of Savernake to drive to the Cotswolds. A rapidly evaporating mist gave promise of a fine day as she drove through Marlborough – already filling with shoppers – bypassed Swindon, took the A361 north to Burford then, deliberately choosing by-ways through villages whose names were as golden as their stonework – Milton-under-Wychwood, Little Compton, Stretton-on-Fosse – reached the market town of Chipping Sneddon around eleven o'clock.

The fresh greens of woods and pasture, the unhurried muddle of cars, horses and pedestrians on narrow village streets and the timelessness of stone and thatch did much to ease the anxieties that had carved the previous night into chunks of wakefulness and troubled slumber. Was it the

English countryside, which she loved with the passion of one not born to it, that was soothing her, or was it escaping from Farrans – with the children? She looked in the driver's mirror for the umpteenth time to check that Toot and Root were still asleep and fastened securely into the back seat of the little Ford. For all Tim's reassurances her imagination insisted in conjuring up images of brutal men marching into Farrans brandishing guns or slinking into the boys' room and grabbing them from their beds. It was these fears that had exercised an unconscious compulsion on her to bring her sons with her this morning. It was going to be inconvenient to have to keep one eye on them while discussing business with Mrs Revesby, but there was no way that Catherine was going to be parted from them at the moment.

In fact the threat of serious distraction easily resolved itself. Mrs Revesby, the Chipping Sneddon festival chairperson, lived in the old rectory and Catherine had no difficulty locating the substantial Georgian building beside the church. She parked on the wide drive and was immediately involved in dealing with a bout of waking tears from Toot. She was cradling him in her arms and desperately hoping he would not set his younger brother howling when the front door opened.

Mrs Revesby turned out to be fiftyish, tweedy and gushing.

'Mrs Lacy? So prompt. Angela Revesby. I won't shake hands. I can see yours are quite full enough. What darling babies. Yours? Silly question – you'd hardly have abducted them en route would you? What I meant to say was, you don't look *maternal*. Oh dear, no, that's not quite right either, is it? But my dear, you're so chic – and slim! I only had two and look at me! Anyway, come in, come in. Shall I take the little one or will he squawk?'

Rupert surveyed the ebullient stranger very warily but he did not squawk. Bearing him like a trophy of war, Angela Revesby marched into the house. Her string of loosely attached observations flowed over her shoulder.

'Rambling old place. Full of draughts. But we love it. I'm going to introduce you to my daughter and granddaughter. Dorrie! Look who I've brought to see Sophie!'

The last announcement was made as they entered a large kitchen. In the far corner, crouched among a jumble of toys, was a well-fleshed woman in her early twenties. Catherine instantly noted the family resemblance. Dorrie was playing with a little girl who was about the same age as Root. Introductions were made and Mrs Revesby busied herself with coffee and biscuits. Dorrie and Catherine sat at the big deal table and talked babies. Toot's eyes lit up at the treasure trove of new toys and he rushed to inspect them, followed, with a more uncertain gait, by his brother.

Ten minutes later Mrs Revesby set down her porcelain mug, nodded towards the three totally preoccupied children and said, unnecessarily *sotto voce*, 'I think we could slip away now, don't you? Dorrie will hold the fort here, won't you, poppet?'

Catherine, satisfied that the boys were in perfectly capable hands, stood up. She smiled at Dorrie. 'You don't mind?'

'Mind?' The matriarch answered for her daughter. 'Of course she doesn't mind. Dorrie adores children and they adore her. Anyway, we shan't be gone long. The chapel's just down the road.'

Dorrie treated Catherine to a reassuring grin behind her mother's retreating back.

Outside, Mrs Revesby guided her visitor up the drive, past the church, towards the town centre.

'Does Dorrie live with you?' Catherine asked.

'Oh, good heavens, no. Just over for the day. She and Simon live in Cirencester. Delightfully happy but not married. That seems to be the thing these days, doesn't it? I sometimes wonder just where my generation went wrong. Simon's an engineer. Good, steady young man. Mad keen on vintage cars. He and my Jack have gone off to a rally at Stratford. Good riddance, I say. It gives Dorrie and me a chance to chat about really important things. Do you know—'

Catherine dived into the verbal torrent. 'You must be very busy with the festival. Are the plans coming on well?'

Angela diverted the stream into the new conversational channel without any loss of impetus. 'The only trouble is it's *too* successful. It's like Topsy – just keeps on growing. When Lord Teddy started it five years ago, there were just half a dozen events. Now the whole week is full to bursting with concerts and exhibitions and recitals and lectures and, of course, the fair, which takes over the whole High Street. This way.'

She turned right beside a corner cycle shop. 'There's the chapel.'

Fifty yards along the side road stood a narrow building with an imposing façade surmounted by a Dutch gable. The date 1696 was carved above the first-floor leaded window.

Mrs Revesby explained. 'We still call it the chapel, although it was deconsecrated, or whatever the Free Church people do, three years ago. It's been many things in its time. It was built by the Congregationalists under the Commonwealth. Then along came Good King Charles and closed them down. That's when it was turned into the village school. Later on the Baptists had it and did a lot of rebuilding. I think they owned it continuously till their numbers dwindled and they were forced to sell. Although someone told me that the building was used as a warehouse for a time in the last century. Anyway, I hope it serves your purpose.'

She led the way in through a side door. Catherine surveyed the interior approvingly. The decor was simple without being severe: whitewashed walls, plain glass windows, and a fine ceiling of bleached oak timbers. A gallery ran around three sides and was very wide over the main entrance where, presumably, an organ had once stood. Catherine walked around mentally installing display stands, panels and banks of flowers. 'It has a lovely ambience. What is it used for?'

'Ah well, thereby hangs a tale . . .'

'Do you mind if I walk around and take a few photos while you talk?'

'Not at all, not at all. You do your own thing while I prattle on. Well, when the Baptists gave it up, the council were all for letting it be sold off to a developer for conversion to a rather superior des. res. They'd certainly have got away with that if Lord Teddy hadn't intervened. The festival had been going for a couple of years and was already very successful. He told them that it would make an excellent venue for festival events and be a valuable asset to Chipping Sneddon. The Baptists were all for selling the chapel to the town, but the council dug their heels in. It was a big *cause célèbre* for several months. Accusations of corruption in the local press. Protest meetings. Slanging matches in the council chamber. We hadn't had so much fun in Chipping Sneddon for years. Then Lord Teddy announced that, if the council would stump up half the money, he would donate the rest. That left them without a leg to stand on.'

'Lord Teddy seems to exercise a lot of muscle round here. Is he some sort of lord of the manor?'

'Oh, no! He lives a long way away, on the Thames near Marlow. But, of course, his biggest children's home is just outside the town. Everyone around here respects the wonderful work he and the staff do there – rescuing all those young people from broken homes or no homes at all. And as for his festival, well it's really put Chipping Sneddon on the map.

'Snobbery has a lot to do with it, of course. He and Lady Masquerier host a very sumptuous and very exclusive dinner party on the first evening of the festival. It's the high point of the social calendar here. People kill to get on the guest list. You will have been invited this year, of course.'

'Yes, I seem to recall a rather impressive card arriving a few weeks ago. I didn't look at it closely, though.' Catherine thoughtfully lowered the camera she had been pointing at one of the galleries. 'I certainly hadn't realized Lady Masquerier was involved.'

'Oh yes.' The other woman nodded vigorously. 'She's one of the directors of Cotswold-Chiltern TV, our local independent channel. They were brought in to the festival right at the beginning. Lady Deb – that's what we mostly call her

– has been tremendously supportive. She makes sure we get good coverage and, of course, that in turn attracts top artists to come and perform. Sponsorship, too. She has lots of contacts in the City. Well, not so much her; her husband. He's a banker – or was. I think he's retired now. Anyway, Lady Deb and Lord Teddy between them have done an awful lot for the town. I sometimes call them our patron saints!'

Catherine carried on with her work in thoughtful silence. Then she said, 'I suppose all the festival profits go to the Downham Homes?'

'Yes, but the town benefits in all sorts of other ways. Extra trade. More tourists. Major events throughout the summer season. The chapel is used, all year round, for all sorts of things – antique fairs, chamber concerts, Christmas charity auctions, stamp collectors' conventions . . .'

Catherine slipped the camera back into her shoulder bag. 'Well, I think I've seen everything I need to.'

'I'll just show you the back premises – kitchen, loos and so forth. Your people will want to brew up from time to time. Actually we've a very good oven. My advice is to cook up your own simple meals here. I'm afraid the local hotel and restaurants tend to up their prices in festival week.' Angela Revesby led the way through a side door.

It was about that time that, back at Farrans, Tim received a phone call from Emma Kerr. She told him, in a voice that trembled between anger and fear, that Gavin had been charged with the murder of Stuart Longton. Once again she begged Tim to do something – anything. Tim said that, as he had promised, he would talk with the police, but warned her not to hold out any hope of his achieving dramatic results. He phoned Sally, his secretary, and asked her if the idea of an afternoon's overtime grabbed her. It did not but she stoically agreed to come in after lunch to assume command. Tim grabbed a sandwich, left a note for Catherine, jumped into the ten-year-old Mercedes and set off for Cambridge.

CHAPTER 10

Despite vigorous thought throughout the two-hour journey, Tim had no clear idea when he arrived in Cambridge of just what he was going to say.

Detective Inspector Tibbs, to whom Tim gained access by dint of being pleasant but firm with the desk sergeant, was tall, moustached and seemed young for his rank.

'Good afternoon, Mr Lacy. Please sit down.' He settled in the swivel chair beside his desk, offered a pack of cigarettes and, when Tim declined, took one himself and lit it. 'I gather you have some information about this business at St Mary's.'

'Yes I have, Inspector. Though I'm not altogether sure you'll want to hear it.'

Tibbs scrutinized him through a cloud of blue smoke. 'Oh, why's that, sir?'

'I gather you've arrested one of the St Mary's undergraduates and I'm afraid my evidence may not support your case against him.'

The policeman displayed no emotion. 'Well, perhaps I'd

better decide that. Suppose you just tell me what you know.'

Tim embarked on a judicious selection of the facts. 'Three months ago I undertook a commission for the Master of St Mary's. I brought a collection of rare and very valuable historical documents from Australia. While these documents were in my possession two attempts were made to steal them. On the day Dr Longton died he telephoned me to tell me that he thought he knew who was responsible for these attempted thefts and he intimated that, in his opinion, the perpetrator would try again.'

'And where were these documents kept?'

'Dr Longton was working on them. I assume he had them in his room.'

'So what you're suggesting, Mr Lacy, is that Dr Longton was murdered by someone making a third attempt to steal these valuable papers.'

Tim accurately read the frown of disapproval. 'I wouldn't presume to tell you your job, Inspector. I merely suggest that this is an alternative line of enquiry you might want to follow up.'

'I can't see that it lets our prime suspect off the hook.'

'Well Gavin Turner certainly can't have had anything to do with at least one of the attempted thefts. It happened in California. I doubt whether he even knows of the existence of these papers. Very few people do.'

Tibbs's eyebrows went up when Tim mentioned Gavin's name.

'I take it you know young Turner, then.'

'I've met him – briefly – once, when I came to Cambridge to deliver the documents.'

The inspector smiled a self-assured smile. 'Would I be

correct in assuming that you also know a young lady by the name of Emma Kerr?'

'I know her, certainly, but—'

'A most forthright, spirited lady, our Ms Kerr. Her devotion to her friend is very commendable. She'll stop at nothing to help young Gavin. I'll wager a month's salary that she's the one who brought you halfway across England this afternoon.'

'You're quite right, Inspector, but that doesn't discount my evidence.'

'Certainly not, Mr Lacy, and rest assured we'll look into it. But there will have to be a lot of substance in what you say to weaken the case against Gavin Turner. He was in the deceased's rooms at an hour well within the timeframe of death calculated by our pathologist. He had the strongest possible motive for wishing to harm Dr Longton. To be honest, I'm not sure that in his shoes I wouldn't have done the same.'

'I was just wondering', Tim made the observation quietly, almost to himself, 'whether you thought Gavin was strong enough.'

'How do you mean, sir?'

'Well, Longton was no lightweight. I gather whoever killed him did so by first knocking him out, then stringing him up to make it look as though he had hanged himself.'

'Death was actually caused by a heavy blow to the head with a blunt instrument. The stringing up was purely cosmetic – or done by someone who didn't know the first thing about forensic medicine.'

'I see. But the fact remains. Dead or unconscious, Longton would have been a considerable weight. My impression of

Gavin is that he's already seriously weakened by a very debilitating disease.'

The phone rang on the inspector's desk.

'I've known men possessed of superhuman strength in the grip of great emotion.' Tibbs picked up the receiver. 'Hello . . . OK, put him on. Good afternoon, sir.' The policeman's voice took on a very respectful tone. 'That's very interesting, sir. What exactly . . . I see. Yes.' His frown slowly deepened. 'Yes, sir and when did you notice this? And you're sure no one else had access . . . Yes, well it may very well . . . No, sir, I don't think we ought to spoil the Chief Constable's weekend. I'll make sure he's kept fully informed. Yes, sir, of course we will. I'll have one of my men come down straight away and take down the details. Thank you for reporting the matter to me so promptly.'

Tibbs replaced the receiver. 'Bloody academics! Ordinary crime isn't good enough for them. Mr Jones taking a kitchen knife to his wife's lover. A demented addict roughing up his supplier for a single shot of heroin. That's the sort of everyday crime we have to deal with. But it's not sophisticated enough for professors and fellows and the like. They batter each other to death over rival theories or plagiarized research.' He scowled across the desk. 'That was the Master of St Mary's House. It seems that he has come around to your view, Mr Lacy. He had just discovered that some very important papers belonging to the college have gone missing from Dr Longton's rooms. He wants us to drop everything in order to find them. He's sure their disappearance is linked to Longton's death.'

Tim maintained a diplomatic silence.

Tibbs stood up. 'I'll have to ask you to go through into the office and make a statement. I'm not saying, mind you, that this makes any difference. It's just that we have to follow up all leads.'

Tim repeated his story to a constable, checked and signed the typed version and left. As he passed St Mary's House on the way out of Cambridge he thought of stopping for a word with Emma but decided against it. All he could tell her was that he had done his best. He negotiated the car back towards the M11 and wondered whether his best would achieve anything. He had to admit ruefully that Masquerier's brief phone call had done more to readjust Inspector Tibbs's view of the case than anything he had said. Was it enough? With so many questions about Longton's death still unanswered it was difficult to see how the Crown Prosecution Service could take the case against Gavin to court.

Tim thought about Masquerier's call. The fact that he believed the Hellfire Papers had been stolen must mean that Stuart had not taken the Master into his confidence. Why not? Was it because whatever he had discovered implicated Sir Evelyn? Was it the Master, after all, who had been trying to get his hands on the Hellfire Papers for his own purposes? No wonder he had put a squib under the police as soon as he was sure they had disappeared.

Only, of course, they had not disappeared. They were lying securely at Farrans Court in one of the toughest safes ever devised by the wit of man. So what, Tim wondered, should he do with them? They were now the subject of a police enquiry and there was no way he could claim ignorance of the fact. Keeping them was a felony. Even handing them over at this stage would involve answering some awkward questions about why he had not done so sooner. Return them anonymously, then, and forget about the whole St Mary's business? That was what Catherine wanted and she was probably right. He had certainly done all he could do. He had spoken up for Gavin, as he had promised. Common sense told him that there was no more that could reasonably be expected of him.

But there were more important things in life than common sense.

Extract from Sir Peregrine Whitehead-Dyer's notes:

The fragmentary nature of my ancestor's account of the next few years is particularly tantalizing because it is clear that these years cover a significant period in the development of his political influence. His parliamentary associates, including Sir Francis Dashwood, created a coherent party – the Leicester House opposition – around the Prince of Wales. Dodington brought into the coalition a growing number of parliamentarians who, for various reasons, were disenchanted with the Pelhams. They orchestrated attacks on the government in both houses and seem to have achieved agreement on at least some aspects of a constructive programme. Their policies, and more particularly their satirical forays against their enemies, were regularly launched in *The Remembrancer* which, week by week, did the rounds of London's coffee houses. Whitehead was closely associated with James Ralph in the production of this journal but this by no means exhausted my ancestor's contribution to the cause. He poured forth a stream of broadsheets, pamphlets and verse lampoons. Now into his forties (though looking older, hence his nickname, 'Aged Paul'), he was at the height of his powers. Friend and foe alike referred to him as the 'Bard of Leicester House'.

Over three hundred strong-voiced men and boys followed the fife and drum and more joined us as we surged down Whitehall, giving way to neither horseman nor carriage. Those who could read took the broadsheets and sang lustily. Those who could not, eagerly roared the chorus:

> When George is in Hanover, Newcastle's king.
> What of Englishmen's liberties then?
> When Pelham and all of his friends hold the ring
> Who shall stand up for good, honest men?
> Cry *'God bless the Prince of Wales!'*

I do not recall all the verses of the catch I wrote for the election marchers in 1750 but the feeling of exhilaration is as vivid as it was on that autumn day when I strode at the head of a mob assembled to support the anti-government candidate, Sir George Vandeput, in the Westminster by-election. Ordinary people in the capital, who otherwise had little opportunity to express their true feelings about the King's ministers, responded warmly. Those who did not join the march stood, two or three deep, along the route to cheer us on. My spirits soared as I paced to the beat of the drum and felt around me, not only the warmth of the sun, but also the ardour of the citizenry.

What was equally gratifying was to know that our campaign

was proceeding so effectively. Every song, every pamphlet, every lampoon, every speech had been planned in great detail at Leicester House. And the government were worried. Not withstanding the bribes Lord Trentham and his backers were able to lay out and the promises of places and sinecures, we had drawn many Westminster tradesmen and property owners into the Prince's party.

The hustings were set up close by St Stephen's Chapel, the Commons meeting place, but we were still a hundred yards from it when it became clear that we were unlikely to reach our objective. A Pelham mob, some hundred or more strong, possessed the ground and were facing us, brandishing placards. Clearly we were in for a fight. There was nothing unusual about that and I doubted not that we could carry the day, but the government's paid ruffians were not our only obstacle. They were flanked to the right by two ranks of mounted dragoons. The troops were there ostensibly to keep order but there was no doubting how they would interpret their instructions if it came to a fracas.

Our march leader was Alexander Murray, son of a Scottish nobleman and in all probability a covert Jacobite. He ordered the music to stop and we advanced to a single drum beat. The enemy held their ground and for some moments it seemed that we would be allowed to take our places before the hustings to hear the speeches. Then there was a shouted order. The government supporters started forward at a run. At the same moment the dragoons spurred to a canter and filled the space between the rival forces.

Their captain faced us brandishing his sword. 'Halt. I call upon you, in the King's name, to disperse.'

We shuffled to a standstill. From behind their protective

barrier of horsemen our opponents jeered and shouted abuse.

Murray stepped forward until he stood by the captain's bridle. 'And why should we disperse? We come peaceably to hear our candidate speak.'

The officer – a young man who ill-concealed his nervousness behind the pomp of scarlet and gleaming brass and the security of his drawn blade – looked down with an arrogant sneer. 'I know you for a troublemaker, Murray. I've Mr Jarvis with me.' He indicated the small civilian beside him mounted on a fidgeting mare. 'Mr Jarvis is a magistrate and if your rabble are not departed in three minutes he shall read the riot act, and I'll not answer for the consequences.'

Murray turned from him and shouted, 'Do you hear that, lads? So much for liberty!' He tossed his hat in the air. 'God bless the Prince of Wales!'

The cry was roared back with such a thunderous echo that Mr Jarvis's horse reared, spilling its rider to the ground. The captain was momentarily distracted. For a few brief seconds he lost control of the situation. It was enough. Someone in the crowd behind him flung a stone into our midst. The response was an angry roar and a surge forward. I was carried along by the wave of human indignation and found myself pressed up against the grey flank of a trooper's mount. Around me men were squeezing through and crawling under the equine barrier. All was sudden, screaming confusion. I heard the order to draw sabres and instinctively ducked. I was knocked to the ground. Prancing hooves stamped the ground inches from my head. I scrambled forwards, my only thought escape from the mêlée.

For minutes on end I was bundled pell-mell, now on my

feet, now on my knees, totally caught up in the motion of the swaying multitude. It was a seething hell of screaming, anguished humanity, like the inner ring of Dante's *Inferno*. At one moment a young man clutched at me, spattering me with blood from a sabre slash down the side of his face. How I avoided a similar fate and extricated myself from the carnage I knew not and know not to this day. All I can record is that somehow – terrified, grimy, bruised, hatless and with torn breeches – I found myself in a side street.

My first objective was to report the morning's events to the leaders of our faction. I made my way on foot to Leicester House and a fine to-do I had to gain admittance in my present state. However, a servant with whom I was friendly took me to a small chamber and provided me with water and towels. As soon as I was tolerably presentable I took my place with a handful of other suitors in the Prince's withdrawing room. His Highness was, as I knew, in council with Dodington, Dashwood and his other close advisers. I was impatient to impart my news but could do nothing until the royal audience was over.

Fortunately, the Prince emerged within half an hour. While he was surrounded by petitioners I slipped into the chamber he had just left. There were seven men sitting or standing around the table. Dashwood saw me and beckoned me over. 'Aha, here is Aged Paul. What news of the election?'

I described the events of the morning and watched my audience display by turns indignation, anger and then pleasure.

'Why, this is capital!' Sir Francis declared. 'We can make much of this. This will show people how Newcastle and his crew abuse our countrymen's liberties.'

Dodington said, 'We must summon Ralph and you must provide a full account for the next issue of *The Remembrancer*. It would be well for you to attend to that this afternoon.'

Dashwood demurred. 'No, Bubb, not this afternoon. I have other plans for Aged Paul today. He is coming out to Wycombe with me. We have things to arrange.'

I indicated my tattered garment. 'Sir Francis, I am scarcely—'

'Don't concern yourself with that, man. We'll find you suitable clothes. Come, I'm impatient to show you something and have your opinion on it.'

He hurried me outside. We took sedans to Dashwood's Hanover Square house where his own valet furnished me in elegant silk and brocade. Yet I scarcely had time to change before Sir Francis rushed me to his carriage and ordered us to be driven at manic speed to West Wycombe.

Throughout the two-hour journey he seemed to be bubbling with suppressed excitement, but not until we were nearing his new mansion did he intimate the purpose of this hastily contrived expedition. I attempted to engage him in conversation about the political situation, the likelihood of renewed war with France, his parliamentary activity, particularly his strenuous attempts to improve roads and highways, and other matters of the moment but his attention was dilatory. It seemed as though he had left all such concerns behind as soon as we quitted the confines of the capital.

It was when we caught our first glimpse of the Chiltern woods, coppery and golden in the sunlight, that he became animated. 'I think I shall abandon politics, Whitehead.'

'Surely not . . .'

'I want to devote myself to art and architecture and . . . other things. The house out here is nearly finished.'

'I look forward to seeing it. It's a couple of years since—'

'But the thing is, my ideas keep on growing. There ain't much left that I can do at West Wycombe Park. The place is full of painters and sculptors, and the temples in the grounds are still a-building, but when all that's done I need other challenges, Whitehead.' He fell silent for some moments. Then, as if making up his mind suddenly, he stared at me intently. 'When I was in Rome, do you know what made the greatest impression? The catacombs. Amazing atmosphere – eerie and yet, at the same time, holy. There's miles of underground caverns; a veritable labyrinth, full of graves and old paintings, little carved-out chambers where the first Christians used to meet for their clandestine worship while the Roman soldiers searched for them. It was that gave me the idea – that and the new road.'

'New road?' Practised as I was at following the tortuous passages of my patron's thoughts, on this occasion I had lost sight of his meaning.

'Yes, I'm putting in a proper highway from the main road up to West Wycombe. You'll see it presently. Long overdue, and it provides work for many of the local men. They're taking the chalk from the hills close to the house. I didn't want them to scar the countryside with quarries, so they're mining the stone, digging shafts straight into the hillside. So, you see, we could have our own catacombs.'

'We?'

'The Order, man! Don't you see? Our own premises, built to serve all our activities.'

Now I understood Dashwood's enthusiasm. The George and Vulture had been rebuilt, at Sir Francis's expense, but members of the Order had no stomach to return to a place with such melancholic memories. For two years we had convened at private houses owned by various brothers in and around London. But everyone agreed that the atmosphere of our original home had been lost. Indeed some of our members had begun to drift away.

Sir Francis stopped the carriage a short distance from the house. A track had been worn up the hillside from the road by carts laden with piles of rock. One passed us while we were making our way up the slope. The grass was white with chalk dust as we approached the entrance to the workings, a large, square hole, within whose depths we could see the glimmer of many lamps.

Dashwood paused before the opening. 'Here we'll have a ruin – a temple or a church completely masking the way into our own sanctuary of pleasure. Symbolic, d'ye see, that we've passed beyond ancient pietisms into the sanctum of true worship; escaped from all shibboleths and discovered the glorious freedom of the human spirit. Then, within, deep in the womb of the mother earth, our chambers for feasting and worship and tupping. We can have as many as we wish, each devoted to whatever pleasures take our fancy. All in our own underworld, our labyrinth, our secret, eerie catacomb. 'Twill be a thousand times more sensuous, more thrilling, more conducive to total abandon than the George and Vulture ever was.'

''Twill be deuced expensive,' I observed. That was, I think, the moment when I began to be wary of my patron's arcane passions. There was a look in his eyes that I had not seen before. The detached cynicism with which he had always entered into our irreverent revels had been superseded by a strange fervour.

The unease grew within me later that night. After supper we sat up till well past midnight in the library at West Wycombe Park. On the table he spread out various plans for his catacombs, inviting my detailed observations. Dashwood's talk was spiced with strange notions of mysterious origin: 'the holy grail of total experience'; 'the fusion of all human passions'; 'reaching the ultimate ecstasy'; 'daring every forbidden thing'.

We returned to town the following day and were immediately re-baptized in the waters of political conflict. Much to my relief Sir Francis made no more reference to the caves at West Wycombe and the rare delights to be indulged therein. He spoke no more of abandoning parliament. Indeed, he pursued with increased vigour the downfall of the government and the forging of a party capable of replacing it.

The administration played into our hands. After the Westminster tumult they arrested Alexander Murray and confined him to Newgate on a charge of public affray. This monstrous abuse of the rights of the citizen provoked angry reaction inside and outside parliament. The Pelhams' attempts to bring the matter to a rapid conclusion turned against them most delightfully. Murray was ordered to appear before the bar of the Commons and earn his pardon by making submission upon his knees. Appear he did but when the speaker instructed him to humble himself, the Scot replied, 'I never kneel but to God.' Many in the chamber cheered but Murray was hustled away to gaol again.

The Prince and his friends engaged themselves in Murray's defence. Dashwood paid for a case of unlawful arrest to be brought in Queen's Bench. I wrote a pamphlet – *An Appeal of the Hon. Alexander Murray to the People of Great Britain*. It was widely distributed and was, I may modestly claim, exceedingly well received. More important than the impact of the case among the populace, however, was the reaction it provoked among the nation's political leaders. It showed men in both houses how low the government was prepared to sink in its silencing of all dissident voices. Murray was eventually hounded into exile by an unrepentant administration but not before many in the Lords and Commons had come over to our side.

With the smell of success in their nostrils the organizers of the Leicester House party were active day and night. Dodington pursued the intrigues of which he was a master. Dashwood was scarcely ever away from the Commons where he voted against the government on every important topic and spoke in several debates with cogency and wit. How do I know this? It was I who wrote his speeches. For six or seven weeks I was scarce away from my desk longer than was necessary for food and the minimum of sleep. I gave little thought to the Order. So did Sir Francis. He and our political allies were working with industry and eager expectancy. No chapter meetings were summoned during those early weeks of 1751. It was something about which I had no regret. The Order had served its purpose and come to the end of its tenure. The joke was well worn. Any attempt to prolong its life could only drain it of its last vestiges of humour – might even transform it into something sinister.

On 20th March I supped at Hanover Square with Dashwood and three colleagues. We were plotting and scheming as usual, though I do not recollect the subject of our deliberations. After eating we removed to the library. It was there, at a little before midnight, that the door was opened to admit Bubb Dodington, even more dishevelled than usual.

He stood in the doorway, forehead glistening and cheeks moist with tears. In little more than a whisper he announced, 'Gentlemen, the Prince of Wales is dead.'

CHAPTER 11

Ingrid Brunhill was nobody's fool. When she arrived at Farrans Court in the middle of the following week she followed Catherine into the house with ill-concealed impatience. She made a Wagnerian entrance to the Lacys' private sitting room. Ignoring Tim's outstretched hand she threw a copy of the *Daily Telegraph* down on the coffee table. 'I suppose you've seen that!'

Tim cast an eye over the brief report on an inside page which had been heavily outlined in red. It was headed, 'Cambridge murder – police hunt missing documents'. He had already read the corresponding piece in *The Times*. It told him what he had feared. Tibbs had decided to go public with the latest development in his enquiry into Stuart Longton's death. He smiled at his guest, whose frown of suspicion only deepened in response. 'Won't you sit down, Dr Brunhill?'

She folded stiffly into an armchair. 'I hope you're not going to insult my intelligence by trying to tell me that there's no connection between this wretched affair at St

Mary's and your invitation to me to come and examine some old papers. As soon as I read this I smelled a very large rat. I nearly decided not to come. Probably I shouldn't have. As a good citizen I ought to have got straight onto the police.'

'I thought kir would be nice on such a warm day.' Catherine poured pink liquid from a jug into tall glasses and tried to lighten the atmosphere.

Dr Brunhill scowled but accepted the drink. 'Well?'

Tim struggled not to avert his gaze from the intelligent dark eyes which were trained upon him. Talking this Valkyrie round was never going to be an easy matter but the untimely revelation about the disappearance of the Hellfire Papers threatened to make it well-nigh impossible. He nodded and assumed an expression which, he hoped, suggested seriousness and honesty. 'You're absolutely right of course. These missing documents – the Whitehead-Dyer Papers – are in this very building.'

'Well, you're very cool, I must say. You steal some important historical documents, then calmly invite me here to vet them so that you can sell them clandestinely for a high price. I take it that's your game? Well, if you seriously expect—'

Tim held up a hand. 'Dr Brunhill, I am not a master criminal. And if I were, I would hardly run the risk of revealing my crime to such an eminent scholar as yourself.'

'So, what exactly is this all about?' She tasted the wine cautiously, as though expecting to detect the presence of a narcotic substance.

'Do you mind if I ask you one or two questions before I try to quell your suspicions?'

'Certainly I mind. If there are any questions to be

answered it's you who must answer them, Mr Lacy.'

'I fully understand how you feel and I certainly don't want to try your patience any more than I already have. But this is a very complex business and I want to go through it carefully, as much to understand it myself as to explain it to you.'

His guest gave the faintest of nods and opened her mouth to respond.

Before she could do so Tim hurried on. 'You will recall, we met at St Mary's House last January?'

'Yes. I didn't know what you were doing there. You told me you were some sort of security expert. Since your phone call last week I've checked that out. It seems you were telling the truth.'

'Didn't someone once say "the man who is going to make a habit of lying needs to have a very good memory"?'

'Very possibly.'

'Did you know anything about the Whitehead-Dyer Papers at that time?'

'There were vague rumours on the academic grapevine that something really significant had turned up in Cambridge. Nothing more.'

'And you had no idea what these papers were?'

'If Stuart Longton was excited about them they had to be eighteenth century. I quizzed him during the evening. He seemed very put out that I had got a whiff of them. He certainly wouldn't tell me anything. You don't seem to be telling me anything, either.'

'OK, I'm getting round to it, believe me. I imagine the name Paul Whitehead is familiar to you?'

'You mean the minor eighteenth-century poet and satirist? Yes, of course.'

'I gather he was mixed up with Sir Francis Dashwood and his circle?'

'Dashwood was his patron – and a very generous one at that.' Dr Brunhill was on her own territory and noticeably more relaxed. 'Whitehead mixed with most of the leading Tories and belonged to several of their clubs. It was said that he knew enough guilty secrets to ruin half the leading families in London. Unfortunately, he destroyed all his letters and diaries shortly before he died. Unless . . .' She looked up suddenly.

Tim nodded. 'The Whitehead-Dyer Papers are, or purport to be, Paul Whitehead's personal journal and the records he kept about the members of the Order of St Francis of Medmenham. Such documents would, presumably, be of considerable importance?'

'Emphatically! And you say you have them here? Why? What are you doing with them? They should be available to researchers.'

Catherine offered more wine. 'Tim and I went to Australia to collect the Whitehead-Dyer Papers on behalf of the Master of St Mary's.'

'Sir Evelyn Masquerier!' Dr Brunhill snorted her contempt. 'That philistine is just about the last person I'd want to see get his clutches on anything so important.'

Catherine said, 'Someone else seemed to share your opinion. They made two attempts to steal the papers.'

Tim took up the story, stripping it to the bare facts and ending with Stuart Longton's phone call. 'Does the name Jenkinson mean anything to you, Dr Brunhill?'

'No, but of course I'd need to see the context.'

Catherine smiled encouragingly. 'That's what we hoped

you'd say. We've hammered our brains over all the papers in the collection. We can't see anything odd. It'll obviously take another expert to find whatever Stuart had gotten onto.'

'That's right.' Tim saw that the formidable Oxford don was interested despite herself. 'The papers obviously have to go back to St Mary's. I thought if we could hang onto them for just a few more days you'd be sure to discover whatever it was that Stuart found. Will you help us?' Tim held his breath. Had they said enough to overcome their guest's scruples?

Ingrid Brunhill looked from one to the other. 'You realize you're putting me in a very difficult position. Obviously I'd be fascinated to look at these papers but you're trying to make me an accessory to something that, even if not a felony, is certainly shady. That's not going to do my reputation any good.'

'There's no reason why anyone should know about your involvement. Whatever you discover we'll say that we found.'

'*If* I discover! I don't know what I'd be looking for. What possible significance can something written by a third-rate Hanoverian poet have for events at the end of the twentieth century?'

Tim shook his head. 'That, of course, is the $64,000 question. Perhaps it has no significance at all.'

'Unless Whitehead was a prophet he can't have written anything that could point the finger at a murderer who wasn't going to be born for two hundred years.'

'I agree. All I know is that Stuart Longton turned up something he believed was important and dangerous, and

219

that a few hours later he was dead. Perhaps there's no connection but that's stretching coincidence a bit far, don't you think?'

The Valkyrie sighed. 'I'm intrigued, of course, but I really can't be involved in something like this. Naturally, I'll keep everything you've told me under my hat. More than that I'm afraid I can't do.'

The Order of St Francis sprang forth from its own dying embers like a phoenix. It was Dashwood who gave it frantic new life but he did not lack for co-conspirators. Sandwich was thrown out of office by the now unassailable Pelhams. With the unexpected death of the Prince and the resultant collapse of the opposition, Sir Francis, Dodington, Potter and their colleagues found themselves powerless. Dashwood removed, almost permanently, to West Wycombe and vigorously set in hand his plans for the catacombs. He had me out into the country for weeks on end to discuss plans, oversee the diggings and attend to the furnishings. The work proceeded at a furious pace. Sir Francis employed an army of labourers and craftsmen and, when progress was not rapid enough for his liking, he took on more. He fixed upon 30 April [1752] – *Walpurgisnacht* – for the extraordinary grand chapter meeting which should inaugurate the Order's new premises.

''Tis the night for it, the only night,' he explained on one occasion when Thomas Potter and I were with him in his library, where the long table was scattered with books. 'Some say it's named after a Christian saint, Walpurgis, who protects her devotees from witchcraft. Yet Glanvil here,' he indicated a large old tome, 'in *Sadducismus Triumphatus*, claims the origin of the word in the German earth goddess, Walburg. One thing is certain, Walpurgisnacht is older than all our religions. Druids were keeping the spring festival on that night a thousand years before Christ. It will be an auspicious time for our chapter meeting. And I look to you, Aged Paul, for some truly auspicious ceremonial. Think what rich veins you have to mine from – druids, witches, virgin saints, Christian catacombs, fertility rites, earth goddesses. Use the library, Whitehead. Order whatever you need; musicians, lamps, hangings, furniture, food, wine. Take no heed for expense. As to our nuns – well, I have some ideas on that score. Round the estate and tenant farms I've noted some fine country girls; browned, supple, glowing with health. Their fathers daren't refuse me – or won't turn away my guineas. We'll have some of the regulars here, of course, to set the dells' minds at rest. It will be better sport if they know not what awaits them. What d'ye say, Whitehead, won't it be the most capital meeting we've ever had?'

I tried to damp the fire of his enthusiasm without making too much smoke. 'I fear the caves will not be ready in time. This wet weather has made it difficult for the waggons. The men are still bridging the underground river and have not yet begun the temple . . .'

'Come now, Aged Paul.' Potter clapped a hand to my shoulder, partly for support, for he had drunk heavily all evening and was betrayed by both his legs and his speech. 'Don't be such a Jeremiah. Because your tackle's shrivelled don't deny us our pleasure.'

Though it was spoken by the drink I resented the insult, as I also resented Potter's growing influence over Dashwood.

'I'm as much the man as you, piss-Potter! I was simply pointing out—'

'Enough.' Dashwood banged the table and glared at us with an intense ferocity. 'It shall be finished! Now, see here, Potter and I have completed the invitation list. With the additional space we now have we can increase our numbers. And we need young blood.'

The character of the Order was changed completely by the men now admitted on the instructions of the founder. It had originated as a select society of like-minded friends. Now, the only qualification for entry seemed to be rejection of all conventions and restraints. Dashwood was past his middle years and, having little else now to occupy his mind, he often fell to brooding on what he regarded as lost opportunities. Increasingly he sought the company of younger and wilder spirits.

At this point I must list some of those who were to play a prominent part in the life of the Order.

Francis and James Duffield were the brothers of our late and lamented friend of the George and Vulture fire. They were vastly different from him and each other in temperament and ability. Francis was tall and had the bearing of a soldier who had fought several times on the continent. After his brother's death he had inherited all the family lands, including the estate at nearby Medmenham, but nothing would induce him to live there because of its unhappy associations. James seemed intent on playing the conventional rôle of the prodigal youngest son. He wasted the provision made for him by his father and, latterly by his patient elder brother, and spent most of his time in alehouses with men and women far below his station.

John Wilkes is a name now known to all, but at the time of which I write he was merely a young, squint-eyed landowner from Aylesbury, where he enjoyed a considerable estate that had come to him by marriage. He had a wicked wit and was intelligent, notwithstanding that he and Potter were fast friends. Their roisterings in London and around Aylesbury were notorious and any man would be hard put to it to say who was the teacher and who the disciple in the arts of debauchery. Yet Wilkes was a man with political ideas and ambitions. He was related to Pitt, assiduously supported his cause and hoped for the reward, ere long, of a parliamentary seat.

[The bottom of this page is missing]

Lord Liverpool was a man cast in the same mould as Lord Sandwich. He devoted himself with equal energy to politics and vice. He was a trustee of the foundling hospital and several of its inmates were commonly believed to bear his image. He contended vigorously in the Lords for reform of the Poor Law. Yet he was a bad man to cross, as many from parliamentary opponents to tradesmen and whores could testify. It was said that one half of London loved him and the other half hated him.

Sir Charles Groom was of the royal household and a young man of an excellent Yorkshire family. His two passions were intrigue and young boys, either of which was like to bring him to the gallows.

Captain Winchester, a mariner, land-bound since narrowly escaping a court martial in the Indies, was a close friend of Groom's and lived much on his generosity.

Jack Laurie was a parliament man, a follower of the

Pelhams and an accumulator of sinecures. To look at, he was sharp of feature, with peering eyes under heavy brows. He bore a striking resemblance to a satyr, as represented in ancient statuary. This may, however, be fantasy on my part who knew, better than many, the real man, though most shared my view that he was vicious alike to friend and enemy. Laurie was a Lowland Scot and ex-Jacobite who had won favour in 1745 by betraying many of his friends. I never detected in him a single moral scruple – a deficiency of which Laurie himself was sometimes heard to boast.

Canon Ermine had achieved high preferment, thanks largely to his connections with the Potters. He drew the incomes from several benefices that he never visited, but staffed with poor young curates. Instead, he devoted his time to membership of several London clubs and to study. His erudition covered many subjects, several of which would have alarmed his ecclesiastical superiors.

Judge Rollo Vesey was a man grown rich on the law . . .

[This passage of the memoirs concludes with
two more pages of names]

The excavation and furnishing of the Wycombe catacombs, were, as you might suppose, completed in line with Dashwood's wishes. By dint of drafting in more labourers and having all his artisans work in relays round the clock, the quarter-mile complex of passages and chambers was finished in time for the inaugural ceremony.

Nature, it seems, was also involved in Sir Francis's grand design. St Walpurgis's Eve ended in a night of storm which set thunder crashing round the hills, and flashes of lightning irradiating the chalk-whitened grass and hedgerows. The brothers assembled at the house. The nuns were brought thither also, but were lodged in a separate chamber so as not to meet the men. As soon as it was dark the brothers left in carriages and were conveyed as close as might be to the Gothic ruins which now masked the cave entrance. Awnings had been set up across the crumbling walls, so that we were not too incommoded by the raging of the heavens. Sir Francis led the way into the shaft. Lamps of green glass spaced along the corridor gave the walls an eerie glow. Here and there grotesque faces and inscriptions were carved in the chalk and there were niches containing items from Dashwood's collection of Roman statuary. All these drew laughter and ribald comment from those who stopped to examine them. A short way in we paused to file into a small chamber on the right – our robing room, where the brothers' habits hung ready to be donned. As soon as we were accoutred in the white garments of our order, Sir Francis took the brothers deeper into the underworld. I and two others returned to the entrance to await the arrival of the nuns.

The carriages reappeared some minutes later and unloaded their lovely cargo, already habited and masked. Standing (some clinging) together in their white robes, fearful of the tempest and the unknown, they looked for all the world like lambs gathered for shearing. An apt simile.

We greeted them and tried to reassure them. Yet only when the bolder spirits walked firmly towards the cave entrance were the rest of the flock induced to follow. I led them at a brisk pace along the passages while my colleagues, like drovers, came behind. I hoped that as the noisy clash of the elements faded they would feel more at ease. However, the tricks of light and shadow, the leering faces carved in the chalk and the echoing drip of water through the porous rock struck fresh fear into my charges. We were forced to stop twice; once when two of the women slipped in the corridor and vowed they would not advance one step further, and again when, on our circuit of Sir Francis's 'Roman catacombs', with their sarcophagi and shelves of grinning skulls, another screamed and fainted clear away. It took many soft words and not a little coin to get our caravanserai moving again.

We emerged, at last, into the Banqueting Hall, an immense cavern some forty feet across, filled with light from wall sconces and a hanging candelabrum. A rousing cheer went up from the brothers, seated at long tables spread with silver and crystal in readiness for our feast. But it was not yet time for food. The brothers stood and bowed to their guests. Then, one at a time, they came forward, led by the Abbot, and scrutinized the nuns. Each selected a companion, and offered an arm to escort her to the Temple.

Thus, in twos, we processed deeper into the labyrinth and many were the gasps and squeaks of mingled fear and excitement as each of our prepared effects came into view. I must confess that even I, who had often walked these subterranean passages and helped to plan their features, felt a chill as we made our way downwards, ever downwards, our shadows forming grotesque, shifting patterns on the walls. At last we came to the tumbling, gurgling torrent which we had, inevitably, christened Styx, the river of the dead. As we crossed the bridge it hissed beneath us, compressed into a narrow gorge, before emptying itself into a huge cauldron of swirling black water. Beyond lay the short slope up to our temple, a circular chamber whose walls were lined with niches devoted to images of Venus, Aphrodite, the Egyptian cat goddess and other deifications of love.

I have no precise recollection of our rites on this occasion. Their devising had been taken over by Potter and Wilkes and they delighted the congregation – or those who understood the lewd allusions of their Latin doggerel.

The feasting and revels afterwards continued long into the night. As was the custom, the food and wine were laid out by servants who then withdrew and left us to our secret pleasures. Everyone entered fully into the festivities except some of the local girls, to whom all this was new and, despite the solicitous attentions of the brothers, very disturbing. Around the perimeter of the Banqueting Hall were a number of curtained cubicles whither couples resorted at various times during the night. Some of the women were clearly unwilling for amorous adventure until they had been well plied with wine.

I noticed Lord Liverpool struggling with a particularly reluctant companion. Twice he tried to draw her away to the nearest bower. Twice she clung firmly to the table. He laughed the matter off but shortly afterwards I saw him produce a small bottle from beneath his habit and pour from it into the girl's goblet while she was distracted. Not much later, he eased her out of her chair. Leaning heavily against him, she allowed herself to be led away to the curtained couch. I was curious to observe the outcome of this encounter and, though not unoccupied myself, I kept a casual watch. It must have been half an hour before Lord L emerged. He was carrying his companion who had obviously succumbed completely to the drug. He laid her gently against the wall.

She was not alone. The floor was by now well spread with bodies. Some were locked in embraces. Some lay singly, overcome by wine or sleep. After a while I, too, slumped across the table. The music, the conversation, the laughter receded to a distant, indistinct murmur and I slumbered.

When I awoke the chamber was silent. Some twenty recumbent figures remained in the vaulted hall. I eased my aching limbs away from the table and staggered through the labyrinth and out onto the hillside, where it was now full day. Thankfully I breathed in morning air, then sat for a while amidst the ruins willing my throbbing head to cease its torment. Servants had now appeared to clear up after our night of revels. They passed to and fro, loading baskets and boxes onto a wagon.

There was a shout. I looked up and saw one of them running empty-handed from the cave. He stared around wild-eyed, saw me and hurried across.

'Mr Whitehead! Do you know where I can find Sir Francis?'

'No, he could be anywhere. What's amiss?'

'Best come and see, sir.'

He led the way back to the Banqueting Hall. It was now empty of monks and nuns – except one. Three servants were kneeling beside a white-robed woman lying against the wall. It was Lord L's woman. The mask and cowl had been removed. It was a beautiful face; the face of a country girl of about fourteen years of age. It took no second glance to see that she was dead.

★ ★ ★

228

They persuaded Ingrid Brunhill to stay to lunch. Disconsolately Tim spent the preceding hour showing his guest over the house and the current exhibition. They were passing through the great hall on their way back to the Lacys' east-wing apartment when a sudden commotion outside shattered the calm of the lofty chamber. They heard wheels skidding on gravel and a blaring car horn.

'What on earth!' Tim strode towards the massive main door. 'Visitors are supposed to drive into the car park.' He heaved open the heavy oak and went out through the porch, followed by Dr Brunhill.

The vehicle that had come to rest before Farrans' ancient portal was still partially obscured by a swirling cloud of dust. As this drifted away Tim recognized, with approval, an old Alvis open tourer, black and gleaming. Behind the wheel, a multi-coloured woollen beret clamped over her hair, sat Emma Kerr. The figure beside her was wrapped in a heavy topcoat and was wearing a cap. Only after several seconds did Tim, with a shock, recognize Gavin Turner.

Emma jumped down and ran across to give Tim a quick hug. 'Look! Isn't it wonderful? They let Gavin out first thing this morning. We just had to come straight here to thank you.'

Tim grinned. 'I'm delighted. But your friend's freedom is much more down to you than to anybody else.'

Gavin slowly descended from the car and walked over to join them. He held out his hand. 'Mr Lacy, I insisted on coming in person. I hope you don't mind. Whatever you said to the Cambridge gestapo certainly shook them.'

With alarm Tim noticed the young man's pallor. The eyes seemed more sunken, the features more bony, than when he had last met the young man. 'I'm glad they came to their senses. You must tell us about it. Come on in. By the way, I like the car; 1948, isn't it?'

Emma shrugged. 'Something like that. My father gave it to me. It's his antiquated idea of what a student ought to drive – "style without excessive speed", quote, unquote.'

Tim made the introductions and led the way to the private quarters. Catherine insisted that the newcomers stay to lunch and calculated that the necessary culinary readjustments would take an extra twenty minutes. At quarter past one they were all seated at the round dining table. Conversation was still general: the youngsters were a little inhibited by the presence of a stranger.

'You must have your results by now,' Tim suggested.

'Yes.' Emma stared down at her plate. 'I got a first.'

'That's terrific. It definitely calls for champagne.' Tim jumped up and went through to the kitchen.

'Congratulations!' Ingrid smiled warmly across the table, glad to be on academic home ground. 'Are you staying on to do research?'

Emma shook her head emphatically. 'I've had enough of Cambridge to last me a very long time.'

'There are other universities,' the Oxford don observed. 'I hope you won't abandon the idea of a higher degree without thinking about it very carefully.'

Catherine looked across at Gavin. 'How about you, Gavin? How did you make out in the exams?'

He smiled sheepishly. 'They were kind to me. I had to miss one paper – I have my off days – but they gave me an overall II 2. That means I can go on to my final year.'

'And will you?' Catherine asked.

He nodded and the sunken eyes took on a sudden intensity. 'I have to. After all that Emma and several other friends have done, I owe it to them to finish the course . . . or at least, to get as far as I can.'

The threatened awkward silence was fended off by Tim's bustling reappearance with bottle and glasses.

When the health of the new graduate had been drunk and they had all settled back to their meal, Catherine asked, 'Do you want to talk about your ordeal, Gavin?'

The young man laid down his knife and fork. 'Sure. In fact, it was in many ways worse for the police than for me. Some of them hated having to come into the cell.' He added bitterly, 'I suppose they were scared I was going to spit at them or try to kiss them. God, people are so ignorant! I gather the station officers gave Oberleutnant Tibbs a hard time of it – telling him I ought to be released on bail or detained in hospital. I overheard a couple of sergeants agreeing that if CID wanted to detain disease-ridden buggers they ought to look after them themselves.'

'Was that why they let you go, eventually?' Catherine asked.

'Oh, no. Tibbs was very determined. If he'd thought he could get a conviction I'd still be there. He grilled me over and over again. I can quite see how some suspects get terrified into making confessions. It's a pretty frightening experience. After one long session, when Tibbs was just about at the end of his tether, he suggested that since I was dying anyway I might as well own up to the murder.'

'Bastard!' Emma growled. 'What did you say?'

'I told him that if he'd care to switch the tape recorder back on and make the point on the record, I'd give him an answer. He went all the colours of the rainbow, then stormed out, slamming the door behind him.'

There was a murmur of enthusiastic approval round the table.

Gavin went on. 'It was pressure from other people that did the trick. Emma virtually slept in the police station. Various gay rights groups were accusing him of prejudice in the local media. Then, Mr Lacy, you came and shook Tibbs up. He was in a particularly foul mood after your visit.'

Tim smiled, remembering the DI's lost battle against rising temper. 'I can't take much of the credit for that. The poor man had Sir Evelyn leaning on him and threatening to take the matter up with the Chief Constable.'

'Moneybags? Speaking up for Gavin?' Emma's thick eyebrows rose with surprise. 'That's a first.'

'I think he was more concerned about the theft of the Hellfire Papers and why the police weren't doing anything about it.'

Gavin nodded. 'That was what finally pulled the rug from under Tibbs's theory. Of course, he spent a couple of days trying to pin that crime on me as well. When he realized that wouldn't wash he couldn't get rid of me quickly enough.'

Emma looked thoughtful. 'Those damned papers have caused a lot of havoc. I wonder who did pinch them?'

The sudden silence round the table was broken by Catherine brightly offering more vegetables. But not before Tim had noticed Emma's quick shrewd glance.

After lunch Catherine took Emma and Gavin on a tour of Farrans. Tim was left with his Oxford guest drinking a second coffee in the sitting room. Ingrid Brunhill had been uncharacteristically quiet during much of the meal.

Tim offered a conversational opening. 'I hope Emma takes your advice about a research degree. She's very—'

'Stop babbling! I'm trying to think!'

While Tim was still searching for an appropriate response, Dr Brunhill went on. 'Those youngsters have been through a hell of a lot.'

'Yes, they have.'

'And whoever killed Longton was quite prepared to see Gavin charged with the murder.'

'Evidently.'

'You don't believe the police stand much chance of catching this monster?'

'Perhaps I do the good Inspector Tibbs an injustice, but I don't see him as a man with the necessary breadth of vision for such an odd case as this. It's somehow all bound up with these Hellfire Papers (as I've taken to calling them – inaccurately I know). The whole tragic sequence of events didn't start until Sir Peregrine's wretched family documents turned up.' He ran a finger along the bridge of his nose. 'If only I could see the connection . . .'

Ingrid Brunhill stood up suddenly. 'I've changed my mind. I realize now that it was churlish of me to refuse. If those young people can take risks sticking up for what they believe is right, it would be absurd for me to stand on my dignity. So, Tim Lacy, lead on and let's get to grips with these Hellfire Papers.'

Half an hour later, having settled Ingrid in a spare room with Sir Peregrine's manuscripts, Tim was sitting on a stone bench in a corner of the walled garden which received the full force of the afternoon sun. His eyes were closed behind dark glasses as his body absorbed the warmth and his mind grabbed a few minutes' relaxation. A shadow and the sense of another presence broke his reverie.

'This is where you escape to, is it? Catherine said I might find you here.' Emma sat on the grass at his feet.

'Where's Gavin?'

'I've left him helping to clear up. I wanted a quiet word with you.' She pushed a wisp of dark hair back from her face.

'So, you've tracked me down. What can I do for you?'

Emma's green-brown eyes stared frankly into Tim's. 'I think you know more about this business than you're telling me.'

Tim emitted a sharp snort of cynical laughter. 'I wish I did. The more involved I get the more puzzled I become.'

'Will you give it up now that Gavin's in the clear?'

'I ought to.'

'Meaning you won't.'

Tim grinned. 'I can see why they gave you a first.' Then, seriously, as though in self-justification, 'I suppose I've passed the point of no return. Easier to go on climbing to the top than turn back.'

'Anything I can do to help? I'm pretty much at a loose end – for a while, at least.'

Tim spoke firmly. 'No. You can and really should walk away, now. You've done a tremendous job for your friend. As you said over lunch, the time has come to put Cambridge behind you and get on with the rest of your life. Take a long holiday.'

Emma shook her head. 'I feel the same way as you do. I'm so far in, I want to get through to the other side. I need to know what it's all about.'

'Sounds to me like a case of post-graduation anticlimax. Life's been so intense for the last three years, what with work and socializing and campaigning, that things are bound to seem a bit flat now.'

'Don't be patronizing!' Emma smiled but the words were sharp. 'I haven't come to terms yet with what the last few months have done to me. There's been so much violence. Two absolutely ghastly deaths – one of someone I cared about a lot, in a funny sort of way. Then the police brutalizing poor Gavin. Someone's behind it all; someone very vicious or very sick. I have to know what it's all about. Haven't you any idea, Tim?' She came and sat beside him on the bench.

Tim shrugged. 'In my experience these things usually come down to money. At first, I thought your esteemed Master was working an insurance scam. Now . . .' He changed tack suddenly. 'Is there anyone by the name of Jenkinson at St Mary's?'

Emma looked surprised but gave the question serious thought. 'I don't think so. I don't know all the undergrads, of course, but it's a small college. I'm sure I'd have heard the name. Why?'

Tim hesitated, considering carefully how much to tell her. He said, 'Stuart Longton phoned me the day he died. He reckoned he'd discovered something important. It was to do with a man – or I suppose it could have been a woman – called Jenkinson. Does the name mean nothing to you at all?'

''Fraid not. Could you have misheard?'

'Very possibly. I'm beginning to wonder whether I didn't imagine the whole thing. It seems so meaningless.'

'We had a sports mistress called Jenkins at school. Bronwen Jenkins, very Welsh and very beefy, but I don't think she collected old manuscripts. Sorry.' Emma gazed at Tim's unsmiling face. 'I'm being flippant. Oh! I wish I could make some sensible contribution.'

'Don't worry. Let's try another angle. Is there anything – anything at all – you can remember about Dr Vare's room or the intruder who brushed past you?'

'I've racked my brains over that dozens of times. It all happened too quickly. Most of what I know about the mess in the Dean's room came from Dorcas.'

'Dorcas?'

'She's the bedder – the cleaner – who looks after the rooms on my staircase. She was highly indignant when the police eventually let her in to tidy up. "Papers everywhere," ' Emma mimicked an outraged, nasal voice, ' "and ash trodden into the carpet and dreadful, melted video cassettes sticking to the grate!" Poor Dorcas felt very put upon. What with Dr Vare, the mysterious stranger and the police the place must have been a real shambles. Sorry, I'm not being any help, am I?' She scowled in frustration. 'Look, Tim, there must be something I can do!'

He stared at her thoughtfully. 'Well, I suppose there's one avenue we could explore, though it's almost sure to be a dead end.'

'Tell me what it is?'

'Do you have access to a newspaper archive?'

'They've got *The Times* on microfilm at the UL – University Library. Is that what you mean?'

'Yes, that would do. Could you see what you can find out about Lord Everton?'

'The self-publicizing philanthropist and Tory grandee? Where does he come into the picture?'

'Probably nowhere. It's just that he seems to be a bosom companion of Lady Masquerier and he has a knack of turning up in the most unusual places. It's very likely you'd be wasting your time, so, if you'd rather not . . .'

Emma jumped up. 'No! I'll get onto it first thing in the morning. Do you think we'd better go back to the others before Catherine suspects me of having my wicked way with you?'

Catherine's thoughts were, in fact, focused entirely on the young man who was, rather inexpertly, putting dishes into the dishwasher.

'You must be glad to be out of the limelight at last.' She stacked the last few plates on the work surface beside him.

Gavin coughed drily and turned it into a laugh. 'Oh I've got used to it. I seem to have been in the limelight rather a long time.'

'It must have been tough.'

'I had good friends; wonderful friends.' He puzzled over fitting in a serving dish.

Catherine busied herself behind him, avoiding eye contact, making it easier for the young man to talk, if he chose to do so. 'Emma must have been—'

'Emma is bloody marvellous.' Half shout, half sob. 'If it hadn't been for . . .' The sentence lost itself in a bout of coughing. Gavin took some deep breaths and recovered. 'I've come to depend on Emma a lot, and that's not fair on her.'

'I'm sure she doesn't mind. She's a very caring woman.'

'Yes, that's true but, more important than that, she's not shocked and she's not frightened.'

'Frightened?'

Gavin turned to face her. 'Oh, yes, that's the worst thing about AIDS, you know. Everyone's frightened of it – my parents, my sister, old schoolfriends, other undergraduates, college staff. They say kind things. Some of them really want to be supportive. But the fear in their eyes gives them away. That, and the way they keep their distance. They're afraid I might touch them or breathe on them, you see . . .' He faltered and rubbed the back of a hand across his eyes. He turned abruptly back to the machine. 'It's unnecessary, of course. AIDS is not infectious.'

'I know.'

'Many people do. My family certainly know. That doesn't stop them avoiding all physical contact.'

'I'm sorry.' It was inadequate but Catherine could find nothing else to say.

Gavin smiled at her. He said, brightly, 'I'm very good with children. May I meet your boys and spend some time with them, this afternoon?'

Catherine avoided his gaze. 'Well, that would be nice . . . unfortunately . . .'

'Sorry. That was unfair of me. I just wanted to drive home the point. You're an intelligent woman. You know I could play with your kids – hold their hands, sit them on my lap – and they would be perfectly safe. Your reason tells you that. But your irrational fear is too strong.'

Catherine leaned back against the table, one hand on Root's highchair. 'You make me feel very small.'

'Catherine, I'm sorry – genuinely. I owe you and Tim too much to want to upset you.'

'It's probably very good for me to be upset. We can never have too much self-knowledge.'

A hole opened up in the conversation which neither could find words to cover. Gavin closed the dishwasher and dried his hands.

Catherine led the way into the sitting room. 'Let's make ourselves comfortable while we wait for the others. Tell me about the course you're doing.'

Gavin sank slowly into one end of the sofa, resting his weight on the arm as he did so. 'I shan't be continuing.'

'But I thought you said . . .'

'That was for Emma's benefit. I haven't told her I'm quitting. It seems somehow so ungrateful after all she's done. Please don't mention it. I'll have to get round to it in my own way.'

'But why?'

Gavin closed his eyes. 'AIDS is an unpredictable virus. It can attack slowly or quickly, without any rhyme or reason, as far as scientists can tell at the moment. Well, mine's accelerating.'

'Can you be sure of that?'

'Oh, yes. The doctors try to keep things from me but I've read up just about everything written on the disease. I know the signs. The night sweats and the spiking temperatures have been getting more frequent over the last couple of months. The skin lesions have started recently – symptoms of what they call Kaposi's Sarcoma. Come October, I shall be in no fit state to return to Cambridge, even if I'm still . . .'

On an impulse Catherine crossed the room, sat next to Gavin and took one of his hands in both of hers. His smile said 'Thank you'. For several seconds the lump in Catherine's throat prevented her speaking.

At last she was able to say, almost in a whisper, 'Gavin, you're incredibly brave, and calm. I don't know how you do it. If I were in your position . . .'

He half-laughed, half-coughed. 'Oh, I'm no stoic, Catherine. I've gone through long bouts of depression, self-pity, anger. But what's the point? I knew what I was doing when I went to a gay club.' He laughed again. 'My God! What a silly word that is. If you want to meet a bunch of remarkably un-gay people, go along to a gay club. Self-conscious? Yes. Defiant? Yes. Insecure? Yes. But gay?' He shook his head.

'You don't feel any bitterness towards whoever is responsible for your condition?'

'I've certainly been through times when I could cheerfully have killed someone.'

'Including Stuart Longton?'

'Oh yes. I came to loathe the man. Not just because of this. He was so arrogant, so cold, so totally devoid of feeling. The extent of his sympathy was telling me that it was my own fault; I should have been more careful.' He looked into Catherine eyes. Read her thoughts. 'No, I did not kill him. If I had, I certainly wouldn't have denied it. What would be the point? I'm already serving a life sentence.'

'Have you any idea who might have done it?'

'That's a question I've had a lot of time to think about, of course. All I can say is what I've already said to the police, over and over again. I spent just under half an hour with

Stuart – at his invitation. We talked about my future at St Mary's. He was actually quite pleasant for once. He said he would see to it that I had a ground-floor room next term with one of the new computer terminals the college has bought. It was really quite a remarkable change of heart. I left soon after nine and Stuart was quite OK then. There were a few other people about in Grand Court but I saw no one go up Stuart's staircase.'

'Was the Master around college that evening?'

Gavin's reply came without hesitation. 'He was certainly in hall. There aren't usually many fellows on high table so one tends to notice. The Master comes in about once a week. I remember noticing that he and Stuart were having an animated conversation.'

'Animated? Do you mean they were having a row?'

'No. They wouldn't do that. Not in hall – *pas devant les enfants*. But they were certainly disagreeing about something.'

At that moment the telephone rang. Catherine crossed the room to answer it.

'Yes, Sally . . . Really? How interesting. OK, put her on. Hello, how nice to hear from you.'

Tim and Emma came into the room. Catherine flashed a smile as she continued her conversation. 'That sounds a splendid idea. Yes . . . just a minute while I check my diary.' She gesticulated to Tim who walked through into the adjoining office and returned with his wife's desk diary.

Catherine flicked over the pages. 'Hm! I don't think I could manage it before 3.30. It is? Good. Well I look forward to seeing you then. Goodbye.'

She clicked the off switch and put the receiver on the low

table beside her. She looked across at Tim with an arched eyebrow. 'Well, isn't that interesting? That was Lady – "call-me-Deb" – Masquerier. She wants to do a feature on the artists I'm showing at the Chipping Sneddon festival. I'm going to her Cheltenham office tomorrow to discuss the project.'

Tim rubbed a finger along the bridge of his nose. 'Sounds plausible. You told me she's an enthusiastic supporter of the festival. On the other hand . . .'

'Watch out for hidden agendas?'

'Precisely.'

CHAPTER 12

Dashwood's physician could not or would not determine the cause of Meg Warrener's death. He probably reasoned that since the poor girl was beyond the scope of his skills there was no cause to jeopardize his own standing with the most powerful man in the locality. The only other evidence presented to the coroner about events in the cave on Walpurgisnacht was confused and confusing. There was nothing he could do but declare that young Meg had died by misadventure. That did not satisfy the girl's family nor many of their neighbours. Over the next few weeks three of Dashwood's hayricks were burned and his favourite hunter was hamstrung.

Sir Francis took no action over these incidents. He knew that his tenants had a right to be angry and hoped that, once they had given vent to their wrath, it would exhaust itself. Such proved to be the case. The Squire of West Wycombe was popular with most of his people. They were convinced that he was mad but they acknowledged that he was a fair landlord who took a genuine interest in their wellbeing. As well as building his own fine house, he maintained their cottages; he had provided them with a decent road and was building them a new church. They were prepared to forgive if not to forget.

Such tolerance did not extend to the caves. From that time forth no man or woman would go near the labyrinth. To keep their children away, mothers told them that devils dwelt inside the hill and would drag them off to hell if ever they strayed too close to the caves. Thus are foolish superstitions born.

As for Lord Liverpool; I had expected that he would come forward to admit responsibility or that, at least, he would make some recompense to the girl's family. Clearly I misjudged both his courage and his generosity of spirit. I could have forgiven him his cowardice. What I could not stomach was his lies and his boasting. At the next meeting of the Order I heard him telling Laurie, Groom and some of his other cronies that Meg Warrener was a victim of his sexual vigour. 'Fair impaled the wench,' he claimed. 'Drove her into a frenzy of rapture! After such an experience what else had she to live for?'

Extract from Sir Peregrine Whitehead-Dyer's notes:

Although my ancestor does not say so in as many words, the Order of St Francis clearly reverted to meeting in members' houses after the disastrous inauguration of the West Wycombe catacombs. The caves were not abandoned entirely. Dashwood permitted brothers to organize their own activities ('private devotions') in them from time to time, but no further chapter meetings were held there. Some brothers lamented the lack of a headquarters but there could be no question of acquiring premises in London. The Order had become notorious, particularly after the Walpurgisnacht tragedy. Garbled accounts of the Wycombe revels received extensive currency and most people who were not privy to the facts were quite convinced that the worship of Satan and its attendant blood rites provided the focus for the clandestine activities of Dashwood and his friends. It was John Wilkes who proposed a new setting for the Order. Dashwood responded warmly to an idea that provided fresh scope for his love of the arcane and picturesque and his passion for building. My ancestor, however, had distinct reservations about the proposal.

Medmenham! I could scarcely believe that Sir Francis was serious when I read the letter delivered to my newly-acquired Twickenham villa one afternoon in the summer of 1755. Dashwood had decided to take a lease on Duffield's house and to transform it and the adjacent abbey ruins into a permanent home for the Order.

I cautiously voiced my feeling the following day when, in obedience to my patron's summons, I took a post-chaise to Medmenham to rendezvous with Francis Duffield, Dashwood, Nicholas Revett (Dashwood's architect), Wilkes and, inevitably, Thomas Potter. We walked among the broken arches, fallen stone and lichen-covered walls of the Cistercian monastery, close by the river bank.

'I own I'm uneasy about this,' I observed to Duffield. 'I hold your brother's memory in great affection and I cannot feel that what we are about would not have distressed him.'

Potter overheard. 'Don't listen to Aged Paul,' he urged waving a bottle (an accountrement he was seldom seen without). 'He's but a flogging cully.* He'll describe amorous congress a dozen ways in verse but can't satisfy a dell himself!'

I ignored the taunt, as did Duffield. He said, 'I was very fond of my brother but I have to balance my reverence for his memory with my family responsibilities. This place is suffering badly from neglect.' He indicated the red-brick house, built in the reign of Elizabeth. Creepers had invaded the terraces and there were jagged holes in one of the oriel widows. 'It sadly needs a tenant – and one prepared to spend money on it.'

Dashwood, walking ahead in enthusiastic conversation with the architect, halted and turned to us. 'You were right, Wilkes. We shall have all we need here. Nick can conjure up pleasure gardens filled with all manner of temples, grottoes and bowers for summer trysting, and yonder is an island for yet more secret revels.' He pointed to where a grove of trees seemed to grow directly out of the shimmering water, then went striding on, talking and gesticulating energetically to Revett.

Wilkes took my arm as we fell in behind. He smiled his twisted smile. 'So, Paul the Wise, what is your real reason for misliking our Abbot's plan?'

'Will you mock me, too?'

'I?' He seemed genuinely pained. 'By no means. You are the pillar of our Order, the king post. Whatever you have to say, we should all listen.'

---

* old lecher, no longer able to perform

'Well then, if you will have it plain, our Brotherhood was conceived as a living satire upon all cant, hypocrisy, religiosity and philosophical pretension. When we took *Fay ce que voudras* as our motto we were defying convention, proclaiming our determination to follow our own inclinations rather than have politicians or preachers tell us how to behave.'

'Why, and so we do still. Ours is a perfect democracy where every man is his own master and Bacchus alone is king.'

'Aye, and that is where we have gone astray. You see, we were a Brotherhood—'

'And still are,' he exclaimed with a laugh. 'Brothers in adversity. Why, here's Dodington losing his parliamentary seat, and me failing in my attempts to get one, and Sandwich out of office and Potter and Dashwood in the Commons but powerless against the government. So, instead of railing 'gainst fortune, we turn our backs on her, fart in her face and come to such a place as this to take our common pleasures.'

'But our pleasures are common no longer. Liberty can never be infinite. When we were a true Brotherhood, that imposed limits on our freedoms. We had a care for each other's sensibilities – even for poor Edmund Duffield, though manifestly not enough. Now there are those of our number who take *Fay ce que voudras* to mean "Do as you please and devil take everyone else". Where is the Brotherhood now?'

'Come, man, you exaggerate.'

'Do I so? What of the little hatreds in our midst?'

'Hatreds? A strong word.'

'But apt. The younger men despise the older. The Whigs snub the Tories. We are sundered into sneering cliques.'

'I think you're alluding to my little contretemps with milord Sandwich.'

'The story's all over town. You don't deny it?'

'Indeed I don't. The man called me a revolutionary and a libertine. Sandwich! Prating on *my* morals! Why the man has five bastards to my certain knowledge! You'll have heard how I turned the tables on him. "Damme, man," says his lordship, "you'll either die by the pox or the hangman." "That depends," says I, "whether I embrace your lordship's mistress or his principles!" '

'Very brotherly! And you've been no less scathing about Dodington.'

'I only asked if he had lost the key to the press where he's locked away his political ideals. I admit I've no love of placemen who think of nothing but their own position and advantage. If I get into parliament it'll be to change things, not to stuff my pockets with sinecures and fees. I shall make more noise than Pitt. Force the government to listen to me.'

'Then I wish you success. As for myself: I'm no friend to faction and no dupe to zeal/Foe to all party, but the common-weal.'

'There's room for both opinions in the Order.'

'I wonder.'

'I still say that you are wrong about Medmenham. It will be vastly diverting when our Lord Abbot has completed his transformation.'

Wilkes was right about that, if about nothing else. Under Revett and the multitude of workmen who descended upon the riverside estate, within weeks the house and grounds were magically transformed into a sumptuous pleasure palace. The mansion provided every facility the brothers and nuns might require: dining hall, chapel, library, bed chambers, all fitted without the slightest concession to economy. Yet it was the grounds which most impressed all who visited them. I think there can never have been gardens more seductively dedicated to venery. Beauty, artifice and wit were all employed to one end: the creation of Elysian Fields where devotees of the goddess of love could worship in any one of a hundred ways that took their fancy on long summer evenings when the scent of flowers perfumed the drowsy air.

Moored where fresh-scythed lawn met the lapping Thames was a purple gondola. Couples might take their pleasure upon its silken cushions or have themselves conveyed to Cupid's Isle where the inner walls of the god's temple were painted with scenes from the story of Dido and Aeneas. Ashore were caves, grottoes, groves, bowers and more temples. Inscriptions were carved in the rock such as might stimulate the scholarly or timorous:

> Ite, agite, o juventes; pariter fudate medullis
> Omnibus inter vos; non murmura vestra columbae,
> Brachia non hederae, non vincant oscula conchae.*

Those less subtle found no shortage of explicit paintings and phallic symbols to unleash their imaginations.

---

* Go to it, youngsters! Both of you strive together to the uttermost.
  Outdo doves in your cooing, ivy in your clinging embraces,
  oysters in your kissing.

But the spirit of *Fay ce que voudras* permitted brothers to indulge a range of other delights. The Order's library was extensive, as was its cellar. Frequently groups of brothers would ride out to Medmenham for an evening of cards, drinking and conversation. As steward of the Order, a post to which I was unanimously elected at the first Medmenham chapter meeting, I can vouch not only for the amount of excellent food and wine consumed but also for the civilized atmosphere that prevailed at most of our gatherings. The Brotherhood enjoyed several happy and successful years, and it seemed that my fears might not be realized. But outward amity concealed internal conflicts.

It took another death to bring them into the open.

Thursday 20th June began badly and got progressively worse.

Opening *The Times* before breakfast, Tim was confronted by a picture of Emma and Gavin smiling and brandishing a bottle of champagne. The Thunderer reported soberly enough on Turner's unconditional release and explained that the police were now pursuing another line of enquiry, connected with the theft of valuable historical documents. Clearly the press had pounced on the youngsters as soon as they had got back to Cambridge the previous night. It took very little imagination to see a brash journalist waiting outside St Mary's with a bottle of Moët et Chandon ready to thrust into Gavin's hands before he knew what was going on. The resulting photos would have been emerging from fax machines in all the national daily offices well before midnight. Tim shuddered to think what the tabloids had made of the story. He found out soon enough.

He was just cracking his first boiled egg when Catherine admitted George Martin to the flat.

'Morning, Major!' The burly figure of Lacy Security's operations manager, immaculate in his well-pressed uniform, strode into the kitchen. 'No thanks, Catherine,' this in answer to an offer of coffee, 'I've got to get the van packed up and take a team to Manchester for a new installation. Just popped in to show the boss this.' He took a folded copy of the *Sun* from beneath his arm. 'Your young lady friend's made the front page.'

Tim spread the newspaper out on the kitchen table. He was confronted by a slightly different, and larger, version of the photograph he had already seen. The headline beside it made him wince: POLICE PORN HUNT. The report dealt summarily with Gavin's release, then went on to describe in lurid detail the 'secret documents' police believed the murderer to have stolen. The 'Hellfire Journals' contained startling revelations about the scandalous sex lives of Britain's leaders two hundred years ago. Sleaze in political circles, the article crowed, was nothing new. It quoted an unnamed expert as suggesting that the missing papers would be a highly desirable prize to a dedicated private collector of erotica and might fetch £400,000 – 'maybe more' on the underworld market. The reporter allowed Inspector Tibbs the final word: 'It's a bizarre crime. Obviously, there's someone out there with a mind so twisted that he's prepared to condone murder in order to be able to gloat in secret over the dirty doings of his ancestors.'

'Well, I guess that lets the cat right out of the bag.' Catherine looked up momentarily from her tasks of coaxing her younger son to eat some cereal and deterring her elder from balancing a slice of toast on top of his egg. 'It could make our Valkyrie jumpy all over again.'

As if on cue, Ingrid Brunhill walked into the room. Without comment, Tim passed her the newspapers. She scanned them quickly and then, to the Lacys' surprise, she laughed. It was a loud, staccato laugh that made both of the boys stare at her wide-eyed.

'What's funny?' Tim asked.

Ingrid tossed the *Sun* aside contemptuously. 'The prospect of these sensation-mongers getting egg on their faces.' She poured herself coffee from the cafetière and gulped down a mouthful. 'That's better! Never feel up to much till I've had my first shot of caffeine.'

'Can I cook you something to go with it?' Catherine allowed herself to be briefly distracted from her demanding offspring and Toot took immediate advantage by pretending that his brother's head was an egg and tapping it with his spoon.

Tim raised his voice above the resulting squawk of protest. 'I don't understand . . .'

Ingrid smiled a light smile which suggested academic superiority. 'No thanks, Catherine. Toast will be fine. Well, Tim, I came in ready to deliver a bombshell this morning. All this press speculation makes it potentially much more devastating.' She spread butter thickly on a slice of brown toast and topped it generously with chunky marmalade. 'I sat up till about three o'clock with these precious Hellfire Papers. I started again at six and I am pretty sure—' she took a large bite of toast and chewed it silently for several seconds— 'I am pretty sure that they're phoney.'

'What!' Tim stared, incredulous.

Catherine stopped hovering over Root's food-spattered highchair. 'You mean all this murder and mayhem's been over a bunch of worthless fake documents?'

Tim said, 'What makes you doubt the authenticity of the papers?'

'At this stage, nothing that I'm prepared to put my name to. When you've studied as many genuine documents of the period as I have you get a feel for the way the language was used, even for the way it changed over comparatively short periods of time. There are parts of these papers, particularly the autobiographical fragment, that don't have the right ring to them.'

Tim frowned. 'So your opinion is just that – an opinion. It can't be substantiated?'

'What do you expect after a few hours' study?' Dr Brunhill snapped. 'However, as it happens there is other evidence: watermarks. The writer has used two different batches of paper.'

'And you think one of them is modern?'

'Oh, no, as far as I can tell they're both right for the period. But you see, it's stitched, like a book and there are several blank pages at the end. We're supposed to believe that Whitehead wrote his memoirs in a pre-prepared note-book. But if that's the case you'd expect the paper to be all the same. In fact, the sheets are mixed up.'

'Couldn't there be a perfectly good reason for that?'

'Probably. But in detecting forgeries – good forgeries – one has to take as many factors as possible into account: paper, ink, literary style, calligraphy. And, of course, provenance. What do we know about Sir Peregrine Whitehead-Dyer?'

'Diplomat. Unmarried. Fanatically keen antiquarian. Seems to have been a semi-recluse, at least in his later years.' Tim swiftly catalogued the facts he possessed about the man who had spread tragedy from half a world away. 'The picture I got of him in his last years was one of intensely introverted gothic gloom. He lived in a big old house with only an aboriginal servant and a computer for company.'

'So, he could well have been quietly perfecting the skills of a forger during those long days in his lonely study. One can even imagine how the idea might have occurred to him. He was gathering material for a biography of his ancestor but he found that it didn't amount to very much. There is a very brief biographical note by someone called Thompson, who knew Whitehead and published his collected poems. Apart from that, references in contemporary writings are very scanty. We know, of course, that he was the MC for Dashwood's high jinks at Medmenham, but since no one really knows what Sir Francis's cronies got up to that doesn't help us very much.'

'If the Hellfire Papers did fill in that gap, then, they really would be useful – and valuable?' Catherine finished cleaning a protesting Rupert and released him from his chair.

Ingrid nodded. 'Indubitably. By the same token it must have been quite a temptation for Sir Peregrine to *invent* material to fill the gap.'

Tim looked doubtful. 'I can imagine him doing that for his own amusement, as an intellectual exercise, but why would he deliberately bequeath them to his old college? As far as I know, he didn't have a score to settle with St Mary's.'

Ingrid shrugged. 'Who knows what fancies fill old men's

minds. Anyway,' she drained her cup and stood up, looking businesslike, 'let's establish the facts first. I'll take the papers to Oxford and have tests done on the ink and paper. It's difficult to fake everything. You can make a document *look* old but the chemical composition—'

'Hey, just a minute!' Tim jumped to his feet. 'You can't—'

'What can't I?' Dr Brunhill turned in the doorway.

'You can't go spreading these papers round the country-side.'

She tutted her annoyance. 'That's a silly exaggeration, Tim. And you're in no position to tell me what I may or may not do. Need I remind you that the papers don't belong to you and that you are holding on to them illegally?'

Tim tried to keep his voice-level down. 'Right now we're the only three people who know where the Hellfire Papers are. We've got to keep it that way. Ingrid, there's a killer out there desperate to get his hands on them – not to mention newspaper reporters looking for a scoop.'

'You can rest assured that I shall be discreet. I shall entrust the manuscript to a friend in the laboratory at the Institute of Antiquities. It won't take him long to do electron microscopy, diffraction and other tests.'

'Let's wait a few days . . .'

'Yesterday you were in a great hurry to find out about the manuscripts.' She was on the point of walking out and thus silencing further argument, but thought better of it. 'Look, Tim, I'm as anxious as you are to unravel the mystery of these papers, though perhaps for other reasons. I happen to believe that fraud is wrong: fraud financial, artistic, aca-demic, anything that parades falsehood as truth. We must expose it whenever we have the opportunity.'

Tim tried calm reason. 'That's fine as a principle and I applaud it. But in this case, the fraudster – the *alleged* fraudster – is dead.'

There was a glint of holy zeal in Ingrid's eyes. 'But there are others and they have to be warned. Look, if you quietly return these papers to Cambridge and someone at St Mary's eventually works out that they're forgeries, what do you think the college will do about it?'

'Probably nothing.'

'Exactly! It will be more important to save face than to say to the academic community, "Be on your guard against fakes. Don't be duped as we were." '

'So, you're going to save them the trouble by exposing the fraud yourself?'

Dr Brunhill was shocked at the suggestion. 'Certainly not! That would be unethical. All I'm concerned with at the moment is discovering the truth.'

'And if your suspicions are correct?'

'Then sooner or later St Mary's will have to be told that I know, and that any attempt at a cover-up would be futile. And now I must be off. I'll be in touch as soon as I've got anything to report.'

The boys' nanny, a cheerful young woman from Little Farrans with seemingly inexhaustible patience, came into the kitchen. After she had collected Toot and Root and taken them into the garden Tim let off steam. 'Well, it certainly was a mistake trusting that bloody woman.'

'She surely has a mind of her own.' Catherine moved quickly round the room clearing the breakfast debris.

Tim snorted. 'Mind of her own! You weren't taken in by

all that high-sounding nonsense, were you? She was gloating like hell! Sheer, bitchy academic rivalry! She's got the chance to put one over on the Cambridge folk and she's not going to let it go.'

'Hm, you could be right.' Catherine's tone of voice proclaimed that she was sure he was wrong. 'Anyway, I can't discuss it now. I've got a pile of paperwork that will have to be cleared away this morning if I'm going to Cheltenham this afternoon. Bye, darling!' She kissed him briefly. 'See you for lunch?'

''Fraid not. I'm in London most of the day.'

He was still fuming over Ingrid Brunhill's behaviour an hour later as he accelerated the Mercedes, hood-down, along the M4. His mood was not improved when he slowed to a standstill near Slough, with the traffic ahead stacked solid as far as the eye could see. When the mobile phone rang his tolerance was at an extremely low ebb.

'Mr Lacy?' An aloof, bored female. 'One moment, please, I have the minister for you.'

While Tim was still puzzling, a man's voice came on the line. 'Good morning, Mr Lacy. John Finsley-Kerr. We met briefly a few months ago but I understand you've been in touch with my daughter recently.' The tone suggested disapproval.

'Yes, I . . .'

'I've just spoken to Emma about this ridiculous business she's involved in. I couldn't get any sense out of her, so I've come to you. You won't be surprised to hear I've had the media on my back since late last night. They've been pestering my wife, and my former wife, too. It's got to stop, Mr Lacy. Being accountable for one's professional activities is one thing; one is a public servant. But having one's family hounded is intolerable.'

Tim thought, 'Pompous ass.' He said nothing.

After a pause the line spluttered into life again. 'Hello? Mr Lacy, are you there?'

'I'm here.' Tim mustered all the calmness he could find. 'I wasn't sure whether you'd finished.'

'I'll assume that was not intended as an impertinent remark.' Finsley-Kerr's tone had become almost a snarl.

'I shouldn't assume anything of the sort.' The car in front edged forward. Tim released the clutch pedal and moved alongside a TIR lorry spewing pungent exhaust fumes. 'All I've heard from you so far is unspecific angry protest. You haven't told me why you've called me, what I'm supposed to have done or what you expect me to do.'

There was a pause. Tim imagined the politician reminding himself of the ground rules for dealing with hostile interviewers. 'Look, Mr Lacy, Emma's a bright girl . . .'

'Well, I don't suppose Cambridge University dish out first-class degrees to idiots.'

'No, well, exactly. She's done very well, and of course her mother and I are very proud of her. But what I was saying was that although Emma is clever, she's still very headstrong. She tends to get involved in things without thinking out the consequences.'

'And that sometimes causes you embarrassment?'

Finsley-Kerr ignored the taunt – with an effort, Tim guessed. 'It was bad enough her being mixed up in the unpleasantness at St Mary's. I hoped that she'd be able to get away from Cambridge and put all that behind her. I've arranged for her to have a break with friends in the

Dordogne for a few weeks. Now she tells me she's staying on in Cambridge to do some research for you. Now you must see, Mr Lacy, that that's very unfair on her. She's been under a lot of pressure and she needs a complete rest, a change of scene.'

'Preferably somewhere far away from prying newspapermen?'

'Yes, all right, I won't deny it. I want her out of the public eye until all this nonsense about the Whitehead-Dyer Papers has died down.'

'Mr Finsley-Kerr, I gave your daughter precisely the same advice myself. It was entirely her decision to get involved.'

'Involved in what, for God's sake!' The minister was losing his cool. 'Just what is this "research"?'

'I'm afraid I can't tell you that just at the moment. All I can say is that Emma is in no danger. She's doing something that interests her and it may even help her to get over her recent trauma.'

'That's not good enough, Mr Lacy. I think I'm the better judge of what's in my daughter's interests.'

Tim thought but did not say, 'I very much doubt that.' He eased the Mercedes past the offending truck and took some gulps of slightly less tainted air.

The aggrieved father continued, 'I insist that you tell me what you've got Emma involved in.'

'I'm sorry. If your daughter's not prepared to confide in you, I'm not.'

'In that case, I want you to call Emma and tell her you've changed your mind. You no longer require her help.'

'Are you asking me to lie? I'm not very good at that. I'm a businessman, not a politician. As far as I am concerned,

Emma is an intelligent young woman. She's over eighteen and quite able to make up her own mind what she wants to do and what she doesn't want to do. I really have nothing more to say on the matter.'

'You could regret that!' Finsley-Kerr was shouting now. 'I understand you do a lot of security work for public museums and galleries. The Heritage Department has considerable influence with such places. It would only take a word from me—'

'Goodbye, Minister.' Tim flicked the off switch.

The traffic congestion eased gradually but Tim decided to cut across country and take a chance on the M40. As he put the Mercedes into top gear on a stretch of open road he went over the conversation again. He wanted to clear the anger from his mind. To think clearly. Something Finsley-Kerr had said had set his brain cells vibrating. What was it? Whatever the politician was worried about, it had little to do with his daughter. So what was really troubling him? He was almost on the motorway approach road when the truth struck him.

Minutes later he called into the office. 'Sally, can you drop everything and pop into town? I want a copy of every morning paper you can lay your hands on.'

CHAPTER 13

The sudden death of King George II on 25 October 1760, as unexpected as it was much looked for, marked the end of our Brotherhood. The son of Frederick Louis, who that day plucked the regal mantle from the body of his grandfather, was a headstrong young man driven by bitterness and idealism. Naturally, he became the lodestone which attracted the ambition and power-seeking of those of the political class who had been excluded from favour under the previous regime. It was clear that there would be ministerial changes; an expectation reinforced by our new monarch's stated intention of sweeping away corruption and creating a government which should unite all the best available talent. It is astonishing that, despite the overwhelming evidence to the contrary, men persist in believing that any change of political personnel will alter the realities of power and advance the common good. Such, however, was the wide-spread optimism which greeted the new reign.

The Earl of Bute, the King's closest friend, now became the leader of the government. Several of the brothers benefited from the new dispensation. Sandwich was restored to his position at the Admiralty. Dodington received the peerage he had so long coveted, but did not live long to enjoy it. The massive constitution which had survived more than seventy summers of abuse succumbed finally in July 1762. Within months Dashwood also made his entrance to the house of peers when he succeeded an uncle as Baron le Despencer.

It was, however, Dashwood's decision to accept government office that created further division within the Brotherhood. Bute prevailed upon him to abandon that studied independency which had been the fundamental article of his political creed throughout his years in parliament. In May 1761 Dashwood was appointed Chancellor of the Exchequer. Inevitably, many saw this as a desertion of principle. Dashwood himself claimed that his decision was a pragmatic one; Bute, he believed, was an honourable man with whom he could work for the realization of those reforms and policies dearest to his heart.

Those of us closest to him discerned deeper, more complex motivations. Dashwood's energetic, questing mind always needed fresh challenges. Over recent years his building activities and his patronage of the Order had taken up much of his time. By 1760 he had exhausted the possibilities of both.

In truth, he had become disillusioned with the 'Mednamites'. The Brotherhood, as I had foreseen, had split into groups which increasingly used the facilities at Medmenham and Wycombe for their own purposes. For several members the abbey provided a discreet rendezvous for adulterous liaisons. It was not uncommon for members to make up small parties including their wives or mistresses and then, during the course of the night, to share the favours of the ladies. Others resorted thither for convivial company and civilized conversation. Wilkes, Potter and their cronies maintained the orgiastic tradition of the Brotherhood. Their 'private devotions' were invariably attended by large number of 'nuns', and they consumed considerable quantities of wine. When Potter died, at the age of forty, surgeons discovered that his liver was almost completely decayed.

Wilkes had by now obtained election to the House of Commons, but he devoted more time and energy to pursuing women and fleeing creditors than to his parliamentary duties. Potter's place in his affections was filled by Charles Churchill, the brilliant poet who by this time had abandoned both his wife and a church career, had published his superb satire, *The Rosciad*, and been enthusiastically taken up by London society. His company enlivened many a meeting of the Order but most of his visits to Medmenham were spent in the company of Wilkes, Bacchus and Cupid.

Whatever feats of debauchery Wilkes and his friends achieved were far exceeded by Lord Liverpool and his associates, who were determined to push the principle of *Fay ce que voudras* to its uttermost limits. Canon Ermine was probably England's leading expert on witchcraft and the black arts. He donated several books on necromancy to the library at Medmenham from his own extensive collection. Yet he could not rest content with the vicarious pleasure derived from ancient writings. He used the chapel at Medmenham or, more frequently, Wycombe's subterranean temple, to recreate the ceremonies they described. In these arcane pursuits he was avidly assisted by Liverpool, Groom, Vesey, Laurie and others, who called themselves the 'Coven'.

When asked whether he believed in the powers of darkness evoked in the Coven's ceremonies, Ermine would hotly reject the suggestion. 'Superstitious nonsense!' he once protested to me. 'But many simple folk still believe it. You'll remember the Osborne case, I'll be bound.'

I certainly did remember the scandalous events that had taken place not twenty miles away at Tring scarcely a decade before. An elderly couple by the name of Osborne had been denounced as witches by their neighbours and submitted to the ancient barbarous ordeal of 'ducking', with fatal consequences. The ringleader of the mob had been hung for that, but the simple local folk had been united in their support for the condemned man and it had taken two troops of horseguards to ensure his safe transfer to the place of execution.

'As long as such ignorance exists,' Ermine insisted, 'we've a Christian duty to combat it. To do that we have to understand it.'

I thought his arguments specious then, and I was confirmed in my opinion when, by invitation, I attended one of the Coven's rituals. I had not been alone in expressing my anxieties, to allay which Liverpool suggested others of the Order might like to be present at one of his little ceremonies. Sandwich, Churchill and I accordingly presented ourselves on the day in question.

It was a warm summer's evening in 1761. Liverpool and Laurie arrived at Medmenham bringing with them in their carriage six boys and girls aged, I suppose, between seven and twelve, and a small puppy. The children had been cleaned up and dressed in fresh linen but, as I was told, they were waifs collected that morning from the streets of the city. When I asked the reason for the young people's presence Laurie replied with words that betrayed his Calvinist upbringing. 'Children are Satan's own wards and must be purged of evil.'

The members of the Coven assembled and were particularly solicitous of their wide-eyed charges. Liverpool was to be seen waddling around the grounds and pointing out Medmenham's attractions with the ebony cane topped with a silver skull which he always carried. Well may the children have thought they had been conveyed to paradise. Their world was one of backstreets and waterfront hovels, where they filled their bellies with whatever they could find or steal and had nothing to look forward to but vagrancy, prostitution and the triple tree.* Now here they were with lawns to run on, trees to climb, flowers to smell and a supper such as they could never even have dreamed of. I own I was much affected to see them cramming food into their laughing mouths as though it might escape if it was suffered a moment longer to lie on the plate.

When we robed and filed into the chapel we discovered the air thick with cloying incense. A pentacle had been inscribed upon the floor around the altar, which was draped in black and had an upside-down cross in its centre. The members of the coven formed a circle round the altar and drew the children into it. Various incantations took place and then goblets were handed to the youngsters to drink. With sudden alarm I recalled the scene in the Wycombe labyrinth and the pallid corpse of Meg Warrener. I was certain that these chalices were drugged and watched anxiously as the children sipped them cautiously and were urged by their elders to drain them. I saw the boys and girls

* gallows

become drowsy and sway upon their feet but nothing worse seemed to befall them. More incantations and parodies of Christian prayers followed. Then someone placed the puppy, now limp and insensible, upon the altar. The eldest child, a boy of about twelve, was brought forward and handed a jewelled dagger. Liverpool guided and steadied the lad's hand to the dog's throat while Laurie was ready to catch the blood in a silver dish. The children stood, eyes dilated and fixed on this barbaric rite. The blood was transferred to a flagon. Lifting it above his head, Liverpool invoked the name of Lucifer. Then the contents of the pitcher were mingled with wine and poured into a large goblet which was passed round the circle for all to drink.

The celebrants filed out with their charges. The rest of us were glad to follow and to gain the fresh, clean air of the garden. Minutes later Sandwich, Churchill and I stood on the terrace and watched as the members of the Coven strolled down the lawn with their young guests, some of whom were still unsteady on their feet. We watched them board the gondola and glide across the water to Cupid's Isle.

Sandwich removed his wig and scratched his head. 'Surely they cannot be . . .'

Churchill glared at him. 'Certain they can, my lord. Don't be naïve. They're vile and they must be stopped!'

'*Fay ce que voudras*,' I whispered, finding the words difficult to form.

The poet turned angrily. He was a tall, heavily built man possessed by the most extreme passions. 'Rabelais never meant that, I'll warrant. Nor did our Abbot. He must hear of this. Whitehead, you must tell him.'

I did so, the following day.

'Yes, I have heard as much,' Dashwood replied. 'But what can I . . .?' He shrugged.

I persisted. 'We have never knowingly sanctioned anything against the law.'

'Well, if Liverpool and his coterie are discreet . . .'

'This sort of thing will out. Never doubt it. And there's no sympathy for this sort of behaviour. I was passing Tyburn last week when those two sodomites went for the morning drop. You should have seen the screaming crowd – mostly women. If they'd broken through the troops they'd have spared the hangman a job.'

Dashwood tuned away, angry and impatient. 'Are we to care for what the rabble thinks? Well, we'll talk of this again at a more convenient time.'

That was as much as I could get from him. When it became clear that our leader would do nothing, other members of the Order took initiatives of their own. Churchill could not keep silent. He expressed his feelings in a poem that enjoyed great popularity. It attacked all forms of sexual perversion.

Women are kept for nothing but the breed;
For pleasure we must have a Ganymede,
A fine, fresh Hylas, a delicious boy.
To serve our purposes of beastly joy . . .

The gallant, seeking whom he may o'erpower,
Drags hapless children to his filthy bower . . .

Though if the Law sleeps, and, through the care they take
To drug her well, may never more awake;
Born in such times, nor with that patience cursed
Which saints may boast of, I must speak, or burst.

Sandwich devised a different stratagem for exposing what he called the 'false brethren'. He thought to shame them into leaving the Order. His plan badly, and disastrously, miscarried.

The studios of Chiltern-Cotswold Television (CCTV) were located in a converted nineteenth-century warehouse on the north side of Cheltenham. Catherine arrived on time, crossed a wide foyer which had a glass-case centrepiece displaying an array of programme awards, and presented herself at a desk where a very young receptionist gave her a professional smile and a breathless, 'Take-a-seat-someone-will-be-down-in-a-moment'.

The someone was a slender brunette sheathed in tight-fitting pink trousers and a black and pink polka-dotted blouse. 'Hi, I'm Cindy.' Another professional smile. 'Deb has someone with her right now. She thought you might like to have a look around for a few minutes.'

Catherine was impressed by the amount of studio space available. As well as the one designated for the daily round of news and current affairs programmes, and a couple of small interview studios, the building housed two large auditoriums, one of which was equipped with several rows of seats and the other swarming with men and women moving scenery, furniture and props.

'I didn't think regional companies made many of their own programmes these days,' Catherine observed.

Her guide motioned her towards the lift and pressed the call button. 'We have a pretty good networking record and we hire facilities to private production companies but, of course, being owned by CTTV means that we do a lot of work for our American partners.'

'CTTV?'

'Cotswold-Transatlantic Television. We're one of the biggest international companies. That gives us a lot of clout in the co-production stakes. That's where the megabucks are these days.'

They entered the lift and Cindy pressed the top button.

As they glided towards the fifth floor Catherine asked, 'Is Deb on the board of CTTV?'

'Deb? Hey, talk about human dynamo!' The PA's eyes glinted with heroine-worship. 'I just don't know how she does it. She's production chief here *and* a major force in the parent company *and* she still manages to do some hands-on production. She's making your programme; she regards the Chipping Sneddon festival as very much her baby. Here we are.'

They emerged into a large open-plan office area where scores of men and women sat in roofless cubicles operating computer terminals or talking into telephones.

'You'd better follow me through the warren.' Cindy led the way along a circuitous route between the desks.

They reached a row of three doors at the far end of the room and Cindy opened the one on the right. 'Do you mind waiting in my office a moment. I'll just check that Deb is free.' She tapped on an internal door and walked into the neighbouring room.

Catherine was immediately aware of a loud voice – a voice that was male, American and angry.

'. . . in writing, signed and witnessed and drawn up by one of the smartest lawyers, on the East Coast. If you try to wriggle out . . .'

'I'm sorry, Deb. I didn't realize . . .' Cindy backed out of the office.

She was hurriedly pulling the door to when the man barked, 'OK, I'm going, Remember what I said, Deb. We've all got too much riding on this deal. Just make sure you deliver.'

Catherine heard the outer door open. She was still standing by the part-open door of Cindy's office. She glanced out and saw a bulky figure making its way through the maze of work stations. It turned a corner and Catherine had a brief glimpse of the man's face. Brief but sufficient. Now what, she wondered, was Professor Zangster doing in the offices of CCTV, and what was bugging him?

If Deb Masquerier was ruffled she did not show it as she greeted Catherine moments later. 'Thank you so much for coming over. Sorry to keep you waiting.'

'Disgruntled viewer?' Catherine nodded towards the outer door.

Deb could not prevent a slight flicker of the eyebrow. Then she laughed. 'Oh, George? He's one of our American directors. I'm afraid he tends to have a short fuse. Now, Catherine, we're very excited about these young artists of yours. What we'd like is a short piece with each of them in their ateliers. You know, "Struggling geniuses in their own environment", that sort of thing. Then when we've edited the films we'll use them as the basis for a studio interview with you. How does that sound?'

They spent several minutes discussing technical details. Then Catherine tried some probes. 'I understand you and Teddy Everton are the prime movers of the Chipping Sneddon festival?'

Lady Masquerier laughed her gravelly laugh. 'Darling, you've met Teddy. You know what a great enthusiast he is. He could persuade the Pope to invest in a condom factory. When Teddy gets an idea – watch out! Well, he decided that he could raise a heap of cash for his pet charities by putting a certain quiet market town on the map. That was that. The good people of Chipping Sneddon had little say in the matter. No, it was Teddy, not me, who set this particular snowball rolling.'

'From what I was hearing in the town you're being altogether too modest.'

Deb waved a hand dismissively. 'Good PR, darling, good PR. CCTV needs viewer loyalty. The best way to get it is to persuade the people in the area we cover that we care about them. Falling in with Teddy's plans gives us some good local programming every year and it carries a couple of bonuses: it regularly demonstrates our commitment to "Middle England" and it enables us to parade our sponsorship of Downham Homes without appearing to blow our own trumpet.'

'Have you known Teddy long?'

'He and Evelyn go quite a long way back. I've only really got to know him since the festival started. Then, when Evelyn was invited to St Mary's to dig them out of their financial hole, Teddy was the obvious person to bring in.'

Catherine was puzzled. 'In what way?'

'Oh, he's a brilliant fund-raiser. Behind that flabby exterior there beats a well-oiled cash register.'

'It doesn't sound as though you altogether like him.'

Deb rose abruptly. 'Darling, I'm not going to say a bad word about him. It wouldn't do to upset the goose that lays the golden eggs. Well,' she held out her hand, 'it's been lovely to see you again. Do give me or Cindy a ring if there's any query. Not that there will be. I'm sure the programme will go terribly well. Remember me to your husband.'

Catherine stood but did not move towards the door. Deb had made no reference to the tragic events at St Mary's. She decided to take the initiative. 'My regards to Evelyn. Do tell him how very sorry we were to hear about Stuart Longton's death.' She paused. 'And, of course, the disappearance of those papers. It must have made life very difficult.'

Lady Masquerier looked up sharply. 'Difficult? What do you mean?'

'I mean media people swarming all over the place, demanding statements, pestering the students and staff – that sort of thing.'

Deb made light of it. 'Yes, well, it's a chastening experience to be on the wrong end of a camera for a change. Goodbye.'

'Hi, darling! Deb Masquerier sends her regards. What are you doing? Taking up origami?' Catherine walked into the sitting room to find her husband in the middle of the sofa surrounded by newspapers.

'Hi!' Tim did not look up from his reading. 'No, just checking something.'

'Do you want to tell me what?'

'Mmn!'

Catherine gave up and walked through to the kitchen. 'Where are the boys?' she called out.

Silence.

She put her head back round the door. 'I said, "Where are the boys?"'

'What? Oh, being bathed.' Tim tossed the *Daily Express* aside and picked up the next paper from the pile on the seat beside him.

Catherine made two mugs of coffee and brought them through. She cleared some of the debris and sat beside Tim. 'Any chance of getting more than a monosyllable out of you?'

This time he did look up. 'Sorry, darling. I just want to finish off reading through these reports in this morning's press.'

'What are you looking for?'

'What I am looking for I am not finding. And that's interesting.'

Catherine sipped the black liquid. 'Well I found out some interesting things, too. When you're not busy perhaps I'll tell you.' She stood up. 'I'll put the supper on. Then I'm going to take a shower. Then I'm going to tuck the boys in. After that, I'm all yours. That is, if you can spare me a few minutes.'

Moments later Tim followed her into the kitchen. 'OK, you win.' He pinned her against the fridge and kissed her. 'Who's going to bat first?'

'You tell me your news while I do the salad.'

'Right. I had a phone call on my way up to London this morning.' He reported his conversation with Emma's father.

Catherine was expertly chopping walnuts, apples and celery. 'Well, I suppose you can't blame him for being worried about her. Cut and wash the lettuce, would you?'

'He was worried, all right, but not about Emma. He's desperate to avoid scandal.' Tim severed crisp green leaves and held them under the tap.

'But surely the publicity Emma attracted by sticking up for her friend is very positive?'

'Yes, he's been playing the chip-off-the-old-block card for all he's worth in his own press interviews.'

'So?'

'So what's bothering him is that he doesn't know what we're up to. Emma wouldn't tell him and when he realized I wasn't going to spill the beans he got very nasty. I reckon he knows or suspects that we could stumble onto something extremely embarrassing. So embarrassing that he's determined to distance himself from it.'

'Are you sure you're not exaggerating? Pass the mayonnaise and cream, will you?'

Tim took the items from the fridge. 'You didn't hear him having hysterics down the phone line. He's desperate to spirit Emma away to France and to stop me doing whatever it is he suspects that I'm doing. No, he's worried all right. He's in a very vulnerable position; well up the political ladder and still young enough to go higher. Ministers of the Crown don't make vicious threats unless they're seriously rattled.'

Catherine arranged the lettuce in a bowl and piled the other mixed ingredients into the centre. 'But how could the troubles at St Mary's possibly affect him?'

'I haven't a clue, but he certainly knows more than he's letting on about the Hellfire Papers.'

'Oh? What did he say about them?'

'He referred to them as the Whitehead-Dyer Papers.'

'What's wrong with that? That's their proper name.'

'But only we and the Masqueriers are supposed to know that. I thought perhaps Finsley-Kerr might have read the name in one of the newspapers. That's why I wanted to go through all the dailies. None of them has anything to say about Whitehead-Dyer. It's pretty obvious that all the reporters have written their copy using the same press handout. The college and the police are playing their cards close to their chest. It seems that the junior minister has a definite interest in these fake memoirs.'

'The pitch is getting pretty crowded with players.'

'Isn't it just? Now, tell me what you've been up to.'

Catherine covered the bowl with clingfilm and put it on a low shelf in the fridge. She leaned against the door. 'Well, I think I've established that the Masqueriers don't associate us with the missing papers and that's a heck of a weight off my mind.'

'Lady M made no attempt to quiz you about them?'

'No, I had to raise the subject. When I did she tried hard not to react but she's obviously bothered about the disappearance.'

'How does she feel about Stuart's death?'

'Irritated. She didn't say so of course, but her body language yelled out that it was "awfully bad form" for fellows to get themselves murdered on college property.'

'No sign of a guilty conscience?'

'Not unless she's a lot better actress than I give her credit for. But you haven't heard the best bit yet. Guess who I saw at CCTV?'

Tim grinned. 'Surprise me.'

'Professor Joseph Nicodemus Zangster.'

'Zangster? I assumed he had finished his course of lectures long ago and returned to the States. Still, there's no reason why he shouldn't be calling on his friend in her place of employ.'

Catherine smiled triumphantly. 'But why should he and Deb have a blazing row and why should she try to cover up the fact that he had visited her?' Catherine reported on the scraps of conversation she had overheard and Lady M's subsequent attempt to throw her off the scent.

Tim sat down at the table, puzzled and intrigued. 'So what interpretation do you put on that little contretemps?'

'I was thinking about it coming back in the car. I couldn't make much sense of it till I remembered something Stuart Longton said to me about Zangster back in January. He was telling me that the professor had come over to collect an honorary degree and that that wasn't the only thing he might pick up.'

'Meaning?'

'Stuart didn't elaborate and that was, of course, before we knew anything about the Hellfire Papers.'

'But you think he might have had them in mind?'

'Well it fits into a very interesting theory. Suppose Sir Evelyn had already done a deal with Zangster to sell the Hellfire Papers to Princeton. We know he wants to raise all the money he can for St Mary's and Stuart was pretty bitchy about him using the rescue of the college's finances to further his own ambition.'

'If that was the gameplan, I can understand Zangster being very disappointed at the papers going missing, but that's no reason for him to storm over to Cheltenham and get nasty with Lady M.'

'Unless he suspected the Masqueriers of a double-cross. Supposing he picked up a paper this morning and saw that the Whitehead-Dyer documents had been stolen. And supposing he thought, "Stolen my eye! These slippery limeys have found another buyer." Wouldn't he drop everything in order to find out what's going on? He was certainly accusing Deb of trying to wriggle out of some important commitment.'

'But why go to her? Why not tackle Sir Evelyn directly?'

'I thought of that. That's why I stopped en route to make a phone call to Cambridge. Masquerier left early this morning for a conference in Zurich. He's not due back till Sunday.'

Tim sat thoughtfully for a few moments. 'It's certainly a good working theory, but does it get us any closer to Longton's murderer?'

'Well, if Stuart had got wind of the Zangster deal and strongly disapproved of it, that would explain why he sent the papers here. He wanted to get them out of the Master's clutches. He planned to leave Cambridge for a few days himself and work out a scheme to keep the Hellfire Papers in this country. That evening Masquerier went to his rooms demanding to see the papers—'

The sound of tiny voices in the corridor interrupted the elaboration of Catherine's theory. She moved swiftly to the dining-room door. 'I'm going to grab that shower. You're on parent duty.' She exited swiftly stage left as two small boys in night attire entered stage right shepherded by their nanny.

The children successfully dominated the next hour or so.

277

They were both wide awake and wanting Mummy and Daddy, whom they had not seen all day. So as a special treat they were allowed to stay up for supper. Eventually they were tucked up and asleep. Then, on the spur of the moment, Tim said, 'Let's go out for a drink.' Tina, George Martin's bookish younger daughter, was always happy to come up from the lodge to babysit and they left her ensconced in the dining room with a pile of homework.

Because it was a warm, still evening with the scent of haymaking in the air, the Lacys decided to walk the two miles into Little Farrans. The Crown and Anvil was a modest hostelry which had stood beside the bridge almost as long as Farrans Court had occupied its nearby hollow. Both buildings had been constructed from the stone transported in flat-bottomed barges when the Merebrook was a wider and deeper river. Nor was that the only link between them. The inn's name commemorated the coat of arms of the Cranvilles, who had once been royal farriers to Edward IV, had become major landowners under the Tudors, and had occupied Farrans Court for four-and-a-half centuries.

Tim and Catherine took their drinks into the garden and sat at a table facing the river and the woods which climbed steeply up the opposite bank. They had spoken little during the walk and neither of them wanted to break the spell of tranquillity and timelessness. Eventually it was raucous cheering bursting through the open doorway of the public bar, where a darts match was in progress, which momentarily shattered the peace.

Tim took a draught of bitter and set down his glass. 'You didn't finish expounding your theory about Stuart Longton's murder.'

Catherine sighed. 'Oh, I don't know. It all looked so obvious when I first thought about it. Now the whole thing seems so sordid and bizarre.'

'Tell me anyway.'

'Well, as I said, it just seemed to me that if Stuart found out what Sir Evelyn was planning, that would explain why he wanted to get the papers out of Cambridge so quickly. Then, if the Master went to see him to ask for them there could well be a violent row. Maybe Stuart accused him of plotting to sell off college property.'

'Yes.' Tim stared across at the darkening belt of trees reflected in the rippleless water. 'It's possible. Of course, there's something else Longton might have said that would have rattled him even more.'

'What's that?'

'Well, knowing how heartily he despised this philistine interloper from the kingdom of Mammon, I can just imagine him looking at Masquerier with that sardonic smile of his and saying, "My dear Master, the fact of the matter is that these Whitehead-Dyer Papers are hopeless fakes." '

Catherine ran a finger down the cloud of condensation on her glass of chilled wine. 'That would certainly provide a motive for murder. He wouldn't want Stuart blabbing. That would screw up his deal with Zangster.' She sipped the sancerre. 'What happens now?'

Tim shrugged. 'I don't know. Nothing probably. All we have is a theory we can't possibly substantiate. Imagine what Inspector Tibbs would say if we suggested he should arrest the esteemed Master of a Cambridge college on the basis of a hunch.'

'But we can't let him get away with it?'

'Why not? A few days ago you wanted us to pull out of the whole business.'

'A lot's happened in a few days. When I think of Stuart and what Gavin and Emma have been through and then the smug Masqueriers . . . God! It makes me so angry!'

'I know how you feel, but what can we do? The devil of it is that we actually hold the trump card. Yet I'm damned if I can see how to play it.'

Catherine drained her glass. 'Then let's go home and sleep on it.'

They walked back hand-in-hand along the deep lane over Stonegallows Top, by the light of a half moon. They cut across their own meadow to reach the drive at an oblique angle and arrived, relaxed and laughing, at the front of Farrans Court.

That was when they saw the car.

It was in shadow but there was no mistaking the Alvis's classic outline.

Tim groaned. 'Oh, hell! What now?'

Tina met them at the front door of the flat flushed with embarrassment and anxiety. 'There's two people in the sitting room,' she whispered. 'I told them you were out but they said they'd wait. They were terribly pushy – well, the man was – and I didn't know what to do. I hope I haven't done anything wrong.'

Tim reassured her. 'That's OK, Tina. I know these people. You'd better collect your things and get off home. Thanks for holding the fort.' He opened the door on the left and was confronted with a silence that was tangible.

John Finsley-Kerr and his daughter were sitting with as much distance as possible between them. The minister, with

280

feigned nonchalance, was going through a small pile of files. Emma sat with red-rimmed eyes, fixing her father with a glare that would have shrivelled anyone less thick-skinned.

She jumped to her feet as the Lacys walked in and rushed across to them. 'Tim, Catherine, I'm so sorry about this. It was his idea. I couldn't stop him coming, so I thought I'd better come with him.'

The junior minister at the Heritage Department stood up. 'I add my apologies to my daughter's. But we really must talk.'

III

DAWN

Let them fly far, and skulk from place to place,
Not daring to meet Manhood face to face,
Their steps I'll track, nor yield them one retreat
Where they may hide their heads or rest their feet,
Till God in wrath shall let his vengeance fall,
And make a great example of them all.

– Charles Churchill, *The Times*

CHAPTER 14

'And just what is it that we must talk about?' Tim advanced to the centre of the room.

The two men stood a few feet apart, eyeing each other like boxers at the beginning of a bout.

Finsley-Kerr was well versed in the politician's art of not answering questions. 'I'm afraid I was a bit short with you on the phone this morning. I'm sorry. I was worried that you might be involving my daughter in something . . .' He broke off, searching for the right word.

'Politically embarrassing?'

'I was going to say potentially dangerous. Emma has a penchant for getting herself into hot water. When neither of you would be open with me I became very worried. Unfortunately, I was down to answer questions in the House this afternoon. Then I had to see a constituency delegation. As soon as I could get away I caught the first available Cambridge train. Regrettably, Emma still refused to confide in me. She seems to repose more trust in you than in her own father.'

Emma turned on him. 'I stopped trusting you the day you swapped Mummy for a bimbo young enough to be my sister.'

'Emmy, believe me, I'm only trying to protect you.'

She opened her mouth to retort but Catherine took her firmly by the shoulder and guided her to the sofa.

Tim began to get the glimmerings of an idea about Finsley-Kerr's involvement. He said, 'I'm having a little difficulty myself in summoning up much trust in your motives for rushing down here at this hour. Call me an old cynic, but isn't there a cabinet reshuffle due in a few weeks' time? Is it possible that that and your unexpected visit here are not altogether unrelated?'

Finsley-Kerr controlled his anger. 'Look, Lacy, I won't beat about the bush. I want to know what's happened to the papers that were stolen from St Mary's House.'

'Why?'

'I'm not in a position to say.'

'In that case my lips are sealed, too.'

'Damn it all, man!' The minister was close to breaking point. 'There's much more at stake here than you realize.'

Tim thought, 'I'll bet there is. But what?' He surveyed the man before him: excellent suit, somewhat dishevelled; club tie loose enough to show the top shirt button; greying hair in dire need of a brush; the shadow of beard beginning to appear; the lines beneath the eyes; the nervous hands. Whatever was troubling the junior minister was troubling him very deeply. Tim was determined to find out what it was. He said, 'We seem to be in a trading situation. Would you like to take this further in private?'

Finsley-Kerr nodded. Tim led the way down to his office

in what had once been the house's stable complex. He settled his guest in a chair and went to the cupboard behind his desk. 'Drink?'

The politician shook his head.

'Suit yourself.' Tim poured himself a generous measure of his favourite armagnac.

The other man made a bid for the initiative. 'Look, it's late. I hope we can avoid any more verbal fencing. Do you know where the Whitehead-Dyer Papers are?'

'You're right. It is late.' Tim sat at his desk and picked up the phone. 'Excuse me a moment.' He pressed a single number. 'Darling, it's just occurred to me that we can't possibly expect our guests to set out again tonight. Could you sort out beds for them? Good . . . Well, not long, I hope.' He put the receiver down and walked across the room. He sat facing Finsley-Kerr. 'Right, Minister, suppose you start by explaining why you're so interested in these papers that you come haring all the way over here on the offchance that I might know something about them.'

The politician sighed. 'Very well, but you must realize that what I'm going to tell you is highly confidential. It must not go beyond these four walls.'

Tim nodded. 'Understood.'

'There's not a great deal to it, in fact.' He paused, collecting his thoughts. 'At the end of last year, Sir Evelyn Masquerier contacted me. He told me that St Mary's was about to receive some very important and valuable historical papers. College finances being as they were, he thought that there was a distinct possibility that they might have to sell them. Because of their importance, he was concerned that they should stay in this country. He asked me if my department could help to ensure that they were acquired for a national collection. It was a perfectly proper suggestion and I was happy to set some exploratory negotiations in motion. Of course, discretion was vital. It still is – all the more so now that the media have cottoned on to the existence of these documents.'

'That's it?' Tim gazed across the rim of his glass as he savoured the burnt-sugary aroma.

Finsley-Kerr levelly returned the stare. 'Yes.'

Tim laughed. 'I think that's what's called, in parliamentary parlance, being economical with the truth.'

'That's an outrageous—'

Tim ignored the bluster. 'I doubt whether it would come as a complete surprise to you to learn that Masquerier has already made a deal to sell the Whitehead-Dyer Papers to an American university.' It was a bluff. Would it work? Tim watched the other man's reaction closely.

Finsley-Kerr stiffened. 'How—' He recovered quietly. 'What Sir Evelyn decides to do with college property is entirely his own affair.'

'In that case why on earth should it matter to you that the papers have gone missing? No, Minister, I smell conspiracy.' Encouraged by the other man's silence, Tim went on, slowly, assembling the details in his mind as he spoke. 'It goes something like this. Masquerier is a very clever financier. He has an asset and he wants to maximize its value. How best to do that? Encourage rival buyers. Better still, attract at least one overseas bid, then leak the news to the heritage lobby. That should up the ante. Now, it would be enormously valuable to have the advice and help of someone on the inside; someone who knows all the top people in the museum world; someone with access to public funds; someone who could oil the bureaucratic wheels if it became necessary to get an export permit. Who better than his old friend John, that up-and-coming chap at the Department of Heritage? He'd help out with a word or two in the right quarters. Especially if there was something in it for him. Am I in the right neck of the woods, Minister?'

Finsley-Kerr attempted a self-assured sneer. 'You spin a very good yarn, Lacy. But of course that's all it is, and if you breathed a word of it to anyone else I'd have a slander writ out against you within hours.'

Tim shrugged. 'Fiction or fact, it doesn't really matter, does it? A word to a few press chums of mine and you'd be facing a nasty scandal. Perhaps in normal times that wouldn't matter too much. But after the run of bad luck this government's had, one more embarrassment at the moment might be considered a bridge too far. You could certainly say goodbye to a seat at the top table. You might even be invited to – what's the expression? – consider your position.'

'Oh, this is preposterous!'

'Is it? In that case, why all this urgent rushing round the country? Why is it so important to you where the Whitehead-Dyer Papers are? The way I see it, their disappearance really set the cat among the pigeons. Not only did it jeopardize the whole plan, it made the potential customers suspicious. If the papers don't turn up soon, someone might start asking awkward questions. Once that happens, it's only a matter of time before the ever-alert ears of the media start quivering.'

'May I change my mind about that drink?'

Tim nodded. 'Help yourself.'

Finsley-Kerr took his time pouring a large scotch and returning to his seat. He used the interval to recover his composure. 'I'm perfectly happy to admit that I have been advising Sir Evelyn about the disposal of the papers – export regulations, that sort of thing. That's my job, and I've no reason to be ashamed of anything that has passed between my department and Cambridge. But I wonder if you can say the same? You brought the papers back to England and while they were in your possession there were two attempts to steal them. Or so you say. We only have your word for it. Now there's been a third, successful attempt. And when I try to find out whether you know anything you clam up completely. Now, that's what I call *really* suspicious.'

'We could go on making accusations and counter-accusations all night and be none the wiser by morning.'

'Agreed. You spoke about trading information. Suppose you tell me what you know?'

Tim paused and drained his glass, with slow relish. Then: 'OK. I've got bad news and bad news. Which would you like first?'

'Get on with it, man!'

'Very well. The first thing is that I don't know where the Whitehead-Dyer Papers are.'

'You're lying!' The politician snapped the words out.

'Tut, tut! Unparliamentary language, Minister. I assure you that that is absolutely true. At this moment I could not take you to wherever these papers are. But the second piece of information is that you probably wouldn't be interested in them anyway. You see, they're fakes.'

'What! How do you know?'

Tim got up to refill his glass. He chose his words with

care. 'Longton examined the papers. He worked out that there was something wrong with them. I think that's why he was killed. Unfortunately for the murderer, Longton had already confided in me. That explains my involvement in the business.'

The minister sat back, shaken and trying not to show it. 'Are you being absolutely straight with me?'

'Absolutely is a very unyielding word. Let's say I'm being as straight with you as you are with me. What I've told you is substantially true. I guess that what you've told me is substantially true. That makes us all square.'

'God, what a mess!'

'That's an understatement. Aren't you missing the point?'

'What do you mean?'

'Everyone's concerned about these vanished papers. No one seems to be very bothered that one, possibly two men have been brutally killed over them.'

'Are you suggesting that the Dean – whatsisname – Vare was murdered, too?'

'I've got an open mind on that. What I do know is that someone wants the Hellfire Papers and will stop at nothing to get hold of them. Now, who do you think that can be?'

'I haven't the faintest—'

'Oh, come on! You must have a good brain to get as far as you have. For God's sake, use it! Look, if I'm right, Longton was struck with a blunt instrument because he'd discovered that the Hellfire Papers were forgeries and also, perhaps, because he'd got wind of your "negotiations". So, who would want to silence him?'

'I suppose, whoever wanted the sale of the papers to go ahead without a hitch.'

'That's how I see it. So, who was in on the deal?'

Finsley-Kerr shrugged. 'I don't know who Sir Evelyn talked to. We only discussed things over the phone. You're not seriously suggesting that Sir Evelyn or I . . . My God! You are suggesting that!'

'I'm not suggesting anything that the police would not suggest if they were in possession of all the facts. I hope you have an alibi for the evening in question.'

'Yes, of course I have. There have been several late sessions in the House recently. I must have been either in the chamber or in my office.'

'Then, as far as we know, that only leaves . . .'

'Oh, that's ridiculous! To imagine Sir Evelyn . . . No, it's unthinkable. Anyway, even if Sir Evelyn did kill Longton and got hold of the papers, why would he put it about that they'd been stolen?'

'Because he didn't get hold of them. I think he went to Longton's rooms for a perfectly amicable chat about the Hellfire Papers. He genuinely wanted to know what Longton thought about them. It was important that he should authenticate them. Longton, of course, hated the Master's guts. It must have given him immense pleasure to tell him that his precious papers were duds. I can imagine him gloating insufferably. Then, for good measure, he added that he knew about Masquerier's schemes to sell the papers. Perhaps he threatened to expose him, to teach him a lesson about meddling in matters best left to academics. They had a row. Masquerier got violent. He picked up something heavy before he realized what he was doing and lashed out with it. Suddenly Longton is lying dead on the carpet. What to do? Grab the papers, try to make Stuart's death look like suicide and get away. Only he can't find the papers because they're not there. He ransacks the place – but no luck. Over the next few days he sweats. He has the rival bidders breathing down his neck. He hopes that the police will turn up the papers without him having to say anything. When they don't, he reports the theft. He's desperate enough to let slip the dogs of law in pursuit of the precious manuscripts.'

Finsley-Kerr drained his glass. Tim could see him wavering over his response. At last he shook his head emphatically. 'No, Lacy, it won't do. As I remarked earlier, you spin a good yarn, but that's all it is.'

Tim shrugged. 'Well, perhaps the police will believe it.'

That did shake his guest. 'The police! Surely you're not going to the police with this extraordinary concoction!'

'Minister, surely you're not encouraging a good citizen to withhold evidence?'

'But you don't have any evidence!'

'On the contrary. I have the information Longton gave me on the day he died.'

'And why should the police take your word for it?'

'Because I can tell them how to get hold of the missing papers.'

'What!' Finsley-Kerr almost choked over his whisky. 'But you said—'

'I said I didn't know where the papers were. That was true. But I do know what Longton did with them. He told me.'

'Why haven't you reported this to the police before?'

'Just checking a few details.'

'And that's what you've got Emma mixed up in?'

'She offered to help. You may find this difficult to understand, but she is a dedicated idealist. Like me, she has a low opinion of people who stoop to chicanery and murder.'

The politician slumped further into his chair. Tim watched him carefully, wondering whether he was now ready to swallow the concoction of half-truth and invention he had knocked together over the last half hour. Would Finsley-Kerr call the bluff? The man had a reputation for outfacing the Opposition across the floor of the Commons and defending indefensible policies against persistent television interviewers. There could be no doubt that he who was stalwart in defence of party interest would do whatever was necessary to safeguard his own position.

'Look here, Lacy, you know what will happen if the police pull Sir Evelyn in for questioning. The dirt-hounds of the press will go sniffing around every tree in the wood. That won't help any of us.'

'Are you saying that we mustn't rock the establishment boat, even if it means someone getting away with murder?'

'I'm saying it will be better for all concerned if I have a quiet word with Sir Evelyn. If he is unable to answer the allegations you are making – allegations which, I must say, still strike me as absurd – I'm sure he will do whatever is necessary.'

Tim laughed. 'Leaving the disgraced officer with a revolver and a single bullet to do the right thing for the honour of the regiment?'

The politician stiffened. 'There's a lot to be said for old-fashioned values and qualities like loyalty and trust.'

'I can't stop you having a tête-à-tête with Masquerier, but if you're going to sup with the devil be sure to use a long spoon. Look at what happened to the last man who had "a quiet word" with the Master of St Mary's House.'

'Now you're being melodramatic!'

Tim replied in a quiet, slow, level voice. 'One of the more important of the many differences between you and me is that you have never killed a man. I have and I can tell you that, contrary to popular opinion, it is remarkably easy, given the necessary emotional stimulus. You might be afflicted afterwards with nightmares and gut-twisting remorse, but not at the time. At the time, you do what you believe is necessary. Now, if you want to face Masquerier with these suspicions that's your affair. Just be very careful, that's all.'

Finsley-Kerr said sulkily, 'Have you got a better idea?'

Tim stood and stretched wearily. 'Yes, I think so. Leave Masquerier to me. I need a little more time to finish getting the evidence together. I shall be seeing him quite casually in a week or so at some arts festival that Catherine's got involved in. I'll find an opportunity for a private chat and I'll make sure the local constabulary aren't far away. It'll all be very discreet. I can't promise that your name will be kept out of things; that will be up to Masquerier and his lawyers. But at least you'll have a few days to put whatever distance you can between you and this sordid business.' Before Finsley-Kerr could reply, Tim went on. 'Right now, I'm knackered and I must show you to your bed.'

He motioned his guest towards the door.

Half an hour later he lay on his back beside Catherine, staring up at the bedroom ceiling. His body was weary but his mind was in overdrive.

'I hope to God our theory's right. I have just made a very influential enemy. I'd hate to think it was all for nothing.'

CHAPTER 15

The Finsley-Kerrs left early on Friday, but not before Emma had grabbed Tim for another heart-to-heart. They walked on the dew-covered lawn in front of the house where the sun threw long shadows over the grass.

'Tim, I am sorry about all this.' Emma linked her arm through his. 'My father's an absolute pig. Was he completely insufferable last night?'

Tim smiled reassuringly. 'Oh, I think we reached an understanding.'

'Are you going to tell me about it?'

'No!' He replied very firmly and hurried on, smothering her protest. 'And that's not because I'm treating you like a child. Your father is right about one thing. You need to get away for a while. Somewhere where the media can't find you.'

'They're not going to be interested in me any more.'

'Don't you believe it. Very soon now this whole sordid business is going to come to a head. I don't know what'll happen. I hope it can be resolved quietly but I wouldn't put my shirt on it. Barring the breaking of some big inter-national story, I can't see the press passing up an opportu-nity to throw around as much mud as possible. I'd like you to be out of range. Now, promise me you'll disappear for a few weeks – preferably without leaving a forwarding address.'

They made their way back towards the house in silence along the line already marked out by the footprints in the dew.

Emma groaned. 'Oh, all right. I suppose I could go to—'

Tim stopped her. 'No, don't tell me. Get into the habit of not confiding in anyone. Just pack a bag and go.'

'May I come and see you again when it's all over?'

'Of course. We'd love to have you to stay when the clouds have blown away. Bring Gavin, if you like.'

'Thanks.' She squeezed his arm. 'Oh, by the way, I've got some photostats for you. That research you wanted me to do. Don't let me forget to give them to you.'

'That was quick.'

'I spent most of yesterday at the UL. Not that there was much to discover. The good guys don't get into the papers. Lord Teddy has a cuddly name and an even more cuddly reputation. I'm sure that's why my father cultivates him so assiduously. You don't reckon he's a secret dealer in stolen antiquities, using his charity work as a brilliant cover, do you?'

Tim laughed. 'I must admit I had my suspicions at one time, but if Lord Teddy turned out to be a crook it would destroy whatever vestige of faith in human nature one had left. I didn't realize he was a close friend of your father's, though.'

Emma shrugged. 'Mutual back-scratchers more than friends. My revered pater gets his lordship on to charity commissions and other quangos. In return he sits on the boards of some of Teddy's children's charities. Good for the image!'

They entered the house by a back door, went up the stairs to the flat and were assailed by the smell of frying bacon.

Lord Sandwich proposed to expose Liverpool and his confederates at the Order's spring chapter in 1762. When we filed into the chapel I immediately recognized, through the haze of incense, the black drapes and the arrangement of the altar adopted by the Coven. Sandwich, who presided at the 'black mass', had added a droll touch: instead of an inverted cross the central place on the altar was occupied by a black staff surmounted by a silver skull. Several of the brothers noted the reference and turned to Liverpool to point it out. His Lordship responded with an aloof smile but he looked much discomfited.

The ceremony proceeded and included every possible parody of necromantic rites. Sandwich and his acolytes were in fine histrionic form and kept their congregation convulsed with mirth. The ritual had two climaxes. The first was intentional. With fine bravura one of the 'high priest's' accomplices laid upon the altar what appeared, in the dim light, to be a young pig lying comatose on a silver platter. Another assistant handed Sandwich a jewelled dagger. With it he made several theatrical passes, accompanied by vivid imprecations. Then he raised the blade high above his head. As we all held our breath, he brought it down upon the sacrificial 'pig'. There was a loud explosion. Gasps and shrieks turned to laughter as we realized that the animal had in fact been some kind of air-filled bladder.

The ceremony moved on to the point at which Sandwich, arms aloft, invoked the presence of Lord Lucifer. Suddenly from close by the altar there was a loud clatter. A red-draped figure leaped into the air behind the celebrant who turned, obviously startled. Women screamed. The 'demon' leaped onto Sandwich's shoulder, gibbering angrily. The corpulent peer jumped backwards. He grabbed at his attacker. He waved his arms. He shouted, 'No! No! Great Lucifer, no! 'Twas but a jest. Spare me! Spare me! I meant no harm!'

While we all stared, knowing not whether this was a masterpiece of witty invention or some unlooked-for visitation, Wilkes stood up, bellowing with laughter. 'Nay, not Lucifer, my Lord. We call her Naomi.'

He stepped forward, grasped a cord which dangled from a collar round the creature's neck and drew her away slowly along the aisle to the chapel door. Everyone joined in the laughter as we saw that Sandwich's devil was, in reality, a small baboon dressed up in a scarlet coat and breeches. The 'black mass' ended in uproar and we all retired for supper in excellent humour.

All except Lord Sandwich. As we crowded around Wilkes, demanding to know how the trick had been managed, Sandwich stood at a distance scowling. John of Aylesbury, as he was known in the Order, explained that he had shut Naomi in a vestments chest behind the altar and fastened a string to the catch so that he could release it at a suitable moment. ''Twas not a jest against your lordship,' he called out. 'I could not know what the frightened animal would do when she was released.'

Sandwich was not mollified. 'Damned creature might have bitten me!'

'What, Naomi? Never. She's the gentlest demon imaginable.' Wilkes went over and took the outraged peer by the arm. 'Come, let us go and feast. I have a gift for you which you shall find more to your taste.'

As we drew towards the end of our meal, Wilkes stood in his place to make what he called a peace offering to 'Brother John of Sandwich'. It was a poem – *The Essay on Woman* – that was later to attain the heights of notoriety, as the bawdiest satire ever penned. It was a brilliant parody of Pope's *Essay on Man*, and whatever the public reaction later, I can testify that it was exceedingly well received on first hearing.

> Awake, my Sandwich, leave all meaner joys,
> To Charles and Bob,* those true poetic boys;
> Let us, since life can little more supply,
> Than just to kiss, to procreate, and die,
> Expatiate free o'er all the female sex,
> Born to subdue and studying to perplex . . .

Lord Sandwich appeared to take it all in good part but he was not the sort of man to forget a public humiliation. The story of the baboon was told around all the coffee houses over the next few days and the Earl was made a laughing stock. The rift between the two men grew wider. So did the fissures within the Order.

* Churchill and his friend Robert Lloyd

Whatever the effect of all this psuedo-satanism on our wider fellowship, it did warn off Liverpool, Vesey, Laurie and their friends. Some of them continued to attend our meetings but they no longer used the Order's premises for their rituals. That, at least, was a happy outcome of our spring escapade. I had read enough about the black arts to know that they were, in large measure, but a cover for all that is most bestial in humankind. The Order of St Francis never sought other than that which is natural to man and woman. We took our pleasures discreetly and by mutual agreement. The laws of the Coven were violence, torture and the corrosion of innocence. When I see educated men of our governing class submit to such laws I can almost bring myself to share Churchill's melancholy:

> Wouldst thou be safe? Society forswear,
> Fly to the desert and seek shelter there,
> Herd with the brutes. They follow Nature's plan.
> There's not one brute so dangerous as Man
> In Afric's wilds. 'Mongst them that refuge find,
> Which lust denies thee here among mankind.

Tim spent most of the weekend catching up on his neglected deskwork. But he found it difficult to concentrate on the mundane, though lucrative, routine of Lacy Security. His mind kept returning to the Hellfire Papers and the violence and deceit surrounding them. Matters were coming to a head. He sensed it. He had warned Emma about it. Yet he did not know what would happen nor could he see how to bring about the dénouement.

He went through the photocopies Emma had obtained, and had to agree with her that they amounted to very little. They provided scarcely more than an extension of Lord Teddy's entry in *Who's Who*. Edward Downham had come into a fortune at an early age, back in the sixties, but while most of his high-society contemporaries had been 'swinging', he had devoted his money and energies to more serious pursuits. As a major shareholder in a number of important companies he had boardroom responsibilities. He showed himself to be an enthusiastic director with innovative ideas and was soon in demand with forward-looking companies. But he was more interested in charity work than commerce. Involved as a student in East End boys' clubs, he had gradually extended his concerns. Because of his genuine interest and his social contacts, charities vied with each other for his patronage.

Overwork and a hushed-up personal crisis over a broken engagement had brought on a minor breakdown in the mid-seventies. It was after his recovery from that that Teddy had resigned several directorships and concentrated on charity work. In 1977 the first Downham Home had been opened as a private contribution towards solving the mounting problem of children taken into care by the social services. The number of homes had now increased to four and they were regarded by most experts as model institutions for the treatment and nurture of emotionally disturbed youngsters. The newspaper articles Emma had gathered frequently repeated the cliché nickname, 'the modern Barnardo'.

The philanthropist's activities had brought official recognition: first a knighthood then, in 1989, a life peerage.

Nowhere in the record was there any suggestion of any antiquarian interests. Lord Teddy's hobbies were listed as sailing and computers. The only suggestion of scandal had occurred in the early eighties when the warden of one of the Downham Homes had been convicted of child abuse. On that occasion Lord Teddy had personally instituted an exhaustive enquiry which had more than satisfied the police and the home office. Thankfully Tim dropped Emma's notes into the wastepaper bin. A loose end satisfactorily tied up.

It was on Monday morning that Ingrid Brunhill phoned. Her colleague had carried out certain preliminary tests and they had proved very revealing. When could Tim come over to Oxford to learn the results of her researches? Tim looked at his full diary, decided to get Sally to reschedule some appointments, and told Dr Brunhill that he could manage Tuesday afternoon.

'Don't keep me in suspense till then,' he added. 'Tell me, was your forgery theory right?'

There was a hesitation at the other end of the line. 'Partially. I'll explain tomorrow.' The line went dead.

On Tuesday afternoon Catherine travelled to Cheltenham to record the feature for Chiltern Cotswold's regional arts programme. Her only previous TV experience had been two interviews with reporters who had come to Farrans to talk to her on her own territory. She had never taken part in a studio–based programme and was rather nervous. However, the expert Cindy took her in hand. After a gin and tonic in the hospitality suite and a long chat with the show's host, Andy Craig, she soon felt at ease. Andy, as well as being professionally charming, had a genuine knowledge of contemporary movements in art. He took her to a viewing room to see the short films that had been prepared on the painters featured in the exhibition. They discussed the points they would cover in the interview. Catherine had a relaxing session in make-up then went to the studio. The programme went off very smoothly and Catherine was surprised when the ten minutes were up and Andy was saying a formal thank you to her. After the show Cindy took her to tea in the executive suite. Catherine remarked that she had rather expected to see Lady Masquerier. Her young hostess pulled a face. Deb was *utterly mortified* at missing her. She had been looking forward to directing the programme but she had had to rush to New York at short notice for an emergency board meeting. Some apparent crisis had arisen. 'Probably nothing at all, but you know how easily Americans panic.' Cindy realized her *faux pas* immediately and went scarlet. Catherine laughed. 'Yeah, we are a pretty excitable people.'

Meanwhile, Tim had driven to Oxford, where by mid-afternoon he found himself sitting in Ingrid Brunhill's rather spartan rooms, drinking a surprisingly good chablis. On the table beside him, wrapped in brown paper, lay the Hellfire Papers which, much to his relief, the Valkyrie had now returned to his custody.

Tim had come ready to do battle and insist on having the documents back. He was glad to be able to change his approach. 'Thank you very much for taking the trouble to examine these. What exactly did you discover? You said that the forgery theory was *partially* correct. What does that mean?'

Dr Brunhill stood by the window looking down into the quad, her remarkably shapeless figure clad in a tartan shirt worn outside baggy trousers. 'I think we'd better wait until Björn gets here. First-class technician but not the world's most punctual individual.' She glanced at her watch. 'I suppose when you spend all your time determining the age of artefacts to plus or minus fifty years, a few minutes one way or the other are of little consequence.'

'Björn, I presume, is your tame expert?'

She nodded but did not avert her gaze from the scene outside. 'Dr Björn Lindgren. Stockholm University. Very bright young man. He's studied and worked in Vienna and Boston. Now he's with us for a year. It's he who's done all the real work on these papers. My efforts were just . . . Ah, here he comes.' She crossed to the door and opened it.

Moments later the space was filled by a very tall, fair-haired, thirtyish man wearing shorts and an open-necked shirt. He had a cardboard box under one arm and with his other hand held a piece of equipment in a carrying case. He set down his burdens, shook hands vigorously with Tim and accepted a glass of wine.

Ingrid said, 'Mr Lacy is very anxious to hear what you've discovered, Björn.'

The young man frowned. 'It was interesting but not so difficult. The forgery is amateur. I must show you.' He spoke with little trace of an accent.

The next few minutes were occupied in unpacking and setting up Dr Lindgren's gear. It consisted of a sophisticated slide projector and a box of transparencies. Ingrid removed a picture from her wall and closed the curtains. The machine was plugged in and Björn adjusted the focus. Then the show began.

'First, here are some simple photographic enlargements. You can see that the differences are quite obvious.'

Tim concentrated on a succession of images flashed on the wall – samples of black-brown lettering on yellowish paper. They meant nothing to him. 'What exactly am I supposed to be looking for?'

Dr Lindgren patiently put the slides through again. 'Here's one example of a "t" and here's another. Do you see, now?'

Tim shook his head. 'Sorry to be thick, but no.'

'Very well.' The young man switched off the projector, added another lens attachment, switched on and readjusted the focus. 'This enables us to see the two images side by side.'

Tim peered intently. 'They still look identical, except that the one on the right is a bit fuzzy.'

'Exactly so.' Björn displayed three other pairs of letters. In every case one had a slightly blurred outline. 'Now here's another picture I took using microscopic photography. You can see exactly why the outline is less distinct. The ink has seeped into the paper.'

'Which proves that the ink is different?'

Lindgren shook his head, impatiently. 'No, no. We come to the ink later. It is the paper that is different. In the sample I worked from there were two different types of paper. Both dated from the middle years of the eighteenth century. But one type had not been written on until very much later. You see, the strands comprising the paper wear and fray over the course of time. If the paper is then written on, the ink will spread slightly.'

'Ah, I see. So, Ingrid, that's what you meant about the papers being partial forgeries.'

'Yes, but this simple test is not sufficient by itself.'

Dr Lindgren hurried on. 'No. The same effect would result from the use of an inferior batch of paper. So, we make further comparisons. Now, here are two "l"s, from one batch of paper. Now, if we superimpose the images . . .'

Tim watched as the two letters merged. 'They fit exactly. I suppose that means . . .'

'It suggests very precise copying, probably with the aid of some photographic technique. Anyone's handwriting is inconsistent. It varies. Yet in what I call sample B there is a rigidity. I made comparisons of a dozen letters. They all gave the same result. It suggests that the forger has made a template from specimen letters in sample A, and used it slavishly in producing sample B. Again, this is not totally conclusive. What we do is build the evidence, layer on layer.' He switched off the projector.

Ingrid let the sunlight back into the room. 'Did you manage to complete the ink anlaysis, Björn?'

'Yes, I ran some minute specimens through all the tests – polarized light and transmission electron microscopy as well as X-ray and electron diffraction. I have the print-outs here.' He took a sheaf of papers from his cardboard box and offered them to Tim.

Tim waved them aside. 'Don't blind me with science; just give me the bottom line.'

Dr Lindgren leaned against the desk. 'Forgers trying to reproduce the types of ink used centuries ago can quite easily use similar components – gums, solvents, colouring agents. Similar, but never identical. Production methods have changed over the years. That means that minor chemical differences can be discerned in all but the very cleverest fakes. In this case our forger or copyist doesn't seem to have done his homework. The ink he has used is very different. Such modern substances as titanium dioxide are present in appreciable quantities.'

'And this modern ink is only used on the pages in specimen B?'

'I have had no time for an exhaustive study, Mr Lacy, but I should be very surprised if that were not so.'

Tim turned to Ingrid Brunhill. 'So what we appear to have is an eighteenth-century document with later spurious bits stuck in.'

She refilled glasses. 'Yes. Not so much a fake; more an embellishment.'

'And what would be the point of that?'

Ingrid shrugged. 'As far as I can see it was an attempt to spice up the original narrative, to make it more sensational. All the specimen B bits relate to the naughtiness of the club's goings on. I can only suppose that old Whitehead-Dyer wanted to make his papers a more dramatic revelation than they are.'

'Does his tinkering affect the value?'

'By "value" I take it you mean financial value.' Her tone suggested that she was dealing with a philistine who could only assess old manuscripts in terms of their market price. 'The answer to your question is "no". There's a great deal of important material in these papers which is going to change our understanding of eighteenth-century society and politics. That and the risqué associations make them one of the most exciting finds for many years.'

Tim mused. So, after all, the Hellfire Papers were worth killing for. He stood up. 'In that case, we must make sure they come to no harm. I'm most grateful to both of you for your help. Now, the sooner I get these back under lock and key the better.' Tim picked up the brown paper parcel.

Dr Brunhill asked anxiously, 'Just what do you intend to do with them?'

'To return them to St Mary's just as soon as it's safe to do so.' Tim shook hands with the two scholars and moved towards the door.

His hand was on the knob when Ingrid said, 'I almost forgot. I've solved the Jenkinson riddle.'

Tim turned abruptly. 'Really? That's marvellous. Tell me!'

Dr Brunhill's smile was almost mischievous. 'As I was walking on the stair, I met a man who wasn't there.'

'No more riddles, please?'

She laughed. 'Very well. Whitehead-Dyer gave himself away by introducing a man into his narrative who wasn't there; who couldn't possibly have been there. In 1760 he listed the Earl of Liverpool among the Wycombe revellers. Now, in 1760 there was no such animal. The title was not created until 1796 to reward one of George III's more able ministers – Charles Jenkinson.'

'I see. By the time there was a real Earl of Liverpool, Paul Whitehead was long dead.'

'Precisely. I ought to kick myself for not spotting it sooner. It's a silly mistake and, I would have thought, perfectly avoidable. Perhaps in his isolated house out in Sydney he didn't have access to all the necessary reference books.'

Tim thought of the embittered ex-diplomat working secretively on his precious documents, surrounded by state-of-the-art technology which linked him to the world's major centres of learning. 'It is odd,' he said.

Ingrid held the door open for him.' It's almost as though he wanted to be caught out.'

Tim slept badly on Tuesday night. There were only four days to go before he proposed to confront Sir Evelyn Masquerier with murder. The sheer enormity of what he had undertaken increasingly dominated his waking hours and haunted his sleep. To accost a prominent and respected citizen and accuse him of unlawful killing . . . how could he do it? His reason readily provided the answer: he would never forgive himself if he simply stood aside and allowed Masquerier to get away with brutal homicide. With anxiety came doubt. Had he really gathered enough information to justify his attack on another man's reputation? Hundreds of times he went over the evidence. The Masqueriers were planning to turn the Hellfire Papers into cash and were being none too scrupulous about it. That much was clear. Their clandestine activities might or might not be illegal but disclosure would certainly do them a great deal of damage. Then there were the attempted thefts. Sir Evelyn had put up a vigorous answer to the charge of masterminding those, but the fact remained that he had had far away the best opportunity and the strongest motive for trying to get hold of the papers. Stuart had certainly had his suspicions – strong enough for him to want to send the papers away from Cambridge for safety. For those suspicions he had been silenced.

But suspicion isn't proof. Tim had nothing that would stick in a court of law. To get a confession out of Masquerier he would have to convince him that Stuart had told him everything before his death. Well, bluffing the suspect was one thing. Carrying it through to the high court? Tim knew that any half-way competent defence counsel would tear him and his evidence to shreds. Reason obliged with the counter-argument: 'It's precisely because the evidence is inadequate for a police prosecution that you have to shake Masquerier into implicating himself.'

There were other worries; facts left over like redundant jigsaw pieces. Tim had made a complete picture, but some things did not fit. Perhaps they belonged to a different puzzle and had simply got into the wrong box. Reason could not eject from Tim's mind the unwanted guest introduced by Ingrid Brunhill – 'It's almost as though he wanted to be caught out'.

The next day Tim drove to London where he had to attend an evening reception at Baron's, the art auctioneers. He went straight to the flat to shower and change. As that left him with an hour to spare, he took out Paul Whitehead's autobiography. Now that he knew what to look for, could he spot the fake passages? He held pages up to the light to check watermarks. He scrutinized the writing with the aid of a magnifying glass. Yes, one really could see where passages had been inserted. The forger, or 'embellisher', had had to stick his contributions in in places where the preceding sentence ended at the bottom of the page. At one point he had actually torn out part of a page. Tim poured himself an armagnac and settled to read Sir Peregrine Whitehead-Dyer's pastiches.

Then it occurred to him that the tremors that had crossed the world had begun as impulses in the cerebral neurons of an eccentric recluse. Tim realized that he wanted to find out more about Whitehead-Dyer. On an impulse he picked up the phone and put a call through to an old friend.

After they had exchanged greetings Tim asked, 'How about a quick drink before you take your train back to leafy outer suburbia?'

'Love to, but it'll have to be quick. My club in half an hour?'

Forty minutes later the two men were seated in formidable leather armchairs in a high-ceilinged room whose walls carried stiff Victorian portraits, watching taxis and tourist buses crawl along Pall Mall. Charlie Spicer was tall, slim and a boyish forty; an effect enhanced, as Tim well knew, by hair dye and regular gym workouts. He smiled over the rim of his champagne flute. 'Why do I get the feeling that this is not a purely social tête-à-tête?'

Tim swirled the ice around in his brandy and ginger. 'We haven't seen each other for six months or so. I just thought . . .'

'Come off it, Tim. When you call me out of the blue at the FO it's usually because you want the lowdown on some rich foreign resident, or how to get round the import-export restrictions of one of our less esteemed trading partners.'

Tim laughed. 'That makes me sound very mercenary, Charlie. The fact is, a few minutes plugged into your computer-like memory saves weeks of formal enquiries through "normal channels".'

'So, what state secrets are you trying to prise out of me this time?' Spicer glanced quickly at his watch.

'I was wondering if you knew anything about one of your own – or, rather, one of your ex-own. There was a chap called Peregrine Whitehead-Dyer. Quite a distinguished diplomat by all accounts. Retired to Australia about ten or twelve years ago.' Tim watched as his friend's eyes narrowed. He fancied he could almost hear the circuitry behind them buzzing.

After a few seconds, the civil servant turned on Lacy a look that was shrewd and revealed nothing. 'What's your interest? What's he been up to?'

'Nothing interesting, as far as I know – unless you regard dying of cancer as interesting.'

'So the poor old boy's snuffed it, eh?'

'Last year. Nothing you can tell me about him can harm him and he had no close family.'

'No. He was a loner and an eccentric – not an uncommon combination in the British diplomatic.'

'You knew him, then?'

'I met him a couple of times. There was some problem over his pension when he took early retirement. I was involved in sorting it out.'

'I didn't realize he left the service early.'

'Only a matter of three or four years.'

'Do you know why he quit?'

'He resigned on health grounds.' Spicer drained his glass and flicked imaginary dust from his lapel. He stood up. 'Good to see you, Tim, but I'm afraid leafy suburbia beckons.'

Tim jumped to his feet. 'Hey, was it something I said?'

'No, Tim. Something you might have said.'

'You mean I might have asked what *really* prompted Whitehead-Dyer's sudden departure from the service?'

The two men crossed the bar, which was slowly filling with dark-suited members who had just left their offices. As they paused briefly before descending the wide staircase to the club's lobby, Spicer nodded almost imperceptibly. 'Something like that.'

'And if I had asked such an audacious question, what might you have replied?'

'I might have said that I had no reason to doubt the official explanation and that, even if I had, I wouldn't dream of passing internal gossip to outsiders.'

After the Baron's reception Tim returned to the flat. He had a long and expensive telephone conversation with Harry Pratos.

It was Dr Thompson who drew my attention to the first issue of the *North Briton*. He and Hogarth came out to dine with me at Twickenham on a warm June day. I now spent more and more time at my modest country home. On taking office, Sir Francis had insisted on sharing his good fortune with old friends. He had pensioned me, provided me with my own permanent quarters at West Wycombe and appointed me to a deputy treasureship of the chamber, worth £800 a year. In consequence of such generosity I was able to enlarge my cottage and look forward to an old age of serene reflection. On that still summer day I looked forward to strolling in my orchard and reminiscing with old friends.

As soon as they descended from the chaise I realized that they were not in the mood for such gentle pastime.

Thompson stumped into the house in his dust-stained coat, threw himself down in my favourite chair and tossed his hat onto the floor. 'Damn you for an old ostrich, Paul!'

'And good day to you, sir,' I replied, too inured to the doctor's unchangeable manner to be offended.

'Ostrich, sir! Head in the sand! Show him, Will!'

Hogarth selected an upright chair and I provided my guests with glasses of sweet calcavello. From an inside pocket the painter produced two folded sheets of printed folio. With a gesture of distaste he laid them upon a tripod table. 'Scurrilous!' he muttered. 'I was for trashing it but the doctor said you should see it.'

I donned my spectacles and took up the broadsheet. Its masthead bore the legend *The North Briton*. A quick glance showed me that it was the latest anti-government paper. Its prose and verse castigated the administration's leading policies and poured scorn on most of the ministers. The language was immoderate but I had certainly read worse. I laid it aside. 'Another savage beast in the satirical jungle. I wonder how long it will escape the establishment huntsmen.'

Hogarth was not prepared to dismiss it so lightly. 'D'ye know who's responsible?'

'No.'

Thompson sneered. '*Brother* John of Aylesbury and *Brother* Charles.'

I was surprised but scarcely dismayed. 'I know Wilkes has no love for Bute but I had not realized that Churchill—'

'Churchill is Wilkes's dupe,' Thompson asserted. 'He's flattered by the unprincipled rogue and doesn't see that Wilkes is only interested in him because he's talented and popular.'

'Churchill is certainly a powerful ally, Will,' I conceded. 'He has no opinion which is not strongly held and his verse is unrivalled.'

'Aye. All London is reading the *North Briton* today. It's like to do the government much harm.'

'It is good for policies to be challenged.'

'Policies be damned!' Thompson roared. 'This has naught to do with policies. Wilkes is furious for being passed over. He's ears over in debt and had looked to his political friends to help him – either with some rich sinecures or an overseas diplomatic post. He's furious with Pitt for not speaking for him and he's convinced Bute rejects him for personal reasons and calls the favourite a sanctimonious prig. D'ye see in that rag how he comes within a ha'penny breeze of accusing Bute of being the princess dowager's lover?'

'If he has not a care, he'll destroy himself.'

'Not before he's destroyed others,' Hogarth suggested. 'He and Churchill have made it known that anyone who opposes them will feel the vicious lash of their pens.'

'Well, well, there's nothing new in that.'

'Indeed, Paul? See if you think the same when you've read this.' The doctor burrowed into several pockets, unearthing soiled kerchiefs, old letters, stubs of sealing wax and tangles of string, before triumphantly producing a crumpled scrap of paper and handing it to me. 'It seems they intend to be particularly vigilant in hounding those they call false friends.'

I read the handwritten lines of verse:

When I look backward o'er the years,
And see protesting patriots turned to peers;
Hear men, most loose, for decency declaim,
And talk of character without a name;

> See men transformed to brutes, and brutes to men,
> See Whitehead take a place, Ralph change his pen,
> I mock the zeal, and deem the men in sport,
> Who rail at ministers and curse a court.

It stung. 'This is unjust! I'm still no friend of the court; no servile, fawning place-hunter, as Churchill knows. I take it this is Churchill's work?'

'Aye. He pinned it up in White's. Scores had seen it 'ere I tore it down,' Thompson explained. ''Tis clear friendship means nothing to him or his mentor. You have been good to them both. So have Dashwood and others of our Brotherhood. Yet they mean to bite like rabid curs at friend and foe alike.'

'Rabid curs is a good simile,' I said. 'For if they continue thus, they must perish of the very disease they carry.'

'Or be put down,' Hogarth growled. 'The doctor and I discussed it on our way. We are agreed that Wilkes and Churchill must be repaid in their own coin. I mean to lampoon them and their set in a new series of engravings. We think you should come in, too. Unsheathe your pen, Paul, and let it flash with its accustomed brilliance.'

The suggestion worried me. 'I would be inclined to ignore them. If we enter the ring it may seem like a contest between the old men and the new. Sympathy might lie rather with the young champions than the aged masters who have had their day.'

I was not able to convince them. Thus matters fell out as I had predicted – and worse.

CHAPTER 16

In 1763 I stayed for a few May days at West Wycombe Park. I was there partly to enjoy the Buckinghamshire air and partly to prepare for the spring chapter of the Order. In truth, I expected a sparsely attended meeting. Wilkes and Churchill and their friends had virtually exiled themselves by their attacks on the Brotherhood, but there were other events to distract particularly our political members. The climate in Westminster and London had become decidedly heated. Bute was immensely unpopular and could scarcely travel abroad without attracting a hostile mob. The *North Briton*, Wilkes's speeches in the Commons and the filthy but powerful torrent of abuse which gushed from Churchill's pen kept the populace in a state of great excitement.

One afternoon a horseman clattered into the stable yard, dismounted and was immediately shown into the library where I was sitting in a window and nodding over a book. The man brought a letter from my patron requesting my immediate departure for Hanover Square, and also a copy of the day's *Morning Post*. I turned my attention to the letter and read, with deepening dismay, the item which Dashwood had marked for my attention.

> We have long wondered about the activities of the Society of St Francis of Wycombe and have frequently striven to discover the identities of *Dashwood's Disciples* – or *Dashwood's Devils*, as they are better known to the commonality – and the precise nature of their secret rites. Hitherto, we have been inhibited alike by the solemn oaths enjoined upon members and the shame which precludes their divulging details of their nefarious pursuits. Now, the protective membrane has been pierced by the honest determination of one of the *monks* to reveal to us – in the interests of common decency – the obscene happenings at Medmenham.

The writer described with tolerable accuracy the customs of our regular meetings but then his fancy took wing.

> The Monastery is served by those versed in chirurgical and obstetric arts so that ladies who wish to curtail or bring forth new life may make a temporary retreat from the world. The offspring of Medmenham's monks and nuns are styled the Sons and Daughters of St Francis and are appointed in due order officers and domestics in the seminary, according to their different abilities, or by drawing lots. Dashwood himself has given the example to his followers. The full number of his bastards is not known but may confidently be reckoned at more than twenty, while Lady Dashwood's womb remains empty. The brothers may take their pleasures but only at the

expense of cuckolded husbands, ruined ladies, ravished innocence and frequent misery.

We shall, in our next issue, expatiate on the necromantic worship of the Order of St Francis of Wycombe. We shall catalogue the names of its members. We shall list the many reasons why this society must be outlawed and no longer suffered to sully the reputation of our Christian nation.

I reached Hanover Square at dusk and waited an hour for Dashwood to return from parliament. At last he hurried in and flung himself down upon a daybed, clutching off his wig as he did so. It may have been my fancy but I formed the clear impression that he had accumulated a multitude of grey hairs since accepting office. Certainly, he had aged over the last year.

'Damnable business, Whitehead!' he observed, closing his eyes.

'Wilkes, I presume?'

'More likely Churchill. Wilkes, as you know, is in the Tower.'

The Member for Aylesbury had, indeed, been arrested on the order of parliament for the publication of a seditious libel. It was the government's only way of silencing a man who had, for more than a year, deliberately agitated city mobs and fomented near anarchy.

'Will he remain long incarcerated?'

'I doubt it. Frankly, his apprehension was an act of very dubious legality; a breach of parliamentary privilege. He has a writ of habeas corpus being heard in the Court of Common Pleas tomorrow and I'll wager he's set free. The thing is, for all that he's a pestilential rabble-rouser, damme if I don't still like the fellow. 'Tis Churchill who's the menace. Great blundering, brainless bull of a man – he charges at anything in sight. Wilkes selects his targets. In the *North Briton* he attacked my new excise on cider. His arguments are cogent, though he doesn't tell us where he'd find the money to pay for the recent war. But Churchill! He's using his pen to bruise as many of his friends as possible, including you and me. I presume you've read his latest couplets?'

'One of the brothers sent me a copy.'

'Why's he tilting at the Order, Whitehead? 'Taint politics and 'taint morality – Churchill's one of the loosest livers in London.'

'I think it must be the preacher in him. Though he's given up his cloth he cannot resist telling others to "do as I say; not as I do".'

'Well, he must be stopped. Aged Paul, you must answer him, expose him. None can do it better.'

I doubted that. Churchill was clever, ruthless and popular. I had little taste for a public contest with such and I still feared that to engage in poetic pugilism would ill serve the Order. However, Dashwood had demanded it and obeying his behests had by now become a habit rather than a duty.

The following day I accompanied Dashwood to the Court of Common Pleas. Hogarth came with us in the coach. The street before the ancient building was thronged with a mob chanting 'Wilkes and Liberty!' They jeered and pressed forward as our coach drew up. It was only with the aid of the soldiery that a way was cleared for us to the door. The court was crowded inside. From our balcony we looked down upon a press of men and women in the body of the court. A great cheer went up when the prisoner was brought in. The bustle subsided as the judge took his place.

Dashwood whispered, 'Chief Justice Pratt, a friend of Pitt. That's why Wilkes has appealed his case here. In King's Bench he'd have been up before Lord Mansfield and after what the *North Briton* has said about him he could have expected but scant justice.'

As the proceedings settled into their ponderous routine, Hogarth took out his sketchbook and pencils. Glancing sideways during the trial I saw, taking shape on the paper, a hideous deformed creature with a suggestion of horns and a leering smile. Only then did I realize the hatred the artist felt for our erstwhile Brother.

The high point of the legal contest was reached when Wilkes rose to speak in his own defence – and to enunciate his political creed.

'The liberty of all peers and gentlemen and, what touches me more sensibly, that of all the middling and inferior set of people who stand most in need of protection, is in my case this day to be finally decided upon; a question of such importance as to determine at once whether English liberty shall be a reality or a shadow.'

Cheers echoed around the rafters and it was a full two minutes before the court officers secured silence.

I looked down at the prisoner. There was the man against whom I had to turn my pen. Yet, with nothing he had said could I disagree. Liberty. It was what we had all talked about throughout our political lives. What we thought we had striven for. What we believed we had found in the Order. How was it that we had become enemies?

When the judge pronounced Wilkes's acquittal I knew not whether to cheer or weep.

On Saturday 29 June the Lacys set out for Chipping Sneddon *en famille*. Since they were going to be away from home for most of the weekend they did not want to leave the boys behind, and when Angela Revesby had volunteered Dorrie's services as baby-sitter they had eagerly accepted. As the car made its way northwards on a grey, showery morning both Tim and Catherine were preoccupied with thoughts of the ordeal ahead but neither mentioned it. They deliberately talked about other things.

Catherine turned to check that Toot and Root were still safely strapped into the small back seat. They were both secure – one asleep and one fighting a losing battle with slumber. 'I hate to mention it, Tim, but we're going to need a bigger car soon.'

Tim slowly applied the brake as the Mercedes joined the queue of Saturday morning traffic going into Marlborough. 'I know. I'm just putting off the evil day as long as possible.'

'The last vestige of bachelor panache?'

'Not really. Buying this was a compromise. I loved the old 356B.'

'I know. George tells me you used to call it your bird trap.'

Tim grimaced. 'I must have a serious word with George.'

'I guess we have a number of important decisions looming as the boys grow up: car, schooling – business plans.' She glanced at her husband out of the corner of her eye. 'Have you thought any more about taking on a partner?'

'Not really. It isn't a decision that can be made in

isolation. It's all tied up with the boys and family life. And the bottom line is, as ever, money.'

'That's why we ought to bring someone in who has capital to invest.'

'OK, supposing I buy that, we still can't just take on any rich idiot.'

'Of course not. It has to be someone you can work with.'

'Someone enterprising, who can make a real contribution to the growth of the business.'

'Someone intelligent, who can learn quickly.'

'And someone rich. I guess that narrows the field pretty considerably. Let me know when you come across this paragon.'

The 500SL escaped from the mainstream of traffic heading for the town centre and Tim accelerated.

They were silent for a while and then Tim added, 'Perhaps we ought to ask ourselves whether it's right to go on living at Farrans.'

Catherine protested. 'Oh, but the boys love it.'

'Sure. But can we really expect them to go on living over the shop and having their parents constantly preoccupied with business? It's not so much overwork that's the problem as never being able to escape from work. Perhaps we ought to sell the London flat and buy something down here where we can be alone as a family.'

Catherine was silent for a while. At last she said, 'That'll be a tough decision to take. I wonder if another answer might be boarding school for the boys.'

'What! I thought you were agin that sort of thing.'

'I'm certainly not very pro it. All I'm saying is maybe we should consider it as an option. Most of the boys' friends locally will be going away to school in a few years. If they were boarding half the year they'd appreciate Farrans all the more and we could make them our priority in vacations – give them more of our time; take long holidays.'

'What schools are the boys' friends down for?'

'Parents I've talked with about it seem to agree that Marlborough's too close. The Stovins want their boy to go Winchester but that's really because Kit Stovin went there himself. Others are talking about Sherborne or Stowe.'

'What!' Tim jolted as though from an electric shock. In fact that was close to the truth. The circuitry in his brain had made an unexpected contact and produced a sudden surge of power.

'I said some parents are considering—'

'Yes, I heard!' Tim snapped the words. 'Quiet! I need to think . . . Association . . . It's all association.' He was muttering almost inaudibly. 'Does it work though? Winchester . . . Stowe . . . Liverpool and Everton . . . But it's only a coincidence unless it works for all of them. Ermine . . . no, it doesn't work.' He pulled the car into a lay-by. He turned to Catherine, almost shouting now. 'What do you know about ermine?'

'Ermine?'

'Yes, yes, ermine!'

'It's a kind of fur.'

'OK. What other kinds are there?'

'Sable, mink, rabbit, ocelot, fox . . .' Catherine's suggestions petered out.

'Right, try another tack. What sort of animal does ermine come from?'

'From an ermine, I guess. Isn't that a kind of weasel?'

'Weasel, stoat, squirrel . . . Damn! I've got to go back into Marlborough. Must get to a library.'

There was no parking to be had in the town so Tim drove to the library and jumped out. 'Meet me here in half an hour,' he muttered and hurried into the building.

The search took him more than thirty minutes. He started with the dictionary. That was little help. He moved to the encyclopaedia and skimmed through every article remotely connected with furs and the fur trade. Nothing. He stood back, scanning the reference shelves for inspiration. He must be wrong. And yet, somehow, he knew he was not wrong. He was on the same trail that Stuart Longton had found when he discovered the 'mistake' about Jenkinson. Desperately, he pulled out again volume one of the *Shorter Oxford Dictionary*. 'Ermine . . . 1. An animal of the weasel tribe . . . 2. The fur of the ermine . . . 3. With reference to the ermine worn by judges . . . 4. *Her*. A heraldic fur . . .' Was that it? Tim went over to the desk and asked what books the library had on heraldry. The assistant went away and returned with a small and obviously dated volume entitled *A Young Person's Guide to Heraldry* by E.A. Peabody. Would it do? she asked. Tim thanked her and went over to one of the readers' tables. He turned the pages with little optimism. But there it was, set out in very simple language, accompanied by coloured pictures: 'There are nine colours or *tinctures* used on a shield. They are in three groups. Metals: Or (gold) and Argent (silver). Colours: Gules (red), Sable (black), Azure (blue), Vert (green) and Purpure (purple). Furs: Ermine and Vair.'

Tim sat back. 'Bless you! Oh bless you, E.A. Peabody!'

The three other occupants of the table looked up, scowling.

Outside, Tim found an angry wife arguing with a traffic warden while trying to calm an equally distraught younger son.

When the official had been mollified by words of calm apology, the children bribed with chocolate, and the Lacys were once more on their journey Catherine demanded, 'Do you want to tell me what all this is about?'

'I'm still working it out myself but the main point is that Whitehead-Dyer deliberately added a fake section to his ancestor's papers, *knowing that it would be discovered as soon as experts studied the collection.*'

'What was the point of that?'

Tim's face creased into an intense frown. 'I think . . . no, I'm sure . . . It has to be . . .'

'What?' Catherine yelled the word.

He shook his head. 'It's one of those things that sounds too horrible to be true when you actually put it into words.'

'Tim, stop that! If you weren't driving, I'd— ooh! You're infuriating!'

'Sorry. Look, think it through with me and see if you come to the same way out conclusions.'

'OK.'

'Right, fact one: three experts have looked at Whitehead-Dyer's papers and they've all, very quickly, spotted fake passages in the autobiographical journal.'

'So, Sir Perry was an incompetent forger.'

'Possibly. But Ingrid – and, I suspect, Stuart – got the impression that there was more to it. Now, the forged sections of the manuscript are all to do with the activities of the most depraved members of Dashwood's very depraved secret society. They got their kicks out of breaking what few sexual taboos existed in their pretty sick aristocratic world. But their speciality was children. It gave them a kind of twisted pleasure to make boys and girls take part in their obscene rituals. They used young bodies for their own perverted purposes. They corrupted minds. They destroyed innocence. They didn't care if they maimed or even killed their victims.'

Catherine stole a glance at the two chocolate-smeared faces behind. 'I couldn't read that part. It was just too ghastly. I don't understand how grown men—'

Tim hurried on. 'Me neither. But who were these men? They have names but, it seems, they don't really exist. That's what puzzled Stuart. In the 1760s there was no such person as the Earl of Liverpool. That made him think about the other members of this paedophile circle. I reckon he'd begun to worry out the truth. That was why he wanted to get himself and the papers away from Cambridge to a place of seclusion – and safety.'

Catherine nodded, frowning. 'Yes, but . . .'

'Hang on. Work it through with me. Why bother to concoct a forgery and then make a deliberate mistake like including a non-existent Lord Liverpool?'

'Carelessness?'

'Ingrid Brunhill didn't think so. She reckoned that Whitehead-Dyer intended the forgery to be spotted, and now I can see that she was right. Ever since we started puzzling over these papers I thought what a coincidence it was that one of old Whitehead's villains was called Lord Liverpool and we'd just met a Lord Everton.'

'I don't get it.'

'Liverpool: Everton – don't you see?'

Catherine scowled. 'No I don't. And don't you turn that "poor little woman" look on me.'

Tim grinned. 'Sorry, you can't help being a Yankee.'

'And what's that supposed to mean?'

'Just that you couldn't be expected to know much about football clubs. If you say "Liverpool and Everton" to your average Englishman he'll immediately think "football". They're both soccer clubs – and great rivals. The point is, it's an obvious word connection.'

'Sounds pretty far-fetched to me.'

'I agree, but the idea kept buzzing round in my head.' Tim slowed for the roundabout that took them off the Swindon bypass and onto the A361 which thrust northwards towards the Cotswolds. 'Then, when we were talking about education earlier you made another, similar, connection – Winchester and Stowe, two top public schools. One of Lord Liverpool's cronies in Perry's yarn is a naval man called Captain Winchester. I suddenly realised that we'd met a lecherous sea dog, very pally with Lord Teddy, by the name of Captain Stow. It looked like another word connection. It couldn't be coincidence.'

'Hmm, you still haven't convinced me.'

'I hadn't really convinced myself either. But there was one way to test whether I was on the right track. If Perry's forgery contained a code it had to work for all the others in the group. The only member of the phoney Liverpool gang I could remember was Canon Ermine – I remembered it because it sounded like a made up sort of name. But I couldn't see any obvious connection. That's why I had to get to a library.'

'And what did you discover that made you so smug?'

'That was the breakthrough!' Tim was talking fast now – excited. 'In heraldry two types of fur are depicted – ermine and *vair*. You see? Canon Ermine equals Dean Vare! The spelling's different but that's a detail. Sir Perry couldn't possibly get his code letter perfect. The thing is, anyone who knows about heraldry would immediately connect the two words. Now I'll bet that if we were to go through the Liverpool paedophile gang we'd find that every member corresponds to someone living today.'

'O.K. I'll buy that but I still don't see where it gets us. Anyway, as far as we know, Whitehead-Dyer had never met Teddy and Captain Stow.'

'*As far as we know*. But let's leave that for the moment. There are some other half-connections that have been bothering me.'

'Such as?'

'Well, for instance, Whitehead-Dyer, his old chum, Charles Vare, and Lord Teddy were all computer buffs, into the latest sophisticated technology. When Perry and Vare died all their papers and computer data were destroyed, too. I thought I'd see if I could get any more out of Harry Pratos on that score, so I phoned him.'

'And?'

'And, when Perry made his bonfire he included a lot of videotapes. Now, I can understand someone wanting to destroy letters, even computer discs, but why does a man make a point of committing video cassettes to the flames?'

'Is it really significant?'

'It is when you realise that the remains of destroyed videotapes were also found in Charles Vare's rooms. His charlady was quite put out by the mess they made.'

They sat in silence for several minutes as the sports coupé negotiated the crowded main street of a small town in which cars slowed to find parking spaces and pedestrians scurried along rain-swept pavements. At last Catherine said, 'Are you suggesting that Perry and the others were all child-abusing perverts who got their kicks out of blue videos and that Perry decided to dish the dirt on them *post mortem*?'

Tim grunted. 'I reckon they were more than voyeurs.' He shook his head. 'I said my conclusions were way out.'

'Damn right they are. Still I guess it would explain why someone was desperate to get his hands on the papers.'

'And why Vare died. When Perry tipped him off he probably went into a blue funk.'

'I still don't get the point of it all. Even if your theory is half way to being right, just what was Perry up to?'

Tim shook his head. 'That's certainly the crux of it. I think I can see at least part of the answer. According to Harry Pratos, Sir Perry was not a happy man. He was always going on about "England home and beauty" and was bitter about not being able to spend his twilight years in his own country.'

'So why did he emigrate?'

'My friend at the FO suggested . . . Oh, I don't know. I thought I was getting somewhere but I just seem to end up with more questions.'

After a couple of silent miles Catherine said, 'So what happens now? Presumably Masquerier is off the hook?'

'I wonder. He still had a motive and the best opportunity for killing Stuart. But I suppose we have to re-open the file on Lord Teddy. If the fake papers are pointing to a modern paedophile gang then it seems he's the ringleader.'

Catherine stared mournfully out at the dripping landscape. 'But he's dedicated his life to children . . .'

Tim whooped. 'That's it! Of course! It fits, doesn't it? Who better to provide his disgusting cronies with their playmates?' Tim's voice took on an edge of bitterness. 'By God, if this is really what it's all about . . . Everton has an endless supply of vulnerable youngsters in his homes – emotionally disturbed kids; kids too frightened to speak out, kids with no families to stand up for them.'

Catherine shuddered. 'I can't get my mind round it. It's too horrible. We must get the papers to the police and explain about the code so that they can check him out.'

Tim shook his head. 'Can you see them moving in on someone as squeaky clean as our fat friend on what they'll consider a half-baked theory? If Teddy got the slightest whisper that they were interested in him he'd destroy whatever evidence exists. So that means . . .'

Catherine looked at her husband – sharply, suspiciously. 'So, what . . .?'

He smiled. 'You don't want to know.'

'Tim! No!'

> Mausolus, a meagre thread on history's loom,
> In death was magnified by sumptuous tomb.
> And still in urn, sarcophagus or bust
> Are reputations saved, which else were dust.
> Where wealth commands memorials in stone,
> Posterity is duped. Virtue alone
> Yet keeps the book and sets in order due
> Names which, though old, remain for ever new.

Death was much in all our minds when I wrote those lines in this library at West Wycombe Park on a wild autumn afternoon scarce six months ago. I had returned to the house with his lordship and the small party of guests who had been out to the nearby hill to inaugurate the mausoleum, Dashwood's latest essay in architectural drollery.

It was Dodington who put the idea into our friend's mind. In his will he left money to Dashwood for the erection of some fitting memorial. For a year or more Baron le Despencer had little leisure to contemplate new building works. The unhappy and tempestuous events of 1763 occupied most of his time. They also exercised me to a not inconsiderable degree.

Our erstwhile Franciscan brothers drained the cup of enmity to the bitter lees. Hogarth published his caricature of Wilkes in *The Times*. Churchill responded with 'An Epistle to William Hogarth', as vile a diatribe as ever sullied the name of poetry. For viciousness and arrogance it had no peer. Churchill presumed to write of one of our greatest painters, 'Thou wretched being, whom, on Reason's plan,/So chang'd, so lost, I cannot call a man.'

Brother William responded with another caricature portraying the poet in the guise of a shambling bear. I was sufficiently incensed to enter the polemic on my old friend's behalf with 'Pug's Reply to Parson Bruin', in which I drew attention to Churchill's vulgarity, his hypocrisy in denouncing the morals of others and the debaucheries of this one-time clergyman. It was composed in the heat of battle and repented of when the rattle of cannon and musket had receded. For the moment the clangour of arms was far from being stilled. The *North Briton* rang with diatribes against all Wilkes's 'false friends' which included Dashwood, Hogarth, Sandwich, Whitehead and other Franciscans.

During those distressing weeks Dashwood and I published notices in *The Times* and the *Morning Post* denying the libels that had been set forth against the Order. Alas, the activities of Liverpool and his friends undid any good we might have achieved. It was at that very time that they were involved in a scandal which shocked London, a city not unfamiliar with every kind of vice. Lord Liverpool's procurers, one day scouring the warehouses and alleyways of Queenhithe, where colonies of the destitute are apt to lodge, chanced upon a child they took for a grubby urchin. In fact he was the son of a prominent City merchant, who, wandering off while his father was engaged in business, had muddied himself thoroughly in waterfront pools. They carried him away to the house Liverpool and his cronies kept for their vile practices. The father, soon missing his son, made frantic enquiry, located the place and demanded the boy's return. The keeper, a great ox of a man, an ex-soldier, Bracewell by name, turned him away with threats. An hour later, the merchant returned with a mob at his back.

They forced their way into the house and soon recovered the terrified boy. Yet, what they discovered else so incensed them that they ransacked the building, forced Bracewell to tell all he knew, then bore him up to an attic where they lynched him. What drove them to such fury was finding room after locked room occupied by pitiable children whose bodies bore the marks of obscene treatment. Letters and papers found in the house contained the names of several people who frequented the premises or ordered boys or girls to be delivered elsewhere. These documents were shown to the magistrate. You will not be surprised to hear that nothing came of it. Lord Liverpool feigned horrified astonishment, claiming that he had paid Bracewell to keep a refuge for young orphans and had no idea that the rogue had betrayed his trust for private gain. Whether Liverpool's influential friends were ever interrogated over the affair I know not. If they were, the magistrate was sufficiently cognisant of his station not to press indelicate enquiries too far.

The hounds of Grub Street, as you can imagine, pursued the malodorous scent of this affair into every last nook and cranny. The odour they claimed to identify was that of 'St Francis and his evil Mednamites'. There was no escape for us. We could not avoid the obloquy poured upon members of the Coven or dissociate ourselves from their activities. You may be sure that Wilkes made full use of the shot so fortuitously provided for his cannon.

By the autumn of 1763 whatever twist the controversy took found us at a disadvantage. In October, the headstrong Churchill plunged himself into a fresh scandal. He eloped with the fifteen-year-old daughter of a Westminster stonemason. The city was once more taken by the ears and assiduously followed the subsequent course of events: the couple's flight to the country; their pursuit by the girl's angry brothers; the return of the ravished Betsy to the bosom of her family; the second flight; the accommodation reached with aggrieved parents on payment of a substantial sum of money. These events should have tended to undermine the Wilkes-Churchill caucus. In effect they reinforced the public conviction that no suspicion of virtue or decency was to be attributed to *any* member of our Order.

This *commedia* formed the second act of a drama which might very well be entitled *All For Lust or The Brotherhood Well Lost*. The closing scenes were dominated by the person of Lord Sandwich. Scarce had the dust of Churchill's amorous adventures settled when his lordship set further events in train. The House of Commons having signally failed to curb Wilkes, he declared his intention of challenging the public hero in the Upper House. When Dashwood heard of this he tried vigorously to dissuade Sandwich from such a course which, whatever its outcome, could only lead to more unwelcome public attention. Unfortunately Wilkes's attacks on the government and, particularly, the humiliation inflicted by the baboon incident (which still rankled in the Earl's breast after eighteen months) would not permit him to abandon his project.

The plot was to indict Wilkes for publishing an obscene libel, the *Essay on Woman*. This would lead to his expulsion from the Commons and, thus, leave him without protection against subsequent charges which would be brought against him. Sandwich relished his revenge and particularly the prospect of hoisting Wilkes with his own petard. He spared neither effort nor gold in obtaining evidence by bribery, forgery and blackmail.

Dashwood secured for me a place in the gallery of the House when the day for the debate arrived. After a couple of Pitt's friends had spoken on Wilkes's behalf and drawn attention to the dubious legality of the proceedings, Sandwich rose in his place on the government side. In rolling cadences which would have done justice to a canting Methodist, one of the biggest libertines in London expressed his disgust at a poem whose equal for explicit and unashamed pornography, he claimed, he had never seen. In outraged tones he read one or two passages of the *Essay* to the house. When he laid it aside to continue with his speech their lordships cried, almost to a man, 'Go on! Go on!' Sandwich was suffered to read the whole poem. Versions of the proceedings which appeared in the next day's press did not fail to point out the irony. When I supped with Dashwood that evening he was disinclined to discuss the affair. All he would say of Sandwich's conduct was, 'I never thought to hear the devil preach against sin.'

With all this occurring we had little leisure to give thought to Dodington's final request. It was not till last summer that Dashwood had the plans drawn up for his mausoleum. When he showed me the architect's drawings and asked my opinion I was at a loss to know how to respond.

'It is like nothing I have ever seen.'

He smiled. 'Good. I intend it to perplex. The common run of men have never understood me, or my chosen companions. Let it remain so.'

It was raining in sudden, hard squalls when the last ceremony of the Order took place. We processed, habited, from the house to the strange hexagonal building close by the church (yet in spirit far removed from it). There, in prepared niches, we placed memorials, not only to Dodington, but also to two other of our original number who had preceded us to the place where, if anywhere, *Fay ce que voudras* has meaning. Dr Thompson's eccentric medicinal remedies had preserved him well into old age but could not win him immortality. Hogarth's health and wellbeing had been severely bruised by the attacks he had been subjected to for over a year; these hastened the end of a great artist who might otherwise have given the world yet more master-pieces. There was no place in the mausoleum for Churchill, who had also recently died, his body wasted by that dissipation he roundly condemned in others. There would be no place for Wilkes, skulking now in France. For Sandwich? Perhaps. It will be for 'St Francis' to decide who shall share with him in this memorial to the Order. I trust that my name shall be engraved there.

We shall have our memorial. Whether we deserve to be remembered, posterity must decide.

CHAPTER 17

Tim deposited his family in the King and Martyr hotel at Chipping Sneddon, with instructions to Catherine to plead urgent business for his absence from the concert and to promise that he would be back in time for Lord Teddy's dinner. He telephoned George Martin en route and arrived in Marlow shortly after two thirty. He went into a stationers and bought a large-scale local map. Twenty minutes later George drove one of the Lacy Security vans into the station car park where they had arranged to meet.

He walked across, a thickset figure but light on his feet, like a boxer, and slipped into the Mercedes' passenger seat. 'Afternoon, Major. What's all this, then? One of our unofficial jobs?'

'Sorry to drag you out on a Saturday, George. Did you pick up that address?'

'Yes. You were quite right about it being in Sally's database. Took a bit of finding, though. I'll get it in the neck on Monday. She always knows when I've accessed her system.' He took a piece of paper from the top pocket of his dark tracksuit. 'What's on then, Major?'

'I want to get inside this place and look for some videotapes before their owner gets a chance to destroy them.'

'Breaking and entering you mean.' George frowned disapprovingly. 'I swear you'll get me into prison one day, Major.'

'I hope it won't come to that, George. We'll play it by ear and be as law-abiding as we possibly can. But we can't afford to be too scrupulous. If I'm right, what we're dealing with here is child prostitution and pornography, and frankly I don't care what laws I bend to put a stop to that sort of thing. However, this is all well beyond the line of duty. If you feel—'

The ex-soldier interrupted. 'The old motto in the mess was "If the officer's paying sup up and say nowt". When we've done a bit of freebooting before it's always been for a good reason and you've always been ready to carry the can. So, what's the plan?'

'Find out if there's anyone in the house, first. I know Lord Teddy's away but he presumably has staff of some sort. If there's someone there we'll try to bluff our way in.'

'And if there isn't?'

'Well then, that'll make life easier, won't it?'

George inclined his head dubiously. 'Don't know about that, Major. Folks in this part are well-heeled and very security conscious. Remember we did the job for that TV comedian with the big riverside mansion? There were no jokes when it came to looking after his precious antiques. He had to have all the latest gizmos and bugger the cost.'

They spread the map out and located Fairlawns, the Everton residence.

Tim drew a circle round it. 'Well, well, well! I suppose I shouldn't be surprised.'

'What's that, Major?'

'Look at that, on the other side of the river, right opposite Lord Teddy's place – "Site of Medmenham Abbey".'

George frowned. 'Doesn't mean anything to me.'

'It was where the Hellfire Club got up to some of their more spectacular capers. I wonder how long his lordship has owned Fairlawns.' He handed the map to George. 'We'd better be off. You navigate. We'll just take the Mercedes. It will be less conspicuous in this particular neighbourhood.'

Fairlawns was one of three houses that shared a private drive from the main road which ran parallel with the river to the south. Tim drove slowly between tall hedges and a belt of trees that guarded the seclusion of the residents, a seclusion reinforced by signboards proclaiming 'Private Property', 'Trespassers Will Be Prosecuted' and 'Guard Dogs'. The drive of Fairlawns was fronted by a pair of tall, solid oak gates. As Tim was looking at them and wondering what to do next, they swung noiselessly open to permit a modest Ford saloon car to emerge.

Tim jumped out and walked over to it. The middle-aged couple inside surveyed him suspiciously but the driver wound down his window. 'Can I help you, sir?'

The 'sir' was the giveaway. Tim assumed a nonchalant, upper-class drawl. 'Oh, hello. Do you work here? Is Lord Everton at home?'

'I'm afraid his lordship's away for the weekend, sir.' The tone was deferential.

'Oh, rot the fellow!' Tim called across to the Mercedes. 'I say, Peter, the old sod's buggered orf for the weekend.' He turned back to the driver. 'Is there someone at the house we can leave a message with?'

'I'm afraid not, sir. My wife and I are just on our way out. If you'd like to give me your name, sir, I'll see that his lordship is told as soon as he returns.'

'Right.' Tim paused as though thinking. 'Well, tell him Toby Templeton called will you?' Tim sauntered back to the Mercedes and climbed behind the wheel.

Lord Teddy's domestics drove away up the lane. Tim turned the Mercedes.

'Are we going away again, Major?'

'Just a precaution. When we get to the main road, see if you can see the Ford.'

Tim paused at the junction. 'Well?'

'Parked fifty yards along on the left, Major.'

'OK, then we'll go right. I was pretty sure they'd check on us.' Tim pulled out and accelerated ostentatiously in the direction of Henley.

Ten minutes later they were back and there was no sign of the Ford. At Fairlawns George jumped out with a small toolkit. He found the junction box at the foot of one of the gateposts, tinkered with it for a few seconds, then stood up and pushed open the massive timber doors. Tim drove through. George closed the gates and jumped back into the passenger seat. 'If the rest's as easy as that, we're laughing.'

The drive curved round to the right but Tim parked the car where it was screened from the house by tall rhododendrons. He donned the anorak he always kept in the car and cautiously the two men approached the building on foot. It was 1930s mock-Tudor – herringboned red brick, leaded lights and an exuberance of exposed timbers. George pointed to a red box high up on one of the gables bearing the legend 'Burke Alarm'. George's wrinkled nose and heavenward gaze registered his contempt for the Burke Alarm Co. The two men split up, worked around either end of the house and satisfied themselves that it was empty and completely locked. They met up on the rear terrace from which a long lawn sloped down to the river, visible through the miasma of light rain which had just started again.

Tim looked along the length of the house. 'I'd like to get in and out without leaving any trace.'

George considered the problem professionally. 'I reckon the alarm control is in a box beside the back door. There's a pantry on the other side. It *might* be possible to get in that way and reach the alarm.'

Tim pointed to a well-trodden path running from one end of the house towards a small grove of trees. 'Let's just explore that first.'

The path brought them to a glade masked on all sides by firs and evergreen shrubs. In the centre stood a building of white stone in the shape of a square Greek temple.

Tim felt a tingling in the palms of his hands. He said, 'I think we're getting warm.'

The impression was confirmed moments later when the two men mounted the steps to the pillared portico and examined the door and the small windows on either side. All were firmly locked and closer inspection revealed that they were wired to their own alarm system.

Tim stood back from the building. 'What do you suppose he's hiding here?'

George pulled a face. 'Looks like a bloody mausoleum.'

'I'll bet whatever's in there stinks a lot more than mouldering corpses. Thing is, how're we going to find out?'

George trotted briskly round the temple while Tim looked more closely at the door. Some words were neatly carved into the oak. Tim nodded grimly as he read the legend, *Fay ce que voudras*.

The older man rejoined him. 'No other entrances. I reckon our only hope is the roof. Unless the place is entirely lit by electricity there must be a skylight.'

There were two, as Tim and George discovered ten minutes later, after they had found a wooden bench, propped it on end against the rear wall and managed to scramble up to the roof.

George peered down through the rain-wet glass. 'Bloody hell, will you look at that!'

Tim and George peered through the skylight into what looked like a miniature version of the control room of a power station or an air traffic operations centre. There were computer screens and consoles and batteries of state-of-the-art communications equipment. Tim thought immediately of Whitehead-Dyer's inner sanctum. He pointed to the satellite dish in a corner of the roof, where it was concealed from ground-level view by the parapet. 'Very sophisticated,' he observed.

He turned to the other skylight. The room below that was very different. Here the furnishings were soft and consisted largely of two divans covered in rose velvet and scattered with silk cushions. 'Voluptuous' was the word which sprang to mind.

'Let's see if we can get in.' Tim scrutinized the edges of the glass. 'Do you think they're wired?'

George rubbed an area of the skylight with his sleeve. 'Doesn't seem so. There's a sort of ratchet arrangement for opening the thing. Looks a bit wobbly.' He produced a small crowbar from his toolkit. 'If I jiggle it a bit . . . Yes, got it.' The window lifted sufficiently for him to get an arm in and disengage the raising mechanism.

'Careful not to get rain inside. That would be a giveaway.' Tim turned down the hood of his anorak. 'Fortunately it's eased off a bit.' He peered over George's shoulder. 'What sort of security system?' He held the skylight while his companion knelt to look inside.

'Infra-red,' George muttered. He withdrew his head. 'Must be fed by a line from the house. I'll go and have a look-see.'

He lowered himself to the ground. Tim watched over the parapet as the master technician produced a small current scanner and moved it along the wall close to the ground. With a grunt of satisfaction he stopped, lifted a small stone slab and revealed a junction box beneath. It took George a couple of minutes to remove the lid, clip another piece of equipment to the exposed terminals and disconnect the wires leading into the temple. He gave a thumbs-up sign. 'All clear now, Major.'

'OK, let's do what we have to do and get the hell out of here.' Tim gazed around at the circle of dark, dripping trees and shivered. Then George rejoined him and the two men lowered themselves into the building.

There were three rooms. The one occupying the rear half of the temple had no windows and was laid out as a small cinema. With the aid of George's powerful torch they saw a dozen chairs facing a large TV screen.

'It's tapes we're looking for, is it?' George shone the beam round the walls. 'Bloody hell!'

There was a display of enlarged photographs. Naked figures: men, adolescents, children; intertwined in various obscene, grinning poses – at least, the men were grinning.

'It makes you want to throw up, doesn't it?' George switched the torch off.

'Just a minute. Let's have the light again. Right. Shine it on that end photo. I thought so. I've seen that girl before.' The teenager in the picture was kneeling on a bed staring straight at the camera while a man behind her leaned over her shoulder, his hands fondling the intimate parts of her young body. 'She was on the sailing ship in San Francisco. What was it Stow called her . . .? Charlie. Poor kid. This picture must have been taken a couple of years ago.'

'She's younger than Tina. My God, I've seen some things in my time, but this . . . Let's get out of here, Major, before I tear the place apart with my bare hands.'

In the control room they located a cupboard well stocked with video cassettes. The labels bore no titles, only code numbers and letters. Tim picked at random K7 and R3 and stuffed them into his anorak pockets. He moved the neighbouring tapes to conceal the gaps.

The two men left the way they had come. With the aid of a piece of thin string, George re-fastened the skylight catch behind them. He disconnected his circuit-diverter and restored the temple's power while Tim replaced the wooden bench. He drove the Mercedes back along the drive while George opened the gates, closed them after Tim had driven through and removed his temporary alterations to the circuitry. He stood up, suddenly alert, ears straining. Then he waved his arms. 'Scram! Car coming!'

Tim threw the Mercedes into gear, raced it further down the track and round a bend. The lane ended abruptly in a wooden fence. Tim braked hard and crossed his fingers.

It seemed an age before George sidled up to the car and slipped into the passenger seat. There was a sheen of perspiration on his brow. 'Whew! That was a close one. His lordship's hired help returning. I made it to the cover of the trees across the lane just in time.'

'You're sure they didn't see you?'

'Don't think so, Major. They drove in through the gates as though nothing had happened.'

'Good. Not that it really matters now. These tapes should give us all we need to justify a police search and there's nothing Lord Teddy and his chums can do about it. Once the vice squad gets inside that temple of lust they'll find enough to put the bastards away for a very long time.'

'Bloody marvellous!' George's face glowed with satisfaction. 'So what's the next step?'

'I want you to pick up the van and take these tapes to the police in Reading. Insist on seeing the CID duty officer and get him to look at the videos straight away. Tell him there's plenty more where they came from and fill him in about what we've seen this afternoon. No need to explain how we came by the videos. Say you were taken to the temple by a friend, or something.'

'Don't worry, Major, I'll think up some yarn.'

'Make sure they get the vice squad out pdq with search warrants and the lot. Impress upon them that there's no time to mess about. If they're quick they can bag the whole network. If Lord Teddy gets the glimmering of a suspicion that we're onto him he'll have everything incriminating out of the temple in a matter of hours. Once tremors start going along the grapevine all the upper-class perverts will be building bonfires.'

'I'll make sure the boys in blue don't drag their heels. Where will you be if I need you, Major?'

Tim started the engine and began turning the car in the narrow space available. 'I've got a couple of bits of unfinished business to attend to in the Cotswolds.'

Tim tracked down Catherine in the kitchen of the Revesby residence with Angela and Dorrie, administering tea to three small children.

Catherine smiled up at him from the table. 'Hello, darling. You missed a marvellous concert.' Her eyes said, 'And what the hell have you been up to?'

Angela embellished. 'Yes, such a pity. We were just saying that the young Chinese soloist in the piano concerto was quite, quite superb. She's another of Lady Deb's discoveries. I really don't know how she manages to find . . .'

The conversation rattled along inconsequentially while the last morsels of food were coaxed down increasingly unwilling throats. Then, while Dorrie administered a damp flannel to sticky hands and faces, Mrs Revesby shooed the Lacys out. 'High time you two were getting changed. Don't worry about the little darlings. We'll get them bathed and into bed, won't we, Dorrie? Off you go! See you later!'

As soon as they were alone and walking hand-in-hand back to the hotel, Catherine said, 'Well?'

Tim gave her a censored version of the afternoon's events and what had been discovered at Fairlawns.

'So you were right about Lord Teddy. That's going to come as a great shock to a lot of people. People like Angela Revesby. She thinks he's the next best thing to God. Oh why, Tim!' She clenched his hand hard. 'What on earth makes him do it? To children! I just wish I could begin to understand.'

Tim shook his head. 'Ours not to reason why. Ours just to make sure the buggers are put away for as long as possible.'

'And you really have handed the whole thing over to the police now?' Catherine looked at him anxiously.

'Yes. Well . . . almost. There's still the little matter of murder. I just want to have a few discreet words with Masquerier and Lord T. See if I can shake them up a bit.'

'What about Deb? She makes a pretty convincing Lady Macbeth in my book. Oh, that reminds me, there have been some interesting developments here while you've been spending a burglarious afternoon. Guess who's turned up?'

'Who?'

'Emma and Gavin.'

'Damn it all!' Tim scowled his annoyance. 'What are they doing here? Emma promised she'd get right out of the limelight.'

'Apparently Deb invited them both. A sort of gesture to make up for recent unpleasantness. She gave them a whole fistful of complimentary tickets to festival events and a special invite to tonight's dinner.'

Tim snorted. 'The best thing she could do for those youngsters would be to leave them well alone.'

★ ★ ★

They met up with Emma an hour later in the King and Martyr's 'function room'. She was talking to an earnest young man in the middle of the small crowd but saw them and waved as soon as they entered the reception area. Instantly she rushed up to them, kissing and being kissed.

'How do you like the glad rags?' She twirled round in her flame-coloured silk dress.

'A distinct improvement,' Tim remarked with genuine appreciation. 'But what exactly—'

She frowned. 'Don't say it, Tim, I know I promised to go away for a bit, but Lady Muck invited us and I had a very good reason for accepting.'

'It would have to be a gilt-edged reason to convince me that you ought not to be several thousand miles away. All hell's going to break loose here tonight.'

'OK, point taken, wrist slapped. Now, will you just listen?' The sudden blush of annoyance on Emma's cheeks matched her dress.

'I'm listening.'

'I went back to the UL to see if I could find out anything more useful about Lord Teddy. I read the newspaper accounts of the trial of this chap who was molesting kids at one of the Downham Homes – some creep named Bagshot. There was an interview with Lord Everton after the bastard was sentenced. "How do you react to the judge's comments? What changes of policy will you be instituting in the homes?", that sort of thing. Well, there was a photograph with the article, taken at some recent charity do in London. And guess who our fat friend was talking to?'

'Surprise me.'

'Sir Peregrine Whitehead-Dyer.'

Tim's eyes showed a sudden surge of interest. 'Are you sure? How did you recognize him?'

'I didn't. But his name was right there in the caption. "Seen talking to Sir Peregrine Whitehead-Dyer, who has recently announced his resignation as ambassador to—" some place with an unpronounceable name. So, he and Lord Teddy knew each other. That's too much of a coincidence, isn't it? I was sure you'd want to know about it. That's really why Gavin and I are here.' She looked at Tim, hoping for approval, but he was absorbed in entering this latest data in his mental computer.

'Where is Gavin?' Catherine searched the elegant throng of dinner jackets and smart frocks.

'Oh, he's resting, poor dear. He enjoyed the concert but he has to take his excitement in small doses.' The smile faded from her face. 'He doesn't realize how ill he is, which is just as well. I just want to make what time he has got as pleasant as possible.'

Catherine remembered her conversation with Gavin and thought about the irony of two people who cared for each other so much that each tried to conceal the same painful truth from the other. She said, 'Well, I don't suppose he'll be missing much.'

'Probably not.' The smile bounced back. 'May I sit with you? There's no seating plan so it's a free-for-all. Or are you on the high table with the fat Baron and Lady Moneybags? My father will be up among the nobs. I want to be as far away as possible.'

Tim said, 'I didn't realize he was going to be here.'

Emma nodded glumly. 'Guest of honour. Probably doing his standard speech on how the government cares about the arts. That should bring plenty of hollow laughter. He collared me a few minutes ago and said if I saw you would I give you a message: could he have a word with you sometime this evening because he's found out something important. If I were you, Tim, I'd forget what I've just said.'

Minutes later someone banged a gong and the guests were invited to take their places. They sat eight to a table and Tim's companions began putting out conversational feelers. It was a game he took little part in. He toyed with his food; the afternoon's experiences had drained his appetite. He spoke little. He half listened to the chatter of others.

'She's one of the most remarkable talents I've ever come across. The value of her work will soar as soon as it becomes widely known.' That was Catherine doing a sales pitch.

'It's supposed to be pronounced "Carr" but that only confuses people, so I really don't bother': Emma introducing herself to a little man with a moustache.

'Your wife tells me you're in the security business. What does that mean exactly?' Mrs Archer, the local chief librarian, making another attempt to prod him into discussion. Tim replied with what he hoped was not discourteous brevity.

All his attention was focused on the top table. He had positioned himself so that he could watch the leading players seated on their raised platform behind an array of gleaming silver and glass: Teddy Everton in the centre, flanked by Finsley-Kerr and Chipping Sneddon's lady mayoress; to right and left the Masqueriers, Janos Vanic, the conductor, and Kim Tsong, the soloist who had so impressed the afternoon audience. Among the other notables Tim recognized Robert Donkin, MD of the potted meat company which was one of the festival's main sponsors. And there, at the right-hand end of the table sat Professor Zangster, still presumably dangling from the Masqueriers' hook.

Tim's eyes roved over the pristine dinner jackets and expensive dresses, the flashing jewels and immaculate coiffures, the laughing, self-important faces. 'So much for the great and the good,' he thought. How many of those glamorous, prestigious masks concealed minds distorted by deviousness, ruthless ambition or vice? Who would know, looking at that totally respectable array of wealth and talent, that one of its members was a child abuser, one an unscrupulous financial manipulator, one a thief?

And one a murderer. Tim brooded while other people's words filled the air around him. Someone at that long table with its virgin-white cloth had clubbed the life out of a harmless academic and then coolly strung him up to give the death the appearance of suicide. Why do that, taking up unnecessary time and running an increased risk of discovery? Because he was following a formula that had worked before. Tim began to see how the murder of Charles Vare could have been managed. But by whom? Which of those so respectable people was capable of ruthless, unhurried assassination? And what was the motive – money or reputation? The moment when he would have to make his move was fast approaching and still Tim could not make the last vital connections that would turn suspicion to certainty. His thoughts jostled in free fall with the snippets of conversation around him. And, suddenly, he knew.

The dinner proceeded at what seemed to Tim an intolerably leisurely pace. The speeches were lengthy orations of mutual congratulation. But at last the formalities were over.

Guests began moving from table to table. The first leavers headed in the direction of the cloakroom.

Tim looked, yet again, at his watch: 10.17. If the police were doing their stuff someone should be arriving in Chipping Sneddon soon to invite Lord Teddy's assistance in their investigations. Before that, it was vital that Tim talk with someone. He gulped down the last of his brandy, said a quick 'excuse me', and strode across the room.

Masquerier was on his feet talking to the potted-meat man. As Tim approached he seemed glad of the interruption. 'Ah, Lacy, good to see you. I hope you don't mind Teddy and Deb roping your wife in to help with this pet project of theirs. I don't think you've met . . .' He made introductions.

At that moment Finsley-Kerr joined the group. The name-swapping and hand-shaking began again. Then the minister said, 'Would you excuse me, Sir Evelyn, if I commandeer Mr Lacy for a moment?' And to Tim, 'Could I just have a quick word?' He gestured towards a door marked Emergency Exit.

Outside, they moved away from the floodlit exterior of the King and Martyr into the hotel's grounds. They took a gravel path between tall hedges. The heavily-scented air suggested musk roses close at hand but in the dusk only blocks of shapes and shadow were visible.

Tim stopped. 'Well, no one can overhear us. What have you got to say?'

The politician was brief, emotionless and to the point. 'You have the Whitehead-Dyer Papers. You will give them to me.'

Tim pretended to ignore the underlying menace in the

voice. 'They belong to St Mary's House, Cambridge. I was just about to discuss arrangements for their return with the Master.'

'Well, you can hand them into my keeping, instead.'

'I don't think so, Minister.'

'Then I must persuade you. Your two children were at the Revesby residence, were they not?'

The words seemed to hit Tim in the stomach.

'What do you mean, "were"?'

'They have been collected by some associates of mine who will keep them – quite safely – and return them as soon as I inform them that I have the documents.'

Fear and anger surged within Tim but he made no move. 'That figures. You hate children, don't you? That's what your disgusting paedophile ring is all about – working out your aggression on the innocent and helpless. Well I warn you, if anything happens to my sons—'

Finsley-Kerr sneered. 'Worked it all out, have you? How unfortunate. Now let's go. And please don't try anything. You are without doubt fitter and better trained than I. You could easily overpower me, but if my associates do not hear from me every hour on the hour . . . We can get to the car park this way.' He pushed Tim ahead of him down the path.

Tim ambled along, hands in pockets, assuming a nonchalance he did not feel. 'You've left it too late. By now the police are swarming all over Fairlawns.'

Finsley-Kerr laughed. 'Nice try, Lacy. And clever guesswork. I suppose those wretched papers put you onto Everton. What exactly do they say?'

'They describe, in some detail, the workings of a gang dealing in the abuse and prostitution of children. They name

357

every member of the ring. It's an impressive list; peers of the realm, foreign dignitaries, senior clerics – even ministers of state.'

Tim heard a stifled gasp behind him. 'The papers actually give names?'

'In code, of course. But very simple. Stuart spotted it, as I presume you know.'

'Tell me about this code.'

'Straightforward word association: Lord Everton became Lord Liverpool; Captain Stow, Captain Winchester; Dean Vare, Canon Ermine. But what will interest you most is the pseudonym Sir Perry chose for you. The penny only dropped tonight. I've known for a long time that the "Finsley" bit is quite spurious, but it was only when I heard Emma say that "Kerr" should be pronounced "Carr" that I made the connection. In Sir Perry's sordid little tale there appears a certain member of parliament by the name of "Jack Laurie". Laurie – Carr; not one of poor Perry's better pieces of word play but good enough for his purpose. As I recall, he described Laurie as "vicious alike to friend and enemy". The definition fits you like a glove. You showed poor Charles Vare no mercy and I can expect none.'

'Charles had a bad attack of conscience. He talked about "making a clean breast" of things.'

'Words which don't figure prominently in the politician's vocabulary.'

'If you can't swim don't get into the deep end.'

Tim's mental cogs were whirling in top gear assessing his options. He could get the MP in a stranglehold or armlock and try to terrify him into revealing the whereabouts of the boys. He dismissed the idea. Finsley-Kerr was vicious and

desperate. Never trap a rat in a corner. Delay him and hope
the police would soon turn up with lights flashing and sirens
blaring? Make him see that the game was up? Make him
phone his accomplices and call them off? That was all very
well as long as the police *did* turn up. Relax the bastard;
keep him talking. For the moment that was all he could do.

'You certainly fooled everyone into believing that Vare
had committed suicide. What was it, drugs in the whisky?'

'That's right, just enough to make him groggy and
convince him that it was time to go to chapel.'

'Bit of luck for you that it was such a dark, wet night.'

'Yes, no one would have thought it odd to see two
muffled figures, stumbling along, heads down against the
wind. By the time I had his coat off and propped him in his
stall he was virtually asleep. The rest was easy.'

'But you still had to ransack his room and make sure there
was nothing incriminating left. And then to bump into your
own daughter on the way out; that must have been a shock.'

'I didn't realize it was her until much later. Through that
gap in the hedge on the right.'

They emerged into the floodlit car park. Other guests
were climbing into their vehicles and driving off. The
politician motioned towards a maroon Rolls Royce in the far
corner. Tim walked deliberately slowly, eyes and ears alert
for any sign of a police presence.

Finsley-Kerr opened the passenger door and saw Tim in
before getting into the driving seat.

When they were both in the car the politician said, 'Now,
where are the papers?'

'At Farrans.'

'Don't lie!' The man's voice was shaking now. 'You were

going to give them to Sir Evelyn.'

'I was going to arrange to give them to Sir Evelyn. After everything that's happened I'm keeping them safely under lock and key.'

Finsley-Kerr considered this for several seconds. 'Very well, we'll drive to Farrans now. But if this is just a ploy to gain time, remember that your children's lives are at stake.'

'You haven't proved that to me yet.'

'We'll phone on the way.' He started the engine. 'The sooner I have the papers . . .'

'The sooner you can kill me? I should think carefully, Minister. Remember how you bungled Longton's supposed suicide.'

'That was spur of the moment. After that idiot Everton failed to get hold of the papers in America I had to grab the first opportunity.'

'So you arranged a private meeting with Longton?'

'I told him I wanted to talk with him in confidence about Emma. It was quite a shock to learn that he'd already started to put two and two together. I had to improvise.' He turned the key in the ignition and the engine roared into life. Finsley-Kerr switched on the headlights.

The beam picked up a figure standing in front of the car, arms spread wide. It was Gavin Turner.

Finsley-Kerr swore. He lowered the window. 'Get out of the way, you bloody fool!'

Gavin silently shook his head and stood his ground.

The minister opened the door. 'I'm warning you! Get out of the way!'

Other people in the car park were beginning to stare. Someone called out, 'Everything all right?'

That was when Finsley-Kerr snapped. He slammed the door, engaged first gear and the car leaped forward. Gavin's attempt to jump aside was too slow. There was a thud as the vehicle roared across the car park. Tim heard a woman scream. The Rolls Royce made – too fast – for the narrow exit. Another car was also heading for the gap. Finsley-Kerr hit it sideways on. That was when Tim threw open the door and rolled out. He picked himself up quickly and ran across to where a small crowd had gathered round Gavin's sprawled body. Behind him the Rolls Royce raced out onto the road.

Gavin's right leg and arm were both twisted at impossible angles but he was conscious. He lay jaundiced in the hotel's garish lights and grimaced with pain. 'Tim, I heard what he said. I was on the other side of the hedge. That's why—'

'Don't talk. Lie as still as you can.' A dozen emotions were churning round inside Tim.

A tall man elbowed his way through the small crowd that had gathered. 'I'm a doctor. What's happened here?'

Thankfully, Tim left the medical man in charge. He rushed into the hotel. The first familiar face he saw was that of Angela Revesby. 'Where's Catherine? Have you seen Catherine?'

'Oh Tim, there you are. Catherine was looking for you.' Angela was the picture of matronly composure.

'But where is she now?' Tim shouted.

'Gone back to my place to make sure the boys are all right. She said she'd have them ready for when you called with the car. I told her there was no need to worry but—'

Tim ran all the way to the Revesbys' house. He punched the doorbell furiously. When no one answered, he punched it again. It opened a few inches, on a security chain, and Dorrie peered out. 'Oh, Tim, it's you.' She released the chain and held the door wide open.

'Dorrie! How are the boys?'

'Fine, unless you've woken them up.'

Catherine came through from the kitchen into the hall. 'Tim what's the matter? You look dreadful.'

'Are the boys OK?'

'Yes, I've just been up to have a look. They're dead to the world. It seems a pity to disturb them.'

Tim turned to Dorrie. 'Has anyone else been here tonight?'

'Yes, the police. Oh, and someone else. It was all very odd. I was just telling Catherine. It was about an hour ago. The bell rang and I went to answer it and there was a young man there. He tried to push the door open, only of course he couldn't because of the security chain. Then the police car came into the drive and the man ran off.'

Tim almost collapsed with relief. 'What did the police want?'

'They were looking for you. Someone had given them a garbled message about where to find you. I said you were at the hotel and off they went.'

Catherine took up the story. 'They paged you at the hotel but no one knew where you were. So the police left a message with me. Would you ring Inspector Quatrain on this number as soon as you can?' She took a slip of paper from her evening bag.

Tim made the call from the kitchen extension.

'Quatrain here.' A tired voice.

'Tim Lacy, Inspector. You've been trying to contact me.'

362

'You bet I have!' The voice woke up. 'What the hell's going on over at Chipping Sneddon? I had a call earlier from Reading CID to detain Lord Everton for questioning.'

'Have you done that?'

'They said you knew about it so I waited till I'd had a word with you.'

Tim almost shouted his frustration. 'But you should have grabbed him straight away!'

'I don't go pulling in personal friends of the Chief Constable without very good reason. Now they've told me there's been an accident over there. I'm just on my way. I can kill two birds with one stone.'

'I think you may well find one of your birds has flown.'

Tim was right. When Quatrain arrived from Cheltenham Lord Teddy had long since driven off into the night.

By the time Tim had finished giving his statement and Catherine had obtained a post-operation report from the hospital on Gavin it was nearly three o'clock. Angela Revesby had insisted that they leave the boys with her for the night and come round in the morning for breakfast. The Lacys dropped thankfully into bed and slept heavily until their alarm call came at eight.

The atmosphere round the Revesbys' kitchen table an hour later was sombre. Tim scanned the *Daily Telegraph* but there was nothing on the night's events at the King and Martyr. Even if editors had heard garbled snippets about the incident in the car park, they had been too busy rearranging their front pages for the bigger story which had broken about midnight.

MINISTER IN FATAL CAR CRASH. Thus ran the

Telegraph's lead headline. Beneath it were the bare facts, padded out to fill two half-page columns. John Finsley-Kerr, Junior Minister at the Heritage Department and rising star of the Tory front bench, had died instantly when his Rolls Royce had spun off the M40 at speed. No other vehicles had been involved. An inside-page feature described Finsley-Kerr's services to country and party, his outstanding parliamentary career and his rapid rise through the Tory ranks. Tim folded the paper and laid it on the deal surface. After such adulation he wondered how the editor would cope with a *volte face* once the facts of the late minister's life and death were known.

Catherine and Dorrie were coping with the children between them. Mr Revesby had already departed for his regular Sunday morning round of golf, a fixture which nothing short of a nuclear holocaust would shift. Angela excused herself after the meal to attend an urgent festival committee meeting, made necessary by the unprecedented events of the previous evening.

Catherine lifted Rupert out of his highchair and watched him shuffle on his bottom across to the toy box. 'Do you think Finsley-Kerr crashed the car deliberately?'

Tim gave a long sigh. 'I expect so. The whole business, ever since Vare's death, has been all about saving his career and his public image. When he realized he'd failed he knew he'd lose everything. He couldn't face that.'

'And you didn't suspect him?'

'Not until it was very nearly too late. There seemed to be two things going on – the financial wheeling and dealing over the papers and the paedophilia; and there was no apparent connection. But of course, there was. I should have spotted the link when Emma told me that her father and Lord Teddy were bosom pals.'

'But you didn't know about the disgusting business at Fairlawns then.'

'Even when I did I was appallingly slow about slotting things together, finding the link between the two. It was only when we were sitting at the table last night that I realized that only one person could have been involved with Everton's paedophile organization and the Masqueriers' wheeling and dealing.'

'You're going to have to spell it out for me.'

'OK. On the one hand we have Vare who is the only person who knows that the Hellfire Papers are dynamite. He confides in someone and that someone has to be another member of the ring. On the other hand only Masquerier knows our travel arrangements for the Sydney trip. If he didn't plan the attempted burglary, he must have confided in someone else and that someone can only have been a person already involved in his schemes. I knew that Finsley-Kerr fitted into the latter category but it wasn't till I made the Laurie-Carr connection that I realized he was also involved with Everton's crowd. *Ergo*, Finsley-Kerr was the missing link. He knew everything that was going on, so of course he would know the papers had turned up safely in Cambridge and that Stuart was examining them.'

Catherine poured herself a fresh mug of coffee. 'When he came down to Farrans to see what we knew and you told him the papers were fakes he must have got a bad shock. He thought we were halfway to working out the story that Sir Perry had planted.'

'He had to stop those incriminating documents circulating

any further, and I as good as told him I was going to confront Masquerier with them this weekend.'

'So he got Teddy to invite him, too.'

'That's right. His lordship, of course, was just as desperate to see the papers destroyed.'

Catherine frowned over the rim of her mug. 'But what was it all about? What made Whitehead-Dyer dish the dirt on his old associates?'

'Revenge. Old Perry was an incredibly bitter man, as Harry Pratos told me.'

'And not just because of his appallingly painful illness?'

'According to Harry, the cancer made things worse but Perry's dislike of Australia was paranoid. That was why he lived as a recluse, never went anywhere and never met any of the locals. Harry told us that he often spoke longingly of England.'

'So why . . .?'

'I believe he was forced into exile. About a dozen years ago Perry and chums had a very nasty scare. There was a scandal at one of the Downham Homes. The police were quickly onto it but the leading members of the ring weren't establishment men for nothing. They paid the warden of the home to take the rap and keep his mouth shut. But they weren't quite quick enough. I'm guessing slightly here, but I think Whitehead-Dyer's name was dragged into the affair. No one wanted a major exposé, least of all the Foreign Office. There was a massive closing of ranks. Perry was pensioned off. He was told to get out of the country and stay out. He hated it but he had no choice. What must have rubbed salt into the wound was that, after the panic was over, the activities of the ring carried on just as before. All his friends were enjoying their sordid games while he was left out on a limb, only able to participate through the computer network and occasional "seminars".'

'I can see how that would make him bitter.'

Tim reached out absentmindedly for the solitary piece of cold toast still in its rack in the middle of the table. He nibbled it, unbuttered. 'It must have been terrible for him having to sell up the ancestral home and go into obscurity on the far side of the world. I guess he often felt like blowing the gaffe. Only, of course, that would have landed him in jail.'

'So he decided to hit back from beyond the grave?'

'That's how I see it. But when it came to it he couldn't resist letting someone in on the secret. That's why he wrote to Charles Vare.'

'Revenge is only sweet if you can taste it? Well, he certainly got back at his cronies.'

'Gosh!' Dorrie stared up wide-eyed from her kneeling position in the toy corner. 'It's like one of those spy things on television. I can never make head or tail of those either.'

EPILOGUE: Encomium

The chapel bell of St Mary's House tolled on a radiant September morning. The door of the senior combination room opened. Sir Evelyn and Lady Masquerier led their small party of guests round Grand Court. They skirted the large square of velvet lawn and passed along the hall's half-timbered façade. No one spoke, but Catherine gripped the hand of Emma, walking beside her and Emma managed a wan smile. At the chapel door they were greeted silently by the new dean – a young man, looking slightly nervous about his first major service at St Mary's.

Inside, sunlight cascading through stained glass made the rows of candles along the stalls redundant. The sense of serenity was completed by the reedy notes of the organ as it filled the air with a quiet passage from the Fauré Requiem. A junior fellow showed the guests to their places. Each knelt briefly, some in genuine, some in conventional devotion. Tim rose from his knees and looked round the small building. There was not a single space vacant and the congregation was made up largely of young men and women; Gavin's friends and contemporaries.

The Dean entered his stall beside the baize-covered door. After a pause he rose and declaimed in a clear, firm voice, 'Let us now praise famous men and our fathers who begat us . . .'

After the passage from Ecclesiasticus, he welcomed the congregation, who had gathered, he explained, not to mourn a son or friend tragically cut down in his prime, but to make a memorial of a young man who had lived bravely and died heroically.

The service pursued its sombre course. There were quiet hymns, prayers, readings by Emma and the Master and appreciations of Gavin Turner by his tutor and two of his fellow undergraduates. Tim only half listened. His mind kept revolving the events of the last tumultuous weeks and months.

On the debit side was Gavin's death. His wounds had not been very serious. Most young men would have spent a couple of weeks in hospital and made a complete recovery. But Gavin's already undermined constitution had swiftly capitulated. After three days he had lapsed into the coma from which he never emerged. Emma had been almost constantly beside him. When there was nothing more to be done for her friend she had stayed to comfort and be comforted by his parents. Tim did not know whether they had talked through her father's rôle in shortening Gavin's life. He simply noted that the tragedy had seemed to bring the three of them together in a relationship remarkably free of bitterness.

There was something else Tim was inclined to throw into the wrong side of the scales. The events of the summer had been for the press like an extended Christmas. The story ran and ran. There was scarcely a day which had not turned up some new salacious development. While those at the centre of the tragedy worked through their private grief and tried to come to terms with what had deeply scarred their lives, journalists played the games inherent in their profession: insensitive intrusion, titillation and hypocritical denunciation of those vices on which their circulation fed.

There was, of course, a credit side. The trail which had begun at Fairlawns had led to the homes and offices of some of the wealthiest and most influential people in Western society. What would go down in criminal history as 'Everton's Coven' was no ordinary paedophile ring. It was a highly expensive club supplying services to those who could afford to indulge their depraved tastes in the most 'refined' ways. Computer links provided the network with texts and images. Diplomatic couriers were the main agents for the dissemination of videotapes. Then there were the 'conventions', sometimes held in Europe or America but more frequently in third world countries where there was a more plentiful supply of unwanted children.

Vice squads in five continents had swooped on private houses to arrest lawyers, media personalities, leaders of industry, diplomats and even a member of the British royal household. They had confiscated boxloads of photographs, tapes, drugs and magazines. One police chief had hailed Operation Excelsior as a 'Waterloo in the war against child abuse'. They had, he claimed, skimmed the scum from the barrel of international filth and added hundreds of names to the index of offenders held on Interpol files; people who would be watched closely after they had completed their prison sentences.

The trials were still going on and public interest was also maintained by the hunt for Lord Teddy. The obese peer was sighted in several places in Britain and abroad and credited with a variety of disguises. As Interpol co-ordinated every snippet of intelligence and conveyed it to London, the press dubbed the elusive Everton 'a latterday Lord Lucan'. But, after seven weeks of hounded freedom, Lord Teddy had given himself up to police in the South of France. TV screens had subsequently been filled with pictures of the peer, covered by a blanket, being shielded by a police escort from banner-waving mobs baying for blood during his journeys to prison and magistrate's court.

Credit and debit. Did they balance? Did the good outweigh the bad? Despite the innocent suffering involved, the answer had to be yes.

Catherine was also busy with her own thoughts as the ceremony moved on. She raised her eyes to the ancient timbers of the vault above. They had seen it all hundreds of times before, the unending pageant of life and death, joy and sorrow, love and hate, grief and exhilaration. The very permanence of the building and what it stood for put the awful events of the past year into some sort of perspective. Small consolation that, though, for the thousands of young minds and bodies mutilated for life by Teddy Everton and his evil côterie. She thought of all the children and adolescents who had been taken to Fairlawns, to similar locations in other lands, to the *Admiral Anson* (which had been little more than a floating brothel) and been forced, often screaming, to take part in acts too vile to envisage. According to the police the ring had been in operation for several years and many of its leading members had been active long before that. 'Once a paedophile, always a paedophile', as a member of the London-based vice squad had told her.

There was nothing new about it. Unnatural sex had been around long before even this chapel had been built. Unbidden, her mind focused, as her worst dreams had done over recent months, on scenes depicted so nonchalantly in the Hellfire Papers. She pictured Whitehead-Dyer gloating, in that monstrosity of a house outside Sydney, over the orgies organized by his ancestor. She reflected on those activities which had shocked even Paul Whitehead. That was the trouble with *Fay ce que voudras*. It licensed unbridled hedonism. It also ignored the fact that there was always a price to be paid for pleasure. The more perverted the pleasure, the higher the price.

In the space of a year three members of this college had died violently. Several prominent careers had been ruined. scores of families had been plunged into grief and shame as the deeds of fathers, husbands and brothers had been exposed by a censorious press. Paedophilia did not only inflict suffering on its victims; it was a slimy fungus whose spores spread far and wide. Catherine glanced at Emma, sitting opposite with downcast eyes, and wondered if she would ever fully recover. Then the organ's trumpet pipes proclaimed the life-affirming first line of 'Now thank we all our God' and the congregation rose to sing.

Afterwards most people made their way back to the senior combination room where a buffet lunch had been laid out.

The Master and his wife circulated professionally and eventually Lady Deb, large gin and tonic in hand, came up to the Lacys.

'God, I hate memorial services! You've no idea how many we have here in Cambridge. Old men like Evelyn get a kick out of them. They're not so much reminders of the dead as celebrations of survival for the living. They just make me feel morbid.'

Catherine opened her mouth to make a sharp retort but the Master's wife, whose elegant black dress had a splash of defiant crimson across the front, hurried on. 'Well, thank you so much for coming, and seeing this wretched business to a conclusion. The last year's been sheer hell for Evelyn. Well, for all of us. My dear, you read beautifully.' The last words were addressed to Emma who had just sidled up to them through the crowd. 'It was so good of you to come – and so brave. Oh, excuse me.' She waved her glass. 'I must go say hello to the Vice Chancellor and his wife.'

Catherine scowled after her. 'Now I know what the word "irrepressible" means.' She put an arm round Emma's shoulder. 'OK now?'

The girl nodded. 'Yes, I think this morning was a help. Do you ever draw a line under unpleasant events in your life? I suppose you have to try. What do you think?'

Tim nodded. 'You certainly have to try.' He recalled scenes that he had witnessed in SAS days: blood, twisted bodies, comrades gunned down – usually to keep unworthy men in power. 'The secret is not to kid yourself that you can, or should, forget. Just to know that it *is* over and to be thankful for it.'

'There's one thing I have to do before I can close this

chapter.' Emma looked suddenly sheepish. 'Tim, I have a confession to make.'

He smiled down at her. 'I'll save you the embarrassment. It was you who had my car broken into.'

Her dark eyes opened wide. 'You knew?'

'Worked it out, eventually. Your curiosity about the Hellfire Papers got the better of you. You guessed they were in the car and while we were having a very enjoyable lunch, one of your devoted admirers did the deed.'

She nodded. 'Tim, I felt awful about it, as soon as I'd got to know you.'

'And as soon as you discovered that the parcel contained old newspapers?'

She grimaced. 'Don't make me feel more ashamed than I am already.'

'I just hope your experience has persuaded you to abandon a life of crime.' Tim laughed. 'Have you, in fact, given any thought to the future?'

Emma sighed. 'My father left me quite a lot of money. In a way that makes it even more difficult to decide what to do. Perhaps I'll give it all away and get an honest job.'

Tim and Catherine smiled at each other. Catherine said, 'Intelligent, enterprising – and rich.'

Tim laughed at Emma's puzzled frown. 'Let me suggest an alternative. Catherine's been nagging me for some time to slow down, find a partner to share the workload. When you've built up your own business it's not easy to hand some of it to someone else and have them making decisions. We agreed not to take the step until we found someone we both liked – someone "intelligent, enterprising and rich". How would you feel about joining us, learning the business and, if it all works out, becoming a financial partner?'

Emma's eyes gleamed but Tim held up a hand and continued. 'You're not to say anything at all now, or for quite a long while. Go off and do something different. Go round the world. Have fun. Then, when you're ready, give us a ring.'

Emma's face lit up with hope and enthusiasm. 'Thanks a lot, both of you. I really appreciate—'

Someone rapped a table loudly and the buzz of conversation died away.

Sir Evelyn was standing in the middle of the room. He looked around. 'Mr Vice Chancellor, ladies and gentlemen. This isn't a speech, just an announcement. Normally this would not be a suitable occasion to reveal the decisions and plans of the governing body, but under the circumstances I am convinced that you are precisely the most appropriate group of people to be the first to hear an important piece of news.

'It is common knowledge that St Mary's House recently came into possession of an important collection of eighteenth-century papers. Those documents became involved with the sequence of sad events which has resulted in us all being here today. Nothing can undo past tragedies but the governing body has unanimously agreed that the Whitehead-Dyer Papers, which in part caused the unhappy happenings of the past year, should be used to help make amends. I can now tell you that arrangements are in hand to sell the manuscripts in question to an overseas academic institution.'

Tim and Catherine exchanged amused glances and Catherine mouthed, 'Zangster.'

The Master continued. 'A full set of microfilm will, of course, be retained here in the college for approved research purposes. A substantial part of the sum realized will be used to set up what we propose to call the Turner Research Fellowship in Medical Science. It will be available for the study of sexually transmitted diseases and we in St Mary's hope that it will play some part in helping to rid our planet of the scourge of AIDS.'

A trickle of applause began and grew rapidly to a torrent.

A selection of bestsellers from Headline